W9-BBZ-196

# THE COURTSHIP

*Dell Books by Stephanie Mittman*

THE MARRIAGE BED
SWEETER THAN WINE
THE COURTSHIP

# Stephanie Mittman

# THE COURTSHIP

A Dell Book

Copyright © 1997 by Stephanie Mittman

All rights reserved. No part of this book may be reproduced or transmitted in any form or by any means, electronic or mechanical, including photocopying, recording, or by any information storage and retrieval system, without the written permission of the Publisher, except where permitted by law.

ISBN: 1-56865-632-7

Printed in the United States of America

This book is dedicated to three incredible people without whom I would be just a lump under my electric blanket:

Alan, who is every hero I have ever imagined and then some. I love you more than all the stars in the sky, times all the grains of sand on all the beaches, times infinity to the infinite. And that's on a bad day!

Sherry, who is a best friend and a half—always and through everything. I couldn't have invented a better friend for me than you. Thanks for being real, in every sense!

Laura, who is the editor of my dreams. Just hearing your voice on the other end of the line makes me think I can do it, again and again. And makes me want to!

Thank you all.

And a special thanks to our cat, Karma, who only ripped up two pages of this manuscript in an effort to remind me that he can't work the can opener himself. Good Karma!

# Chapter 1

*Oakland, California*
*1888*

Above Ash Whittier's head the courthouse ceiling fans droned rhythmically as they circled round and round. Behind him, in the heavy oak pews, an impatient crowd stirred restlessly. And beside him his sister-in-law Charlotte's skirts whooshed with her every move. Yet despite all the commotion surrounding him, it was a tiny, constant chirping that was grating on his nerves.

He laced his hands out in front of him, cracking the knuckles, and silently counted the seats in the empty jury box.

"Nervous?" Charlotte asked him, her huge hazel eyes scanning the courtroom as she adjusted the hat resting on her open satchel. Like her suit, it was a no-nonsense dark blue—without a frill, a ribbon, a bow—as close to a man's hat as it could be. With delicate fingers she turned the hat over to rest its brim on the case's edges, so that it now sat like an empty nest. At least it appeared empty. If not, he'd swear it was the source of that chirping that was crawling up the back of his neck.

"Where's Cabot?" he asked, twisting in his chair to check yet again the back of the courtroom for any sign of his brother.

"He's got a jury summation down the hall," Charlotte told him for what he supposed was the third time. She opened her mouth just enough to allow a small pink tongue to run quickly back and forth over her bottom lip before catching herself in what was apparently a nervous habit.

"There's really nothing to worry about," she said a bit too glibly as she caught a wayward spiral of chestnut hair and poked it into her very tight bun. It was unclear whether she was reassuring him or herself with her words. "Judge Hammerman will ask to have the charges read. The district attorney will state *arson* and probably also insurance fraud, for motive. Brent, the old windbag, will state his case, which will take forever, or at least feel like it. We'll say it's circumstantial, which of course it is, and then the judge will ask how you plead."

"This is ridiculous, you know," he said. That only made a half-dozen times he'd said as much since he'd been led into the courtroom to find her sitting at the defense table instead of his brother. All of it was crazy: that the police would imagine that he'd set fire to his own warehouse just a few hours after he'd sailed the *Bloody Mary* back into Oakland Harbor; that his business partner would accuse him of the crime; and that a lady lawyer (his brother's wife, no less) was preparing to defend him.

Talk about a short plank over a deep pier.

"It's all very routine," Charlotte said, fidgeting with that ugly hat of hers as if she found it more interesting than his legal proceedings. "We stand. I say you're represented by Whittier and Whittier and—"

"Whittier and Whittier . . . ?"

"Cabot and me."

She said it so matter-of-factly that Ash was almost forced to wonder whether Cabot had actually broken down and made her a partner in his practice.

"Change the sign, did he?" he asked. "The stationery?"

His sister-in-law glanced quickly at the floor and ignored his question, busying herself with looking over the papers in front of her. For Ash, who knew his brother all too well, that was as good as answering. Cabot would never give a piece of himself away.

"You can prove where you were last night between midnight and three or so, can't you?" she asked, looking at him with eyes so big and innocent a man could drown in them.

"Sure," he said, then hedged. "Maybe." He tried to remember a name, but the truth was they'd probably never gotten past *sweetheart* and *honey.* He knew she was blond. That is, she was blond on top. And she'd been walking the street somewhere between the pier and the bar where he and Moss, the best damn foreman any warehouse operation ever had, had stopped to have a few too many.

"Where?" Charlotte moved her hat over to the edge of the open Gladstone, where it perched precariously, and peeked in. Again he could hear the chirping, louder, crawling on his nerves like ants over a ripe peach. He gripped the edge of the table while beside him his sister-in-law checked the watch hanging from a golden bow that, while small, wasn't much bigger than the breast on which it hung. Well, leave it to Cabot to be above such things as choosing a woman by the size of her . . . he reined in his thoughts.

"I was on the *Bloody Mary,*" he mumbled at her.

"That's fine. Crew members saw you, naturally?"

Someone had rowed him and the girl out to the boat—Jonesy maybe, or Flint, after he'd left Moss back in the bar to pay the bill and go home to his wife and kids. And someone had to have taken the girl back to shore later. She hadn't been there when the police arrived.

"Did anyone see you?" she repeated.

He hadn't sold tickets, for Christ's sake. "I suppose, coming or going. . . ." he said, his voice trailing off. Where the hell was Cabot? This wasn't the sort of thing he could talk about with his sister-in-law.

"Coming when? Going where?" she asked. Before he could answer she laid a small hand on his arm and nodded toward the side door. Things were about to begin. And about time, too.

A clerk came out and went directly to the district attorney's table. At Ash's side Charlotte sat up straight and tall, the itsy-bitsy pink nails of one hand tapping expectantly on the table.

"Where the hell is Cabot?" he couldn't help asking, as sweat broke out on his upper lip. The DA nodded at something the clerk said while Ash continued to badger his sister-in-law. "He wouldn't leave me to you, would he?"

"Ashford, he's at least as worried about you as you are about yourself." She rose abruptly, taking her briefcase carefully with her. "Would you excuse me for a moment?"

"Are you going for Cabot?" he asked. He was not about to spend another night in jail just to avoid insulting his sister-in-law's prowess as an attorney. "I think you'd better get him now."

With that tiny hand of hers she patted his weather-worn one reassuringly, even patronizingly, then walked over to the prosecution's table and leaned forward to speak quietly with both the bespectacled man who sat there and the clerk. When both men nodded, she bent over and picked up her valise.

So that was where she'd hidden her softness. Whether it was bustle or actual bottom he couldn't tell, but his sister-in-law surely improved a courtroom when she conferred with the enemy. His gaze followed her all the way to the back of the courtroom until she passed through the double oak doors.

He ought to be ashamed of himself. This woman was Cabot's wife. And it had taken his brother long enough to find her. Well, women weren't exactly lined up outside Cabot Whittier's doors, no matter how impressive those mahogany and cut-glass panels were.

There were some magic tricks that even Cabot couldn't pull off.

That Cabot had found Charlotte Reynolds attractive was easy enough to understand. According to Cabot (whose standards had always been impossible) Charlotte was smarter than three quarters of the men he knew, and all of the ones he'd opposed in court. And Ash had to admit, despite the man-tailored clothing she had on, that she was pretty in an innocent way—which was to say that she had no cleavage and her wide eyes were smolderless. She was pleasant enough too. She hadn't mentioned that he'd repeated himself a hundred times, or complained when she'd had to repeat herself on his behalf. And she was young, practically a child when Ash compared her to Cabot's years.

But no doubt what Cabot found most attractive had to be that she clearly worshiped the ground beneath him.

Ash did concede, however, with her third trip down the hall, that in contrast to her many assets, she apparently possessed the smallest bladder in California.

He stood politely as she returned to the table and took her seat once again. When she'd finished adjusting her hat and bag to her own satisfaction, opening the bag and carefully putting her hat atop it again, he demanded to know if Cabot was coming.

"Oh," she answered, those big eyes so bright he nearly had to shield his own. "You should see him! He's in courtroom number three waving some photographs in front of the jury, and jaws are falling faster than pigeon droppings on the cupola at City Hall."

"Charlotte," he begged, not even trying to feign enthusiasm. "Does that mean he's almost done?"

"I told you," she said, frustration finally tinging the edges of her voice. "They've got nothing on you to warrant your being held for trial. This is just routine. Cabot lets me handle these kinds of proceedings every day."

"Not for me," he grumbled, tired of waiting for things to get started. If he ran his shipping company the way Oakland ran its courts, there wouldn't have been anything in the warehouse to burn. He had no patience for mistakes and the Oakland police had obviously made a big one.

He stretched out his legs, knocking her hat from its perch. He reached down for it, his head almost level with the top of the alligator Gladstone he'd bought her as a wedding gift in Argentina, and stopped.

There, in the bottom of her monogrammed lady's version of the same case he'd brought Cabot, was a small box lined with straw. A tiny baby bird strained his neck up at Ash, opened a beak smaller even than Charlotte's fingernails, and chirped.

Well, at least he wasn't crazy.

Charlotte was.

Without sitting back up he cocked his head and took a long look at his sister-in-law, the only lady lawyer in all of Oakland. With the exception of that Clara Foltz person his brother had told him about, she might have been the only lady lawyer in the whole state of California.

At the moment she looked like some schoolgirl caught with someone else's lunch pail at recess. Her cheeks glowing, she shrugged and tried to wave away the bird with her hand.

"He needs to eat every few hours," she explained.

It was a struggle to keep the smirk from his lips, but he thought he succeeded admirably as he nodded at the esteemed Charlotte Whittier, Esquire, respected member of the bar. "I see. We wouldn't want your bird to be hungry."

"He isn't *my* bird," Charlotte said, her chin so high, he could hardly see those long dark eyelashes of hers.

"Then he belongs to Cabot?"

"Oh, yes," she said, not even trying to hide the sarcasm. "And judges never sleep on the bench. It's no one's bird. But someone has to feed it or it'll die."

Well, he'd wondered when Charlotte's nesting instinct would surface. He just hadn't expected it to be quite so literal when it did. Although it'd been five years since she'd married Cabot, there'd been no mention of little Whittiers to date. Even his mother had stayed away from the subject, focusing instead on Charlotte's incredible achievements in the legal field.

Without a word Ash replaced the hat over the opening of the Gladstone bag. Charlotte didn't seem to be in the mood to be ribbed about her hungry feathered friend, and Ash wasn't in the mood to tease her anyway. He had a bird of his own, a parrot, on board the *Bloody Mary*, who was no doubt screeching to be fed himself.

"Cabot *is* coming, isn't he?" He'd gone beyond begging. Now he was groveling.

"I told you, it's just routine," she began again just as a haggard clerk with a droopy mustache and a hacking cough opened the door beside the judge's bench and yelled, "Hear ye! Hear ye! Hear ye! The Superior Court of the County of Alameda is now in session, the honorable Judge George Hammerman presiding. All persons having business before this Court shall draw near and ye shall be heard."

Beside Ash, Charlotte rose, exerting a slight pressure beneath his elbow until he realized that he, too, was expected to rise.

"I—" Ash began, indeed having business with the court.

Charlotte stopped him, signaling him with a finger against her lips that it was not time for him to speak.

"Oh, it's you, Charlotte," the judge said, grimacing. "I expected Mr. Whittier to be here to represent his brother in a matter so grave as this. Not that I have any doubt that you, dear, couldn't do the case justice."

Charlotte's meager chest rose and fell sharply. Beneath her charming veneer and behind her pleasant smile, the woman next to him was seething.

"Mr. Whittier is next door explaining the finer points of the law to Mr. Cohen," she said, eliciting a smile from the judge. Everyone knew that Alfred A. Cohen hardly needed lessons in the law from Cabot or anyone else. She pulled back her shoulders and appeared ready to do battle. "So I'm afraid the court will have to settle for *Mrs.* Whittier for the present."

"All right, Charlotte," the judge said, signaling her to slow down with a show of his palm. "No need to get all huffy with me."

While behind her skirt Charlotte's fist balled, she turned a dazzling smile on the judge and nodded, corrected and ready for her next lesson.

"Mr. Brent," the judge said, looking over his half-spectacles, "are you ready to proceed?"

The district attorney nodded.

"And you, Charlotte? You're ready, too, dear?"

Her intake of breath was audible, but rather than utter a word (which Ash thought was likely to be profane—if the white knuckles dotting her clenched fists were any indication), she simply nodded.

If he were being perfectly honest, Ash Whittier would have to admit that he was wholly unaccustomed to upholding a lady's honor. Still, in the case of one's sister-in-law (especially when that sister-in-law was attempting to represent one's interests in a court of law), he supposed an exception should be made. And so he cleared his throat.

"Excuse me, Your Honor," he said, amazed at how loud his voice sounded in the quiet courtroom, how far it carried and echoed back at him, mocking him for this sudden solicitude of the fairer sex. The judge looked over his glasses at Ash, waiting. It appeared too late to turn back, so he continued.

"As a defender of the law," he said—paused with the hope of finding the right words, abandoned that hope, and forged ahead—". . . and an obviously forward-looking person who'd allow a lady attorney to appear before you, I take you to be a man who believes in parity. Right?"

"Charlotte?" The judge asked, dismissing Ash as if he had suddenly lost his hearing. "Are you having trouble with your client? It seems he doesn't realize that he will most certainly have his chance to speak, but that right now is not that time. Would you like a moment to explain to him the purpose of being represented by an attorney?"

"No, Your Honor. I'm sure that there will be no further outbursts from my client," Charlotte said sweetly. Her tone, though, held a note of warning for Ash, which she followed with a discreet kick to his shin that brought tears to his eyes. His reflex action sent her Gladstone skating across the floor and her scurrying after it, affording the entire courtroom a delightful view of her bustle. Anxious to get on with it, Ash captured the bag with a single stride and returned it to its place between them.

"To continue, Your Honor, I feel it is only fair," he said before she could get in another kick, "that if you call Mr. Brent *Mister*, you should accord my attorney the same courtesy. That is, you should call her *Mrs.* Whittier."

The ceiling fans, which had no business being on in February anyway, got louder.

Other than that there wasn't a sound. Not even that pathetic little bird had the nerve to chirp in the silence. The entire courtroom refrained from drawing a breath until the judge signaled to his clerk, who stepped up on the rise, yet still needed to stand on his toes to hear the judge's request.

"There will be a short recess," the clerk said. He glared pointedly at Charlotte. "One minute!"

Charlotte looked up at the judge, saw that he was busying himself with the papers on his desk, and whispered at Ash through clenched teeth. "Didn't anyone ever teach you to pick your fights carefully? Would it do us any good to have him call me Mrs. Whittier and slap you in jail? Good glory! They must have used up all the Whittier common sense on Cabot and left none for you."

"Anyone with a shred of common sense can see that the law is stupid and needs changing if it doesn't insure you the same dignity as your adversary," he hissed back, convinced he had made a good point.

"My adversary wants to put you in jail," she reminded him in hushed tones. "Are you bent on helping him?"

"So we don't care what's right, is that it?" he whispered, knowing she was right but not knowing how to back down. "I just need to know how the game works, so I can play it along with you."

"Okay," she said, crossing her arms over a blue suit jacket that was doing its best to negate her even being a woman. "The game goes like this. You pretend you're gagged and let me do the talking. Is that simple enough?"

"Are we ready?" Judge Hammerman asked, his voice filling the room as he looked over his half-spectacles at Charlotte expectantly.

"*Simple enough* would be to allow a man to defend himself," Ash muttered. "Or to find his damned brother. . . . Sorry, I shouldn't have said that in front of you." Mixed company and all that. He knew better, he just didn't hang around ladies much. Not the kind whose eyebrows rose at a word like *damned.*

"You can say anything you want to your lawyer," Charlotte whispered. "But not to the judge. Where you sleep tonight is going to be up to him."

"I asked if you were ready, Charlotte, dear. Do you need me to explain it to him?" The judge motioned for Ash to step forward, but Charlotte put a restraining hand on his arm.

"No, Your Honor. He understands perfectly."

"I guess you'd better tell him I'm sorry," Ash whispered.

She smiled, and Ash realized that he'd been stingy in his assessment of her. Cabot's wife left *pretty* in her wake—before she seemed to remember that smiling was definitely not lawyerly.

"Now you whisper?" she asked quietly. "Had you done that before, we wouldn't be risking a contempt-of-court citation." She addressed the judge politely on his behalf. "Your Honor, my client wishes to apologize for his outburst, and assure the court that it will not be repeated."

The judge nodded. "The defendant will stand for the reading of the charge."

This time he needed no prodding from the woman beside him. He stood and stared down at the plain dark-blue hat beneath which was hidden the fledgling, and wondered idly what the austere fedora would look like atop his sister-in-law's small head.

"In the matter of the *State of California* versus *Ashford Warren Whittier.* Defendant is charged with the following crimes in connection with a fire occurring at one-thirty A.M. on the morning of February ninth, 1888." The clerk stopped to cough and clear his throat. Ash wondered if he did that regularly just for the dramatic effect. It was surely working in this case. "One count of arson in the first degree; one count of arson with the intent to commit insurance fraud, and three counts of murder in the first degree subject to the felony-murder provisions of the State of California—"

"What?" Ash dragged his gaze from the clerk to the man sitting smugly on the other side of the aisle. In the benches behind them, people gasped. The hum of the crowd grew so loud, he could hardly hear himself ask, "Murder? Are you crazy?"

"Murder?" Judge Hammerman repeated, pounding his gavel and demanding silence. The judge made no effort to hide the shock that registered blatantly on his face. "I thought this was a simple case of business gone bad. Nowhere in the papers is there . . ." He shuffled the papers before him, sifting through them haphazardly and glancing toward the back of the room. "Get Whittier the hell in here," he said to the guard standing at the rear door. "I don't care what he's doing next door."

"Your Honor," Charlotte began.

"Sit down, Charlotte. This is a serious matter, not one of your silly little cases. I won't have some woman fainting in my courtroom. Especially not when she's Cabot Whittier's wife!"

Ash looked down at his sister-in-law. She looked a lot closer to exploding than she did to fainting.

But obediently, she sat, her fists clenched tightly enough to turn coal into diamonds.

Behind him people spoke out of turn and shouted questions.

In front of him the judge banged his gavel while the clerk called for order.

And inside him his stomach turned sour and breakfast teased his tonsils.

After what seemed to Ash like a very long while—but not so long as to produce his brother in the courtroom—Judge Hammerman shook a chubby finger at the district attorney and grimaced. "What in hell is this all about, Brent? There's no mention of murder in these papers. You can't just—"

"Your Honor," the district attorney said, approaching the bench somewhat cautiously, "page four of the indictment specifically begs leave to amend the charges should person or persons be discovered to have been injured or annihilated by said conflagration."

"And I take it that there was a body found?"

"Three, Your Honor."

"Whose?"

The attorney turned and looked at Ash, his eyebrows coming down until they melded with the frames of his glasses. "Burned beyond recognition." Ash sat down heavily in his seat. No one ordered him to come to his feet again. "According to the coroner, probably a woman, and two small children."

Ash put his face in his hands, and fought the nausea that threatened to embarrass him.

"The doctor thinks they might have jumped to their deaths down the lift shaft."

Ash felt Charlotte's hand on his shoulder, warm even through his jacket, and surprisingly strong.

"Then the charge stands as murder in the first degree," the judge agreed. "Where the hell is Cabot Whittier?"

"Your Honor, if it please the court, we're ready to proceed with the preliminary examination," Charlotte said. "And we ask that any and all witness be produced so that—"

"Open the damn door!" Cabot's voice was the one thing that hadn't changed in all the years. It still sliced through Ash like a fencer's foil—clean, neat, and deadly.

While the clerk hurried to open the double doors at the back of the courtroom, Charlotte reached down for her hat, placed it in the little metal rack beneath her seat, and silently closed the satchel that sat open between them. She looked at Ash blankly, innocently, as if she had no knowledge of any baby bird at all, or of the reaction Cabot would have had upon finding it in the courtroom. And quite as if she dared him to suppose otherwise.

"Your Honor," Cabot said from the back of the room, as if he'd been in the court from the very beginning. Ash sensed the movement behind him, knew that everyone had turned to watch his brother's rather dramatic entrance.

Everyone, that was, but Ashford Whittier. He kept his eyes on a point just above the judge's head and listened to the slow sound of rubber wheels turning against the polished wooden floor.

Once again he was out on some goddamn precipice and his big brother Cabot was coming to save him. The last time it had cost Cabot the use of his legs.

Ash wondered what it was going to cost him this time.

* * *

He was doing it again, Charlotte thought testily. What had been the point of all the coaching, the teaching, the studying to be admitted to the bar, if he was going to rush in like some white knight every time she faced a challenge in court? Oh, he was perfectly content to let her flounder when it came to representing her indigent clients, the ones who could only pay her in freshly laid eggs or cords of chopped firewood, but let it be a matter of any interest to him . . .

A tiny *tsk* sound escaped her lips. Of course this was of interest to him. It was his own brother, for heaven's sake. She slid her chair closer to Ashford's and nudged him to move farther still to make room for Cabot's wheelchair at the defense table. Cabot's manservant, Arthur, with him since the day he'd been placed in his invalid's chair, pushed the wood-and-cane chair up the aisle slowly, as he'd no doubt been instructed to before the doors had ever opened.

Sometimes she wondered if Cabot wasn't more actor than lawyer; the way he used the area in front of the jury box as a stage; the way he paused, sighed, shook his head. His voice, too, was a well-honed tool. He could shout without raising the volume of it at all. He could whisper and be heard in the last row.

Now he sat in front of the prosecution's table, shaking his head as though he were thoroughly disappointed with the district attorney.

"Without me here, Brent?" he asked. "Springing a murder charge on an unsuspecting woman whose bailiwick consists largely of apple-stealing urchins and women whose drunken husbands attempt liberties that liquor tends to nullify? I'd thought better of you than that."

Charlotte's wedding band dug into her fingers as she balled the fists in her lap. The ragged thumbnail on her left hand nearly broke the skin of her right. *The ends,*

*Charlotte* . . . he would no doubt say once they were back home, raising his palms while he waited for her to conclude his statement with *justify the means.*

"The facts are the facts," Brent said, straightening his lapels, as if that could give him back the dignity Cabot had clearly stolen from him. "And the charge is murder."

Cabot waved his hand in the air as if the charges were merely so much smoke and could be dismissed as easily. Charlotte wished that it were so. Three people dead! And two of them children. She rubbed at the corner of her eye, a gesture that didn't go unnoticed by her husband.

"Proud of yourself, Mr. District Attorney?" he asked, handing Charlotte his hanky with more show than concern, and letting the courtroom suppose her so distressed by the sudden turn of events that it had brought her to tears. If there was a trick he didn't use, she wasn't aware of it. And the fact that they involved her every now and then never stopped him, not even after she'd made it clear, *damn clear,* he'd said, chuckling at her frustration, how much it irritated her.

Times like this, she wished he had feeling in his legs just so that she could give him a good swift kick in the shins.

"Charlotte?" Judge Hammerman asked solicitously. "You all right?"

"Of course I'm—" she began, only to be interrupted by one of Cabot's convenient coughing fits. She refused to look at him, knowing full well that he was trying to catch her eye. *Time,* he was telegraphing her. They needed some time. "Your Honor," she asked, "if I might just go down the hall for a moment?"

"Again?" Brent said, then clapped his hand over his mouth and turned three shades of red. "The prosecution has no objection," he added quickly.

"I'm relieved," Cabot said, obviously amused by his own choice of words.

As she came to her feet, her brother-in-law gently lifted her alligator bag and offered it to her. "Need this?" he whispered, raising one eyebrow in question.

Was he taunting her? Could the man have so little sense of self-preservation? He antagonized his brother at nearly every visit, and now he was alienating her. Who did he think was going to do the work involved in getting him off on a murder charge? A chill ran up her arms as she thought of the babies killed in the fire. Good glory! Was that really a tear? She hadn't cried in so very long.

*Lawyers don't cry, Charlotte,* Cabot had counseled her, shaking his head at her in disappointment when she'd broken down after losing her first case. *They file appeals, they serve writs, they submit memorandums of law and affidavits in support. They don't crawl off in a corner and bawl.*

Of course, he was right. She had a whole sex to vindicate. She was paving the way for her sisters (in the figurative sense), her daughters (again, symbolically speaking), the young women of generations to come. And every sign of weakness was a giant step backward not just for her, but for them all. At first she'd hidden herself in the closet to cry, but Cabot had heard her through the wall. Then she'd moved her tears to the cupola's high room. Finally she'd managed to move them out of her life altogether.

Pacing in the ladies' room, she gave Cabot five minutes. It wasn't as if any amount of time would enable him to pull a rabbit out of his hat—not even for his brother. Oh, in the long run they'd clear him—Cabot always saw to it that the justice system worked—but the plan to keep him out on bail was surely burned in the bottom of the pot.

How would they ever tell Kathryn that instead of sitting

down to the delicious meal of *salmi de perdreaux* she had planned, her son would be feasting on greasy fried chicken and bread and water in the county jail until his trial? Kathryn's younger son seemed too big to cage, and much too fine.

Well, Kathryn was strong. Hadn't she supported Charlotte fully in her quest for recognition, helped her to conquer the weaknesses that kept her separate from her male colleagues, and advised her on everything from her boots to her bun?

And now Kathryn would be called upon to practice what she preached.

"Three *people,*" Brent was saying when she returned to the courtroom. Naturally they hadn't waited for her. She was only the attorney of record. A formality with which men like Judge Hammerman and her husband had no problem dispensing. "Not *vagrants.* People."

"Uh, uh, uh," Cabot said, waving one finger back and forth to show Brent the error of his ways. "Not *people.* Vagrants."

Hurriedly she took her seat, whispering for her brother-in-law to explain what she had missed.

"Someone's killed three people," Ash said quietly, his voice cracking. "One just a baby. And he's—"

"My point is that under the law, if there were occupants of the warehouse at the time of the fire, which for our purposes we shall call 'nighttime'—that period referred to in the penal code as the time between sunset and sunrise—they were not 'lodgers,' a category of protected occupants which constitute an 'inhabited building'; but rather 'vagrants,' unlawfully occupying, or more specifically trespassing, at said time and therefore not entitled to the protection of the law."

"They're still dead," Brent said dryly, removing his

glasses and tossing them carelessly on the table as he rubbed at his eyes.

"Dead, yes," Cabot said, wheeling himself around in a wide circle until he faced Judge Hammerman. "But murdered? No. This is a case of arson. If that. For all we know, those vagrants were responsible for the fire. Trying to keep warm on a cold night with no thought to the public safety—"

"This is California, not Siberia," Brent said. "Your Honor, please!"

But Charlotte could tell from the way Judge Hammerman was lapping up every word Cabot was saying that, at the very least, Ash Whittier would be released to his older brother's custody.

"Surely the charge of murder seems excessive," the judge argued on Cabot's behalf. "There is certainly not the required malice aforethought here. And while death could possibly have been the result of arson, which would certainly make it fall within the purview of a felony, I think manslaughter is the best you could hope for, Brent, considering that the vagrants were likely to be foreigners."

Beside her, Ash threw up his hands. "Are they less dead if they're not citizens?" he asked her under his breath. "If they made my roof theirs, then they weren't people?"

"I'll go for manslaughter," Brent agreed, while Charlotte studied the anguish on her brother-in-law's face. It was a nice face, too, weathered by his trips at sea, burned by the sun of exotic ports and crisscrossed with smile lines by his eyes and his lips. "And arson in the first degree with intent to commit insurance fraud."

On the pad in front of him Ash set to doodling with a pencil. A lefty, his hand curled around his work, hiding what he drew and no doubt smudging it. "Sure you don't want to add that I was toasting them to eat for breakfast?

Or that I torched the Piedmont Springs Hotel while I was still away in Argentina?" Ash asked the DA.

Charlotte clapped her hand over her mouth while Cabot glared at his brother. "My client apologizes to the court, Your Honor."

"Again," Brent added.

"Again?" Cabot asked, raising an eyebrow at Charlotte as if she had any more control over his brother's behavior than he did.

"Your Honor," Charlotte said, coming to her feet, "Mr. Whittier arrived last night from a six-month sail in connection with his business. After only a few hours' sleep he was arrested on his boat, brought to the mainland, and interrogated extensively without benefit of food or sleep. He is tired, his nerves are frayed. I beg the court's indulgence on his behalf."

"You left out the part about being told his business was well into the red because the coffee beans he'd bought on the last trip were rotten and couldn't be sold. That surely didn't soothe your client's nerves."

Only Charlotte Whittier could sense the change in Cabot. Five years of marriage had taught her the subtle signs that others missed. Two fingers traced the spokes of his chair wheel. He sucked for a moment on the corner of his mustache.

"And tired? Not surprising after the knock-down-drag-out fight he had with his partner, Mr. Greenbough, over the receipts," Brent added, gesturing toward the judge as if he'd made his case.

Idiot. He ought to know better than to show a single card to Cabot Whittier, never mind his whole hand.

"My client admits to being tired and unnerved," Cabot said. "Within hours of his arrival he learned that his warehouse had been burned to the ground, then was accused of the crime, arrested, and deprived of sleep. Now he learns that deaths occurred on his premises. He apologizes for any thoughtless statements arising from that condition."

Judge Hammerman nodded unenthusiastically. If Ashford weren't Cabot's flesh and blood, Charlotte had no doubt he'd be looking at a contempt-of-court citation by now. Instead the judge asked Brent to produce his witnesses.

Brent's smile was nothing if not chilling. "Prosecution offers the sworn testimony of Moss Johnson," he said, feeling around for his glasses, which Charlotte supposed Cabot had somehow moved when he'd wheeled himself around to face the judge. When he finally located them, Brent handed over several papers to the clerk. "And calls Selma Mollenoff to the stand."

*Think about what you ate for breakfast, Charlotte,* she could hear Cabot coaching.

Folding her hands on the table, she watched Selma make her way to the stand, and pretended it didn't come as a shock that the prosecution would call to the stand Selma Mollenoff, the sister of Dr. Eli Mollenoff, a man Charlotte considered her dearest friend.

Selma, the same woman for whom she'd secured a position as bookkeeper in her brother-in-law's company, the same woman with whom she'd attended Miss Tracy's Secondary School for the Education of Women, the same woman to whom she'd lent her watch at the last meeting of the Ebell Society for the Advancement of Art, Science, and Literature for Women, so that Selma could time Charlotte Perkins Gilman's speech. Selma was Charlotte's most ardent, if not her most vocal, supporter in the case for Virginia Halton's right to disseminate scientific information to women regarding the functioning of their own bodies.

Of course, Selma took her oath defiantly, shooting needles at Brent with her eyes.

"Did you see Mr. Ashford Whittier yesterday, Miss Mollenoff?" Brent asked.

"Yes, but—" she began, her eyes connecting with Charlotte's apologetically.

"Where?"

"At the warehouse. That's the G and W Warehouse. But—"

"Just answer the questions, Miss Mollenoff," Judge Hammerman said. "This isn't a trial—here all we want is the truth."

Charlotte covered her smirk with her hand. If whether or not Ash went to trial didn't rest squarely on Selma Mollenoff's shoulders, Charlotte would have laughed out loud at the judge's comment. As it was, several spectators behind her did.

"So, Miss Mollenoff, Ashford Whittier was at the G and W warehouse on the afternoon of February eighth?"

Selma's shoulders sagged under the weight of her answer. She sighed, making it appear she had already convicted her employer. "Yes, as I said, but—"

"Seeing to the unloading of . . . ?"

"The Cuervo, but—"

"Excuse me?" Brent waited for Selma to explain.

"José Cuervo," she said with a heavy sigh. "Tequila."

"What is that?"

"Alcohol. From Mexico, but—"

"Alcohol." He let the enormity of the sin sink in before continuing. "And when the shipment of . . . hard liquor . . . was unloaded, you saw Mr. Whittier leave the building?" Brent asked, his eyebrows reaching for the ceiling.

"No." She had given up adding her qualifiers.

Brent whirled around as if there were actually a jury to

which he could pander. "No? You mean he was still there when you left the premises at four-thirty on the eighth?"

"He was there when I left," she agreed. Then she added quickly, running all the words together to prevent Brent from stopping her, "But he always stayed late when he came home from a buying trip."

Brent nodded. The statement hadn't done his case any harm. It also hadn't exactly put Ash at the scene at one-thirty in the morning.

"That's all."

Charlotte looked at Cabot, hoping he would signal for her to question Selma, disappointed when he shook his head slightly and wheeled himself within a few feet of the witness box. She could have handled the cross-exam herself. She squeezed the fingers of her left hand within the confines of her right. Harder, and harder still, until all of the anger flowed out her fingertips. And then she sat forward and tried to learn from the master.

"Hello, Selma," Cabot said warmly, letting the judge know that they went way back, which wasn't so true, but was Cabot's style. "This is obviously very difficult for you, isn't it?"

Selma nodded, grimacing, and threw her shoulders back. "It's ludicrous. Mr. Whittier wouldn't hurt a—"

Cabot didn't allow her to finish. Lord knew what Selma might say, given the opportunity. "Well, I'll be very brief. You saw Mr. Whittier at the warehouse in the afternoon. Is that unusual when he came back from a trip?"

"No. He always came just as soon as he got into port." She smiled, apparently grateful to be able to say something helpful. "And he always brought a little gift for everyone in the office, something you can't get here, or something for their children, and—"

"Thank you, Selma," Cabot said, cutting her off. "And

you say that Mr. Whittier was still there when you left. That unusual?"

She shook her head, twisting a handkerchief with her hands. "He always remains as long as the men will work. But they only stay until dark, and so sometimes he stays on with Moss and they finish after the others have gone."

"Well, this is February. It gets dark early, doesn't it?" He didn't wait for her to respond. "I noticed you referred to the Mexican liquor as Cuervo. Are you a big drinker, Miss Mollenoff?"

She rolled her eyes at Cabot's foolishness. "We've been importing tequila from the Cuervo Company as long as I've been with G and W. And it was on the books when I started."

Cabot wheeled back to the defense table. "So, all in all, it was a pretty normal day down at the warehouse. That right?"

Selma agreed, neither of them mentioning the fistfight between the partners.

"Thank you, Selma. No further questions, Your Honor."

"The clerk will read the statement of Moss Johnson into the record," Judge Hammerman said, apparently not much more impressed than Charlotte with the evidence.

The clerk cleared his phlegmy throat. "I, Moss Johnson, do swear that I am the foreman at the G and W Warehouse and that on February eighth, 1888, I saw Mr. Ashford Whittier have words with Mr. Greenbough, which came to blows. And I heard Mr. Whittier say that he'd be best off if he just burned down the place and walked away with the insurance money."

There was dust in Charlotte's mouth. There had to be. What else would explain the fact that she couldn't swallow?

"I didn't mean—" Ashford started to say, but a hand on

his arm quieted him. "It's something you say," he whispered to her, and she nodded understandingly as she watched Brent come to his feet.

"Motive, Your Honor," he said, putting his hands up as if everything was self-evident. "Tequila—means. At the premises—opportunity. I don't know what more you could want to hold the man over for trial."

The judge, biting the inside of his cheek, nodded his agreement, and thumbed through some papers on his desk. "On the weight of the evidence here presented, the court has no choice but to insist that the defendant be bound over for trial. The matter will be heard in this court on March twenty-second, 1888." He banged his gavel.

*March 22.* The dust in Charlotte's mouth turned to boulders around which she couldn't even speak.

Cabot ran his fingers up and down the spokes of his wheels until the tips turned white.

"Your Honor, as Ashford Whittier's attorney, I ask that bail be set in the amount of five hundred dollars and that he be released on his own recognizance until such time as his presence is required in this Court."

"Ha!" Brent choked out, looking at the judge as if Cabot had clearly lost his mind. "Three people murdered, Your Honor."

"You agreed to manslaughter," the judge reminded him. "Offense isn't punishable by death. The man's entitled to bail."

"And five hundred dollars is supposed to keep a man whose home is on a boat from sailing off into the sunset to spend his days sipping milk from coconuts?" Brent demanded, throwing his glasses off again, and then reaching out to keep one hand on them.

"The Whittier honor and integrity is what will keep him here," Cabot answered somewhat smugly. Unfortunately it was rather widely known that it was Cabot Whittier who had cornered that particular market in the Whittier family, so Brent just crossed his arms and stared at the judge as if daring him to set foot in that pile of horse manure.

"Five thousand and into your custody, Whittier," Judge Hammerman said, banging his gavel and rising before Cabot could argue further—which the judge, and Charlotte, and probably the DA, as well, knew full well he wouldn't, since they were luckier than ladybugs to have gotten away with all they had.

"God bless the prejudices of the Californians," Cabot said quietly, brushing a speck of lint from his thighs. "And the preponderance of Chinese vagrants."

"I can't believe you did that," Ash said, crumpling up the piece of paper he had been scribbling on and throwing it to the floor. "Just like that. Three nonpeople. Someone killed them, Cabot—"

"Not one word," Cabot told him, pointing for Charlotte to retrieve the paper for him and then smoothing it out. On it were a woman and two children, coffins drawn awkwardly around each of them. Cabot handed the paper back to Charlotte, who held on to it, rather than open her satchel and place it in there, which was clearly Cabot's expectation.

"Can we go?" Ash asked, rising and stretching out a body that seemed all the taller next to his brother's sitting form.

"When they're all gone," Charlotte told him. Cabot didn't like impeding anyone's exit with his chair maneuvers. She placed her hat onto her head, adjusting the angle until it could accommodate her bun beneath it.

"It's nicer than I thought," Ash said, obviously trying to take his mind off his troubles as he tilted his head to look at her. "At least it doesn't compete with that pretty face of yours."

Charlotte felt herself blush. Crying and blushing in one day. What would she stoop to next?

Good glory! The last time anyone had called her pretty, well . . . she couldn't remember the last time! Cheeks positively on fire now, Charlotte busied herself with opening her briefcase and carefully laying the scrap paper inside it. Any reporter would have made an editorial out of Ash's doodle, and one of Cabot's first lessons had been never to leave in a courtroom anything she didn't want splashed on the front page of the *Oakland Enquirer.*

"I do believe the brim on that hat is too wide, Charlotte," Cabot said, assessing her hat and shaking his head. "Have it cropped before you wear it to court again. It wouldn't do to have you looking frivolous, featherbrained."

Ashford stifled the laugh, settling for tapping gently on her briefcase.

Inside it the little black-capped chickadee strained up toward her and let out the loudest cheep he could. "As soon as we get home," she whispered. Fortunately, Cabot had made his way over to the prosecution's table, where he was busy exchanging pleasantries as though the fact that Brent had charged his brother with murder had nothing to do with the price of tea in China. Which, when one thought about the circumstances and the supposed motive for the fire, was more to the point than anything else might have been.

Did Ash, in fact, import tea? She shrugged. In five years of marriage to Cabot she didn't think that Ash had been to Whittier Court more than half a dozen times or so. While they'd have the occasional Sunday dinner at the Tubb's Hotel with him when he was in town, the meetings were what Cabot would call short and sweet. Or maybe simply short. And though Kathryn received occasional letters from him, she never shared their contents.

"Much as I hate to admit it, he is pretty amazing," Ash said, pointing to his brother. Cabot sat with one hand raised, gesturing toward the ceiling fans and explaining something about how a reversal of their direction was bringing the warm air down into the room.

Charlotte agreed. It seemed to her there wasn't a subject about which Cabot wasn't well versed, or one about which he didn't have an opinion worth hearing. "Was he always so smart?"

Ashford Whittier closed his eyes and swallowed hard, his features softening with the pain of remembrance. How stupid she was, how unkind! She should have known better than to bring up those awful memories—she was careful enough with Cabot, after all.

"Cabot was already twelve when I was born," Ash said, his easy smile pasted back in place once again. "He was a man in even the earliest of my memories—and brilliant, even then. Of course, to a four-year-old anyone who can figure out how to peel a banana seems smart."

"What about bananas?" Cabot asked, having shaken hands with the opposition and shooed them from the room. "You still like them?" he asked his brother.

A look passed between the two men, years melting away until they both were boys again. And then it was gone.

Ash studied the marquetry floor, his hands pushed down deep into the pockets of his pants.

"It'll be all right," Cabot said softly, in that same smooth voice with which he'd comforted Charlotte when her grandmother had died and left her all alone in the world at seventeen. The voice he used for pitiful clients facing death sentences, and reluctant witnesses who had information he needed them to reveal. "It only looks so bleak because we haven't had a chance to present our defense yet."

Ash nodded soberly. "Right. And what's the worst I could get, after all?"

Charlotte and Cabot exchanged looks, Cabot leaving it for her to say. If she complained about it later he'd no doubt tell her it was part of a lawyer's job, informing his client about the risks and options. And so it was. Still, she couldn't bring herself to be quite honest and truthful with her husband's brother, and so she answered, "With Cabot defending you?" and tried to leave it at that.

Ash's clear brown eyes met hers. "That bad?" he asked.

She nodded. "Arson alone can be as much as fourteen years. Brent'll go for the maximum on each count, I'm sure."

The air rushed out of him and he sat heavily in the wooden chair at the defense table, his hands hanging limply at his sides. "All together?" he asked, summoning up resources she was forced to admire. "How much all together?"

Cabot rolled up close to his brother, pushing at a chair in his way, signaling Arthur to back off just a bit. "Have I ever let you down?" he asked. "I haven't saved your hide over and over again to let it rot in some jail now."

Charlotte stood where she was, not sure Cabot was even aware of her presence and not wanting to be noticed. Emotion was a stranger to her husband's way of life, and she felt him fighting now to rid himself of it.

"I'm the best damn lawyer in the East Bay," Cabot said, his voice filling the empty chamber. "No matter what Alfred Cohen thinks. The best. Maybe even in San Francisco too. I'll get you off, Ashford, without serving a day."

"You got some kind of magic wand tucked back there somewhere?" Ash asked, his hand on Cabot's shoulder as he tried to peer behind him.

"I'll take care of it," Cabot answered. "You know I will.

There's just one thing I'd like to know—as your brother, not your lawyer. For curiosity's sake."

Ash nodded, his tall body leaning forward as if he was poised and ready to tell him anything.

Cabot looked around the courtroom, making sure they were alone. He seemed surprised to see Charlotte there, but made no move to exclude her. "Well," he said, one eyebrow raised in question, "did you do it?"

# Chapter 2

They could still hear the peacock squawking even after they'd all rushed into the front hall and Cabot's brother had slammed the door behind them. Somehow the bird, intended to show the Stanfords and the Lathams that the Whittiers had as much money and taste as their neighbors, had gotten his function confused with that of a guard dog. And as if his awful catlike calls and charges against pure strangers weren't bad enough, he had developed a distinct dislike for Cabot and was bent on biting the hand that fed him.

"Incogitant bird," Cabot said. "He's lucky I don't roast him and serve him in his own feathers!"

"Cabot!" Charlotte wasn't any fonder of the peacock than her husband. Still, she did understand the difference between a pet and a meal. "Maybe he was just trying to protect the house from a stranger." She gestured at Ashford, who came around so rarely that Charlotte didn't think even the staff would recognize him.

Cabot examined his sleeve. "That gormless pile of feathers ate another button! Arthur, I want that bird confined to a pen when I'm out and about. I want—"

"Can we just forget the ridiculous bird?" Ashford asked, pulling at the tie around his neck as though it were a noose.

"Bother you to think of something being confined?" Cabot asked callously while he handed his hat to Arthur and told him to let Maria know they would be in his office awaiting tea.

"Of course it bothers me," Ash said, removing the tie and shoving it into his pocket. "But not as much as your little question did. That you could even think I would set a building on fire, *our* building, no less. I willingly admit I've been stupid, maybe even reckless from time to time, but you must know I've never willfully, knowingly, gone out and—"

"Of course you haven't." Kathryn Whittier's smooth, even voice welcomed them home as warmly as open arms. She came into the dark wood-paneled front hall slowly, leaning heavily on her ivory cane. On the far side of sixty now, the years had clearly taken their toll on Kathryn's body, but had been kind to her face. A thick mass of silvery hair done up in the latest style surrounded fine features and soft gray eyes. She eased herself down into the softly cushioned chair that Charlotte had suggested be left in the hall for her. "How did it go in court?"

Cabot's tight little shake of his head warned Charlotte not to reveal too much. Before she could carefully frame her words, Kathryn waved the question away and looked beyond them for her younger son.

"Mother." Ash said the word with reverence, coming out from the shadows of the dark hall to kneel by Kathryn, taking both her hands in his as he looked her over from head to toe. "Why, you haven't changed a bit! As beautiful and young as ever," he said while a slight grimace touched the corner of his mouth.

"Don't put him on the stand if he's got to lie about anything," Kathryn said to Cabot. "It's not his forte."

"I don't have to lie," Ash said, standing to his full height and maybe then some, as the lines of his face hardened again. "Despite what my brother might think."

"Oh, Cabot," Kathryn said with a heavy sigh, "why are they all mad at you this time?"

Cabot's innocent look was priceless. Charlotte had been there, had watched him do away with three dead people and question his brother's honesty to boot, and still, if she were sitting in the jury box and staring at that face, she'd be fooled into thinking her husband guiltless. How many cases had he won on that face of his?

Still, the thought of those children, burned beyond recognition, wouldn't let her be. "He obliterated three lives," she told Kathryn. "Negated their very existence, transformed them from victims into criminals themselves." She turned to Cabot. "You cheapen the value of life itself when you do that."

"Oh, Charlotte. There you go climbing on that high horse of yours. Would they be any less dead if I'd let the murder charge stand? Or would it just have left us explaining to Mother why her baby was crossing his hands behind his head in the Alameda County Jail and facing the prospect of a noose around his neck?" Cabot dusted an imaginary piece of lint from his lap as he gave her time to accept his logic. Irrefutable, as always.

"But it was offensive," she said finally. "It offended me as an officer of the court, as a servant of justice."

"No," Cabot argued, "it offended you as a woman. As a lawyer you know it was a brilliant legal maneuver. And in court, as I've told you time and again, you are a lawyer, not a woman."

"Is that like a vagrant and not a person?" Ash bent over to yank at the laces of the boots he'd probably had on since the previous morning. "Or an arsonist who's innocent?"

"In a lawyer's portfolio, Charlotte, there is no room for emotion. When you read for the law you learn to deal in crime, precedent, and punishment. If you're looking for sentiment, I suggest you read a romantic novel," Cabot said with disdain, then signaled Arthur to wheel him into the offices at the front of the house. "If you'll excuse me," he said, gesturing toward the files he held in his lap, "I've work to get done."

"*You* don't like sentiment in the courtroom?" Charlotte called after his back, nearly laughing at the irony. "What was that about me crying this morning?"

His hand came up and stopped Arthur's progress. He leaned over the arm of his chair to get a better look at her. "Indeed. What were those tears, Charlotte?"

She shook her head at him. "Nothing. A cinder in my eye. From those damned fans." Guiltily she looked at Kathryn. "Sorry."

"Charlotte, you sound more like a man every day," Kathryn said. "The next thing we know, Cabot will have you puffing on cigars and swilling brandy."

"I just might," Cabot responded. "Don't think for a second that every decision in the law is made in a courtroom. It's in the back rooms where the real work is done, and if Charlotte wants to ever progress beyond dog bites and landlord-tenant disputes, she's going to have to get into those dens of iniquity and leave her sensibilities outside."

"It doesn't seem as if you've left her any sensibilities." Cabot's brother looked up from his boots to examine her slowly from head to toe. From his grimace it appeared that he was not impressed with her court clothes.

"*Any* is more than she needs," Cabot answered. "Crying in court! Really, Charlotte! Leaving me to turn your little soft spot for children around and throw it back at the DA. . . ."

"For heaven's sake, Cabot," Ashford said, finally managing to spring his swollen feet from his oxford ties. "She's a woman. She's got tender feelings."

While he spoke, he motioned toward her squawking alligator valise as if it contained the proof of her maternal instincts. As if just because she was reluctant to let a living creature die, she had some innate need to mother it.

"I'm a lawyer," Charlotte told her brother-in-law. One brother was nearly as bad as the other! She snatched up her Gladstone and headed for the stairwell. "A lawyer, Mr. Whittier," she repeated. "Not a twit."

Of course, pressed to the wall, she would have had to admit that there was a certain amount of dignity lost as she carefully carried up the stairs a legal case full of angrily chirping bird.

"Where are you off to?" Kathryn called after her. In her voice was that slight quiver which was usually reserved for discussions with Cabot.

"My study," Charlotte said, for want of a better name for the bright room in the cupola of the house. The room where, because the elevator only went as far as the second floor, her secrets were safely hidden from Cabot.

"You mean the high room?" Kathryn asked. Charlotte stopped in her tracks without answering and waited for her to continue.

Finally, when there was no further word from her mother-in-law, Charlotte took another step.

"Is that where you mean?"

When Charlotte had married Cabot she had taken

great pains to assure the older woman that she had no interest in taking over the running of Kathryn's house. Becoming a lawyer would take all the energy and attention she could give it. As far as Charlotte, and everyone else, was concerned, Kathryn was the lady of the house. Charlotte had even gone as far as to make sure Kathryn had no objection when, after just a few months of marriage, she moved certain of her belongings into the high room and her plants to the rooftop surrounding it.

And it had been fine until now. It inconvenienced no one and gave Charlotte a place where she could be . . . well, just Charlotte.

"Of course that's where I mean," she answered, anxious to get the little chickadee fed without missing any further discussion of Ashford's case. "Why?"

"Well, dear," Kathryn hedged, "I do realize that the house is yours now, yours and Cabot's, that is, and you are certainly free to make whatever arrangements you wish. But considering the boys' tendency to argue . . ."

This last she said as if the two men were still quite young, as if it were before the accident, and she was worried about them getting into a scuffle around her antique urns.

What she meant was that if Ash's room was on the same floor as Cabot's, it could prove an embarrassment to the latter.

It was something Charlotte should probably have thought of herself. But then hadn't Cabot spent two years before their marriage and the five years since drumming that feminine sensitivity out of her, all so that she could be the second best lawyer in all of Oakland?

Of course, it didn't take a woman to notice the details. Cabot didn't miss a trick, a nuance, a hint, of anything in his household or his cases. She, on the other hand, was as likely to miss a trolley going through the parlor as the subtle problems that accompanied her husband's condition. And if Kathryn thought it best, well, she certainly knew her sons better than Charlotte.

"You'd like to put Ashford in the high room?" She tried to keep the disappointment from her voice. After all, she still had her bedroom, her office, the back porch—a hundred places on the grounds to find solitude when she still needed it. It was just that the high room was *hers*. Hers alone.

"It does seem the most obvious solution, doesn't it?" Kathryn asked while Charlotte fought to keep the resignation from showing in her nod.

"I could go to a hotel," Ash offered from the bottom of the stairwell, obviously wishing as fervently as she that he were anywhere else.

"Remanded to your brother's custody," she reminded him. Maybe Ashford didn't understand the letter of the law, but she had a very clear picture of the next few weeks, and in it the sun wasn't shining over Whittier Court.

"Well, then, the couch is fine," he said, looking at the walls as if they were already closing in on him. "Heck, it's a big house, Charlotte, and it's yours. I certainly wouldn't want to put you out of your study."

"I've no objection to you taking over the high room," Charlotte said, brushing off calling the room her study, or the house hers. Kathryn had little enough in life to call her own. Charlotte was not going to take the woman's house from her just because she'd married her son.

And if Cabot didn't need a study, why should she? "Really," she added, wishing she felt half as generous as she sounded, and thrice as generous as she felt.

She couldn't help loving that high room, with its eight arched windows, two in each direction. At every hour of the day there was something to watch—the sun rising, playing on Lake Merritt, dappling the trees, and finally setting at the end of the day. She loved taking down her hair up there and brushing it until it glistened, then pulling it back into its bun to face the world. She loved the lace curtains, and the flowered slipper chair she'd taken down from the attic to set beside the windows.

"You'll no doubt want me to remove a few of my things," she said, imagining the wrong impression Ash could get from the condition she'd left his room in. "But the room is yours, of course. I was only borrowing it while you were away."

"You aren't practicing your cigar smoking up there, are you?" Ash asked. "Or have you other vices even Cabot doesn't know about?"

Kathryn rapped her cane on the hardwood floor. "Don't you go teasing Charlotte," she said, though Charlotte had the sense that he wasn't teasing so much as he was accusing her of something. "I'm quite sure she hasn't a single vice."

"Charlotte!" Cabot's angry voice implied otherwise as he shouted her name from his office. "Charlotte Whittier, get your corpus calossum in here at once and explain this! I thought we agreed that your little Comstock case for Virginia Halton was ancient history."

His sister-in-law looked as though she'd been caught with someone else's fish on her line.

"Charlotte?" Cabot demanded. "Are you out there?"

"Coming!"

She glanced down at the valise in her hand and then at the doorway, looking nearly vulnerable for a moment despite the tight bun and the starched collar. Ash noticed that when she wasn't carefully sucking it in, the woman's lower lip was full—lush, even. And, at the moment, he thought it was trembling slightly.

"I'll put him upstairs," Ash said, climbing the couple of steps and trying to take the case from her hand. She hesitated, clinging to the briefcase handle while his hands gripped the sides.

"Charlotte!"

Hesitantly she released her hold on the bag. There was no question the lip was indeed quivering when she called out to Cabot that she was coming.

Ash remained on the stairs, watching as she straightened her shirtwaist, threw back her shoulders, and lifted her chin before crossing the threshold into the offices that had been built as part of the house when his father had begun the construction years before Ash had even been born. Two offices, one for father and one intended for son. His father would die all over again if he knew that they now were for husband and wife.

Once Charlotte was gone, he put the briefcase down with a quick promise to the bird within. On flat, tired feet he padded through the foyer into the front vestibule, unable to resist a quick look out onto the wide green lawn to satisfy his curiosity. More than likely he'd have noticed on the way in if it hadn't been for the damn peacock.

Naturally, the old sign was there, just as he suspected. The back of it was still and forever peeling, assuring him that it read as it always had: WHITTIER AND SON, ATTORNEYS-AT-LAW. *Whittier and Whittier,* she'd said. He didn't think that Cabot's wedding vows would have extended to the sharing of his little empire. It wasn't like Cabot Whittier to share anything he felt belonged exclusively to him.

"When Cabot's interested in hearing who I suspect might have done it, send Rosa up, will you?" he asked his mother, stooping to kiss the top of her head as he passed her on his way to the stairwell.

"You don't mind being back in the high room, do you?" she asked when he reached for the briefcase that waited on the steps. "Other arrangements could certainly be made if that room disturbs you."

"Of course not," Ash said over his shoulder as casually as he could. He took the steps two at a time, stopping at the second-floor landing for a quick look to see what had changed. Seven eight-panel mahogany doors, all closed, still lined the hall. On the papered walls that separated the bedroom doors were portraits of his ancestors, many in judge's robes, some even complete with wigs. A bench across from each painting allowed a resting place for the contemplation of the Whittier roots.

That was how his father had put it. The *Whittier roots.* The phrase always left Ash feeling like the one rotten apple the family tree had produced.

In the bag at his side the bird chirped weakly to remind him of its hunger.

Up the second flight of stairs his old room waited for him. The curtains were drawn and the sun streamed in, pointing to his old desk, the pages of an open book flipping in the breeze, a hairbrush with a few dark strands set beside it. The desk was still there, but now it was haphazardly redecorated with shawls and feminine gewgaws and yard upon yard of lace. Even his dresser, where once mighty soldiers fought battles over blocks upon which to stand, was covered with a frilly runner. The lacy doily was nearly hidden by a collection of small bottles, a mortar and pestle, and a stack of fresh clean cloths.

And from the sounds coming from beneath his bed, it appeared that his sister-in-law's feeding station was attracting more than simply birds.

Kicking the door shut, he pulled back the chair from his desk, and started to set Charlotte's satchel there. He stopped at the sight of a pair of ladies' cotton hose that lay crumpled on the seat. Apparently his sister-in-law had made herself quite at home in his old room. He held up one of the stockings, its top banded with the same delicate edging that covered everything else in the room, its ankle embroidered with intricate little flowers, and let it hang from his raised arm. Nothing he'd removed from his own person had ever shown quite so much shape.

But a grown woman's foot couldn't be that small, could it?

The bird shrieked at him and he dropped the stocking guiltily. "Well, she shouldn't have left it around," he said in his own defense, placing the satchel on the trunk at the foot of the bed. Upon opening it he found that the bird, apparently angry at his confinement, had taken out his frustration on the contents of Charlotte's Gladstone, ripping papers and decorating them with his droppings.

"Where's your lace collar?" he asked the bird, gently taking him out and cradling him in his palm. "Or doesn't she let you wear it outside this room?"

She was something, that Charlotte. Fooling the world into thinking she didn't have a feminine bone in her body, tricking him into feeding her little runt of a bird when his own parrot was probably starving to death. Moss Johnson's job was strictly to be Ash's man in the warehouse, not on board the *Bloody Mary.* Had it occurred to him, then, to go onto the ship and feed Liberty? He hoped so, or the whole harbor would be deaf from the parrot's version of "Little Brown Jug." Deaf and scandalized.

He looked over the various bottles on his dresser, wondering what he was supposed to feed the tiny thing in his hand. He really ought to be downstairs, helping Cabot sort out the details of his return to Oakland. Of course, Cabot would do it better than he could. Cabot had always done everything better than Ash ever could.

The way they told it, Cabot had been faster than the

wind before the accident. He'd probably swum across the bay in record time, though it didn't seem anyone had ever bothered to clock him.

Now the man had to settle for just walking on the water.

Rolling on it.

"Charlotte, this case is too dangerous, too controversial, for you to be taking on. You're trying to build a career here, not change the world," Cabot said, throwing the letters she'd received into the wastebasket.

"I'm trying to do both," she said, digging the letters back out. "Women have rights, Cabot, or they should have."

"Oh, please," Cabot said, raising his hands in mock defeat. "Don't start in again with your damn suffrage talk. If I have to hear about the forward-looking territory of Wyoming one more time, I think I may just buy you a ticket and let you go freeze your tail off out there for a month or two."

"But I don't see why if Wyoming allows women the vote, and to serve on juries and in its courts, that the great state of California—"

"Charlotte, we've been over this a million times. Wyoming precedent won't apply here because it's not a state. When you've got a population of forty-two thousand in the whole territory, you'd let the damn dogs have the vote!"

"And do you put women and dogs in the same category?" she asked him, pacing around the room rearranging whatever wasn't nailed down.

"From what I've heard, they both have cold noses," Cabot said. "And they are noisy and messy and they don't give you any peace."

He sighed heavily and, pushing his papers aside, rested his elbows on his desk.

"We don't have time for this, Charlotte. We've got to hire a private investigator for the legwork and we've got to go over every shred of evidence with a fine-tooth comb. I have a bad feeling this is going to be our toughest case."

"But you're tired," Charlotte said, watching as Cabot rolled his head, stretching his neck out first this way and then that. "Maybe we should do this later?"

"If we wait until I'm not tired, Charlotte, they'll have hanged my brother and buried my grieving mother as well." He reached for his glass on the desk, found it empty, and grimaced.

"I'll get you some more," Charlotte said, hopeful for the opportunity to leave the room and check on whatever had happened to the fledgling she'd left in Ashford's care. If what Cabot was always saying about his brother was true, the bird was probably already dead from neglect. And then there was Van Gogh, the little one-earred rabbit she'd named for that poor artist Cabot's friend from Paris had told them about, who'd no doubt left a welcome present right on Ash's coverlet.

"Sit," Cabot directed her as she stood and reached out for his empty glass. "You can make better use of your time researching the penal code than playing at the domesticated little woman. Did you ask him if he had any alibi?"

Charlotte set the glass down on the desk, careful to center it on the coaster the way Cabot preferred. She pulled the servant's cord for Maria and then took her seat again. Cabot's face was drawn; his fingers played relentlessly with the spokes of his chair wheel. "Are you all right? It's not like you to snap at me so."

"I'm sorry, little one," he said, studying her with eyes that softened the longer they looked. "Have I been a beast?"

"Grumpy," she admitted, shrugging it off. "Nothing that I can't handle."

"You're a good girl," he said, returning to his papers and ignoring Maria so that Charlotte had to once again get up, hand Maria the glass, and gesture for her to refill it. When Cabot read, he didn't like the chaos of chatter, and it amazed Charlotte how the staff could keep silent and anticipate instructions without a word being spoken.

"His alibi?" Cabot asked when Maria closed the door behind her. Cases were never discussed in front of the servants, as well they shouldn't be. Charlotte certainly wouldn't appreciate her private business bandied about in the back halls. Not that she had any private business. Still, if she had . . .

"He seems strangely vague on that," she admitted. "Apparently he was on the ship all night, but he's not too sure who saw him. He mentioned something about coming and going."

Cabot smiled knowingly and shook his head. "I'll just bet he's not sure. Probably doesn't even know her name or where he picked her up. We'll have to get the investigator to find out where the hell he was. And who it was he took back with him."

"Good glory! Don't say that in front of your mother. I think she holds him in slightly higher regard than you do."

"Women, mothers especially, have a tendency to be blind to a man's faults," he said without looking up from his work. "Consequently they overlook the obvious."

One more thing to overcome. Filed up there with *Women have a tendency to talk too much, consequently their point is lost; women have a tendency to dress too warmly in the winter, consequently they become overheated indoors; women have a tendency to ask for the impossible, consequently they are disappointed.*

"Well, no doubt we'll find out who she is if we offer a

big enough reward to come forward. Of course, I can't guarantee my mother will like it. Nor will you, for that matter. We might as well start with who rowed them out and back."

"Wouldn't that be enough?" she asked.

"Not if I was the DA," Cabot said, and folded his arms across his chest. "Now you tell me why not."

Charlotte didn't have to think long. She rose and looked down her nose at Cabot. "And can you swear, Mr. Witness, that he didn't leave the boat and come back between the time that you ferried him in and out yourself?"

"Good girl," Cabot said. "Unfortunately I don't think it will take Brent any longer to see that than it did you."

"But your brother would certainly remember the woman, wouldn't he? I mean, he'd know her name, would recognize her, she'd know him. . . ."

She could see from the look on Cabot's face that not only wasn't it a surety, it didn't even appear likely. "I'm sorry, Charlotte, but my brother doesn't take women very seriously. He'd probably be stoned in Wyoming."

Not even remember who he was with. She tried to hide the shock that must have been written all over her face by busying herself with the library ladder that was resting by the window. Outside a large black man was lumbering up the front walk. On his shoulder was the biggest, most colorful bird Charlotte had ever seen. Had it not been flapping its spectacular wings, she'd have supposed that it wasn't even real. Even Argus, the peacock, was too surprised to make a move.

"Moss Johnson is here with an enormous red-and-yellow-and-blue—"

"That's Liberty," Ashford said, coming up behind her to peer over her shoulder. "He's a scarlet macaw. From Peru. I'll let them in."

"Go easy on him, Ash," Cabot warned as his brother headed for the door. "He was only telling the truth."

Ashford turned to stare at his brother, his eyebrows lowered in question. "Oh, the statement in court. He must feel bad as"—he paused and looked at Charlotte—"all get out."

"Mmm," she agreed. "*Damned* shame."

"I think I've some cigars in my luggage," he teased. "Should I pull out one for you?"

"Haven't taken to them," she said, pulling at her lapels and standing straighter. "Yet."

He shook his head at her. "From the looks of my room, it doesn't appear that's imminent." Then, before hurrying out, he had the audacity to wink at her.

"Charlotte?" Cabot had apparently stopped his work to study her, and was staring hard. "Why, Charlotte . . . are you blushing?"

Whipping around so quickly that her skirts tumbled a book off the table, she faced the window and fought with the lock. "Some fresh air might be nice," she said, flipping the catch and throwing up the window sash to invite in the cold wind.

"I haven't been up in that room in nearly twenty years," Cabot said, his voice soft and distant behind her. "I suppose it's still too messy for him to find anything as small as a cigar."

"I'm sure that's what he meant," she said, willing the flame in her cheeks to pass. Had they only had some warning, she could have removed her things from the high room before Ashford discovered her . . . her what? Treason to her calling? Her weakness for frills and lace? Her affinity for . . .

"Oh, my word!" Kathryn gasped from out in the hallway. "Have you ever seen anything so lovely?"

"If you two could come out here for a moment," Ashford asked, tipping his head into the office and beckoning them with a crooked finger. "It isn't quite the way I'd planned my homecoming, but I've a few gifts and such. . . ."

Charlotte tamped down the excitement that bubbled in her chest. Ashford had brought her presents before. Her wonderful Gladstone from Argentina, a silken nightgown from China, a beaded reticule of ocean pearls—not much she could use, of course, but all of them treasures to own. She just hoped that the parrot wasn't their gift. If Argus the peacock was any indication, birds didn't seem to like Cabot overmuch.

"You coming?" she asked Cabot as she came down from the library steps with a volume of *Black's Law Dictionary* in her hand.

He backed up from the desk and turned his chair slightly, backed up and turned the chair again. Charlotte knew better than to offer him any help. She understood his pride, but it hardly explained why he insisted on keeping the desk at what he perceived to be a "normal" distance from the wall when it meant that he could barely maneuver his wheels in and out of the narrow space intended for an office chair. Without assistance it was difficult, and Arthur was the only one ever permitted to help him. She supposed it was that Arthur was paid to see to Cabot, and Cabot respected the man's desire to do his job and do it well.

When she'd first assessed the situation, she'd accused him of being stubborn and pointed out how much simpler it would be to move the desk an extra foot or eighteen inches into the room. But *no,* he'd told her, *the world does not adapt itself for a cripple. It would rather inconvenience those who can't, than remind those who can of our existence.* Quickly she'd learned to allow Arthur to help or to stand to the side and let Cabot do it himself.

And so she waited while he extricated himself, hands jammed into her pockets to keep from helping him.

"Go ahead," he said when he was free of the desk. "Let's see what we have no use for this time."

Liberty hopped happily from Moss's shoulder to Ash's own as Charlotte came into the foyer. The bird gave out with his usual complimentary whistle that he reserved for females, and added, "Oooh! Pretty! I want some of that!"

Knowing the rest of Liberty's vocabulary, Ash considered the immediate removal of the bird's vocal cords.

"It talks!" Charlotte said, her normally husky voice coming out a high-pitched squeal of delight.

"Oh! Oh! Oh! Don't stop!" the bird said in his best falsetto. Dropping his voice several octaves, the parrot added, "Shut up, you stupid bird!" just moments before Ash would have said the same thing. "Don't stop!"

Jeez, but that bird was looking to be stuffed like some piñata from South America.

"What does it want?" his sister-in-law asked, craning her neck at the bird and biting on that little pink tongue of hers.

Ash stared at her, trying to decide if she was just feigning innocence, while Moss Johnson coughed loudly and pulled several nuts from his pocket, shoving them at the bird and encouraging him to eat. "This ought to keep your mouth busy," he grumbled at the bird. "Don't you know a lady when you see one?"

"Hats off," the bird said, taking a peanut in one of his claws and deftly manipulating it until it was ready to be eaten.

"Oh, Cabot, come look!" Charlotte said, taking the nut Moss offered her and holding it out bravely to Liberty.

"What do you say?" the bird asked, still unable to get

the idea that *thank you* was the appropriate response. He took the nut from Charlotte and left a smile in return. For a moment he was quiet, chewing on one nut, studying the other, until Cabot rolled into the room and sent the feathered monster into fits of apoplexy. Flapping his enormous wings dramatically, Liberty set about squawking as if someone had set his tail on fire.

Now, even under the best of circumstances Liberty's voice was not what one would call soothing. He was, after all, a parrot, though Ash had to admit that there were times the stupid bird did double duty as his priest, his friend, and even his conscience. But when he was frightened or unnerved, as he was now at the sight of Cabot's wheelchair, Liberty's call was a deafening caterwaul that went through a man's head like a toothache.

And Moss's screaming at the bird to shut his beak wasn't helping matters. Kathryn had her hands over her ears, motioning for Charlotte to do the same, though his sister-in-law seemed to be taking her cue from Cabot rather than the older woman. She took far too many cues from her husband in Ash's opinion, but it wasn't any of his business what pains she took to hide her lacy stays beneath a show of manly-looking business suits. Perhaps it was exciting to Cabot to know that, under it all, his wife was just as feminine as any other woman. But it surely didn't float Ash's boat.

To his mind (what there was left of it with Liberty flapping wildly as if he could get up enough steam in the small confines of the hallway to actually take off and fly), there were enough tough-minded men in the world going around swashing their buckles. The fact that a woman could be strong and still be soft, be worldly without being jaded, that she could see things with equal clarity but from a different point of view—that was a woman's strength, as surely as a man's need to protect and guide was his.

In an effort to prevent them all from becoming deaf, and himself from being beheaded by one of Liberty's powerful wings, Ash lifted his arm and somehow managed to get it wrapped around the fully hysterical bird. "I'll put him upstairs," he shouted over the din while trying to calm the macaw down.

He was close to deaf, but not blind, and he couldn't miss the panic in those wide eyes of Charlotte's, or the slight gesture with her hand pointing up the stairwell and making tiny flapping signs. The little chickadee. He'd forgotten all about it. Clearly putting Liberty in the same room as that runt would be the end of it.

"On second thought," he said, pushing the screeching pile of feathers at his foreman, "take him out to the kitchen, will you, Moss?"

Moss took him, the bird turning his head clear around to keep an eye on Cabot, but at least quieting some so that all they heard now was the ringing in their ears.

"And tell Mrs. Mason if he doesn't stop that noise she can start plucking him for dinner," Cabot called after the big man's lumbering back.

"That's not funny," Charlotte said distractedly. Ash supposed there weren't many things Cabot said that anyone would consider funny.

"Tell me that squawking psittacine isn't your idea of a gift," Cabot shouted, pressing with his palm against his left ear and then releasing it as if that would restore his hearing.

"We've hardly room," Kathryn agreed, equally loudly. "Unless, of course, he could stay in the conservatory."

"Out of the question," Cabot yelled. "He'd eat my best specimens."

"Aren't some plants poisonous to birds?" Charlotte was rubbing both her temples as she spoke. "I've been doing some reading—"

"You don't have to yell," Ash said softly. "I can hear you just fine."

"A miracle you're not deaf," Cabot said. "That bird has got to go, Ashford. Naturally, I thank you for the thought but—"

Ash reached down for the sack that Moss had brought in along with the bird and pulled out a small wooden box. "Cigars," he said, handing the case to his brother and winking at Charlotte as if they were friends. "The bird's mine. Lives on the *Bloody Mary* with me and goes with me everywhere since I won him from a coffee merchant down in the Andes. I expect you to be a good boy, Cabot, and share these with your wife."

Cabot left the box in his lap, unopened. Ash knew he loved cigars, especially these Cuban ones. He also knew his brother was an ungrateful bastard who wouldn't want Ash to think his gift was truly appreciated and so he tapped the box, said a perfunctory thanks, and added that Ash "shouldn't have," as if he truly meant it.

"And this is for you, Mother." Ash found the small velvet pouch within the large burlap sack and placed it in his mother's upturned palm. He'd planned this gift for a long time, ordered it the last time he was in the islands, and had to wait months for it to be ready. Finding an Italian cameo carver who had relocated to the South Seas was a stroke of luck, but the design on the piece of jewelry was quite deliberate.

"Oh, my!" His mother's eyes misted over. "Look, Cabot!" she exclaimed, holding out the pale pink shell with four children glistening in cream on the cameo's face.

"How lovely," his sister-in-law said as she leaned over Cabot's shoulder to get a better look. "I've never seen one with any children on it. Wherever did you find it?"

"Like a newsman, an importer never reveals his sources," Ash said, sorry he hadn't brought her back a cameo as well, since she was so obviously taken with it. Perhaps when he got out of his present troubles and had the chance to return to the islands he could have one carved for her with a little bird upon it.

In the meantime he had something he was sure she would like just as much. Especially now that he'd been up to his room and seen her fondness for lace.

He took out the carefully wrapped package from the sack, neatened the ties on it to more properly present it, and bowed slightly at the waist. "For you, madam."

Charlotte fingered the strings, savoring the moment as if she'd never before received a present. Delicate fingers toyed with the crisp brown wrapper until Ash feared the gift would disintegrate with age.

"Charlotte, we've work to do," Cabot reminded her. "Unless he's brought gifts for all the jurors, I think he'll be relying on us to save his hide."

"You just have to spoil her moment, don't you?" Ash didn't mean for the words to come out, but once they had, he realized that it was something Cabot did with great regularity.

Charlotte looked tentative now, fingering the package more gingerly than before, as if it might be the last he ever brought. Just as disconcerted with the idea as she was, Ash cleared his throat. "Open it," he encouraged.

Without further ado Charlotte pulled at the strings and removed the wrappings. Her intake of breath was all the thanks Ash required and then some. Small, well-manicured fingers caressed the white silk reverently, then traced the lacy insets, one row after the other, with awe. She held it up by the shoulders against herself and stood on tiptoe to get a glimpse in the mirror. Then she turned to face the rest of them with a smile on her face that could have led sailors safely into port in the dark.

"Do you suppose it would fit Mother?" Cabot asked,

tilting his head and looking from his wife to Kathryn. "She's nearly as small as you."

"What?" The smile was gone from Charlotte's face. Replacing it was a nervous gnawing at the edge of her bottom lip, which seemed fuller every time Ash bothered to look at it.

"It doesn't have to fit Mother," Ash said. "It's for Charlotte, who it suits rather well, I think."

"Shows how little time you spend around here," Cabot said. "Not that it isn't a lovely . . . whatever . . . but it's much too frivolous for a woman of Charlotte's position and taste. Why, can you imagine a courtroom taking a woman seriously in *that*?"

Ash bit his tongue to stop himself from reminding Cabot that a courtroom took a man in a chair with wheels rather seriously and he doubted that a woman in lace would fare much worse. "There's always the weekend," he said instead. "You do let her have the weekends off, don't you? Church and all that? Wouldn't look good if she didn't get out to pray."

Charlotte took one last wistful look in the big gilt mirror, which was hung too high for her to see anything but her very sad face. Then she folded the blouse and held it out to Kathryn, blinking furiously as she did.

"Cabot's right. I thank you for thinking of me, Ashford, but a woman can't be all frills and lace one day and starch and wool the next. I've a reputation I'm proud of, and my image is a part of it."

"Isn't there somewhere you could wear it?" Ash asked, rolling his eyes toward the stairwell.

"No," she said with a sigh that would have broken a lesser man's heart, but seemed to go unnoticed by her husband. "It would be a shame to hide so lovely a blouse in my armoire. You enjoy it, Kathryn."

"It's a pity," Kathryn said as she took the blouse and,

just as Charlotte had done, covered her chest with it. "But I don't suppose anyone would take you seriously if you wore it."

Ash wasn't so sure that was so. He stared at his sister-in-law, knowing that beneath the navy boiled-wool jacket and under the starched white shirt, covered by the serge skirt and above the no-nonsense boots, there was at least one band of lace on her stockings. And, if his room was any indication, yards more of it intimately caressing her body.

And there was no question about it. He was taking her seriously. *Damned* seriously.

# Chapter 3

It had taken Cabot only a day to break down and enjoy one of the cigars that Ash had brought him. His face was nearly lost behind a cloud of smoke that Charlotte swore he was purposely blowing in her direction. Burning the soles of her shoes couldn't smell any worse, but she smiled at him as though swallowing in gobs of putrid air didn't bother her at all. She even took a few deep breaths before sitting back smugly in the wing chair in Cabot's office. It would take more than one rotten cigar to make her cough and wheeze and complain as if she were some delicate little flower that was being choked by an infernal weed.

Cabot extended the wooden box and gestured for her to help herself. Without taking his gaze from her, he tilted his head back and blew a steady stream of smoke toward the plaster acanthus leaves that ringed the ceiling, watching her, daring her to take the cigar.

"Or would you rather wear a frilly blouse and sit demurely in a drawing room with some embroidery?" He continued to hold the box out with his left hand while he tapped off the ashes of his cigar with his right.

"It was a beautiful blouse," she said, wishing she didn't sound quite as wistful as she did. "I'd have worn it to Judge Pollack's chambers the day we were married if I'd had it then."

"And gone down to assist me in the Ehrlich case afterward? I think not," he said, and smoke came from his nostrils as he snorted at her.

It had been a foolish, wayward thought. Not her dream at all. Her dreams had always been different from other girls'. Whereas Abigail wanted to play house, Charlotte wanted to play court. While Marjorie always pretended to be the bride, Charlotte was always the judge.

Cabot left the cigar box at the edge of the desk in front of her, and with his left hand he thrummed the pads of his fingers against the heavy mahogany desk, waiting.

"You're angry about the shirtwaist," he said, allowing for her to deny it.

"Disappointed. But you're right, of course." Wasn't he always? Wasn't that his most admirable quality? And his most exasperating? "My image would indeed be compromised by such a . . ."

Words failed her. Lovely was too mild. Elegant too cold. *Exquisite.*

"—ridiculous-looking thing," Cabot finished for her. "No doubt Mother will like it, though. She has a weakness for that sort of thing."

"And you, Cabot?" Ash stood in the doorway. He crossed his arms, and leaned against the door frame. The sleeves of his shirt were rolled high on his forearms, his tan skin contrasting sharply with his wilted white shirt.

Charlotte could nearly smell the sea just looking at him. "What is it *you* have a weakness for?"

Cabot looked at his brother, startled by the question. She could see he was thinking about it, running his tongue against his teeth, squinting his eyes slightly. His lips parted as if he were ready to reveal some private truth, but then he waved away the question with his hand. "We've a case to prepare. Go busy yourself while Charlotte and I get to work."

Ash winced. "There's got to be something I can do to help. I realize I'm no lawyer, but it is my ass . . . ashes . . . on the line."

"You can answer the door," Cabot said, gesturing toward the hall where someone was employing the brass knocker Charlotte had all but fondled that first time she'd come to see Cabot to beg him for a job. Oh, but she'd been full of herself back then, not even out of school and already sure she would be the best woman lawyer west of the Mississippi if only Cabot would allow her to clerk for him. Pigheaded and single minded, her grandmother had called her, demanding to know what was wrong with marriage and babies.

As if there were any security in that. Hadn't her own father swindled her mother out of her inheritance and then vanished into the night? And hadn't her mother been reduced to cleaning other women's houses and cooking other families' meals while Charlotte's grandmother flitted merrily around Europe? Her grandmother hadn't been there to see the woman lose her pride, her hope, and finally her health.

Well, at least the old woman had come back to take care of Charlotte after Mina Reynolds had given up and died.

"It's Greenbough," she told Cabot, looking out the

window and watching Ash's partner shift his weight nervously from one foot to the other.

"Do you want to do the interview?" There was a smirk on Cabot's face that said he knew she did, how very much she did.

She shrugged as if it made no difference while her heart pounded so hard inside her chest, she thought the watch on her shirtwaist might just take flight. "If you like," she said, relieved when her voice sounded like her own and not some banshee's. The truth was, the law gave her a rush like nothing else did, a heady wild feeling of power and strength to which a woman hardly had a right. Well, they had a right to the feeling, but no avenue, no opportunity, to experience it.

"Go straight for the jugular, Charlie," he said, backing his invalid chair away from the desk slightly. "Only, don't give him an inkling it's his own blood dripping on the floor."

"I know my business," she snapped at him, stretching up on her toes to check her appearance in the high mirror that faced her husband's desk.

"Yours and everyone else's." He pointed a finger at her in warning. "And plenty that doesn't even concern you and me."

He was never going to let that case of Virginia Halton's go. But then, neither was she. Dr. Mollenoff called it a matter of life and death, and she couldn't agree more. That Cabot didn't see it that way was his problem, not hers, she told herself.

She extended her hand to Sam Greenbough as he came into the suite of rooms, and pointed him toward a chair in her office, hoping to stop him before he could get a foot into Cabot's.

"Sam!" Cabot bellowed from his doorway with an enthusiasm Charlotte was sure he didn't feel. "You take it easy on my wife, now, you hear? She's still learning the ropes, so cut her a bit of slack. Just tell her everything you know and count on her forgetting half of it!"

Charlotte knew he was merely trying to give Sam a false sense of security so that he'd let down his guard and she might learn something helpful that he'd otherwise not reveal. No doubt that was why Cabot was allowing her to conduct the interview. Just the same, it grated, and she found that she couldn't bring herself to meet Ashford's eyes as she slipped by to trade places with him, her skirts swishing against his trousers as she did.

"Do you mean to sit there and tell me"—Ash could hear her clearly, right through the wall—"you're trying to tell me, in all seriousness, that you have no recollection to whom you sold one thousand pounds of coffee only three months ago?"

Cabot's beard had gone slightly gray while Ash had been away. Now the salt-and-pepper hairs around his mouth were split by a wide smile that revealed his brother's clean white teeth.

"I don't see what that has to do with anything," Greenbough answered her. "And even if I did, I couldn't help you. All the books were burned in the fire."

Cabot leaned his head toward the wall as if to hear better. Ash could see that he was holding his breath.

"Was your memory burned in the fire too? Because I find it hard to believe that a transaction of such magnitude—"

"I said I don't remember." Ash didn't like the tone his partner was taking with Charlotte. He rose from his chair but Cabot signaled him back down.

"It's a simple matter, Mr. Greenbough," Charlotte said evenly. It seemed the more agitated Sam got, the more civil and calm Charlotte stayed. "There are a limited number of coffee merchants in the Bay Area. Perhaps if I provided you with a list, it would jog your memory."

"What difference does it make who I sold them to?" Sam demanded.

Ash was wondering the same thing. He wanted Cabot to prove that Sam had set the fire, not mismanaged the business. Still the fact that his partner was being so evasive led Ash to believe that Charlotte, the lady lawyer, was onto something.

"Indeed," she agreed, and he imagined her hazel eyes dancing. "What difference *does* it make—*if* you did what you said?"

The woman was as brilliant as she was beautiful. His brother was one lucky man.

That thought, so ironic, coupled with the fleeting idea that if he could find himself a woman like Charlotte, Ash might just settle down once and for all, made him laugh right out loud.

"You hear him laughing?" Greenbough asked Charlotte. "Everything's one big joke to you, isn't it?" Sam shouted through the wall. "No respect for anything."

"What did you ever do to that guy?" Cabot asked, then put up his hand to stop Ash from telling him. "I don't want to know any more than I suspect."

"If that chip on his shoulder was any bigger, his knuckles would be scraping the sidewalk," Ash told him. Was it his fault that Sam's wife thought Ash could sell sand in the desert and that Sam couldn't give away boats on the bay? Or that she was probably right?

Ash hadn't given her so much as the time of day, so he couldn't see what it was Sam had to grumble about.

"Hey," Sam shouted. "You've really done it this time, Whittier. Alls I can say is, I'm glad this partnership is over and I hope you rot in jail. Even if they are Chinks."

"*Were* Chinks," Ash mumbled, wondering how he could have ever gone into partnership with a man like Sam Greenbough. Granted the man had connections up and down the whole West Coast and was related to half the brokers back East. Still, it hadn't turned out worth it, financially or morally. Of course, his brother's "vagrant defense" wasn't any better. "I didn't set that fire," Ash shouted, hitting the wall that separated Cabot's office from Charlotte's with the side of his fist. "And you know it!"

"Isn't he the most irritating man?" he heard Charlotte ask. "And you here doing all the real work while he goes sailing off to places like the Sandwich Islands and the South Seas. Doesn't really seem fair, does it? You stuck here to make the very best deals you can. Like on those coffee beans. That couldn't have been easy, getting someone to take beans that had been ruined by the rain, Mr. Greenbough, and get a decent price. . . ."

"You hear her?" Cabot whispered. His eyes were shiny with excitement, his vest straining with pride. "Isn't she something? Nothing I ever taught her was wasted. Not a thing! I even amaze myself sometimes!"

Ash fought to keep his mind from wandering, from speculating on the other things that Cabot had no doubt taught the pretty young woman in the next room during five years of marriage. It wasn't like him to give any thought to someone else's private doings. Why did those lace-topped stockings refuse to go away? Why did he wonder what they would look like against that soft part of a woman's thigh? Dear God! This was his sister-in-law!

Cabot asked him something, and Ash looked at him dumbly. "What?"

"Have you a copy of the insurance policy?" Cabot repeated. "And try not to daydream while we're all busy saving your skin."

"I'm trying," Ash said, studying his brother's hands and wondering if they were gentle enough, noticing how very long his fingers were, and shocking himself with where his thoughts were going. "The insurance policy? Me? No, you must have it. When have you ever entrusted to me something that had value to you?"

Those long fingers of Cabot's played with the spokes of his chair wheel. "Does it bother you that I've a piece of that warehouse?"

"There isn't any warehouse anymore," Ash replied. "But, yes, it bothers me that you refused to let me buy you out when I was in the position to do so and that now you'll have to settle for the insurance money instead."

"Not if it's arson," Cabot said, reaching for his copy of the *California Penal Code* and flipping it open to the bookmarked spot. "Section Five forty-eight, burning or destroying property insured. Every person who willfully burns or in any other way destroys . . . blah, blah, blah."

"Hey—I didn't burn the place, Cabot. And you certainly didn't burn it, so—"

"So who did?" Cabot asked, fingering the ends of his chair arms as he looked over at Charlotte's room, where a low drone signified that she was still discussing the case with Greenbough.

"I don't know, but I'm sure as hell going to find out," Ash told Cabot, coming to his feet and running his hands through his hair.

"You'll do no such thing," Cabot told him. "I've an investigator for that and you've been remanded to my custody, which means you are not to leave this house."

"But—" Ash began. Cabot put his hand up and signaled for him to listen to Charlotte's interrogation of Greenbough, as if Cabot's wife could possibly save his tail.

"So then, what you're telling me is that because of the fire there is no way to know to whom, or for how much, you actually sold those coffee beans?" he heard her ask, the ludicrousness of Greenbough's assertion mirrored in her voice.

"You just might be a very lucky man," Cabot said as he maneuvered his chair back and forth to get it free of the desk.

"Well, it's certain you are," Ash said, fighting the urge to help his brother. He was sure that a third wheel on the back of the chair, a small one that could pivot, would make all the difference, but so far he hadn't managed to get Cabot to listen to reason. "She's quite a woman."

"She's quite a lawyer," Cabot said proudly, obviously taking full credit for Charlotte's ability while he seemed to be dismissing any other attributes she might possess. "She's given him a motive. We've a second suspect, you see. Now, let's go say good-day to Mr. Greenbough, shall we, and thank him for coming in."

Charlotte looked up with a start as Ash opened the door to her office. He nodded at her and at Greenbough and held the door open for Cabot to go through.

"Sam," Cabot said, extending his hand, "I can't tell you how much help you've been. We'll be in touch."

Sam Greenbough looked at Cabot and Charlotte, clearly confused by their civility, their pure and obvious delight at his presence. After all, he'd come to nail Ash's skin to the wall, and here they were, shaking his hand and thanking him. Cabot did have a right to be proud. He and Charlotte made quite a team.

"When you're done getting what we need from Mr. Greenbough, meet me in the conservatory, Charlotte, will you? I'd like to dispense with this case in the next few days and get on to something more challenging."

Sam turned around in his chair to watch Cabot leave. "I'm not here to help you," Sam called out after him, as if that could change what he'd apparently told them unwittingly.

"No," Cabot agreed, wheeling the chair around to face Sam, "I'm aware of that. But stranger things have happened. It's a funny thing. They say that when a man loses one of his senses, the others are heightened. A blind man hears better than most sighted men. A deaf man can smell a fire a mile away.

"And a cripple . . . well, a cripple hears, sees, smells, everything that goes on around him. And doesn't miss a trick." He looked at Ash accusingly, as if he'd been reading his thoughts and had surmised—from what was really nothing more than a casual interest—that his brother had designs on his wife, when nothing could have been further from the truth.

Cabot fingered the spokes of his wheels. "No, not a trick."

# Chapter 4

Davis Flannigan squinted his one good eye at the sign on the lawn. It was dark, so he wasn't making nothing more out than some name that started with a *W*, then a bunch of fancy letters after that. He did his best to keep up with the doc, but his side was still stinging something powerful where his father's boot had clipped him by surprise when he'd fallen.

Not that the beating was anything out of the ordinary, mind you, but over the last year he'd figured out that if he tightened his muscles and kept them like a knot he could withstand the blows till tiredness had stopped the old man where Davis himself couldn't.

Then his father'd fall to his knees, crying and moaning, pulling Davis against him and blubbering about how sorry he was.

All things considered, Davis would sooner take the beatings.

But twice now he'd had to sneak away to beg help off old Doc Mollenoff. He couldn't set a broken rib himself, now, could he? Still, he didn't know about this lawyer business the doctor was insisting on. His father wasn't going to like it one bit, that he was sure of, and when Ewing Flannigan didn't like something . . . well, generally Davis had to pay for it in the long run.

"You all right?" the doc asked him. The older man stood waiting for him, his head slightly cocked so that Davis thought his hat might fall right off his bald head and set him glowing in the lamplight. His big sad eyes looked real wet, like he was hurting for Davis. As if Davis wasn't hurting enough himself. "You want I should help you?" Doc Mollenoff put out his hand, but Davis just pretended it wasn't there, wasn't reaching out for him, hoping to steady his step.

If there was one thing Davis hated, it was pity. He threw his shoulders back, but the pain was so bad that he had to suck air, and the old man wasn't blind enough to miss him wincing.

"We're almost there," the doc said, and Davis just avoided the old man taking his arm.

He was thinking it wasn't such a good idea, this coming to see a lawyer, even before he walked up the ramp to the two front doors that met in the middle like one wasn't enough. From the looks of the place nothing was enough for these people. He'd be willing to bet that the people in this house had never wanted for anything in their lives. A coddling house for coddled people. What could they know about him and his da?

He turned to go, sure now that he'd made a mistake in coming, and wondered how he hadn't figured that little piece of brilliance out before he'd walked halfway across Oakland to get to the house.

"You don't got to be afraid," the doctor said in his

funny accent, while one hand rested on Davis's good shoulder just firmly enough to stop him from bolting. "Mrs. Vittier is a very nice lady. And she could help you."

The doctor was taking him to the lawyer's wife, who, the doctor claimed, was a lawyer herself. *A lady lawyer.* His father'd get a good laugh about that one . . . after he beat the tar out of Davis for airing their dirty laundry in public.

He coughed and looked around for a place to spit. Heck, even the dirt in the flower boxes was clean. The doctor handed him a handkerchief, waited while he used it, and then took it back. Pretending not to be checking, the man stole a quick look at it, swearing under his breath. Hey, but a doctor ought to be used to some blood every now and then. Davis surely was.

Doc Mollenoff grabbed the brass knocker on the left door and clapped it hard enough to send it smack on into the parlor, then pounded on the hard polished wood with his fist for good measure.

At the same time he turned to Davis and put on one of those smiles Davis had learned not to trust. After all, the man was mad enough to spit teeth and here he was showing his pearly whites to Davis instead. "You'll like Charlotte Vittier," he said as if he really expected Davis to believe him, a man who couldn't even pronounce the lady's name right. When Davis had asked him who Mrs. Vittier was, the doctor had corrected him. *Vittier,* he'd said, like *Veather* or *Vindy.* "She's a good voman," he added.

*Vomen,* as the good doctor called them, came in two varieties, like marbles. There were the *taws,* the shooters—those were the ones that did the hitting—and there were the *ducks*—the ones that got hit. They were all made of glass and Davis could see through them all. Except, of course, the aggies. His mama had been an aggie—so fine that even his father had had the sense to prize her.

Now that she was gone, Davis's home was overrun by the common types. They were all after his da, willing to be ducks if the mood struck him, just so as they wouldn't have to be without a man. Half of them wanted to mother Davis, as if he still needed that, and the other half didn't want nothing to do with a ten-year-old boy. That was the half he preferred. Always best to know where he stood, he figured.

He turned, heading for the steps since the doctor was blocking the ramp they'd come up, and figuring he didn't care much which way he went down so long as he got away from the lawyer's house.

"Might as vell talk to her," the doc said, his grip on Davis's shoulder about as tight as a pipe wrench, which was pretty surprising for a man as old as he was, what with his having practically no hair and all. "We've come a long vay, and I know I'm not going back vitout something should fill my belly. It's a long valk back, no?"

Davis didn't like being taken for a fool. He knew the food was a bribe. He thought that maybe since he knew up front and had no plans of falling for it, then it was him pulling the scam. It'd been a while since he'd had a good meal, and so long as it was clear that they'd be leaving soon as they ate, Davis supposed it was all right with him. It was a long trip back, what with the doctor not taking a horsecar after dark on Fridays, and Davis was tired as a bartender's arm on Friday, inside and out.

"B-bu-bu-bu . . ." He gave up without getting the word out, pulling at his lips as if that could fix his tongue and make the words flow smoothly like everyone else's did. No doubt the doctor would just promise to leave and then break his word anyways. At least when he got his words out, Davis meant what he said.

"You just let me do the talking," Dr. Mollenoff said, a warm hand gently rubbing Davis's back through his thin coat. "You don't gotta say a word." And then he rapped again with the brass knocker and muttered something Davis thought might be German.

At Maria's sharp knock Charlotte and Cabot both looked up. They'd heard the knocker, Charlotte noting the urgency, and they'd made guesses as to the caller. "At this hour?" Cabot had said. "No doubt a visitor for Ash. Female. Pretty. I'd guess blond."

"The Stanfords," Charlotte had suggested. "Argus has flown the coop and is eating their gaudy purple bougainvillea."

"Better their bougainvillea than more of my buttons," Cabot said, checking his cuffs as Maria entered the room.

"Dr. Mollenoff is here," the maid announced, moving her gaze from Cabot to Charlotte. "He wants to see you."

Cabot seemed relieved. He'd been happy to give the doctor and his pathetic patients over to Charlotte, telling her Dr. Mollenoff's ragtag-and-bobtail band, as he referred to the doctor's patients and friends, was a fine place for her to cut her legal teeth. After all, he'd said with a wink, she couldn't make them any worse off than they already were.

He smiled at her and waved her from his desk, reminding her to take a paper and pencil, saluting her with what was left in his glass of iced tea.

"Lawyer Whittier," he said with a nod of his head, a row of fine white teeth peeking through beneath his heavy mustache.

"Lawyer Wittiest," she said, giving him her usual reply and toasting him with her pad and pen. "You're sure you can spare me?" Despite it's being after nine, she and

Cabot were still ironing out some last-minute changes in the summation that had been interrupted by Ash's arraignment.

"I've been practicing law for almost twenty years now, Charlotte," he said, raising his eyebrows at his framed diplomas for verification. "I think I can write a summation on my own."

Despite taking pains to hide her hurt, he apparently caught her mood and quickly amended his answer.

"Now, don't go being offended. I'm sure the summation would be even better for your touch, of course. I'll leave it here and you can look it over if you have time before you go up to bed."

"You needn't patronize me," she said. "I only thought you might want my help. I never thought you needed it."

"Charlotte, don't start this now," Cabot said, a grimace replacing his smile. "You've a client waiting for you."

His eyes returned to the papers in front of him, his shoulders hunching forward privately as if to claim ownership of his work.

"Good night, then," she mumbled before leaving the room. If her help was so unnecessary, why had he kept her down in his dark little office on such a beautiful night, a night that was meant for sitting by the window and seeking out the first star, for watching the reflection of the moon on the ripples of the lake? Because she was a lawyer now, not a silly schoolgirl. And she had a client waiting, waiting while she contemplated wishing stars and waning moons, of all things!

She should have known from the look on Maria's face when the maid had come to get her that Dr. Mollenoff hadn't come by to pay a social call. It was Friday night, after all. Only something of great importance would have kept him from the synagogue. Nevertheless, she wasn't prepared for what waited in the foyer.

In the poorly lit hallway stood her good friend Dr. Mollenoff and a boy of maybe nine or ten. The boy's face bore several fresh bruises, including an awful one that shut one eye. His left arm was in a sling. Still, his chin was defiantly raised, and his one open eye glared at her as if he dared her to comment on his appearance.

Charlotte took a deep breath, fought to swallow the horror creeping up her throat, and offered him a smile. For all his bravado the boy was shaking like there was an earthquake.

"Maria, would you be so kind as to get this young man a nice tall glass of milk? Or would you prefer some hot cocoa?"

The boy shrugged, at the cost of great pain, if his wince was any indication.

"Milk, then?" she suggested, and waited for a nod, then passed the request on to Maria, who ran from the room quickly, dabbing at her eyes with the corner of her apron. Oh, sure, Maria could cry, but Charlotte had to stand there and act as if it were a perfectly normal everyday occurrence for a boy beaten to a pulp to appear on her doorstep.

Afraid her office might put the boy off, Charlotte led Dr. Mollenoff and the poor child into the front parlor. There she motioned for the boy to sit on the sofa, allowed the doctor to sit next to him, and pulled a chair close enough so that she could take the child's hands, should they be offered to her. From the look of him she doubted it.

She introduced herself, explaining that as a lawyer she was sworn to help those who needed it. Then she asked, in what she hoped was a soft enough voice, if there wasn't some way she could help him.

The boy shook his head, his jaw clenched.

"Well," she said, "Dr. Mollenoff must think I can do

something to help you, or he wouldn't have brought you here. And the doctor is a very smart man, isn't he?"

The boy made a face that seemed to imply that either the question was stupid, or the doctor was. Or perhaps it was Charlotte herself he thought was an idiot. He was trying for all the world to look as if none of this concerned him at all, when quite unexpectedly his one good eye honed in on the doorway and opened wide.

Charlotte heard a knock, despite the fact that the doors were open, and then a male voice, which said, "Come in. . . . Shut up, you stupid bird. Come in. . . . Shut up, you stupid bird."

Charlotte's head whipped around. Ashford stood in the doorway, feet bare, hair mussed, and Liberty perched on his shoulder, twisting his head this way and that in an apparent attempt to eat Ashford's ear.

"Heard the banging at the door and thought it might be some sort of trouble," he explained to her with a shrug. "When I saw the boy I thought—"

"A pa . . . pa . . . par," the boy said, pointing at Liberty.

Ashford came forward and knelt down at the edge of the couch, his arm brushing Charlotte's skirts.

"Liberty, this is . . ." He paused, looking to Charlotte for the boy's name. She realized with embarrassment that she hadn't even asked.

"Ach!" Dr. Mollenoff said, squinting at the large bird, as if he could possibly be hard to see. "This is Davis Flannigan, and you should pardon my manners I didn't introduce you yet. An old man, I forget hands are for shaking."

He put out his hand to Ashford and when the younger man took it, the doctor quickly clasped it with both of his.

"You look good. I hear from my sister things are not so hunky-dory with you. They're not so hunky-dory with my friend here neither. This is Mr. Vittier, my friend."

"A pleasure," Ashford said, bowing slightly toward the boy, which set the bird to pacing across his shoulders. "It's been a long time, Eli. Tell me, how is it your accent gets thicker every time I see you and Selma's is barely a trace anymore?"

"Age versus youth," the doctor said with a smile. "The older you get, the more you become vhat you always were. A nasty boy becomes a mean man. A selfish girl becomes a stingy old woman. And a Russian peasant becomes . . . well, my roots are my roots. Sometimes I svear it's my father's vords coming out of my mouth. But Selma, my little Selmala, she came along late in my parents' life, here in America."

"And she'll always be your little Selmala." Charlotte laughed. Selma, two years older than she was, was a grown woman with a job as a bookkeeper, but to her big brother, who was nearly twenty years her senior, she would never grow up. "Well, Davis, what do you think of this bird?"

For Charlotte's part the parrot scared her just a little. He moved slowly, more like a reptile than any sparrow she might spy on the branches outside the high-room windows. Granted, his feathers did look like satin, but his beak was big and hard and his light eyes were old, ringed with white feathers that were lined in black like wrinkles, and he stared at her unblinkingly.

"Oh, pretty, pretty, pretty!" the bird said in yet another voice. "Hoist the sails and get the rigging up!"

"H-h-how does it t-t-talk?" Davis asked, the wonder on his face making Charlotte almost forget about the bruises.

"I can't take credit for that," Ashford said. "Or blame. Won him in a poker game from the captain of the *Trustworthy*. Came with a few bad habits, I have to admit."

"Shut up, you stupid bird!" the bird squawked, as if he understood what Ash had just said.

"Actually, that phrase would be mine," Ashford said

sheepishly, bending so that the bird would be within reach of the boy on the sofa. "You can go ahead and pet him."

There was just a touch of gray in Ash's deep brown hair, a single strand here, another there. It surprised Charlotte, as much because Cabot still spoke of his brother as if he were a child as because, with his footloose ways and fancy-free air, he'd seemed too carefree to have the gray hairs that came with age and worry. But the few silver strands shone enticingly in the lamplight as he crouched beside her, talking with the frightened boy who was mesmerized by the giant scarlet macaw. She all but sat on her hand to keep from just touching the wavy strands.

Either the bird or Ashford smelled faintly of astringent. A tiny nick on his jaw where a bit of dried blood revealed a recent shaving error led her to believe it was her brother-in-law. It smelled good, more like citrus than her husband's old-fashioned bay rum. She closed her eyes and imagined the faraway island where Ash had probably purchased it, a combination of exotic fruits held out to him by a half-naked woman with dark eyes and even darker hair, and . . .

He stood up beside her, his full height leaving her staring at his thigh. It took her a moment to raise her eyes to him, and when she did, she found him staring down at the boy. "You're looking kind of tired, son," he said, reaching for one of Kathryn's satin pillows and putting it behind the boy's head.

"And it's no vonder. He's had, by anyone's standards, a hard day," Dr. Mollenoff said. "I should have expected it. It's Friday, after all."

"Payday," Charlotte said with a tight nod.

"So his father gets drunk. And for every beer Flannigan has, Davis here gets a contusion. If the man should ever discover Scotch, ve vould be in real trouble." Dr. Mollenoff cleared his throat.

Instead of responding, Ash reached into his pocket and handed the parrot a cashew nut shaped like the crescent moon. Slowly, the bird took the nut in his claw and tilted his head to get a good look at his gift, as if he was deciding whether to eat it or put it into Ash's ear. Daintily, which wasn't easy for a bird whose tail came nearly to Ashford's elbow, he brought the nut to his beak and broke off a small amount with a dark tongue that looked like leather.

"You want to give him one?" Ash asked the boy after having shown by example that there was nothing to be frightened of. It was all Charlotte could do to keep from nodding herself.

The boy smiled and his misshapen face looked younger and less bruised.

"Go ahead, he won't hurt you," Ash assured him.

The boy held out a second nut to the bird. "Don't be afraid," Ash told him. "You're safe here."

It was apparently the opening Dr. Mollenoff had been waiting for, and he pounced on it. "We've come to keep him safe," he said to Charlotte and then spoke to the boy. "Mrs. Vittier helps anyone vhat needs help, Davis. I think maybe she could help you."

"How?" Charlotte asked. "What is it you want me to do, Eli?"

"I vant you should get him taken from his father." He said it simply, as if it were in her power to do it, even if she could be convinced it was the right thing to do.

"Is that what *you* want?" she asked the boy, Davis, whose one open eye alternately watched her, the parrot, and Ash, but avoided the doctor altogether.

Davis shook his head.

"But you'd like him to stop hurting you, wouldn't you?" she asked.

The boy grimaced. "I guess," he said. It was the first full sentence he'd uttered.

"Of course you would," the doctor said. "Nobody vants he should be a punching bag."

"Let's start slowly," Charlotte said as reasonably as she could. The boy was frightened enough. "Where's his mama?" she asked the doctor.

"Died years ago in some sort of boating accident. Drowned trying to save her baby, I think."

Davis leaned back, his eyes closed.

"So it's just him and his father?" Charlotte asked.

"Every Friday." The doctor maneuvered the boy until he was lying back on the soft cushions, Kathryn's pillow beneath his head. He struggled to sit up and keep his dignity, but his eyelids drooped despite his efforts, and his body sagged tiredly against the arm of the couch. "I gave him something for the pain. Tonight at least, he'll sleep good."

"Here?" Charlotte asked, looking over her shoulder at the sound of the curved accordion door to the elevator closing in the hall. Cabot was going up to bed. The decision was apparently hers.

"Shame to wake him up," Ash said softly.

"Ssh," Liberty said, his loud voice making a mockery of the word. "Oh! Oh! Shut up, you stupid bird!"

They waited, but the bird actually had in fact shut up, and finally Charlotte sighed and nodded.

"He can spend the weekend," she told the doctor. "You tell his father that he's safe and that he can come for him Sunday night if he's stone sober. And tell him Moss Johnson will be here if he's not." Moss had been a fighter once, and there wasn't a man who lifted a glass in Oakland who didn't drink one to old Moss, who'd had to give up the ring when age had gotten the best of his reflexes. He was still a worthy adversary most men wouldn't dare cross.

"So next Friday? Vhat then?" the doctor asked, easing the boy's arm out of the sling and placing a pillow beneath it.

"We'll catch that streetcar when it stops at our corner, Eli," Charlotte said. At the very least the boy could spend his weekends with her while his father slept his anger off.

"Ach, but she's an angel, isn't she?" Eli asked Ashford, who nodded reluctantly, staring at her as if she'd suddenly sprouted wings. Eli rose and took her hands in his. "I guess He had enough up there, not like down here vhere ve always need."

"If you were Irish, Dr. Mollenoff, I'd say you were kissing the Blarney stone." Charlotte tried to appear annoyed, but was sure she failed. What was it Cabot always said? *That face, Charlotte, is your greatest liability. When you lie, it gets in the way of your sincerity.*

She saw the doctor to the door and bade him goodnight, then crept back into the parlor to take another look at her newest client.

"Oh, *feces equitum!*"

"Care to translate?" Ash asked. He recognized a curse when he heard one, even if it was in a language he didn't speak, but didn't mind putting her on the spot just to see her wriggle out of it.

She didn't try, leaving him ashamed to think she would. "It's Latin," she said quite honestly, "for horse dung."

He felt himself grimace. She sure was blunt. And unabashed. Not like any woman he knew. "Cabot teach you that?"

She shook her head. "The seminary. Learned three languages there. A girl can't be too cultured! I can curse in Latin, Greek, and French. *Merde!*"

"I never realized a fine school like that would offer

elementary gutter dialect," he teased. It was refreshing the way she opted not to play those foolish games so many other women did, pretending never to have heard a dirty word, pretending one had never crossed their lips. And it was electrifying to see her smile, positively heart stopping to hear her laugh.

"Oh, yes," she said, big hazel eyes sparkling devilishly in the dim lights. "I'll have you know I got an A in that course too."

"I suppose you got an A in everything." It was hard to imagine her being less than perfect at school. She was certainly perfect at everything else he'd seen her attempt. The woman seemed like a ready sponge, anxious to learn everything. No wonder Cabot found her irresistible. If Ash had anything to teach, he'd surely enjoy Charlotte as a pupil.

"Absolutely," she confirmed, while she made sure the boy was settled in, the afghan was pulled nearly up to his nose, the pillow was centered just perfectly under his head—and all without disturbing him. When she was done she turned that wonderful smile on him again and added conspiratorially. "Of course, nothing but the cursing has ever come in handy when I needed it. Except, of course, with Cabot."

"Well, Cabot has a tendency to make me curse too. And did you get him at the seminary as well? Don't tell me. You were taking husbandry." That smile was surely something. It was a wonder it had taken Cabot as long as it did to snap her up.

Ash had been on one of his first trips to the Hawaiian Islands when his mother had mentioned a young lady in the house doing filing and such for Cabot. He supposed in all the intervening years he'd never been around long enough to hear the "Courting of Charlotte Reynolds" story. Amazing that he hadn't wondered before this very moment.

She stood there with that dazzling smile, her hair glistening in the glow of the gasolier, and it occurred to him that there was really no rush for him to get on up to bed. "So you met my brother at the seminary?" he asked. It was about time he got at least one version of the story.

Charlotte's head bobbed up and down, all those glints from her hair nearly blinding him. "Oh, yes! But not in husbandry, Mr. Clever! Nor in the classics lectures or the botany field trips or—well, certainly not at roller skating!"

She squatted down next to the couch, and he handed her a nut, which she offered without hesitation to Liberty. There weren't many women brave enough to put out their hands to the huge macaw, whose beak could probably snap off fingers as delicate as hers were.

"Not that I skate anymore. Anyway, Cabot was speaking there—part of a lecture series about the law—and he was magnificent!" She sighed, rolling her eyes. "I can still remember him looking out over the crowd of girls and telling us that we could make a difference in every major case that came to trial. It was the first time I had a sense of worth as a person."

"The first time? Surely when you were accepted at the seminary you knew you were special." Ash had forgone college, opting for experience and the chance to get away from home, but he'd been sorry later. Regret was like a big pot of stew for him, and college was just one of the many ingredients that went into the tasteless meal he couldn't avoid.

"Oh, I was just sent there by my grandmother to learn the fine art of being the wife of someone of importance." She seemed to consider what she said and find it amusing. "I suppose that's what I became. I really wanted to go to Hastings Law School, you know, not that my grandmother would have stood for it. After she died, the cost was such that I could never . . . so when Cabot . . ."

Even in the dim light he could see her blush as she stumbled to correct the impression she had inadvertently given. "I don't mean that I married Cabot because I couldn't go to law school. You shouldn't think that. I'm not the kind of woman who would take advantage of a man, or a situation, or . . ."

"Oh, no. I don't think that at all," he was quick to reassure her. "You're a stellar example for all women—" he said, stumbling over his words.

"If I am, it's because of your brother. Because that afternoon he said that how women felt and acted impacted the world at large. That our opinions carried weight."

"And you fell in love with him, then and there?" he asked, amazed at how her skin glowed in the semidarkness. He supposed that a man who could make a woman feel important was probably worth his weight in gold. Had he ever made a woman feel like anything more than a pleasurable moment in a pleasure-seeking life? No instance sprang to mind.

"Fell in love?" She seemed taken aback by the question. "No. Well, maybe. I was only seventeen. I just knew that I wanted more. More of him, more of the heady feeling of making a difference in the world."

"You certainly make a difference," he said, nodding in the boy's direction.

"Well, if I do, it's because of Cabot. I actually begged him to let me come and help him. You should have seen me, nearly prostrate, begging him to use me."

Still seated on the floor, she demonstrated, bending over herself so that her head nearly touched his bare toes, and looked up at him with pleading eyes. He didn't suppose she could have looked much younger then than she did at that moment. Or more appealing. "And Cabot succumbed." It was more a statement than a question.

She remained on the floor, rising enough to clasp her hands together. She begged with her eyes, big and innocent; with her lips, soft and pouty; with her chest, which rose and fell with every breath. It didn't take much to imagine her as a teen. She was barely a woman now. *"Oh, please,"* she said so sweetly he could taste it in his mouth. *"I'll do anything,* I begged him. I thought if I could only convince him . . ."

Ash crossed his legs, and shifted in his chair, grateful when she finally sat up and brushed the hair from her eyes. "And he took you up on it. You were, what did you say? Seventeen? That's pretty young." She still seemed young. Still seemed innocent, fresh. He could imagine his brother being quite seduced by her joie de vivre, her thirst for knowledge, her slim body with those slight soft curves just where a woman's curves ought to be. His brother must have found that bottom lip impossible to resist. His brother must have wanted to run a finger, just one finger, or perhaps the back of his hand, against that cheek to see if it could possibly be as soft as it appeared.

"Oh, not too young for Cabot. He says you can't be too young. That way you've no bad habits to break."

But his brother should have known the hell better than to let this woman, this *child,* offer herself up like some sacrifice. "No? I suppose bad habits get developed as you age."

When he tried to draw a breath he found his chest was hot and tight. With great deliberateness he worked at rolling up his sleeves while she continued to tell him the intimate details of her infant association with Cabot.

Details he had no desire to hear. And yet he couldn't pull himself from the room, couldn't pull his body from the chair, couldn't pull his eyes from her face.

"Oh, Cabot doesn't permit bad habits. He's very demanding, you know. You'd guess he was soft, but he can become rigid in an instant. You know, just like that!" She raised her index finger up, then, studying his face, she hedged. "Well, maybe you don't."

He uncrossed his legs and tried to put his weight onto his feet. He wanted to get up, to leave the room, but his lower half refused to obey anything he wanted it to do. Or not do. He recrossed his legs, his hands in his lap. Rigid was something he understood perfectly at the moment.

"Of course, he was patient with me," she said. "Despite all that insistence that I use my hands and not my mouth. And all that practicing, practicing."

"I would really prefer not to hear this," he said. He knew damn well he was misunderstanding everything she said. He had to be, or his brother was about to lose the use of his arms along with his legs.

"He was right," she said in defense of the man whose wife she now was. Ash had to give Cabot that. He'd married her, kept up his end of the bargain. "I'd never have learned, otherwise. I've such a big mouth, and I'm so quick to use it."

There was no question that he wasn't hearing right. That he had a dirty, filthy mind and that he was putting words in her mouth she couldn't be saying. And because he was a hopeless reprobate he was now forced to sit on one hip, curled nearly in a ball, still too mesmerized to simply get up and leave the room. In all his experience, no woman had ever been so blunt, so . . .

"I mean, the written word is so much more effective than the spoken one. And Cabot is right. A judge makes his decision on the strength of the papers before he even walks into the courtroom to hear oral argument, more often than not."

"Oral argument?" Ash choked out, his voice breaking high.

"My forte, Cabot says. He could see that right from the beginning. That's why he made me write out everything, *ad astra!* I didn't get to use my mouth till I got to say 'I do,' in the judge's chambers. And even then, I thought he'd make me write out my vows!"

He tried to catch his breath, control it, smooth the hairs that stood on end down his arms and up his neck. He concentrated on the Latin phrase she used, trying to overcome his body's reaction to what he'd thought he'd heard. *Ad astra? Ad astra?* To the stars.

"What exactly was it you did for him?" he asked, ashamed of himself for wanting to know but unable to resist knowing every detail of their lives. "When you started out with him . . . at seventeen . . . before you married him . . . then." He stumbled over his words like a schoolboy. He wondered if it wasn't her very presence that had made the young boy sleeping behind her stutter so. Another conversation like this one, and Ash, too, would be stuttering hopelessly.

"Filed. Edited the papers he wrote. Let him practice on me," she answered. He choked on air and she watched him sympathetically until he motioned for her to continue, elaborate. "Speeches, summations. Just like now. Not much changed when we married."

He couldn't keep from wondering if she was doing it on purpose.

"Except of course that you live here now. Share a table . . . an office . . . a bed."

There was something in her eyes—there for a second, then gone. He could have sworn it was pain that flickered there, and then the innocence returned, more genuine even than it had seemed before.

"Charlotte? Did I say something wrong?" he asked when she came abruptly to her feet and stretched.

"Do you think he'll be all right here?" she asked, gesturing toward the boy. "Or should we put him up in one of the bedrooms?"

"Best to leave him here. If I try to move him, his injuries will probably wake him up. I think it's pretty wonderful of you to try to help him," he added, not willing to allow the evening to end.

She smiled sadly. "I hope Cabot won't mind."

"I'm sure you'll make him see reason," Ash said, wondering how Cabot could resist granting his wife anything she asked for. He stayed where he was seated, his hands in his lap to hide the effects of their conversation.

"I haven't yet, but I haven't given up trying," she said with a shrug. Instead of leaving, as he'd expected, she knelt, picked up another nut from the hand that rested upturned in his lap, and offered it to Liberty, all the while worrying her bottom lip. He waited, staring at her mouth, sure she wanted to say something more, but nothing was forthcoming.

Finally she let go a ragged sigh and asked, "How do women get you to do what they want, Ashford? I mean, when you've refused to see things their way, don't understand what it is they need, how do they . . ." She covered her face with her hands, but not before he saw the pink creep over her cheeks.

"They look at me about like that," he said, tipping her chin up so that he could look into those huge eyes of hers. "And sometimes—on very rare occasions—that's enough."

She stared back into his eyes, unblinking. If the warmth in them should ever be meant for him, he would be a cinder at her feet. She struggled to give him a smile. "Would that were always the case," she said softly. "I guess I'd best get up to bed."

"Yes," he agreed, coming to his feet and allowing Liberty to pace across his shoulders until he found the spot he wanted, before turning down the lamp.

Charlotte rose and stood just beyond his reach by the doorway. She looked tired, sad. What he'd said wrong was a mystery, but he had the urge to tell her how sorry he was, nonetheless. Instead he just stroked her arm and steered her toward the stairwell.

At the landing she turned and whispered good-night. "And thank you for helping with Davis. I think if you hadn't come in with Liberty when you did, he'd have insisted on going back home."

He nodded, brushing away her praise. He'd done nothing but show off his parrot, while she had offered the boy her home, her expertise, and her protection. And all without losing that soft, innocent vulnerability she strove so hard to hide.

Just outside Cabot's bedroom door she came to a stop and waited for him to pass, smiling politely as he did. Three steps up the next flight he still hadn't heard her open the door. He stopped and leaned over the railing just in time to see her leave Cabot's door and enter the room next to it.

*Except now you share a bed,* he'd said.

And she hadn't answered, had she?

# Chapter 5

Many had been the mornings he'd woken up with a small ear and long silky hair resting on the pillow beside his head. This was the first time, though, Ash had awakened to a long silky ear and a small hare just inches from his nose. Somewhere in the early hours of the morning, when he'd finally stopped tossing and turning in a vain attempt to smother notions better left unthought, he'd heard the scratching under his bed again. The patter of rodent's claws forced him out of the bed and left him eye-to-eye with a one-eared rabbit who clearly thought that the high room was his. The rabbit's left rear leg impatiently tapped the floor as he waited for Ash to clear out.

"No dice," he'd told the rabbit, who'd eyed him suspiciously and then, apparently deciding Ash was not worthy of his fear, had hopped up nimbly onto the bed and wiggled his cotton-tailed behind between the covers and the pillow, and shut his eyes.

Ash had been willing to share his bed—provided the rabbit was willing to listen to the troubles of a man with a clear path to hell by way of the gallows. He'd spent the rest of the night regaling the rabbit with tales of the high seas and low ports, neither of which appeared to impress the furry creature.

Long about dawn he'd begun to question the bunny, figuring that a critter his size, with a demonstrated penchant for hiding under beds, would know quite a bit about what went on at Whittier Court.

Evidently, the rabbit felt it was none of Ash's business, because he kept his mouth shut regarding his mistress and her exploits.

Exploits?

What did he think Charlotte was doing, other than tending a few miserable creatures and brushing her hair where Cabot couldn't see her?

The rabbit was right. It was none of his damn business.

But that didn't stop him from wondering. And worrying.

And so he'd talked himself blue while the rabbit had listened politely in the dark, offering a reassuring paw on Ash's shoulder and a nuzzle to his neck just when he needed it.

They didn't share a bed, Cabot and his wife. What stupid, ridiculous assumptions Ash had made over the years. Too young when Cabot's accident had happened for it to have even occurred to him, Ash had never so much as wondered whether Cabot was still able to function as a man. Hell, Cabot had been just eighteen when he'd fallen from the roof.

Had he ever known a woman intimately? Had he ever felt that surge of passion filling his loins to bursting?

Had he ever burst?

Ash groaned and flipped over on the bed, startling the

rabbit. "He should have let me take my damn chances," he told the animal, who stared at him with unblinking eyes, "instead of risking his life for me. I'd have come in sooner or later, you know."

How could he face Cabot now, now that he knew the full extent of what he'd done? *Horse dung!* as Charlotte said. *Feces* whatever! *Merde!* Why hadn't anyone ever told him?

"Damn!" He threw back the covers and sat up on the side of the bed, his head in hands. So he hadn't only cost his brother the use of his legs—which was hardly an *only,* though Cabot had seemed to rise above it—he'd cost him the use of what lay between them.

*You share a bed. . . .* Had he really said that to his sister-in-law? As if it were any of his business! He smacked his forehead, shook his head, and smacked it again. He should never have come back home. The Hawaiian Islands were warm and sunny. The pineapples and the women were both ripe for the picking.

But no, he had to get his beans back to Oakland Harbor, the dung heap of San Francisco Bay. And somehow manage to get himself arrested for murder.

*Manslaughter,* he corrected, reminding himself that the people in the fire he hadn't set weren't people at all. Cabot was as good as ever at what he did, better maybe. But, of course, now his brother had Charlotte's help.

Charlotte. It kept coming back to Charlotte, with that wide, wonderful smile and those big bright eyes. Jeez, she couldn't be more than twenty-three or twenty-four. What was she doing married to someone as old as Cabot, who couldn't even . . .

He really was disgusting. People didn't marry just to copulate. Marriage was a merging of the heart, the mind—not just the body. Charlotte wasn't looking for

Cabot's physical perfection any more than Cabot was looking for hers.

Though he could have found it if he'd just open his eyes.

The problem was that, the way Ash saw it, Charlotte was a tumbler of cold, fresh milk, condensation on the outside of the glass, maybe a drop or two still clinging to the lip; and Cabot, well, Cabot was a fine cut-crystal goblet full of well-aged wine.

He wouldn't want a life without either of them, but they sure as heck didn't belong on the same table!

Beside him the rabbit nudged his thigh.

"Hungry? Oh, *merde!*" Charlotte's word again, he thought, as he jumped up to feed the bird, which hadn't been fed since the previous afternoon. He ran to the dresser, only to find that the bird and all his paraphernalia were gone.

So were the woman's stockings.

"I'm telling you, Charlotte, that there is a nest in the eaves somewhere," Cabot was saying to her when Ashford joined them in the dining room. "I heard a bird chirping half the night."

Ashford's mouth opened, then closed again, and Charlotte swallowed hard, hoping he'd have the sense to keep it that way. Not that she liked lying to Cabot, but it was such a little lie, and for a good reason. Still . . .

"I'll have a look outside," she said, wishing Cabot wouldn't put her in this position, knowing she'd done it herself. Again.

"I could look," Ashford offered. He seemed lost amid the disarray that passed for breakfast at Whittier Court. Cabot was already done and wheeling back from the table,

Kathryn was just coming in from the kitchen, Davis in tow, and Charlotte was halfway through her meal.

"Am I late?" he asked.

Cabot halted Arthur before the servant pushed him through the door. With his finger waving first at Charlotte and then at Ash, he said, "Don't you go climbing ladders, either of you. I have a gardener who gets paid to risk his neck."

She bit her tongue. Had Ash not been there, she'd have asked Cabot if he believed the gardener actually had a neck, or that it could indeed be broken. But she was not about to goad him into a fight in front of his brother. In fact, she didn't want to do much beyond stare when Ashford was around, nor could she seem to.

"I'll make sure no one gets hurt," Ashford said. His gaze was fixed on Cabot's hands, which fidgeted uncharacteristically in his lap. "Can I get you anything, Cab?"

"No one is to climb anything," Cabot ordered, his face reddening. "Is that understood? In all likelihood it was a cricket, and not a bird at all."

Kathryn, having made her way slowly across the dining room, patted the handle of Cabot's wheelchair and kissed her younger son Ash on the cheek. Waiting while Arthur pulled out the chair for her, she motioned for Davis to take the seat beside her.

Cabot studied the slight boy, who shifted his weight self-consciously under her husband's scrutiny. Finally he pointed with his chin. "This him?"

Well, no one had ever accused Cabot of being friendly. Charlotte forged ahead, regardless.

"Davis, may I present my husband, Mr. Cabot Whittier. Cabot, this is Davis Flannigan, my newest client." The introduction was met by silence on both sides.

Finally Cabot spoke. "Do you think this is the best time to take on a new case, Charlotte? I would think it abundantly clear our priority has to be my brother's situation right now, and our calendar was quite full before he landed himself in hot coffee in the harbor."

Charlotte looked at the boy. He was tall for his baby face, and reed slim. The swelling on his eye had gone down just enough to reveal a matched set of sapphires nestled in purple-and-brown sockets. His lip was stiff and in the corner caked blood cracked when he grimaced.

"The best time?" she repeated. *Well, I could wait until the boy is dead.* "I think it's the *right* time," she corrected.

"Do you expect that his father will simply allow him to take up residence here with us?" he asked.

Charlotte was about to answer when she caught sight of Van Gogh silently inching his way through the dining-room doors. She looked to Ash for help, but the man was still staring at Cabot's lap as if he was waiting for it to do something extraordinary.

With the rabbit hugging the wall and rounding the bend, she had no choice but to jump to her feet. "I believe I left something upstairs," she said, hurrying toward the doorway, where she tried to gently steer the rabbit in the opposite direction with her feet. "If you'll excuse me for just a moment."

She was through the doorway in a second, scooping Van Gogh into her arms as quickly. Behind her she could hear Kathryn offering some inane excuse for her behavior. "Imagine coming to the table in her slippers," she said. "I don't know where her head is some of the time."

Her brother-in-law, nice as he was, was going to get her into a lot of trouble if he didn't keep his door more tightly closed. With one hand holding up her skirts, and the other securely tucking Van Gogh to her side, she hastened up the two flights of stairs to deposit the rabbit in Ash's room.

Good glory, but he made a mess of his sheets when he

slept. Not that it was any of her business, but his linens had more twists and turns than an interesting case. She reminded herself that her brother-in-law's thrashings about in bed were certainly none of her concern and forbade her active imagination from running its natural course. Instead she concentrated on Van Gogh's antics long enough to return the smile to her face. Swinging around to leave, her skirts brushed something off the nightstand by the bed. Cursing the stupid bustle she could never seem to account for, she stooped down and picked up a leather photo case. Probably a photograph of Ashford's latest girl. Cabot had guessed blond, so she opted for brunette, and opened the small booklet to see who was right.

Staring back at her were two boys. The younger one, perhaps four or five years old, was sitting upon the shoulders of the older one, whose legs were spread slightly to juggle the young boy's weight. Both faces were vaguely familiar, and she felt her knees buckle as she lowered herself to the bed with the two smiling boys staring at her.

Cabot—without the beard, the weight, and the years, was standing on two good legs, carrying his baby brother, Ash. Behind them, nearly out of the picture, a dark-haired woman was combing a young girl's hair while another waited her turn, apparently unaware that the film was catching them before they were ready.

Kathryn! But the little girls? Were they summer guests, some distant cousins, neighbors? Charlotte looked more closely at the photograph. One girl's hand rested on Kathryn's hip while her eyes were focused on the boys. The other girl held up a ribbon toward Kathryn.

"I didn't realize anyone was in here," Rosa said in her soft Mexican accent, the door opened only a crack. "Oh, it's you. I'm sorry about the bunny, señora, but nothing is the same with Mr. Whittier's *hermano* up here."

Charlotte nodded her head in agreement. Nothing had been the same since they'd brought Ashford back from the courthouse into their home. She stood to put the photograph back on the night table. "How long have you been with the Whittiers?" she asked, her hand still clutching the leather case.

"I come about a year before you, maybe less." She kept her eyes on the floor, watching for escapees.

"What about Maria? Or the gardener, Mr. Newcomb? Have any of them been here longer?"

"Mr. Newcomb was here a long, long time. Maybe twenty years. Since before."

*Before.* That would be before Cabot's accident. Like every family, the Whittiers told time by some major occurrence. For Charlotte and her mother, *before* had meant before Charlotte's father abandoned them. For Charlotte and her grandmother, *before* meant before her mother had died and Glenda had had to return from Europe. For Rosa it was probably the year her family came north to the United States.

For Davis it would either be the year his mother died, or the year he was taken from his father. Better that, she reminded herself, than for Mr. Flannigan to mark things by the year he killed his son.

She looked at the photograph again and recalled the cameo Ash had brought his mother. Four children. And now there were only the two. The frame back where it belonged, she thanked Rosa for her efforts and headed back downstairs, lost in thought.

From the doorway to her own bright and sunny office, she could hear Cabot and Ash's voices. She followed the sound through to Cabot's darker room.

"Sorry to make you work on Saturday," Ash said, rising when she entered and sitting only after she did. "I'm sorry to have dumped the whole mess on you, but I didn't know where else to turn when the police showed up. It was all so crazy. Still, I suppose things must be tough enough around here." His voice dropped off and he worked at a hangnail on his thumb.

"Here," Cabot said, handing her several envelopes. "More letters of wild approval for your efforts." His voice was heavy with sarcasm. She said nothing. The popularity of a position had never determined its correctness for Cabot, yet he expected her to buckle under because she'd gotten a few vitriolic letters.

"Wild approval?" Cabot's brother asked. "May I see?" He held out his hand, and with a shrug she put the letters into it. He'd know sooner or later, living in the same house, that Charlotte wasn't winning any popularity awards for taking Virginia's Comstock case.

Ash's face fell. "*Baby Killer? The Antichrist?* What in hell is this?" He put the papers under Cabot's nose.

"Why don't you ask her?" Cabot said, putting on his best unruffled act. "It's her case and I can't exactly forbid her from taking it."

Not that he hadn't tried. And she understood his position, truly she did, but she couldn't let it influence hers.

"My client is being prosecuted for the dissemination of certain information which is vital to women," she said simply, hoping that would be enough.

"Not all women," Cabot corrected. "Some of them are your most ardent enemies. This letter is from a God-fearing Christian, as she calls herself, and she doesn't find your information vital. In point of fact, Charlotte, *you* don't—"

He stopped and looked at Ash.

"I never knew information to hurt anyone," the younger man said, sifting through the letters with steam pouring from his ears. "And I never knew you to side with those who did," he said to his brother.

"What would you know about whose side I've ever been on?" Cabot demanded. "What would you know about anything that's gone on in the last six or seven years? What am I talking about? When have you ever been aware of anything outside yourself?"

"Cabot! What's gotten into you?" Charlotte asked, coming to her feet. "Don't you dare take your anger at me out on your brother."

The room went stony silent. It had been years since anyone had defended him to his brother, years since his brother had shown any anger. Ash remembered his mother, bless her, coming to his defense when Ash had been what, sixteen? seventeen?

*He's jealous,* his mother had told him when she'd gotten him alone. *Life isn't as easy for Cabot as he makes it look.*

Oh, God, he'd been an idiot. Indiscreet and insensitive. Blind.

"I don't really want to intrude," he said, standing and wavering. "Maybe you two want to talk . . . ?"

"You're putting yourself in danger, Charlotte," Cabot said, slamming his fist against the arm of his chair. "First the challenge to the Comstock Laws, and now this boy. You can't just take a child from his father and harbor him in your home."

"I've already told Dr. Mollenoff that he can stay on the weekends until I can work something out with his father or the judge. He can work for us to earn his keep. I'm sure he'll want to do his share."

"Well, he can't. Last time I looked, the deed on this house belonged to me, Charlotte, and if you think I'll allow you to risk my home in addition to you risking life and limb, taking in strays—"

Ash coughed and Charlotte glared at him as if he'd actually thought that what Cabot had said was funny. Cabot glared at him, too, and demanded, "I do still have some say in whom I hire, don't I?"

Charlotte nodded, crossing her arms over her chest. "Indeed you do. He'll work for me."

Ash tried to remember anyone else standing up to Cabot the way Charlotte was doing. His brother had ruled Whittier Court since their father had passed on. Before that, Ash could remember very vaguely, as a little boy, the tirades his father would hurl at his older brother.

The last one was a week or two before the accident. Ash remembered that one because Cabot had brought it up again after the doctors had told him he'd never walk. He'd told his father he still wasn't sorry, and that he was sure to never be.

*Well, you're the only one with a reason to be sorry,* he could still hear his father yelling. *And you've no one to blame but yourself. Keeping all this from your mother is going to kill me.*

Not six months later their father was dead.

"Work for you?" Cabot asked, wiggling his finger in his ear as if he hadn't heard right. "And what is it a boy with one good arm is going to do for you?"

"Teach me to throw a lasso," Charlotte spat back at him. "Hold my left hand. There are a million things he can do while he's mending."

"It's a shame that talking isn't one of them," Cabot said, sighing deeply and resting his cheek on his hand. "I swear, Charlotte, a person gets a splinter and you're making up a cot for them in the guest room and sending a note to the butcher to double the week's order."

"Cabot," Ash started, but Charlotte interrupted him.

"That boy'll talk when he wants to," she said.

"Not in this house, he won't," Cabot said. "If he's to be

here, he'd better know I won't tolerate that stuttering and stammering."

"What?" Charlotte, obviously baffled, looked from Ash to Cabot, who smacked his forehead and rolled his eyes at Ash as if to say *See, what did I tell you about my wife?* when in fact Cabot had never told him a blessed thing.

"You didn't notice, did you?" Cabot asked.

Her eyebrows lowered over those lovely hazel eyes of hers, clearly revealing she hadn't.

"Charlotte, the boy can't spit out a single word. Dear one, he simply cannot talk. How you can be so blind to a person's faults, I just don't know."

"Better to be blind to their faults than to their virtues," Ash said softly, enjoying the bewilderment on Charlotte's face as she tried to see that poor beaten child as anything less than perfect.

"This from a man with more faults than virtues, of course," Cabot said, examining his fingernails as if the secrets of the universe were hidden there.

"I want to help him," Charlotte said, ignoring the bitter words he and Cabot were exchanging.

Cabot's sigh of resignation was more eloquent than anything he could have said. As a final touch he added, "You want to help everyone."

She reached her hand out across the desk, palm up, as if she wanted Cabot to put his into it. "Is that so bad?"

Cabot put his hands up as if he didn't think he knew the answer, which was as close to a joke as Cabot came, since everyone knew that he had all the answers. "You can't help *everyone,*" he said matter-of-factly.

"You're right, of course," she said, pulling her hand back into her lap. "I'll only help the ones that come to me."

And then she got up, turned on her heel, and, without

so much as a look over her shoulder, left the room. It was hard not to applaud at her exit.

Ash heard her voice in the hall, along with his mother's and the boy's hesitant attempts, and turned toward his older brother.

"You're one cold son of a bitch."

"Circumstances make a man what he is," he said. "And as Haliburton said, *circumstances alter cases.*"

"Yeah, yeah. And Pope said that *circumstance is not the thing.* Somebody's said something wise about everything, but words don't change the facts."

"No, they don't." Cabot rubbed his thighs with the heels of his hands. "Some things can never be changed."

"Never is a long time," Ash said, wondering if Cabot never took his wife's hand when she offered it, never invited her into his room, never said her hair was pretty or her smile could light a man's way home in the dark.

"Never is forever," Cabot agreed, balling his fist and hitting his thigh soundly so that the dull thud filled the room.

"How are you feeling?" Charlotte asked Davis, whose bruises were receding to reveal a tight jaw and narrowed eyes. "Better?"

He stared at her, sullen.

Well, any child whose father beat him, and on a habitual basis, was bound to be downcast. She'd just have to try a little harder to win him over.

"Have you seen a rabbit this morning?" she asked.

The boy raised one eyebrow. "In the d-d-din . . ."

". . . the dining room," she finished for him. So he'd seen Van Gogh's attempt to steal breakfast and her quick outmaneuvering of the rabbit. And if she read his eyes right, he heartily disapproved of her handling of the matter. "Much as I wish we could, we really can't let a rabbit, however adorable, have the run of the house, now, can we?"

The boy waited while she floundered around for an acceptable reason a grown woman would hide the existence of a small bunny.

"Mr. Whittier prefers that our pets . . ." What did Cabot prefer? That she have no pets beyond the showy ones their neighbors could see, like Argus? What was it he had said when she'd brought Griffin along with her meager belongings following their wedding and the dear cat had jumped up into what it had mistaken for Cabot's waiting lap? *That I have to abide the ease with which two-legged creatures scurry about me while I sit confined is difficult enough, Charlotte. To watch the four-legged, lesser forms of life perform feats I cannot even aspire to is degrading. And beneath you to suggest.* The cat was banished to the outdoors. Where Argus, the ingrate, poked his right eye out. The poor cat had spent the rest of his life in a dark cellar waiting for Charlotte's visits, which never lasted long enough.

"Mr. Whittier doesn't like animals," she admitted, "so I pretend we don't have any."

The boy began to say something and then thought better of it. Instead he simply pointed to himself and raised an eyebrow as if to ask if they would pretend he wasn't there either.

"Oh," Charlotte said, tucking her hands up into her armpits so that she wouldn't cup the boy's chin or something just as awful as that. "Mr. Whittier just likes to sound gruff. Lawyers have to be very tough, you know. They've got to keep their soft spots well hidden or someone might just discover their Achilles' heel and—"

"So they tend to let calluses form until that soft spot is so well protected even they don't know it's there."

Charlotte's hands fell to her sides at her brother-in-law's words. She took a deep breath and then another before responding. "You make that sound like something undesirable." He also made it sound rather unappealing. And just when she was beginning to like the man too. Perhaps Cabot was right about his brother—his kisses were always the Judas kind.

"To each its place. I wouldn't like to do battle without a suit of armor, but at the end of the day we all need a soft pillow on which to lay our heads."

"Soldiers sleep on the hard ground," Charlotte corrected, "not in some cushy bed surrounded by—" She caught herself before she mentioned lace, but Ash didn't seem to notice.

"Their loss," he said with a shrug.

"I suppose you feel that a woman doesn't have any place on that battlefield," she said. All the while she could feel Davis's eyes studying her, studying her brother-in-law, sizing them up and already declaring Ashford the victor.

"I guess I never considered the question one way or the other."

"Consider it," she all but demanded. *Go ahead, say I don't belong in the courtroom.* He clearly disapproved of her dress, her manners, her vocabulary. Why not her profession? He'd hardly be the first.

"I think that if women were in charge," he said after an interminable silence, "there wouldn't be as many battles. And that the battlefield would be a more compassionate place."

She thought there was actually a compliment buried in there somewhere, but she'd lost the thread of the argument—something Cabot had trained her never to do. Ashford brought her back to it.

"But this is a house, Charlotte, not a battlefield. Home

is where your soft spots are safe. Or ought to be." He turned his back on her, claiming victory with his finality, and addressed the boy. "I'm not all that good at guessing ages. Twelve?"

Charlotte wasn't at all surprised when the boy shook his head.

"Ah, eleven, then."

The boy didn't confirm or deny, and Ashford dropped the question, probably as sure as she was that the boy wasn't a day over ten. She did notice, however, that the boy came down off his toes, satisfied that Ash hadn't taken him for some mere child.

But then it seemed to her, hidden somewhere in their verbal duel, that Ash hadn't taken her for some mere woman, either.

# Chapter 6

Ash sat with Cabot in his office, hearing the quiet voices of Charlotte and Moss next door. Spread out across the desk were pages of notes Selma had managed from memory.

"So the theory is that Sam's been skimming off the top all along?" Ash asked. "I still don't see how that would tie in with the fire, even if I could get myself to believe that he's been clever enough to steal from me for years."

Cabot raised an eyebrow as if to say it didn't take a genius to manage some thimblerigging where Ash was concerned. "The idea is to cast aspersions on your partner and feed him to the jury as a rational alternative to you. If the man can be proven to be a thief, it isn't so big a leap to assume he could have set a fire to cover up his crime as well," Cabot answered, drawing an asterisk beside each of the edibles that Ash had brought to Oakland over the last while.

"It doesn't seem to you a rather wide chasm between pocketing a bit of profit and torching a warehouse?" Ash pointed to an entry Cabot had missed and his brother added a star to it.

"Whose side are you on?" Cabot asked with a theatrical sigh as he continued drawing lines between the buyers and the merchandise on his papers. "You seem, if not anxious to lose your freedom, at least resigned to it."

He supposed, in a way, he was. Actually, he'd been waiting for it for years, expecting it, maybe even looking forward to the day he would finally be handed the bill for his brother's injuries. In the beginning he'd expected a first-class whooping for venturing out onto the roof outside the high room. After all, he'd been six and only knew the kind of punishment that came from his father's hand or, on rare occasions, his strap.

But everyone had been so busy with Cabot and the doctors that it seemed they'd all but forgotten him. He'd waited for the blame to come home, waited for them all to turn on him, to take their love away, waited for them to banish him from his home.

And when they didn't, he banished himself, became a vagabond whose only home was a ship with a fickle anchor. And he asked them for nothing at all, accepted nothing from them.

Occasionally, he would buy love wherever it happened to be for sale—something to do while he waited.

But there had never been any question in his mind that someday there would be a price to pay. Maybe it was what made him so reckless.

"You could be right," he said, watching his brother pore over each of Selma's scribblings as if the arsonist's name were hidden in there like one of those puzzles they sometimes stuck in the back of the newspaper. "Maybe it's just time to pay my debts. Still, it doesn't feel quite right for me to be rotting in jail for something I didn't do when there are so many things I have. I mean, where's the divine retribution in that?"

Cabot stopped fiddling with the order of his papers and stared at him uncomprehendingly. How could Ash explain that he had expected a more appropriate punishment in the end? That he was still looking for meaning where there was none, and searching for forgiveness in a house where the blame still hadn't been assessed?

"Divine retribution isn't in our hands," Cabot said, trying to pull their focus back to the matter before them. "Our job is to see justice done, to bend the system to the circumstances, to wrest your freedom from twelve men heady with their own importance. Our job is to see you found blameless in their eyes and to hell with the Divine!"

Charlotte heard Cabot raise his voice and smiled apologetically at Moss Johnson, who sat across from her in her office. She knew how protective Moss was of his boss, how he was Ash's right-hand man whenever his boss was in port. Yesterday Selma had sworn her undying devotion to Ashford. Today it appeared to be Moss Johnson's turn.

Over the flowers that had mysteriously appeared on her desk, she studied the big man who filled to overflowing the leather chair across from her. On his face was the evidence of every fight, legal or otherwise, in which he'd ever had the misfortune to take part. His left eyebrow was bisected by a scar, his right one was half gone beneath a mound of bumpy blue-black skin.

Beneath his brows two deep brown watery eyes blinked furiously, fighting tears.

"I didn't wanna give no statement," Moss told her again. "They made me, I swears it."

"Did you say anything that wasn't true?" Charlotte asked.

He studied the hat in his hands and shook his head so slightly that Charlotte would have missed it if she hadn't been looking for it. "Then don't worry about the statement, Mr. Johnson," she said softly. "It didn't do Mr. Whittier any harm."

He looked at her doubtfully, and she hedged.

"All right. It didn't do him any more harm than was already done." She laced her hands and leaned forward across the desk. "Now the question is, how can you help him? And the answer is, by telling me everything you know about Mr. Greenbough's business dealings in the last few months. Miss Mollenoff has already told me about how poorly the business is doing. I understand that a ship went down off the coast about six months ago and they took quite a loss."

"Not that you could tell by Mr. Greenbough," Moss said with a huff. "He still be smokin' them two-for-a-quarter cigars like nothin' be wrong."

"Really?" she asked, not all that surprised. Greenbough would be where she'd put her money, if she were a betting woman. She'd been on the qui vive when it came to him right from the beginning, but Cabot had warned her not to jump to any conclusions. His goal was simply to exonerate Ash, not necessarily to place the blame on someone else. She'd like to know what he'd make of this little piece of information.

"I can't do no testifyin' against that boy Ash, Miz Whittier. No one can do nothin' to me that ain't already been done, and they ain't gonna make me say another word against him, true nor false." He crossed his arms over his chest as if that was the end of it.

The door from Cabot's office opened and Ash stepped through it, nodding to her politely and placing a hand on

Moss's shoulder as he passed. "Thanks for believing in me," he said, his voice gruff, his eyes on the floor as he passed through her room toward the hall.

She wondered which of them he was talking to and decided it was Moss. "You're very fond of him," she said to the big man when Ash had shut the door behind himself. Was there, she wondered, anyone as fond of her, or of Cabot, as Moss and Selma were of Ashford Whittier? Surely she and her husband were as well respected—more so, actually.

But loved? She doubted either one of them engendered such loyalty, and couldn't help wonder what it was about Ash that had even her in his corner.

Moss hunched his shoulder and rolled it in a few big circles. "Ain't nothing like a few good thrashings to make a man old before his time," he said as he massaged his left shoulder vigorously.

Was it Davis Flannigan's left arm or his right that was in a sling? She couldn't remember. Why hadn't Dr. Mollenoff given her any instructions about tending to the boy? She could see for herself he was better, but for how long? And would Cabot allow him to stay? Maybe Ash could convince him if she could not. Ash could probably convince a squirrel to lay eggs if that was what he set his mind to.

"That's all for now," she said abruptly, coming to her feet so quickly that her cup of tea went spattering to the floor, sending a hundred tiny shards in every direction. Her hands shook as she crouched down to pick up each tiny piece of the last of her mother's old china cups.

She needed to talk to Cabot, needed him now, to tell her that Davis wouldn't spend his life as someone's punching bag. Tell her, too, that someone cared for her as much as Moss did for his boss. And most of all she wanted his assurance that the world of law she so desperately wanted to be part of wasn't as inhuman as Ashford kept trying to imply.

Instead she waved away Moss's clumsy attempts to help her, and gathered into the trash the remnants of her precious cup while Moss moved the saucer into the center of her desk and out of harm's way.

"Mr. Flannigan's here, señora." Maria's voice followed a soft knock and then was drowned out by several sets of footsteps.

"It's my son I'm coming for," the man said. Charlotte came to her feet quickly, taking his measure as she did. He was cleaner, better dressed, and more presentable than she'd expected. He was also a good deal handsomer. He didn't reek of alcohol, his nose wasn't red and bulbous. He held his hat in one hand and rubbed the fingers of the other nervously against the buttons of his coat. "And I'm trusting the lad weren't no trouble."

"Davis is hardly the problem here," she said, extending her hand just the way Cabot would. "I'm Charlotte Whittier. You are Mr. Flannigan, I presume?"

"Ewing Flannigan," he said with a slight nod of his head. Behind him she could see Ashford, his hand on Davis's shoulder.

In the other room Charlotte heard Cabot cough. It was his signal for her to come into his office for instructions. She ignored him and introduced Moss to Mr. Flannigan.

"Mr. Johnson was a fighter of some renown," she said, though she had no doubt that Ewing Flannigan knew him by reputation and that if he had any doubt whether this was *the* Moss Johnson it was removed when Moss came to his feet and towered over him.

Flannigan nodded. And swallowed.

"I hope you don't mind," she said as sweetly as she could feign under the circumstances, "but I've invited Davis to visit us again next weekend."

Cabot coughed more loudly, pointedly. Flannigan's eyes darted to the inner office door, but Davis's, Ashford's, and Moss's all stayed glued to her.

"Dr. Mollenoff will bring him here on Friday and you may come to pick him up Sunday evening, provided you are in a condition to do so."

"You've got no right," Flannigan mumbled, apparently too afraid to speak up in the presence of Moss.

Charlotte motioned to Davis, who came and stood next to her. He came up only an inch or two higher than Moss's silver belt buckle. "You talk to me of rights, Mr. Flannigan? What of his rights? The right to be loved, cared for, safe? I can't do anything about the first two, but I can secure his safety in a court of law, if I have to—"

"Charlotte!" Cabot's voice shook the paintings on the wall.

"I will!" she said making sure she was loud enough for Cabot to hear.

"Would you like me to show Mr. Flannigan and Davis out?" Ash offered softly. "If you're through, that is. It appears that he needs you," he said, gesturing with his head toward Cabot's door.

"Thank you. I believe we're finished." She tipped her head sideways toward Mr. Flannigan, waiting for him to differ.

"He's my boy," Mr. Flannigan said, putting a protective arm around him.

"You'd do well to remember that," Charlotte said in response, before turning away to wipe her sweaty palms down her brown serge skirt so that she'd be able to grasp the knob on Cabot's door.

Behind her she felt Ash's breath against her ear. The knots in her stomach tightened. "Well done, counselor."

She had been scared to death facing Ewing Flannigan. He was a man with a temper and she was bound to rile him. Moisture had collected between her breasts, her mouth was dry, her legs shaky. At Ash's kind words her eyes flooded with tears and she yanked the door to her husband's office open, and hurried in.

"I'll be out back with Kathryn," Ash called in over her head. "She wants to sit and look at the lake. Call me if you need me," he said as he closed the door behind him.

She was halfway to Cabot's desk before she could see him clearly through her tears. With a frown he pointed to the chair across from him, indicating that she sit in it.

"Well, you've made quite a mess of things, Charlotte. The boy will be lucky to make it home before his father beats the tar out of him for your meddling."

It was what she had feared more than anything, yet she'd forged ahead heedless of the consequences. She buried her head in her hands and felt the enormity of what she'd done descend on her.

"For heaven's sake, don't come all to pieces now," Cabot said, reaching into his pocket and pushing a hankie at her. "It isn't that bad."

"But I broke my mother's cup," she said before dissolving into a puddle at the edge of his desk.

"Yes, I know," he said. "I heard it break. Sit down and try to compose yourself. Do you want a brandy?"

She shook her head.

Cabot thrummed his finger pads against his desk while he stared at her, his lips a thin line, waiting impatiently for her to calm down.

"I broke her cup," she said again. With all that had gone on in her office, why was that the only thing she could say? "And he has scars all over, Moss does. And Selma keeps saying it's her fault and"—she sniffed loudly—"I broke my mother's cup."

"I can't deal with you when you're like this," Cabot said as if he were dismissing her, then began thumbing through the papers on his desk. "Perhaps you'd like to go wash your face. My comments can wait a few minutes."

"What comments?" She took the hankie he held out to her and blew her nose.

"Charlotte, your actions have just put that boy in a most untenable situation," he said, backing away from his desk while she blew her nose and searched for her dignity in the folds of the soggy hankie. When he was finally free of the desk he rolled the chair over to the front window and looked out. "Well, no blood on the steps at any rate. Perhaps I'm just overreacting. Go wash your face and meet me in the conservatory in half an hour or so. That long enough?"

He stopped his chair inches from the one in which she sat and studied her, waiting for an answer.

Silently she nodded and watched him struggle with the door. At last, Arthur showed up and wheeled him from the room.

Ash had found Kathryn in the parlor, watching as Davis and his father made their way down the long walk to the front gate. She had shaken off his invitation to sit out back and watch the doings on Lake Merritt, and instead he had helped her up to her room and gone on up to his. He wondered just how long he'd be able to amuse himself within the confines of Whittier Court before his need to find out who'd set his warehouse afire sent him out. Just how long would he be able to obey the rule of law his brother lived by before he listened to the rule of man that governed his own heart.

Earlier he had tried in vain to introduce the rabbit to Liberty, hoping that Liberty would then at least be able to share his room instead of being relegated to the kitchen, where he scandalized the cook with his language. Van

Gogh had sought refuge under his bed and now Ash lay on his back beneath his bedsprings trying to convince the little fellow that Liberty was gone and it was safe to come out.

With the mattress above him and dustballs tickling his nose, he heard his door open and close. Tilting his head to the side he could see her boots as she walked past the bed. He heard her sigh and the sobs that followed it, then watched the bed as it curved slightly toward him under her meager weight. He lay stock still, his outstretched arm just inches from her foot, listening to her ragged breathing and wondering whether he should make his presence known.

It could be that she would simply take a minute to collect herself and be gone, none the wiser that he'd been privy to what she'd no doubt consider an embarrassment. Best, he decided, to wait her out.

And it might have been a good idea, too, and probably worked if that sneaky rabbit—after giving Ash a disdainful look—hadn't crept out from under the bed and rubbed up against her shoe.

"Hello, cutie-pie," she said, and he watched her hand come down and gently scoop up the bunny. "I suppose you're not surprised I've done it again."

*Now,* he thought. *You'd best come out from hiding now before she says something you aren't meant to hear.*

But he didn't move.

She adjusted herself on the bed, and her feet disappeared from view. Stretched out across his bed, she sighed heavily. Above him the bed undulated, taking his insides along for the ride.

"I should have let Cabot handle it," she told the rabbit. "I don't know who I thought I was to take on the boy's father."

He put his hands up against the bottom of the mattress,

easing his fingers between the cords that supported it as best he could, and stroked it gently, softly, so she wouldn't feel it—so that the solace was his alone.

"I try so hard," she told the bunny. "But I'm quite the sow's ear still, aren't I?"

He swallowed hard, feeling it in his temples, nearly bursting them, and pushed his fingers farther beneath the ropes until the weight of the mattress pressed them tight. For a moment, a second, the pain distracted him. But then she spoke again.

"And despite my best efforts I can't control these silly tears. I'm ridiculous, you realize," she told the rabbit. "Cabot is right, of course. He's always right."

Ash closed his eyes and sucked his lips between his teeth, biting down hard on them to keep from uttering a hundred words of comfort. *Cabot's an idiot, a fool. You are a wonder just as you are. Extraordinary. Perfect.*

"Just look at me, talking to animals and crying like some child when I ought to be taking care of business. All right. I'm done feeling sorry for myself." She sat up, crushing Ash's fingers mercilessly as she wiggled her behind to the edge of the bed.

He forgot to take a breath, but she took a deep enough one for both of them and he imagined the starched white shirtwaist she wore filling out its pleats and then returning to itself.

One foot was on the floor.

He pulled his left hand from within the mattress ropes.

A second foot. A swish of serge. The creak of his window being raised. Like some intruder—and what else was he if not that?—he silently freed his right hand and scooted far enough so that he could watch as she climbed from his window out onto the roof beyond the high room.

"No!" He gagged on the word, scurrying from under the bed, scraping his hip, clipping his elbow, banging his head, in his haste to get to her. The railing that had been placed out there after Cabot's fall could stop an accidental catastrophe, but if she was bent on destroying herself . . .

She looked up at him, startled, as he came barreling out through the window. From the pot over which she was bowed, a pair of pruning shears in her hand, she stared at him with wide eyes. "I thought you were down at the lake," she said, dabbing at her eyes with the cuff of her very full sleeve. "I didn't mean to intrude. It's just that I haven't seen to these plants in several days and I . . ." She let the sentence trail off, looking everywhere but at him, shaking her little head, putting the pruners down, picking them up, putting them down again.

"Are you all right?" He rubbed at his elbow and then felt for a bump on his head.

"Your fingers are all white," she said, reaching out for his hand and studying the crisscross of lines the ropes had left. She took his hands in hers and traced the marks across his palms. "What in the world have you been up to?"

"Just fixing something," he said lamely. "Or trying to."

"Oh." She let go of his hands, reluctantly. Or did he just imagine that she didn't want to let him go before she started rubbing her hands up and down her arms and giving him that sad little smile that sat heavily in the pit of his stomach?

"You all right?" he asked again. *Go ahead, talk to me. Pour out that little heart of yours.*

"Of course I'm all right," she said brusquely, clipping what appeared to Ash to be a perfectly formed green leaf off some flowering thing. "Why wouldn't I be?"

He stared at her, hard, trying to tell her without words that he knew—and, more, that she was safe telling him.

"Everything is fine."

"And Cabot, is he fine?" *That is, are you and Cabot fine?*

"Of course. Cabot is . . . well, Cabot."

"What I'm really asking is are things fine between you and Cabot? He seemed a bit angry down there and I wouldn't want you two fighting on my account."

"Cabot and I don't fight, Ashford." She seemed unable to meet his gaze.

"You don't seem to do much else either," he said, tipping up her chin. Then he realized the implications of what he'd said and added, quickly, "I mean you don't seem to go out much, or socialize, or sit in front of the fire or—"

"Cabot and I work together," she said, pulling her chin from his touch. "What we do is a lot more important than going to the theater or nonsense like that. I'm not the 'little lady'—Cabot's or otherwise—and if you've been imagining me sitting around embroidering pillow slips while Cabot smokes a pipe, I'm afraid you've got the wrong household in your mind."

Imagining her? She hadn't been in his mind once in the five years she'd been married to Cabot. Not until now, when he couldn't seem to have a thought without her in it. "I just meant that you and Cabot seem more like partners than like man and wife."

Oh, jeez! He'd done it again.

"We are partners, Ashford. Nearly equal partners. And I mean to outlawyer my half of the Oakland bar."

"I'm sure you're a great lawyer. Probably as good as Cohen. I only meant that . . . he doesn't seem, and you don't seem . . . that is, you don't . . . well, you both don't . . ."

He put out his hand and took hers, holding it up for her to see them intertwined. Touching her, he had to remind himself to breathe. And he was certain this time that she didn't want to pull away. Still, she did.

And he should have let it go at that, he knew, yet he didn't. "And you don't do this," he added, and squeezed her shoulder gently.

And when that should have been enough, he still went on. "Or this." He rubbed his knuckles against her cheek, and she closed her eyes for a brief second before pulling back.

"I've got to go meet Cabot in the conservatory," she said, putting down the shears and fingering the blossom on one of the plants. Had he imagined that she warmed to his touch?

"Does he have roses for you there? For Saint Valentine's Day?"

"Is it February fourteenth?" she asked. "Good glory! I've got papers due tomorrow in bankruptcy court!"

He plucked a flower from one of her plants and held it out to her, along with his heart. "Does he at least say nice things to you, Charlotte?"

"What?" He couldn't tell if she hadn't heard his whisper, or didn't understand.

"Does he compliment you much, my brother?" he asked, noticing how the sun played with her hair while the breeze set a strand or two dancing.

"Whenever I've done something to deserve it," she said, ducking her head under the window sash and waving away his help.

He let her leave the room and close the door behind her before he allowed himself the last word. "I suppose," he said softly, surprising himself, "that would apply to every breath you take."

# Chapter 7

Overnight the house had become too small. Ash didn't care if it did have fourteen rooms. Since he'd stood on the roof with Charlotte, the walls of each and every one of them had begun to close in on him. He needed to stretch his arms out. Like Liberty he needed room to flap his wings. He needed to put his muscles into something, to fight the elements, to . . .

He kicked the heavy oak foot of his bed in frustration and winced as the sharp pain danced up his leg and dissipated in his belly.

He needed to get new boots with stronger toes in them. In fact, he might need new toes if he didn't get his emotions under control.

Surely he knew better than to try to tell Cabot anything, so why was he even considering marching downstairs and telling the idiot that all the stiff muslin shirtwaists and blue serge suits in the world weren't going to change that sweet wife of his into a cigar-smoking, curse-wielding, tradition-flaunting trouser-wearer?

And what good would it do to tell Charlotte that he'd looked into the eyes of a hundred women and none were as soft as hers, as full of life and love and all that was feminine? Especially when she was trying so hard to deny it?

He needed air.

Pulling at his shirt collar, he unfastened two buttons. He threw open window sash after window sash until breezes whipped the curtains around him. And still he couldn't draw a breath.

Salt air. Brine. That was what he needed. To be at sea again. Out of this house. Away from this family.

Away from her.

Her? Charlotte?

Ridiculous! Even if she wasn't his brother's wife—which she was and he had no intention of forgetting that—she wasn't his type at all. He preferred women who relished their femininity, waved it at him like a cape at a bull, and enjoyed the charge as much as he did.

Charlotte?

He could see her in the bullring, her arms crossed over her chest, trying to stare down the bull. He sat on the bed, running his fingers through his hair and fighting the image of heeling to her command.

She was interesting, that was all. As a sister-in-law.

Naturally he felt warmly about her. Wasn't she a relative? Didn't they break bread at the same table? Sleep under the same roof?

She was a curiosity. The lady lawyer.

If only he hadn't seen those stockings, he was sure he wouldn't imagine the lace around her thighs every time he looked at her tailored dark skirts. If he hadn't come across her damn hairbrush again, hadn't conjured up pictures of her sitting on the window seat brushing out that chestnut hair and watching some sailboat on the lake, he could just have put her from his mind. If he hadn't heard her sobs, he might have been convinced that she was as tough as she pretended to be.

But now that he had, even days later, he couldn't forget she was a woman. So how the hell could she? How did Cabot do it?

The *how* puzzled him. The *why* left him with his jaw open, staring off at Lake Merritt. He was wholly startled by the knock at his door.

Rosa poked her head in and told him that the señor wanted to see him. He took no offense that Cabot was the only one referred to as the mister of the house. It was Cabot's house, after all, his staff, his life, into which Ash had come barreling at full speed. It was a wonder he hadn't smashed it to kingdom come.

In the conservatory, surrounded by his precious gardenias, orchids, and gloxinias, a pair of tweezers in one hand and a magnifying glass in the other, Cabot sat waiting for him. He turned at the sound of Ash's footsteps, each one echoing deafeningly off the tile floor.

Ash stopped walking and the noise became an awkward silence. The cloying sweetness of gardenias made the place smell like a funeral parlor.

"Think Greenbough could have set you up?" Cabot asked, bending his head once again to his work.

"I didn't think he was smart enough, but I don't know who else to suspect," Ash admitted.

"Well, that's what the investigator is for. That and to find the woman you were with. Charlotte's spoken with a couple of your crew and says that the truth is your alibi is weak, at best." Cabot placed the tweezers down carefully next to several other implements on a clean white cloth that all but covered a silver tray.

"Well, Charlotte's an intelligent woman," Ash answered. Cabot, who had been reaching for a small brush, stopped, his hand in midair, to stare at his brother.

"Did you think I would marry just any woman? A twit to stand beside my chariot here and impress my associates? Did you doubt for a moment that when I wed, if I wed, it would be to the crème de la crème? *Stone walls do not a prison make,* nor rubber wheels an object of pity."

The brush remained suspended in air as if it, too, waited for Ash's response. "I don't believe anyone pities you, Cabot," Ash offered finally.

"Not even you?"

The man had a home, a calling, a wife, all of them exalted, and he thought that Ash might pity him? "Especially not me," he answered honestly. He gestured toward the brush. "What is it you're doing?"

"Pollinating," Cabot said.

Ash held his breath, hoping that Cabot wouldn't remind him it was the only method in which Cabot would ever, could ever, propagate.

"Making perfect specimens," Cabot said after a while. "If I could, I would surround myself with only perfection."

Ash took the insult for what it was, and shrugged it off. One couldn't pick one's brothers, and Cabot had every right to be dissatisfied. "Well, it seems as if you've managed that with Charlotte."

"Ha! Do you think so?" Cabot asked. "Sometimes I imagine she's all that I've planned for her to be, worked so hard at. You know it wasn't easy teaching her to rise above her emotions. Even now I'll catch a tear or, worse still, hear a sob when she fancies me occupied."

Ash smiled indulgently and waited for Cabot to admit he was joking. When no admission came, he demanded one. "You aren't serious, are you?"

"You don't know how far she's come," Cabot said. "Or you'd understand. Why, she cried when that mangy cat of hers finally died! Sobbed like a five-year-old who'd lost her mother! And throw things! I'd hear china crash against the wall at all hours of the night. Couldn't handle unhappiness. Couldn't abide frustration. Couldn't resist temptation. But she's learning. She wanted to be the best damn lawyer in Oakland and I promised her she would be, next to me, of course. And if I promise it, I see to it. You know that."

"And if she were only a good wife?" Ash asked, remembering the sound of her sobs in his bedroom. "Cabot, the woman's your wife and you're her husband. Maybe she wouldn't be throwing things against the wall if you just treated her like a wife now and then instead of a partner."

"What's the difference?" Cabot asked, putting down the brush and dusting his hands off over the cloth before folding it up carefully and placing the tray at the edge of the table. "In our case a partnership is enough."

"Enough? I've been here over a week and haven't once seen you hold her, touch her, comfort her. I haven't seen—"

"Looking for a show, are we? Then I suggest you go back down to the docks and put on one of your own. There are half a hundred women down there who would gladly match you thrust for thrust and half a hundred more that would let you watch. Maybe you can even find the one you spent the night fiddling with while Rome burned."

Bile puddled in Ash's mouth. "Don't debase your wife with talk of two-bit pokies, you bastard. This is Charlotte I'm talking about—about decent, tender expressions of emotion with a good woman who has needs and desires that ought to be seen to by you."

Cabot shook his head as if Ash's words were senseless,

baseless. "Do you suppose my wife to be common because the women you know are of that ilk? Is it so hard for you to imagine her and me on a higher plane? Above needs of the flesh and satisfied with intellectual excitement?"

"Is that why you don't even send her flowers? Cabot, the woman needs a pair of arms around her to hold her and tell her everything is gonna be all right—is that so demeaning to a man of your high standards and moral stature?" He was pacing now, something his brother hated, no doubt for its excessive show of ability.

"And what would you propose she do? Crawl up into this chair with me? You of all people should know better than to point out what my limitations are. You, who—"

"I'm not suggesting you . . ." He was stuck for the right word, a word that was fancy enough for Charlotte, refined and demure enough to describe the loving of a woman who would never know the fulfillment of her marriage to his brother. "Damn it! All right. All right. I'm not suggesting you dance with her, on your feet or on your back. Don't you know there are a million other ways to love a woman? God in heaven, Cabot, haven't you done any more than kiss your bride?"

The room was stony silent as the truth settled in.

Cabot sucked on his mustache and rubbed his hands on his thighs nervously. Finally he said softly, "I made her a partner." Then he wheeled back until he could get around Ash's shaky frame.

"Oh, dear God—not even a kiss?" he asked the back of Cabot's chair. "Not so much as that?"

Cabot gave a tug on the bell pull by the door. "You mind your own damn business when it comes to my wife," he said just before Arthur opened the twin doors.

"Don't you mean your partner?" Ash corrected, as Arthur struggled with the conservatory ramp and left him surrounded by brilliant flowers, alone in the rapidly darkening room.

Cabot was as abominable at breakfast as he'd been at dinner the night before. At Charlotte's suggestion that perhaps they call Dr. Mollenoff, Cabot had stonily rung for Arthur and left the room, ignoring her questions and his mother's pleas.

"I don't know what's the matter with him lately," Charlotte told Kathryn, pushing away her plate and rising to follow her husband to their offices.

Kathryn's gaze fixed on her younger son before answering Charlotte. "Sit, Charlotte dear. Finish your tea and we'll talk a bit."

"But Cabot needs—" Charlotte began, gesturing toward the open doorway through which Cabot's voice could be heard clearly as he berated Arthur for everything from poor steering of his chair to leaving the curtains open to the morning sun.

"Sit down, Charlotte," Kathryn repeated. "Cabot needs some time to come to himself and a bit of space to do it in. Ashford, aren't you done with those eggs yet?"

For a moment her son looked surprised. For a good ten minutes he'd been playing with the food on his plate, hardly aware, it seemed, that it was there for eating. But he took her hint gracefully and excused himself, looking relieved to be released from what was sure to be "girl talk."

Once he'd left the room, Kathryn made a ceremony of pouring them each another cup of tea. Then, settling against the back of her chair as if ready for a long discussion, the older woman asked after the small bird that had accompanied Charlotte to court for Ashford's hearing.

"He's doing well," Charlotte told her mother-in-law. "Feathering out and eating up a storm."

The older woman nodded. "And that one-eared rabbit?"

"Van Gogh is fine too. He seems to have taken a liking to your son."

Kathryn laughed, a hearty, throaty laugh that sat oddly with her delicate looks. "Is there anyone who hasn't taken a liking to Ashford?"

Charlotte smiled her response. The man had turned out to be ever so much more likable than Cabot had led her to believe. He was friendly, easygoing, earnest. Everything she spoke of seemed to interest him. There was a warmth about him that enveloped her, a softness despite his manliness that wrapped about her even when she was across the room from him.

"It's what irritates Cabot so much about him, you know. That easy way of his that makes people take to him so. I think Cabot would give anything to spend one day in Ashford's shoes."

Charlotte opened her mouth, but Kathryn continued quickly.

"I don't mean because of his injuries either. Ashford always had that nimbus—that sort of being comfortable in his own skin—that made Cabot all the more uncomfortable by comparison."

"Are you saying that Cabot is jealous of Ashford?" Charlotte asked. She had to believe that Kathryn was surely off the mark, no matter how well she knew her sons. Cabot's assessment might have missed the mark as well, but surely Cabot thought that Ash was a ne'er-do-well, a rotten apple, a bad seed. While Cabot was becoming the most well-respected lawyer in the Bay Area, he claimed that Ashford carefully, deliberately, became a success at nothing. What was it Cabot called him? A jack-of-no-trades?

"I'm saying he always was, right from the start, and I suspect he always will be." Kathryn fingered the rim of her teacup and leaned closer to Charlotte. "What else do you suppose is causing this bad humor of his? He's as petulant as he was as a child when Ashford was receiving what Cabot thought was an unfair share of the attention."

"Cabot was petulant?" Charlotte tried to imagine Cabot's bottom lip protruding, his foot stomping in aggravation. She tried to imagine him as subject to the same feelings and emotions that ordinary people had. The exercise proved futile.

"Cabot is a competitor. It's what makes him such a good lawyer, don't you know. But it made him a difficult brother, and it left him very little room for other emotions. He was too busy always trying to win. . . ."

"Win what?"

"His father's affection, at first. Then, when it became clear to him that Ashford had all the love that Charles had to give—which was never very much, to be frank—he shifted to his father's respect. And there he cornered the market, so to speak. Charles admired Cabot's intelligence, and so that was where the boy's energies became focused."

"I suppose that was a lucky thing, considering," Charlotte said. What if his father had admired his physical abilities?

"Respect is not enough, though," Kathryn said. "I suppose it never is."

Arthur knocked courteously by the open doorway before entering the breakfast room. "If you'll excuse me, madam, Mr. Whittier has requested that particular glass this morning." He pointed to the tall water glass still at Cabot's place.

"Oh, dear," Charlotte said, placing her napkin on the table and rising. "Has he taken his bitters, then?" He always liked to follow the medicine with the largest glass of water possible. She reached for the goblet just as Cabot's manservant did.

"Let him take it in, Charlotte," Kathryn said, her hand on Charlotte's arm.

"But he needs me," Charlotte said, pulling away and reaching for the pitcher of water to refill the glass.

"Arthur can bring him his water, dear. Finish your tea."

It was rare that Kathryn ordered Charlotte to do anything, rare enough so that Charlotte retook her seat and waited while Arthur filled the glass. "If he needs me—" she began, but Kathryn waved Arthur away.

"How's that dog with the missing leg?" Kathryn asked her out of the blue. "You ever see him anymore?"

"Occasionally," Charlotte said. She'd convinced Dr. Mollenoff to take in the dog once she'd gotten him fattened up and cured of the infection the fox trap had caused when it had severed the poor animal's leg. Her mother had hated living in an apartment above Dr. Welles's veterinary office, but the barking of dogs and the odor of animals had made the rent cheap enough for even Mina to afford. At first Charlotte had simply made a nuisance of herself, but eventually Dr. Welles had come to rely on her, exchanging a room for her help once Mina had died.

"And the squirrel?" Her mother-in-law asked.

"What is it you're trying to say, Kathryn?" Charlotte finally demanded. "There's no need for a bone in your throat with me."

Kathryn patted her hand gently, leaning in so closely that the stray silver hairs from her head tickled Charlotte's cheek. "You're a good girl, Charlotte, good and kind to all God's poor unfortunate creatures. But sometimes I worry that you've mistaken my son for one of those helpless animals you keep taking under your wing."

Cabot a wounded animal? Charlotte had never heard of anything so ridiculous. "That's insulting to both of us," she told her mother-in-law through tightly clenched lips.

"I know you admire him greatly as a lawyer, Charlotte. But don't pity him as a man."

"I never would," she said, rising. She tried to keep the surprise from her face. If the truth were told, in all the years she'd known Cabot as a lawyer, it hadn't, until that very moment, even occurred to her that, aside from being a lawyer, Cabot Whittier was also a man.

"Excuse me," Ashford said, appearing at the door so suddenly, she nearly walked right into him. "Oh, the party breaking up? Just in time. There's something I think you're going to want to see."

There was nothing she wanted to see, she was sure. Most especially not if it meant letting Ashford Whittier take her arm and lead her to the window where he stood so close that she could feel the rise and fall of his chest against her back.

"Look!" he said, pointing out the window at a small man dressed in white overalls who was carefully, diligently, painting new lettering on the sign that had been on the front lawn so long, it seemed to have grown there.

"I think you'll want to come out and see this," he said, grasping her elbow and gently guiding her away from the window and toward the front parlor.

"What's he doing?" she asked, sure that it couldn't be what she suspected, what she'd waited for all her life, it seemed.

"Come on," he said, his excitement almost as palpable as her own. He helped her down the stairs and kept her hand in his as he led her down the path to the far side of the old sign.

WHITTIER & WHITTIER, ATTORNEYS AT LAW, it now read, clear as crystal for the world to see. Ash squeezed her shoulders as he stood behind her. "Congratulations," he said warmly. "I didn't think he had it in him."

She turned and threw her arms about his neck, squeezing tightly and letting loose a shout of pure triumph. She was so comfortable within his arms that she nearly forgot herself and kissed the poor man before letting go of the stranglehold she had on him and spinning around.

She searched the front window for Cabot's face and, finding it, waved to him and pointed at the sign. Then she hugged herself and waved again just as Argus began squawking at her, trying to eat her elbow right through her freshly pressed shirtwaist.

From within the house Cabot nodded, waved back, and let the curtain fall.

His silhouette was still there as she darted around the peacock and raced up the ramp toward the house to thank him.

Ash had pulled out the champagne as soon as they were back in the house, but his old grouch of a brother had insisted it was a workday for—as he put it—people who actually worked for a living. Charlotte had looked at the bottle longingly, clearly wishing they could celebrate, but agreed with Cabot that lawyers—she'd pointedly added "especially law partners"—had their reputations to uphold, and had joined Cabot in his office, the smile on her face so wide that Ash feared her lips might split in several places.

And damned if he hadn't thought about touching his own lips to those places. A stupid foolish thought.

Jeez, but it was nice to see her happy. She was entitled to it. There was no need for her to know about his talk with Cabot and the fact that it had probably forced his brother's hand. As stingy with his emotions as he was with his purse, Cabot had kept a lid on the morning's excitement and was actually meeting with some investigator instead of taking part in the evening's celebration. Ash supposed he should be grateful, but wished Cabot could have just put it off until the morning and let Charlotte have her moment of glory.

"It would be a nice night for that frilly thing I brought her from the Orient," he told his mother, placing a rose on Charlotte's plate while they waited for her to come down to dinner.

"She won't wear it," Kathryn answered, frowning as they both turned at the sound of Charlotte's voice at the top of the stairs.

"Oh, you'd be surprised what she'd wear," she said, coming down two steps and pausing, then coming down a few more until Kathryn actually gasped and it was all Ash could do to keep his jaw above the celluloid collar of his new blue shirt.

There was no mistaking it. After all, her legs were at his eye level. And legs they were, covered not by one of her many tailored dark skirts, but by a pair of trousers!

"Charlotte!" Kathryn leaned heavily on her cane and sank slowly into the nearest chair, apparently horrified. Squinting to watch Charlotte descend the rest of the way into the dark hallway, she blinked several times as if she hoped she were simply seeing things, and fanned herself with her free hand.

As for Ash, he was now acutely aware of why it was that women did not wear trousers in polite society. Seeing the light slice a path between Charlotte's legs to just beneath where legs and womanhood came together, like some sunbeam pointing to where the treasure was buried, well . . . try as he could, there was just nowhere else to look!

"Every inch his partner, don't you think?" she asked, pulling a cigar from her breast pocket and clenching it between her teeth, barely cringing at its foul taste.

He stared once again at the point where trouser leg met lap. *Not every inch,* he thought.

"Dear Lord, Charlotte!" his mother said. "You didn't actually go down to Capwell's and buy that suit, did you?"

"Doesn't fit too badly, does it?" Charlotte asked, sashaying this way and that as she came the rest of the way down the stairs.

Ash was familiar enough with a woman's underclothes to know that there wasn't room for them within the confines of those trouser legs. His tongue was thick inside his mouth as he thought of a tailor fitting the fabric to her legs, reaching for the inner seam . . .

This was Cabot's wife, damn it! He had no right to these thoughts. Her eyes were sparkling in the lamplight as she shimmied her shoulders, fairly dancing around his mother and himself. He had no right to these desires.

"Isn't it perfectly wonderful?" she asked, trying to unobtrusively scratch at her leg through rough wool that he suddenly recalled all too well.

"You find that in the attic?" he asked as she rubbed at her left calf with her right foot.

Nodding, she said, "Just look at the condition it's in! I don't think it's ever been worn."

"The attic?" Kathryn asked, fingering the edge of the jacket suspiciously. "I don't recall . . ."

It had been his first suit with long pants and his mother, as indulgent as always, had allowed him to pick it out. It wasn't until Sunday in church that it became clear why the suit had been the least expensive one at Pennoyer's.

"Anything wrong?" he asked Charlotte as she squirmed slightly and ran her hands down her thighs.

"Wrong?" she asked, leading the way into the dining room and sitting down quickly, then wriggling in like some bird in a nest. Ash hid his smile, trying hard to think only of the poor woman's discomfort and not the fact that it certainly served the little hussy right for going around in men's trousers with very likely nothing at all underneath.

She wriggled again and he coughed to keep his laugh at bay. What did she expect from woolen trousers that cost seventy-five cents? They weren't her lace underthings, that was for damn sure.

"Problem?" he asked when he noticed her tearing at the back of her neck like some angry mama scrubbing at tar.

Her hand returned quickly to her lap, where, under the cover of the tablecloth, he imagined it was offering her some slight relief from the cheap cloth's effects.

However, thinking about those soft, delicate *womanly* parts being savagely assaulted by the coarse masculine fabric set his own parts to itching. And the more she squirmed and wiggled and rubbed, the harder it became for him to sit still and think of anything beyond what his wicked imagination had begun to conjure up.

"You haven't taken in a dog, Charlotte, have you?" Kathryn asked when Maria brought in the mullagatawny soup.

"No, ma'am," she answered, inching forward in her seat to offer still more relief to some beleaguered spot Ash's depraved mind was at that very moment longing to comfort for her.

"A cat, then?" Kathryn asked, reaching for the silver dish of chutney. "Anything that might be carrying fleas?"

As he watched, uncomfortable enough himself, she sidled still farther forward in her chair, so far that Ash was forced to consider the possibility of her sliding right off and onto the floor.

Tears glistening in her eyes, she politely tasted the curried soup as she rocked gently from one side to the other, her shoulders dipping as her hips shifted back and forth, back and forth. Ash's body, traitorous as always, was beginning to respond to her rocking as if it were meant for him—as if it were an invitation to a party he was forbidden to attend.

"For heaven's sake, Charlotte," he shouted, coming to his feet and shaking out his legs as if his mother had been absolutely right about the possibility of fleas. "Go upstairs and change out of that ridiculous suit before we all begin scratching our skin off in sympathy!"

"I can wear a suit if I please," she shot back, now openly attacking her elbows with enough vengeance to tear them right off her arms.

"Not that one." He gestured at the suit she wore and clawed at his own arms. "Just remembering it makes my skin crawl."

"Now I recall that suit," Kathryn said, her eyes dancing with the memory. "We had to leave the church before the poor reverend had even begun the sermon, your brother pretending to have something caught in his throat, or some such nonsense."

"And Cabot telling you that you should have expected I'd go for style and not quality. And your insisting that the best lessons were often learned from our mistakes. And Cabot suggesting it was a perfect suit for church because it was certainly a penance to wear it!"

"Then all men's clothes don't—" Charlotte interrupted herself to stand and pull off the jacket, then commenced rubbing at her sleeves. Ash had the fear, and the hope, that her shirtwaist would be the next to go.

"You stubborn little thing! You'd have just sat there through the whole meal, wouldn't you?" Ash asked her.

She smiled a Cheshire-cat smile, leaning against the

door frame and using it like a scratching post. "Mmm-hm," she purred. "We law partners can't be thin skinned."

Good God! The woman hadn't an ounce of guile, or she wouldn't be moving the way she was moving in front of him. In front of him *in front of Kathryn!* Had she ever tried that little manuever in front of Cabot? That ought to get the man off his we're-above-such-base-thoughts high horse. It would take more than paralysis to not feel *something* when she moved like that. A man would have to be dead . . . for a long time . . . longer than Ash could imagine.

"I'd thought to give the suit to Davis tomorrow, but I think the poor child surely has enough troubles," she said as Ash retook his seat. He crossed his legs, slipped the chair beneath the tablecloth, put his hands in his lap. But he still felt as if his mother could surely see that he was the son with the dirty mind, while Cabot was the one with all the moral integrity.

"Go change," he said as calmly, as coolly, as casually, as he could make the words sound when what he really wanted was to shout them at her.

"Yes, dear," Kathryn said. "Do get comfortable."

Leaving the cigar beside her plate, Charlotte pranced from the room and Ash caught the quickest flash of hand to bottom before she was out of sight. He loosened his collar and took a long drink of wine.

He was in deep trouble, and once again, only Cabot could help him.

Cabot, whose job it was as the woman's husband to reach out to her, to take her hand, touch her shoulder, unbutton the back of her blouse. Cabot, who had tutored the girl into a lawyer, should now have the pleasure of ushering her into womanhood. Cabot, whose responsibility it was to see that Charlotte was happy, satisfied, fulfilled. If his brother was so bent on Charlotte being all she could be, how about that side of her?

He could feel his mother's eyes boring into him, just the way they had when he was younger. All the world's oceans hadn't hampered her ability to read his thoughts and disapprove. Yet even knowing his weaknesses, she managed to remain full of unconditional forgiveness for his every wayward thought and act. And the more she forgave, the more full of self-recrimination and self-loathing he always became.

And why shouldn't he hate himself, salivating over his brother's wife like she was a two-bit tart?

"Lovely, isn't she?" Kathryn asked him.

"Who?" He gave her his blankest stare, which she didn't even pretend to buy.

"She's just what your brother needed." Kathryn stared at him as though he actually required the extra warning. "She's the light to his darkness. The warmth to his coldness. She's the laughter to his—"

"And what is he to her?" Ash heard himself ask. "When she cries, is he the comfort to her sorrow? When she's lost, is he her beacon in the night? When she doubts herself, is he there to tell her who she is? Or just who he wants her to be?"

Kathryn was quiet, fingering the edge of one of her teaspoons, aligning her silverware as if her children's happiness depended on where each implement rested on the table, when Charlotte returned. She was clearly not in "something comfortable" as his mother had suggested. He could hear the rush of petticoat beneath a heavy wool skirt as she hurried to her chair. And while she might have forgone the stays, her shirtwaist was as starched and stiff as ever.

"It's just you and me and Mother," he said with as much exasperation as he felt. "Why can't you once wear something lovely? Something full of lace and fluff and femininity? We'd swear never to tell, wouldn't we, Mother?"

"I don't care for all that frippery, that fuss and feathers," Charlotte said, pulling at her cuffs to straighten them. "I am not some decoration for a man's pleasure. If you want lace, you wear it!"

"Really? I see. I stand corrected. Then I suppose those stockings I found in my room, the ones with all the lace, weren't yours?" he asked. "Just some stranger's, who left them there in passing?"

Beet red. Strawberry bright. Ripe-apple shiny. Oh, but the woman could blush a robin's breast pale by comparison.

"Are you implying," she asked, trying to busy herself with catching up on the main course of deviled rump steak, "that I would wear something as frivolous as lace-topped stockings?"

"Ashford Whittier!" his mother scolded. "Such a topic of conversation! And at the table! I never!"

Ignoring his mother, he leaned forward and stared at her while she struggled to swallow the last of her meal. "Are you saying they weren't yours? Because if I remember my fairy tales right, there would be a way to prove to whom they belong. Think they would fit, princess?"

"Ashford! Stop this before it goes any further!" Kathryn pounded her cane against the floor for emphasis, but darned it if the girl hadn't gotten his dander up with all this ridiculous denying of who and what she really was, inside, deep inside.

"Why would I have a patently capricious piece of—"

"You denying it or sidestepping the question, counselor?" He was leaning over the table now, his nose nearly touching hers.

"What if they were mine?" she asked, her eyes over-bright.

"Is that an admission?" He signaled for Rosa to wait where she was, holding the dessert he had requested be made in Charlotte's honor. "Answer the question," he demanded. There was a flush of power that surged through him and for the first time ever, he could understand what his brother saw in the law.

"Am I on trial here?" she asked, folding her arms over her chest.

He stared at the pretty face above the no-nonsense white shirtwaist. "Yes."

For a moment the room was silent, and then Kathryn rapped her cane once again.

"Ashford, sit down! Stop this at once," she sputtered, reaching for her goblet and knocking it over. Water flew across the table, trails of it reaching out for Charlotte, who ignored the cold wetness that was seeping through her sleeve.

"On trial for what?" she asked.

His breathing was coming hard now, his frustration pressing against his chest like a stone. "For the abduction of Charlotte Whittier, the woman."

Kathryn gasped.

Charlotte swallowed hard.

And he forged ahead, his words pouring forth on their own, out of his control. "Or have you actually killed off the woman, Charlotte? Have you and Cabot succeeded where God failed?"

"I won't have it!" Kathryn said, coming to her feet. "Not such blasphemy in my home and at my table!"

"You're jealous!" Charlotte shouted right back at him, not relying on Kathryn to end her battles for her. "Every man but Cabot is jealous because I've succeeded where they've failed. I've done what they've only wished they could do. And I've proven a woman can do it. I've done it for every wife at her husband's mercy, for every daughter that's made to learn the graces at the expense of common sense, for every woman whose rights are canceled by a man's tyranny. You watch me, Ashford Whittier. I'll be on the bench one day. And someday I'll vote too. And then there will be no stopping women. First in the courtrooms and then in the polling places. Eventually in every branch of government right up to the Congress and the White House itself!"

"And what will you have accomplished for women if you can't be who you are? What good will you have done them or yourself if all you're doing is emulating a man? Charlotte, you aren't a woman lawyer, you're just one more male lawyer, only you're wearing a dress."

Kathryn had made her way to the hall. She was stopped in the doorway, looking first at Ash and then at Charlotte as if the two were batting a lawn-tennis ball. She was stooped slightly, more weight than usual on her cane, and she balanced herself by holding on to the door frame. It appeared she was going nowhere without hearing Charlotte's response.

"Do you think that I could have gotten where I am, allowed to practice in any court in California, if I wasn't as tough and strong as I've become?" Charlotte asked him. She still sat at the table despite the fact that he towered over her now, shouting at her, berating her as if it were her fault he had fallen in love with her.

The knowledge staggered him, and he sat in the nearest chair, his knees just inches away from her thigh.

"Listen to me, Charlotte," he said softly, reaching for a dry cloth and patting at her sleeve for her. "You are a brilliant and talented woman. But you *are* a woman, and that's where your strength lies. Don't you see that as a woman you bring something special to the table? To the court? To everywhere you grace?"

"You don't understand," she said, and her bottom lip trembled so that she had to bite on it to get it under control.

"No," he said, signaling for Rosa to place the fancy cake in front of her. "It's you who don't understand. A woman doesn't just see the issues, the way a man does. She *feels* them. And to deny that gift, to shut off that caring side, that womanliness, is to throw away all that you've gained for women just for Cabot's misplaced respect."

"He does respect me, you know," she said softly, her hazel eyes swimming in tears. "And I deserve that respect."

"I don't doubt you deserve it," Ash agreed, cutting a piece of the cake for her. "And a lot more."

"What is this?" she asked, looking at the cake ringed with upright ladyfingers and filled high with whipping cream. There was also, according to Mrs. Mason, just a touch of almond liqueur.

"It's a charlotte russe," he said softly, licking off the bit he had gotten on his fingers in serving her. Mrs. Mason had done his request justice with the recipe she'd found in Mrs. Beeton's *Household Management.* He found himself entirely satisfied with her interpretation of the French confection. "The sweetest thing in the world."

He watched her eat every drop on her plate, delighted with how well she fancied it. *Charlotte Russe,* he thought. *Indeed, the sweetest thing in the world.*

Still and all, the celebration went flat, the rest of the cake was returned to the kitchen, untouched.

# Chapter 8

He coulda just gone straight to old Doc Mollenoff's place instead of dropping by the tavern. His pa would have found out when he got home—if he wasn't too far gone to notice Davis missing from the couch. That's what anybody with a lick of sense woulda done. He coulda left a note reminding the old man that he'd be rubbing elbows with the silver-spoon crowd. But no, he had to go right into McGinty's and push his pa's nose in his own droppings.

He brushed at the fresh bruise on his cheek and gingerly touched an ear. The darn thing was probably still bleeding even with all the packing the doc had done.

*"I—I . . ." he'd started to tell the old man sitting there on the stool like Her Majesty's own consort, with Deirdre hanging on his every word as she filled his small glass with another whiskey and the large mug with still more Oakland's Best.*

Ewing had glared at him, waiting, and then turned away when Davis's tongue decided on its own that the old man wasn't worth the effort. Instead he'd just thrust the card the woman had given him at his father.

*"And you think I wouldn't be knowing where me own son was wettin' the pillow with drool?" his father had asked. "The one lady in all of Oakland that's got 'er nose higher in the air than old Judge Mallory, and she's gotta take a shine to me own millstone. I know where them Whittiers are and I know what they be up to at any given moment."*

Then he'd launched into one of his nothing-happens-in-this-town-of-which-I-ain't-aware speeches and proceeded to tell Deirdre, and anyone else who could stand hearing him crow like some peacock again, about how important a carrier of the mail could be. *He was a bloomin' mailman! Lord give him patience!*

Meanwhile his da had blabbered on about how he knew the ins and outs that nobody else had put together, not even the coppers, bless their stinkin' hearts.

Davis shoulda left right then. He'd done what he come for, telling his da where he'd be. No need to rub his nose in how Davis had been invited to stay with the upper crust cause his da couldn't hold his liquor and went crazy every Friday.

It had taken him long enough, trying to get the whole thought out, everyone waiting for enough words so that they could just fill in the end themselves.

And before they could, he'd gone and got his ears boxed.

He deserved it, he figured. Deserved a lot worse than his da had ever managed to dish out. Always breaking down and being sorry before he ever really let that last punch loose.

Course, he didn't seem too sorry earlier in McGinty's.

The horsecar ride over'd been bumpier than usual. Too much rain, Doc Mollenoff had told him, trying to make Davis lean against him like some baby. Too little rain, the doc's sister had said before rolling up her shawl and handing it to Davis to hold for her. He didn't mind much about holding her wrap, though, since it made him a pretty good pillow against all the banging and bumping that had gone and woken up every pain he had.

She'd wrapped it about herself when they'd gotten off the trolley a few blocks from Mr. Whittier's place and hummed some tune that was real familiar to him, all the way to the house on Oak Street.

"I tried to refuse to speak to him at all," Miss Mollenoff was telling anyone who would listen just as that old geezer, Arthur, was pushing Mr. Whittier into the room. Arthur was so old, he made Mr. Whittier look kinda middle aged.

"Selma, it's all right," the missus said, a bunch of papers in her hand. She was a lawyer, Davis thought, looking at her and trying to figure out what her angle was. *A lady lawyer.* Now, that was something, all right. Probably thought she was too smart for the likes of him to outwit. "After dinner you'll tell me exactly what was said."

"After dinner my eye!" the mister said. "Be a good girl and give us something to sink our teeth into, Selma dear. No doubt it's salmon instead of steak for our bellies, so how about something tougher for our minds?"

"It's Friday," the really old lady, the lawyer's mother, said. "Of course it's fish."

"Thank you, Mrs. Vhittier," Dr. Mollenoff said with a slight bow as he held out the chair for her and helped her sit in it. When Davis was that old, he hoped he'd be dead.

"Yes," Selma agreed. She was kinda pretty, in a plain way that reminded Davis a little of his mother. Not that his mother was plain—'cause she wasn't. She was beautiful. But Selma did look a little like her without some of the details drawn in. "Thank you. You're a wonder at remembering our laws."

"They're Jewish," the other Mr. Whittier, the one with the parrot, whispered to him. "So they keep kosher."

Davis nodded. He didn't know what a kosher was or where they kept it, but he figured wherever it was, it was probably the same place they were hiding their horns, which everyone knew Jews had. Selma had a lot of hair, piled high, and wide enough to hide a good-size set of horns, but the doc . . . he couldn't hide a single hair on his head without it sticking out plain as a pikestaff with the flag of Ireland waving on it.

"Foolish nonsense," Cabot said as he waved away the pottage of love apples and leaned forward at the table. "No offense intended, Mollenoff. I have no quarrel with Judaism specifically, but with religion in general. Archaic laws to bind a people to an unproven force and keep them subservient by the exploitation of their fears and the comfort of their traditions."

"Cabot," Charlotte said, outraged on her guests' behalf. "That's insulting. Judaism goes back thousands of years and their dietary laws are rooted in strong health concerns that have proven correct over the centuries."

"Yattita, yattita, yattita," Cabot said with a sigh that was meant to put her in her place. "And we're supposed to eat fish on Friday because Christ did. Take a man's idiosyncracies and—"

"Not in my house," Kathryn said, signaling the servants to stop in their tracks. "You will apologize to me, to our guests, and to the Lord, Cabot Whittier, or you will leave my table and, very likely, my heart."

She was stonily silent, her hands remarkably still, not a shake in them as she waited for Cabot's contrition.

"I'm sure Cabot didn't mean—" Charlotte began when her husband said nothing. Why here, why now, did he have to bring up his quarrel with God? She had understood, even accepted, his rejection of some all-powerful being's allowing him to be ruined as a man in his prime for the heinous crime of saving his little brother.

Under his tutelage she had kept her faith private and to herself until it had all but vanished. But to challenge the strong beliefs of others was an unforgivable breach of the social etiquette he embraced almost as strongly as others worshiped the Lord.

"Apologize," his mother demanded.

His brother, Ash, sat sadly shaking his head. "You know, Cabot, there are people who, in the face of adversity, actually embrace their faith instead of abandoning it."

"Well, I suppose some people have a need," Cabot answered. "And hope."

"You've left out gratitude," Dr. Mollenoff said, fingering tassels that escaped from just beneath his vest.

"Gratitude? Am I wrong that the Cossacks came to Poland and forced you from your home, Mollenoff?" Cabot asked. "Is that what you're grateful for? Weren't your relatives and friends left behind to die?"

"Cabot!" Charlotte didn't know how Kathryn managed to find her tongue. Her own was thick and lodged in her mouth where she fought against it to draw a breath.

"Are Selma and I not here, in America, where we are safe and free? For that I thank my God," Dr. Mollenoff said in the lyrical cadence his accent provided. "God is good, Cabot Vhittier. Just because ve are not vise enough to understand Him doesn't reveal a veakness on His part, but on ours."

"Amen," Charlotte said softly, ignoring the widening of

Cabot's eyes. Let him worship the law. After all, the *California Penal Code* had become his bible, the judges who handed down opinions, his gods.

Maria took a step forward with the silver platter on which the salmon and green peas were artistically arranged, but Kathryn raised her hand and shook her head.

"I'll have your apology, Cabot, or your good-night."

"And so you have it," Cabot said, bowing slightly with his head. "My apologies, Mother. My point being made, I see no reason to leave my belly any emptier than my head."

"That would be rather difficult from where I sit," Ash said, squeezing his mother's hand gently and refilling the doctor's goblet with wine. Next he reached over the table and carefully poured the deep red wine into Charlotte's glass, winking at her as he did.

"Don't you take anything seriously?" she asked him.

"I take a great many things seriously," he said, staring at her as if she were suddenly the only one in the room with him. "But my brother's opinion of religion is not one of those things."

"How about my opinion of the status of your case?" Cabot asked. "The meeting I had with our investigator last night? Miss Mollenoff's meeting with the district attorney? Who I believe Sam Greenbough sold those damn beans to and for just how much? Any of those concern you, or is your mind occupied elsewhere even as we speak?"

There was a note in Cabot's voice, a warning, perhaps, that Charlotte wasn't sure she had ever heard before. There was an edge, a gruffness, that belied the gentility in which he so prided himself.

"Contrary to public opinion, as well as your private opinion, I'm sure," Ash said to his brother in a surprisingly similar voice that only served to remind Charlotte of their relationship, "I can concentrate on more than one thing at a time. In fact, I can button my shirt, sing some ditty, and still have a thought in my head quite at the same moment."

"It's when you are *un*buttoning your shirt that all that ability seems to hide under the sheets, then. Is that it?"

Across from her, Davis's eyes widened and his jaw dropped just a bit. When he caught her watching him, he quickly lowered his head and busied himself with the last drops of soup in his bowl.

"Why don't you tell us about what the district attorney asked?" Charlotte said to Selma, trying to steer the conversation, and her mind, away from the thought of Ashford Whittier unbuttoning his shirt. Pulling her gaze from his collarless shirt and leaning forward so that she could focus on Selma, who sat two seats away from her, she fought to rid her mind of her brother-in-law's chest.

It didn't work. Instead, Michelangelo's *David* came to mind and she sighed, caught herself, and tried to hide it with a stretch and mumblings about being tired. Selma was repeating how she had not wanted to tell the DA anything at all and how he had tried to trick her into admissions that she cleverly fought off at every turn.

Of course, Ashford Whittier didn't look one bit like *David*.

For one thing, he had clothes on.

She felt her cheeks burn and tried harder to concentrate on what Selma was saying.

"On and on he pressed me about the books. Did Mr. Whittier ever ask me to change an entry? Did he ever question my figures?"

And, too, Ashford Whittier had hair on his chest. Charlotte had seen the dark wiry strands escaping the confines of his unfastened collar twice now, looking like some springs gone haywire.

"And I told him that Mr. Whittier showed very little interest in the books at all," Selma continued. "That he took care of the importing and any dealings with the clients overseas."

*David,* now full blown and in all his naked glory, reached across the table for the platter of gratin of asparagus by her elbow. With a gasp she grabbed for her wine, took a small sip, and followed it with a very unladylike mouthful, swallowing it quickly. Too quickly. Choking for a breath, she wheezed as if the wine had been laced with bones.

Ash, once again fully clothed, thank goodness, was on his feet and behind her practically before her breath had caught in her throat. He grabbed her wrists and pulled her arms above her head with one hand while he pounded gently on her back with the other. Still coughing, her eyes swam in tears while everyone around the table shouted directions for her well-being.

Her voice croaking and broken, she tried to tell them all she was perfectly all right.

Actually, it was a wasted effort and she needn't have bothered trying, since Ash was reassuring them all of the fact while he gently massaged a spot between her shoulder blades. "You're okay," he repeated over and over while his hands investigated her back and no doubt learned more than he had any business knowing. The tips of his fingers seemed to be searching for her corset. Tender circles made lower and lower on her spine announced that he had found none. He squeezed her shoulders in what felt like full approval, and she realized that she'd left her hands high in the air and that she was surrounded by five pairs of very wide eyes. Sheepishly she lowered her hands, and her gaze along with them.

But not before seeing the daggers that shot from Cabot's eyes at his brother. What did he want? For her to choke to death? She hadn't seen any move on Cabot's part to help her. Had Cabot ever touched her back? Anyplace but the top of her hand, which he patted frequently enough to make her feel like an obedient pet?

She hardly knew the feel of his hands, but his brother's had been warm, strong, and reassuring.

"Are you all right?" Selma asked her when it was finally clear that she certainly was, but no one seemed to know quite what to say.

"She's fine," Cabot said before she could get the words out herself. "I thought we'd done the wine thing, Charlotte, and that I'd taught you to sip rather than gulp it down as if it hadn't fermented yet."

"Thank you, Cabot, for embarrassing me further. I certainly hadn't suffered enough," she said with a tight, polite smile.

"I hardly think choking on a glass of wine is cause for recrimination." Ash made an elaborate ritual of placing his napkin on his lap, then shifted his body so that his back was to Cabot. "You're looking especially lovely tonight, Mother."

"Yes," Charlotte agreed. There was a distinct pinkness to her mother-in-law's cheeks despite the worried look on her face. "Very pretty, actually."

"Oh, Pretty! I want some of that!" Liberty shouted from the kitchen. Despite his banishment he seemed to follow conversations from the distance, and always had an inappropriate comment at an appropriate time. Each outburst was usually followed by "Shut up, you stupid bird!" said either by the parrot himself or by a disgusted diner or two.

Dr. Mollenoff blotted at his lips with his napkin and then, pinkening a bit himself, raised his glass toward Kathryn. "Prettier than the Vhittier vomen, they don't come," he said, lifting the glass toward Charlotte as well, and then taking a small sip. "Not that my Selmala isn't the first crocus of spring herself, mind you."

*"All beauty comes from beautiful blood and a beautiful brain,"* Cabot said. "Whitman. *Leaves of Grass."*

*"Nothing radiates beauty so much as a good heart,"* Ash said, looking at Charlotte so intently that she could feel the blush creep up her cheeks like warm winter sun through the conservatory windows. "Whittier."

"John Greenleaf Whittier?" Cabot questioned, his eyebrows lowered over his doubting eyes. "From what poem? Is that 'Ichabod'?"

"Whittier," Ash repeated, fighting to keep a straight face and losing. "Ash Whittier."

"Is there more to it than that?" Charlotte asked, touching a cool hand to her warm cheek.

"What was the first line? *Nothing radiates beauty like a good heart?* Knowing my brother, the second line is likely to be: *And nothing relieves gas so well as a good fart."* He looked accusingly at Ash, as if he'd been the one to be so uncouth at the table.

"There isn't any more," he said softly, the look intent on her again. "Yet."

"Perhaps you've been lacking in the inspiration department," Dr. Mollenoff said, lifting Selma's chin with a finger as if he were offering her to Ash. "The right voman, she could make you breathe poetical."

Ash pulled his gaze from her and smiled at Selma. "I'm certain you're right," he agreed, while Charlotte chewed on the inside of her lip and wished he'd look her way again. "The right woman might even turn a man like me into a soul worth saving."

And then he did look Charlotte's way again and the breath caught in her throat all the while his eyes held her.

"Lord, save my soul!" Liberty shouted from beyond the swinging doors. "Again! Again!"

Squashing the napkin in his hand and flinging it to the table, Ash began rising. He did it slowly, deliberately, moving the chair back, then forcefully returning it to the table before him. "Shut up," he said distinctly, each word ground out from between clenched teeth. "Shut up, you stupid, stupid bird."

Cabot's laughter nearly drowned out the *crack, crack, crack* of boot against wood as Ash marched across the dining-room floor and flung the door to the kitchen wide.

"How would you like to spend the next thirty years in the cellar?" they could all hear him threaten before the door swung closed and the real squawking began.

Cabot appeared amused, leaning back with a smirk and tapping the arms of his chair while the rest of them bit at their lips, wrung their hands, and furrowed their brows. "No! No! No!" the bird yelled, accompanying himself with sharp whistles and calls. "Oh, my! So big!"

"Shut up!" Ash shouted. "Get over here before I turn you into parrot soup!"

"Awk! Awk!" Liberty's screams pierced the walls and struck like knives against their eardrums.

Charlotte squeezed her eyes shut and felt her shoulders heading for the ceiling.

And then there was quiet. An eerie, unnatural quiet.

Cautiously she opened one eye and saw the stricken look on Davis's face. She gestured toward the kitchen door. "Go ahead and check on them. I'm sure everything is fine, but you'll feel better if you see it for yourself. You know Mr. Whittier wouldn't hurt a thing, don't you?"

Cabot raised one eyebrow and backed his chair away from the table. "I need you to change the date on Ash's case, Charlotte. Are you still planning on going to court on Monday?"

Was Lake Merritt wet? Of course she was still planning to go to court. "I do have Virginia Halton's case to move forward," she said, busying herself with straightening her silverware. Of all the houses in Oakland, she supposed that the Whittiers' had the most perfectly laid tables and decided that there were certainly worse habits than lining up silverware to table edges. "Even if there isn't a judge in all of Oakland willing to listen to my argument. In Wyoming, not only do the women vote, but—"

"We're not in Wyoming, Charlotte," Cabot interrupted. "And you play with the hand that you are dealt and argue in front of the judge you draw."

"But there's a—what is it they call it?" Charlotte said, searching for the right words. "Oh, yes. 'A stacked deck,' I believe."

"It is what it is," Cabot said, shaking his head. "And it seems to me that your expenses on this case must have exceeded your retainer by now. You'd be perfectly justified in—"

"I have no desire to withdraw from this case, Mr. Whittier," she said formally. "You know that my heart and soul are in those papers, and I can't believe you would even suggest that I drop so important an issue as a woman's right to information regarding her own—"

"Charlotte! Not at the table! Please!" Kathryn pulled a lace-edged hankie from her sleeve and waved it in the air before dabbing at her nose.

"Your heart and soul are in those papers?" Cabot leaned forward and narrowed his eyes as if he could get a glimpse of that very soul from across the table. "After all I've taught you? Sometimes you make me think I've wasted my breath altogether."

"I do believe my son prefers that his lawyers not have a heart or soul," Kathryn explained to Eli Mollenoff with a slight laugh meant to lighten the situation.

At just that moment Ash came back into the room,

straightening his collar and dusting off his shoulders as he did. At his mother's comment he stopped in his tracks and looked from Charlotte to Cabot. "I do believe he feels quite the same way about his wife as well."

# Chapter 9

Charlotte could just make out Selma, her smile wide, her hand held up triumphantly, at the very edge of the crowd that gathered around her as she made her way to the back of the courtroom. Being Eli's sister, she had to be careful about associating herself too closely to the cause or someone might begin to wonder just what Dr. Mollenoff's views were. And it wouldn't matter that he was innocent, that he spent those nights in his back room repairing the damage that other doctors, or women themselves, had done.

No, guilt by association was ugly and Charlotte didn't want to find herself defending the good doctor from a witch hunt.

"Congratulations!" they said, one after the other, as she tried to fight her way through the throng.

"It's only the first step," she reminded them. Getting the court to hear the case was hardly the same as winning it. But Virginia would have her hearing and Charlotte would settle for one victory at a time.

"The first step on the road to hell," someone toward the back of the crowd shouted. "You're doing the devil's work."

"If your husband was any kind of a man, he'd keep you at home where a woman belongs," someone else hollered.

"Silas," some woman replied for her, "if you were a man you'd be holding down some job and not here harassing this woman for doing hers."

"If she were doing her job she'd be on a first-name basis with the midwife instead of with the judge."

"You been testing the evidence for accuracy, little lady?" some man asked, trying to wrest her briefcase away from her.

Well, there it was. Just as Cabot had warned. Someone—probably a lot more than just this one man—was inferring that because she was defending her client's right to send information related to the avoidance of conception through the mail, she was practicing the methods herself.

"She's given women a voice," someone said while Charlotte struggled to keep hold of her briefcase and exit the courthouse.

"I got my own voice," another woman said. "She don't speak for me."

"I speak for my client," Charlotte said, throwing back her shoulders and pushing her way toward the door.

"And for me!" several women shouted. "For us!"

Something hit her face, moist and clingy, and she reached up with her hand and wiped at it. Against her serviceable chamois gloves, glistening in the sun that streamed through the cut glass of the courthouse doors, was someone's spittle. She spread her fingers, expecting it to flow between them like the white of an egg, but it clung on determinedly, seeping into the leather while she simply stared.

"Let me through," she said, the sea of people unwilling to allow her an easy path. She kept her hand in front of her, palm upward as if the saliva would somehow evaporate in the warmth of the sun, and bent her head into the crowd until she was free of them all. Gulping the fresh air, she stood on the sidewalk for a moment and fought to get her breathing under control.

*You asked for this, Charlotte,* she could just hear Cabot saying. Cabot, who hadn't come with her this morning because he'd had too much to do on his brother's case.

His brother. Had she really lied to Ash, told him that it was simply a landlord-tenant matter to which she had to attend? What else, she'd asked him, would Cabot allow her to take care of herself?

Ash Whittier would have taken apart, limb from limb, the man who had spat at her. He'd have hung him from a yardarm, or whatever it was that sailors did. He'd have fed him to the sharks.

The spittle shine had dulled, leaving several wet patches on the plain beige gloves Cabot had purchased for her to wear to court. Unsnapping the dull flat buttons at the cuff, she peeled the chamois glove from her hand and let it fall to the sidewalk.

Ash Whittier would have ground his heel in it and taken her arm to help her cross the street.

And for some reason she couldn't fathom, that wouldn't have insulted her in the least.

There was something she hadn't told him, and Ash didn't like being played for the fool. Oh, her arguments had been plausible enough—if the case had any import at all Cabot would never have allowed her to go off and slay her own dragons—but her cheeks had been just a little too pink, her eyes a bit too bright. She'd tugged too hard on her gloves and had gripped her Gladstone too tightly. And then she was gone.

He handed the piece of paper he'd been writing on to Cabot. "If there are other merchants in California we've sold to, I'm not aware of them," he said.

"And competitors? Other people who would benefit by the shortage of goods the fire caused and the lack of competition you're likely to offer in the next while?" Cabot asked as he looked at the list and moved a bowl of nuts out of Liberty's reach.

"You plan to have the investigator looking into this, as well, I take it?" he asked his brother, moving the nuts back to where Liberty could help himself.

Cabot's mouth twitched. "I'll get him on it tomorrow. He's had no luck with your lady friend, despite a decent reward, and I've had him concentrating solely on the fire, but I don't know that he's come up with enough to raise so much as a doubt about your guilt."

"In whose mind?" Ash asked him.

"Don't start with me, Ashford," Cabot said. "I've got Charlotte off getting into who knows what depths of trouble, and I'd just as soon not go any rounds with you." His fingers played with the spokes of his wheels, and he ran his tongue against the rough bottom bristles of his mustache.

"You're worried about Charlotte?" He knew there was more to it than she'd let on. "Why? Is it that woman's case?"

Cabot shrugged. "Don't concern yourself. You've never given a damn about anyone else before. It'd be a shame to ruin a perfect record."

"Is she in danger?" He was looking out the window, watching for her, before he realized he'd come to his feet.

"She's going to a court of law. What kind of danger could she be in? And do you think I'd have allowed her to go if I thought for a moment she was?" Cabot asked him. "Don't forget, she's my wife."

"I haven't forgotten," Ash said, keeping his back to his brother. "I wasn't so sure you were aware of it."

"As I said, don't concern yourself. What goes on between Charlotte and myself is none of your business."

"Business! Mind your own business!" Liberty snapped. It was good advice, and Ash wished he could take it.

"It appears to me that nothing goes on between you and Charlotte. And since I'm to blame for that, I think I have no choice but to make it my business."

Cabot opened his top left drawer and placed the dish of nuts into it. "Out of sight, out of mind," he told the bird as he shut the drawer.

"Do you really think that that applies to your wife as well? That separate bedrooms will keep her from needing the affection that a woman, a person, needs?"

"You're such an expert, are you? On what a woman needs?" Cabot swung his arm toward a long row of books behind his chair. "Read any one of these and you'll find the truth—that sex is a burden to a woman. It's demeaning and degrading, and any woman of virtue would prefer avoidance if it wouldn't cost her the affections of her husband or rob her of the opportunity to bear children. Since the latter is not a possibility, I've simply spared her the humiliation of spreading her legs for a pleasure in which I can't partake."

Ash gripped the curtains tightly as if they were his temper and he could rein that in as easily. It took him a moment to compose himself, to remember the circumstances and that no one was more responsible for them than himself.

With all the self-control he could find, he sat calmly in

the chair across from his brother. "Look," he started softly. "There are things you just don't know, haven't experienced, that aren't in those books of yours. If you'd ever seen the look in a woman's eyes as you leaned above her, heard the sigh of contentment after you've taken her places she's never dreamed of going . . ." This wasn't easy. He'd never put into words the sheer wonder of giving someone else pleasure, though it had been a by-product often enough when all he was seeking was enjoyment himself.

Cabot laced his fingers and leaned forward on his desk. "Aren't you leaving out the best parts? How her fingers feel wrapped around your manhood, guiding you into that slippery nest of tangles? How her breath quickens with your every thrust until you think you'll burst and end it all? Didn't you forget about the way her nipples strain toward you and brush against your own naked skin while her nails dig into your back and she begs you not to stop?"

Sweat beaded on Cabot's forehead, and he swiped at his upper lip.

"What about the slime that covers her belly as you shrink back to reality and become two sweaty bodies who couldn't control the animals within you? Is that what you see when you look at my wife, Ashford? An animal that can't rise above those base needs—like some serving girl that a man could fire for serving two masters?"

Ash's eyes were closed, his mind a mess of memories that only now began to make sense.

"Matilda?" he asked, remembering the pretty maid he'd been so fond of and who had left so suddenly just days before the accident.

Cabot shrugged noncommittally. He was right. What did it matter?

"Charlotte is unsullied and will remain that way. She's a masterpiece that I created for better things than lying on her back." His hand curled in on itself and he tightened his grasp. "She is intellect. She is strength. She is brilliance."

"She is a woman," Ash said. "A creation of something much more powerful than you or I could ever understand. You're like some Greek myth gone mad, Cabot. Like Pygmalion, making a sculpture and falling in love with it and asking Venus to bring her to life. Only, you took a creation so perfect already that it should have taken your breath away, and you sought to suck the life from it, from her. You tried to take out the softness, the heart and flesh and blood, and make her as cold and unfeeling as, as . . ."

"As me. Go ahead and say it. I was a man once. I walked and ran like any man would. I thought and acted like any man would. Hell, I enjoyed a woman like any man would. It galls you that Charlotte won't succumb to you like the rest of them. That she's above and beyond all of that. She can do without the physical side of love just as I can. . . ."

"But it's not Charlotte's debt," Ash said softly. "Don't make her pay it."

"Whose debt is it?" Cabot shouted back at him, pounding his desk with his fist while Ash rose and stared out the window, blinking at the strong winter sun. "Is it mine?"

Lightning could have struck him then and it all wouldn't have been any clearer. He'd spent more than twenty years waiting to be handed the bill for his brother's pain.

And here it came, glistening like gold in the sunshine, coming up the walk and giving him a triumphant wave.

Davis watched as Mrs. Charlotte Whittier, who really was a lawyer, if Mr. Whittier was to be believed—and he couldn't imagine anyone not believing what Mr. Cabot

Whittier said—leaned against the closed front door from the safety of the inner hallway. He watched her tug at the plain gray hat she wore and then raise her little finger, turning it this way and that to get a good look at it in the stream of sunshine shining through the fancy glass in the front door.

She was lucky that stupid peacock was so slow. And she was lucky she still had her finger, from what he could see. The bird was nothing like Liberty, who the mister had him talking to while he watered the plants in that plant room for a dime a day. Every time he stuttered, the parrot cocked his head and made noises that Davis would have gotten smacked for in church. It wasn't any wonder the bird had learned to say, "Shut up, you stupid bird!" He was always saying it just when Davis had a mind to.

"M-m-mis . . ." he started, silently cursing his tongue as he struggled to tell her that the mister wanted to see her. She jumped at the sound of his voice and then tried to guess at what it was he wanted. Patience. Everyone was telling him he ought to get some, but he didn't think there was much extra laying around. Maybe if he closed his eyes and pretended she was that hardhearted parrot—"Mist—" His tongue seemed frozen in his mouth and he gave up, pointing toward her husband's office.

She nodded. "Oh, he does, does he?" she said in a huff, straightening her hair and her jacket and her back all at the same time. "Wants to hear about it all, does he? Well, he'll just have to wait."

She rushed past him, then turned around in her tracks. He could see then that her eyes were sparkling, but not with any sort of cheer or nothing. If he had to guess, he'd figure something bad had happened and she didn't want to talk about it. Well, it wasn't any of his business, and he wasn't even a mite bit interested, anyways. Leastwise he wasn't till she smiled that real soft smile of hers at him and he felt his insides go to mush.

There wasn't much that was sadder than a lady smiling with tears in her eyes. When he pictured his ma, more than not, that was the face he saw.

He didn't like looking, and didn't figure she'd want him to stare at her anyways, so he glued his eyes to the floor and set to wondering how she could stay upright on such tiny little feet.

"Did you remember to feed Van Gogh?" she asked him in this whispery voice that made it sound as if they had a secret, which as far as he was concerned, they did not. Not that he'd told the mister about the rabbit. But he wasn't making any promises that he wouldn't neither.

He nodded. Did she think he'd let the ball of fluff starve just because she had better things to do?

"Thank you." She didn't make a big thing of it, and he appreciated that. Sometimes when you did something for a lady she made this big fuss like you'd all but saved her from the path of a runaway trolley or something. Just saying thank-you the way she did made it seem more like she really meant it.

"It's okay." Both words came out clear and he could see the surprise in her eyes, as if for a second she thought he was cured or something. He remembered himself the first few times his tongue didn't turn on him. But he knew better now than to trust it. His tongue was like some tease or bully, taunting him to try and laughing at him when he failed. He'd known for a long time that it would take a better man than him to beat it.

"Charlotte? That you?" The old lady, the mister's mother, came through the doorway from the parlor, her eyes so squinty that Davis thought she looked like some sort of owl outta a picture book. "How did it go? Did you give as good as you got?"

"We'll have our day in court, Kathryn," she said with a sigh.

"Well, that's a victory for our side, yes?" the old lady asked, and got a nod from the missus. "Ironic, isn't it?"

Davis didn't know what the word meant, but he didn't like the way the missus bit at her lip before answering. "It's not a war, Kathryn," she said, and he saw her look toward the mister's office.

"Perhaps not, but I think he's feeling that he trained the enemy." She tapped that cane she always carried against the floor like she was applauding.

"I truly believe he agrees with me in principle," the missus said, shifting that satchel of hers to her other hand. "I don't want to be anyone's enemy, least of all Cabot's. I'd always want him on my side." She headed for the stairs and he was about to remind her that the mister wanted her when the old lady called after her.

"Where are you going?" she asked, taking a few slow steps toward the staircase. "Not up to the high room, I hope."

The missus put one hand on the banister as if she had to pull herself up to get there. "I've got plants to see to and I thought that with Ashford busy with Cabot, now might be a good time."

"What is it you do up there, Charlotte?" the old lady asked, looking up to the top of the stairs as if the landing were very, very far away.

The missus gave one of them quick shrugs. "Hide."

"From who?" the old lady asked. "Cabot?"

Lord, if it wasn't the saddest look he'd ever seen when that little missus shook her head. "Me," she said, nearly choking on the word.

And then she was up the stairs faster than even Van Gogh could get to the top.

* * *

"To Charlotte," Cabot said, raising his wineglass to her and encouraging everyone around the table to join him. "Your milk will do," he said quietly to Davis, who sat just to his left, taking the seat that was usually reserved for Dr. Mollenoff.

As they all lifted their glasses to her above the glow of the candles that her mother-in-law had insisted the table be set with, Kathryn added, "You've done your sisterhood proud," while she held her glass aloft, in danger of losing a good bit of wine from the angle at which she held the goblet.

"Posh!" Cabot said. "This has nothing to do with her sisterhood. This is the law, and she has done me proud. They said I wouldn't be able to pull it off. No one would take her seriously. They said that a woman would be laughed right out of court. Three female attorneys in the whole damned state and I'm responsible for one of them. The best of them." He took a mouthful of the dark red wine and swallowed it slowly, savoring every drop.

"I was so proud of you," Selma said. "I took notes on everything you said so that I could tell Eli later. Oh, how he wanted to be there!"

"It vas bad enough that you vere there," Eli said, his smile laced with concern. "I've varned you and varned you about being discreet. You and I could both be in hot borscht and then vhere vould the ladies be?"

"I sat at the back of the courtroom, Eli," she defended herself. "With a hundred other women. No one noticed me any more than anyone else. Surely I was less noticeable than the man who spat at her."

There was dead silence in the room and Charlotte studied her plate as if the beautiful array of veal escalopes with mushrooms, cream, and sherry was the most interesting display of dead calves she had ever beheld. With her head tipped so low that she thought her gaze would go unnoticed, she risked a glance at the man seated across from her.

Ash's chest was rising and lowering like the piston on some steam engine, ready to explode if it couldn't move forward.

"You know," she began, "it was so warm today you'd have thought it was May. I could have worn my—"

"Who?" Ash's voice was quiet, but firm.

Selma, sitting next to him, reached for her wineglass with a shaky hand.

"Who spit at you?" he demanded, ignoring the wine that had spilled, ignoring Rosa's efforts to blot at his sleeve with a wet cloth, ignoring Selma's tearful apology and Kathryn's assurances that it was an old cloth and, knowing Ash, an old shirt. "I asked you who spit at you?"

All right. A better woman would have told him she didn't need or want his concern. Clara Foltz would have called his response typical of what was wrong with modern man and his view of women's role in society. Charlotte Perkins Gilman would have blamed a breakdown on him. Charlotte Reynolds Whittier, on the other hand, had to put the heel of her left foot onto the instep of her right and press very, very hard to prevent herself from enjoying fully—oh, so fully—the concern of the handsome—oh, so *very* handsome—man seething across the table from her.

"It was nothing," she said, waving the incident away with her hand. "Some zealot who was convinced that a woman ought not know how her body works."

She'd said similar words to Cabot a hundred times and they'd never embarrassed her. Even his response, implying that she had no knowledge herself or any need to know such things, had never sent the scarlet waves of heat up her cheeks the way they were climbing now as Ash studied first her and then Cabot.

"You will not," he said, returning his gaze to her, "ever go to the courtroom alone again."

Cabot seemed highly amused by his brother's outburst. "Do the words *remanded to the custody of Cabot Whittier* mean anything to you? Charlotte is not some little priss that would be bowled over by some spittle-laden wind, however strong, that might come within a few feet of her."

"Hit her cheek," Selma said. "Didn't you tell them, Charlotte? I do admire you so. There were bets, you know, that you'd cry. Silas Haring lost fifty cents!"

Ash Whittier's knuckles were white as he gripped the edge of the table. "If my brother cannot accompany you, I will see that Moss Johnson is there," he said through gritted teeth that nearly made his words unintelligible.

"Charlotte can take care of herself," Cabot said. "She needs to overcome the odds, and I understand that need. There are few things in this world as we know it that a woman can take pride in, and I'll not let you rob my wife of them."

"Your wife?" Ash said, coming to his feet. "Do you know that may be the first time I've heard you refer to her as that? Look at this table—you across from Mother, Charlotte on the side like a guest. Oh, you'll no doubt say she'll eat all the same. I've no doubt you're quite right about Charlotte. She can take care of herself. She's had to, hasn't she? There are many things a person *can* do. Why, they can even manage to spend their life in a chair if they have to. But how many would you actually *choose* for yourself?"

His mouth was still open, but there seemed to be nothing left to say. His hands were raised, but they pointed nowhere until one finger warned her. "No going to court yourself. Understood?"

He didn't wait for her to nod, and she wasn't sure she could. Could one nod without breathing? Without moving a muscle at all?

Something seemed to satisfy him, a look, perhaps, or her very silence, which he might have taken for some sort of affirmation, since after his warning he simply strode from the room with just a quick nod of politeness at Eli and Selma.

"He doesn't understand pride," Cabot said. "Not the way I do."

# Chapter 10

Two nights later, when he heard the footsteps on the stairs, he knew they belonged to her. After all, they were too light for anyone but an angel. He shook his head at his own foolishness and suffered Liberty's derisive laugh.

"Someday it's going to happen to you," he warned the bird, watching him break his nuts into smaller and smaller pieces so that the little chickadee could share his meal. "If it hasn't already," he added.

He waited for her to tap on the door, anticipating her knock as if it were a reprieve from the governor. Not that he cared all that much about his case anymore, except that it was a shame for the guilty to go unpunished. Still, Cabot would get him off, or he wouldn't, and Ash would leave Oakland, one way or the other, and none of it made any difference because she wasn't going to be a part of it. Sometimes, in his darkest moments, when he lay alone on his bed in the middle of the night and knew she was alone, too, just a floor beneath him, he thought it might be best if he pleaded guilty just to keep her safe from him.

Not that he would force himself upon her—no, never! He wanted to put the twinkle back in her eyes, not see it gone for good. What a mess he'd made of Cabot's life and what a mess Cabot had made of Charlotte's. She might as well be a nun for all the pleasure afforded her by his unloving, unlovable big brother.

The knock was soft. Hell, beneath all the starch and serge everything about her was soft. He made sure his shirt buttons were closed, his sleeves rolled down, and then opened the door slightly. Best that they kept their distance, after all.

And then he saw those sad eyes, that tiny pink tongue licking that lush bottom lip, and he swung the door open wide, grabbed her arm, and yanked her inside.

"I was looking for the little chickadee," she said as if to explain why she had chosen just that minute to breathe life into his mundane existence.

"He's here with Liberty," he said with a jerk of his head toward the birds, pretending that he hadn't been wishing, wanting, making deals with himself and bargains with God, if only she'd come to him.

Her jaw fell slightly, in clear concern for the tiny bird's safety, before she could fully comprehend that the bigger bird was making a meal *for,* and not *of,* her little friend. "I thought I'd better get him fed," she said. Her hair had lost its willingness to stay pinned up and was falling softly around her face like streamers around the prize float at the parade.

"He's eating," he pointed out unnecessarily.

"Yes, I see." At the rate they were going they might actually get to the weather by midnight.

"You don't seem very pleased." Actually, she was sniffing and fishing around in her pocket almost frantically. He handed her his handkerchief, grateful Rosa had left him a clean stack just that morning, and lifted her chin, only to drown in her eyes.

"Oh, I'm pleased," she said, her nose twitching, her bottom lip caught between her teeth.

"Good," he said. "That's what we want."

"We?"

"Yeah, all of us," he said, spreading his arm to include Liberty and the chickadee and even Van Gogh, who'd nosed out from under the bed at the sound of his mistress's voice.

"Well, I'm happy." She smiled at him, or tried to.

"Good."

There was only the sound of the birds breaking seeds and nuts for a moment.

"You happy?" she asked, and for the first time let her eyes meet his, search his, pierce the ridiculous shield he'd raised to fight the dazzling effect of her. "Are you happy, Ashford?"

He wanted to be honest with her. Really, he did. He wanted to tell her that he couldn't be happy as long as she was trapped in a loveless marriage to his coldhearted brother. He wanted to tell her that, no, he wasn't happy, would never be happy, because the one thing that could bring him happiness in the world was forbidden to him forever, that he'd tossed away those rights unwittingly before she'd even learned her letters.

"If you're happy, I'm happy," he answered, as honest an answer as he could find in his heart to give.

"Good," she said again, resolutely, as if that settled the matter.

"Yes," he agreed.

She made her way to the desk and handed Liberty a nut, watched him crack off the shell, break the meat down into small bits, and lay them at the chickadee's feet. "We don't lie very well, do we?" she asked finally.

"Well, I wasn't trying all that hard," he said, defending his acting skills.

"Really?" She turned and looked up at him, those piercing eyes stabbing him with their pain again. "I was trying with all my might."

"Then we'd better hope you never have to convince anyone of something you don't really believe."

"I'm not a good liar," she agreed, tilting her face up toward his. "I'm not much good at anything but the law, and that relies rather heavily on the truth of things."

He wanted to tell her that it didn't seem that way from where he sat, not as someone who'd always been privy to the machinations of a family involved in the law from as far back as they could trace and then some, but it seemed to cast aspersions on something she treasured. The notion that the law was imperfect and that justice was neither blind nor evenhanded merely sullied it, and her along with it. And so he just nodded, his head getting that much closer to hers, his lips nearly brushing her temple, yearning to ask her if she cared for him, terrified to know. "Do you always tell the truth?" he asked, letting his lips taste the warmth of her skin.

Before she could answer he heard the uneven tap of his mother's cane on the steps—rap, step, step. Rap, step, step. Charlotte's wide eyes and her dash for the window told him that every now and then she at least attempted to keep the truth to herself.

"Charlotte, don't be ridiculous. There's no reason for you to go out there," he said as he fought her efforts to raise the sash. "There's nothing wrong with you coming up to my room."

"Look at my face and tell me I hadn't better hide," she

said. There might as well be big bold letters spelling out a guilt she had no reason to feel.

Unless, of course, she was feeling what he was feeling, had come for what he had been hoping she'd come for.

He lifted the sash and handed her out the window, then hurried to the door, opened it, and leaned against its frame.

"And what canary have you swallowed?" his mother asked him as she went around him and into the room.

Charlotte positioned herself between the windows that faced north and those that faced east and leaned back against the overlapping wooden boards, grateful she was short enough to avoid the mansard roof. Cabot had always said her honest face would be her undoing, and here she was, out on the roof in February hiding from her mother-in-law to prove it.

"Have you seen Charlotte?" she could hear Kathryn asking. "I do swear this room gets higher every time I manage to get up here."

"You never swear, Mother," Ash answered, obviously trying to avoid the question rather artlessly.

"I've looked for her everywhere. I've been down to the cellar where she kept that poor cat with the horrid eyes, and out to the carriage house where the squirrels have all but taken over. Did you know she feeds those rodents?"

"No," he answered, coming and sitting on the windowsill so that she could watch his back expand and contract with every breath while he talked with Kathryn as if not a thing had passed between them.

She reminded herself it hadn't. Not beyond her mind, anyway.

"Though I admit it doesn't surprise me. She seems to have a weak spot for all living things."

"Even Cabot?" Kathryn said. "Is that what you're thinking?"

"What would make you come looking for her here?" Ash asked. Apparently he enjoyed playing with fire after all. Maybe Charlotte ought to rethink his innocence with regard to the warehouse. "For heaven's sake, Mother. Sit down and catch your breath."

"It's those stairs. I believe there's a new one for every year. The older I get, the more of them there seem to be. Isn't that her bird?"

"Go ahead, Mother dear. Out with it. I've seen you do it with others, but never known you to play cat-and-mouse with me before." His fingers traced the window ledge, reminding Charlotte of how Cabot traced the spokes of his chair wheels, reminding her they were brothers.

"What is it you think I have to say?" his mother asked. "That I'm concerned about you? That I see time hasn't healed that pain, that—"

Ash cut his mother off. "Did you really come to talk about me, Mother, or about Cabot? Or about Charlotte and Cabot, perhaps?"

"You're right, I'm worried about all three of you. I admit it. You want me to say it? All right. I'm concerned that perhaps you've decided that Charlotte deserves more than Cabot is capable of giving her."

"Isn't she?"

Charlotte swallowed hard. The air was cold and bit at her nostrils and her throat.

"Oh, Ashford," Kathryn said, and Charlotte could hear the fracturing of her heart in her voice. "You don't understand Charlotte at all. There is nothing more important to her than the law. There never has been. Her name is on that marriage license and I know she sees it as a contract with Cabot. Charlotte would sooner let one of her precious animals die than go back on her word. If you think otherwise, Ashford, you'll find yourself wrong, and you'll be terribly, dreadfully hurt. I know that child as well as one of my own, and there's no doubt in my mind that she's made of better stuff than you give her credit for."

"It's a contract between them, then?" Ash asked. "And nothing more?"

"You aren't listening to what I'm saying. Yes, there are limits to their marriage imposed by his condition, I would say. She gave up some things in order to obtain others. That's what contracts are all about."

"And his part of this so-called contract? What did my brother give up? Where's his compromise?"

"How can you, of all people, ask that?" Charlotte could hear the gasp and the indignation through the open window and tears stung her eyes as they always did for all that Cabot had lost. "He will never father a child. What more must a man do without?"

"But that's not her fault, is it? Nor is it his choice. You can't give up something you don't have. She's the one who's given up children, she's the one who has given up any kind of physical love. From what I can see, she's given up any love at all. Was that part of their 'bargain'?"

He got up from the window, leaving Charlotte quite alone on the roof. But he was speaking loudly enough for her to hear him as clearly as if she were in the room with him, and she knew that what he said was as much for her benefit as for his mother's.

"He took her as his wife, not his partner. But he offers her no love, no comfort, no warmth. Didn't that contract call for him to love, honor, and obey? Aren't those the usual vows to which they had to say *I do?* Didn't he promise to put her above him, to cherish her?

"I want to know why she's the only one held to those vows, vows that he has never bothered to embrace, just like he's never bothered to embrace her."

"You should have taken up the law yourself," Kathryn said. "You present one side of the argument very well. But Charlotte herself knows the other side. Knows that she got what she wanted from the arrangement. Do you know how many lady lawyers there are in California? Do you—"

"So I've heard a great deal of lately. And I've heard about arrangements and contracts and agreements. What I haven't heard about is love."

"He can't," Kathryn said, her cane striking the floor for emphasis. "You know he can't."

"Can't what, Mother? Can't love?"

"You know very well what I mean," Kathryn said. She was standing by the window now. Charlotte, trapped, leaned back in the hopes of staying out of sight.

"I know that my sister-in-law is married in name only. I know that my brother has broken his vows to love and honor." He was standing by his mother now. Charlotte could see his arms on her shoulders, leading her away from the window.

"With whom did he break those vows?" she demanded.

"With his wife," Ash said, leaning out the window and looking directly at Charlotte. "There's nothing wrong with the man's arms, nothing wrong with his lips, and without being crass, I simply say that if he loved her, he could make her happy and make their marriage a real one."

"They have a real marriage," Kathryn said, "considering everything."

He ducked back into the room and Charlotte ran one finger over her lips. They were soft, pliant. She closed her eyes and pressed two fingers against them as she had every night since she had married Cabot. *I will never,* she told herself, barely able to control her breathing, *kiss myself good-night again.*

"A real marriage, you say? With you at the head of the table across from Cabot? How fortunate for you that

Charlotte had no 'high calling' to become the lady of the house. Almost like having one of your daughters back, isn't it?"

"I didn't know you had it in you to be so cruel," Kathryn said. "Or perhaps so observant either."

"Oh, my God! The bird!" Ash ran back toward the window and looked out, his mouth open as the tiny black-capped chickadee flew past Charlotte and swooped unevenly down toward the trees below.

His eyes searched hers and reluctantly she shook her head. The little bird was gone.

"Has it made its escape?" Kathryn asked from deeper in the room.

"Yes," Ash said softly, looking at Charlotte. "It's free."

"Maybe you should go after it," Kathryn said. "I wouldn't be able to bear seeing Charlotte unhappy."

"Charlotte will find something else to love," he said, fingering the paint on the windowsill's edge, pulling away a rotting chip and flinging it out onto the roof. "And maybe this time it will be something more worthy."

"I see. You can tell her who she should love, as well as who she shouldn't. Isn't that really Charlotte's decision?" Kathryn asked. "I mean which broken bird it is that's worthy of her affection?"

"Her birds are all flight worthy, Mother. She'd do well to look after herself for a change instead of giving that heart of hers to anything she thinks needs it—even an ingrate who flies off at the first opportunity."

"She understands loyalty better than most," Kathryn said softly. Charlotte heard her cane strike the floor. "You should recognize the signs, Ashford. You're no stranger yourself."

"I understand the difference between loyalty and love."

"Is there a difference?" Kathryn asked. "Can you have one without the other?"

"Undoubtedly," Ashford Whittier answered with a sigh so deep, it rattled in Charlotte's own chest. "And it hurts."

"Loyalty is important, son, but I don't suppose that if you are lucky enough to have the opportunity, a body should have to live without love. Maybe it would be best if you go see whether you can catch that bird?"

"Someone else will have to catch it." Charlotte sensed him back at the window, but refused to take her eyes from where she thought the chickadee was. She watched the green leaves get blurrier and blurrier, and still she kept her head turned away. "I've been *remanded* to my brother's custody. Never forget that, Mother."

"Then she'll get away," Kathryn warned. Charlotte heard the door to Ash's bedroom open.

"With all my heart I hope so," Ash answered, closing the door behind his mother and returning to the window only to crawl out beside her.

He hated the roof, not surprisingly. It dredged up memories better laid to rest. Carefully he set his feet on the flattest part of the heavy slate shingles, and tried to block out the image of his brother coming toward him on two good legs, smiling, his hands out for balance, while Ash backed farther and farther away, clinging to the ridge of the roof in fear.

None of it ever made any sense. It had been Cabot, his bear of a big brother, coming to rescue him. And yet his strongest memories were filled with terror and confusion.

He pushed the thoughts back to the corner of his mind that was reserved for them, where he kept his guilt carefully preserved so as never to forget what he'd done, and eased himself down next to Cabot's wife, both of them leaning against the wooden slats that overlapped each other and cut into their backs. He was forced by the height of the window sash and all the moldings that punctuated the frieze to keep his head forward as if he were eager to tell her something that he'd vowed would never pass his lips.

"He'll die," she said at great length.

"No, he's stronger than you think," he answered, confused about whether they were referring to the bird or the man who had come to depend on her so heavily.

"Do you think so?" Huge hazel eyes, swimming in tears, were only inches from his face, so close he couldn't see them clearly anymore, couldn't see *her* clearly anymore, couldn't see anything clearly but the pain.

"Look," he said, pointing down to the garden, where Davis had just appeared. "What's he doing?"

They watched as Davis gestured toward one bush and then to another. He nodded his head and then pulled out his clippers. Before each move the boy studied the house, made elaborate motions with his hands, and then nodded.

"Somebody's directing him," Ash said, finally catching on.

Beside him Charlotte smiled tightly and brushed at a tear. "Cabot must be having him bring in some pussy willows. He likes to bring them indoors to bloom."

Cabot liked to bring everything inside, out of the sun, out of the natural order of things, and have it answer to his whim. He wanted to cultivate the woman who was huddled against the cold beside Ash, wanted to train her to grow just the way he thought best, like some topiary taken to the extreme, and damn nature in the process.

"Cold?" Ash asked, rocking his weight forward so that he could get up and help Charlotte in. Beside him she made no move to rise.

"Are you sure he'll be all right? What if it gets cold tonight? What'll he eat? Where'll he sleep?"

He settled back, putting his arm out for her to lean

against, and searched the trees below for any sign of Charlotte's little bird.

"There!" He pointed to one of her many feeders just as the tiny bird was lighting there. "You've taken care of everything, Charlotte. Just relax now. I'll open the doors to the carriage house tonight so he'll have a warm place to sleep."

"But he'll be alone. . . ." She snuggled closer against him, robbing the heat from his body while stoking deeper fires they couldn't afford to risk.

"Not once he finds a mate," he answered, stiffening to keep some distance between them. "The right mate."

"Maybe if I left my window open," she began.

"A little Charlotte Russe," he said as he stroked her hair and inhaled the sweet freshness of her skin. "So sweet. There are a million starving souls, and you keep trying to feed the ones that aren't hungry."

"Everyone's hungry," she said, her head against his chest so that he could feel the words penetrate his shirt and tease his skin.

He had thought he knew all there was to know about hunger, how it rose from his loins, how it swelled his manhood. But all these years he'd mistaken mere desire for absolute need. Now it was as if someone had set fire to his skin where her body rested against his side, and no ointment, no salve, no cream, would ever be able to cool or soothe it.

Words strangled in his throat, played havoc with his tongue, and mocked his sincerity. Hadn't he said *I love you* to a hundred women before her? And now wasn't he forbidden to even relish the thought?

He had stolen from his brother the chance to be a real husband.

Someone else would have to take away the man's very real wife.

# Chapter 11

Charlotte's hand was on the conservatory door when she heard Cabot's voice. "Slowly," he said. "This isn't a race, it's a lesson. And it ends not at a set hour, but at a set goal. Do you understand that?"

How well she remembered that creed. *You research a case until you're done, Miss Reynolds. The facts, not the clock, dictate your completion.* Charlotte waited along with Cabot for Davis's answer. There was no response.

"I don't hear nods. A simple *yes* will suffice. A *yes, sir,* would actually please me, and a *yes, sir, Mr. Whittier,* might get you the sight of me spinning a little circle in this chair."

"Yes, s–s–sir," she heard Davis's halting answer. "M–M–Mister Whit–ta-ta . . ."

She pushed the door open slightly. If Cabot was doing roundabouts, Charlotte was not about to miss them. "I do believe I'll have to start practicing those circles," she heard him say. There was almost a lilt to the man's voice, nearly a chuckle in his tone. "Now, you will stay in this room and practice while I take care of a few matters. You will water all the flowers on the far wall, but this time not more than this beakerful, understood?"

"Yes, s-s-sir," she heard Davis respond.

"Pressed for time as I've been, I've still done a good deal of study on the subject of stammering and stuttering—you do realize there is a difference and that you are a stutterer?"

The boy nodded. *No!* she thought. *Answer him!*

"Your affliction will not be overcome with a nod of the head, but by perseverance, determination, good diet, good habits, good morals, and, most importantly, good teaching. Is that understood?"

"Yes, s-s-sir." If she had a nickel for every Brussels sprout he'd insisted she eat, a penny for every glass of water—oh, he was a tough taskmaster, Cabot Whittier was, and never had she learned so much. She remembered coming into his office from the brisk walks he insisted she take, her cheeks tingling from the excitement of some new discovery, thinking herself a genius for figuring out the lessons of the law. Of course, he always set her straight, but that rush of exaltation—it was almost like being in love.

The thought stopped her cold, and she listened with only half an ear while Cabot issued orders to her charge.

"There is a bicycle in the carriage house. I can think of no better exercise for a youngster who has completed his studies, eaten his vegetables, and performed his chores."

"Yes, s-s-sir."

The man who had started her dreaming, had pushed her along when her hopes had faded, and had propped her up when her confidence had faltered, was focusing intently on Davis's mouth, manipulating the boy's jaw, examining his teeth. "There is, according to this book, and more importantly to my own observations, a certain rhythm in all good speech, a stroke of the voice followed by a partial rest. Lewis here recommends the use of poetry."

The boy yanked his head away from Cabot's prodding fingers and stood just out of the chairbound man's reach.

"Excuse me for assuming that you wish to recover from your affliction. If I am wasting my time, I'd sooner know it now than waste another moment on a boy as lazy as Ludlam's dog."

"No p–p–p–"

In the overheated greenhouse, frustration seeped along with sweat from every pore of Davis's body. Cabot sat in his chair, watching the boy without offering so much as a guess at what he wanted to say, though clearly it was a comment on the idea of poetry. Charlotte bit her tongue, caught between her admiration for Cabot's devotion and her need to rescue Davis from his own inadequacy.

Cabot, for his part, sat very still. His fingers didn't tap, his lips didn't twitch. "Think what you wish to say," he told the boy. "Let the words become clear in your mind."

Davis pointed at the watch that sat neglected in Cabot's hand.

"I have as long as it takes," he assured the boy. "You were about to tell me something with regard to poetry, I suspect."

The boy struggled to answer him and Charlotte lost the battle to remain outside the room. "He probably hates it," she said, coming in and approaching the pair. "Boys always hate poetry."

The boy nodded emphatically. She'd only seen him from the back, but coming around him she found a new bruise had joined several other faded ones on his face. She hated boxing, hated fisticuffs of any sort. Still, she couldn't help wishing that once Moss Johnson could go a few rounds with Ewing Flannigan. Without gloves. Or a referee. Or a bell for him to be saved by. All right. Twice. Or every day . . .

Davis glared at her, daring her to say something about his appearance. Instead she continued her attack on poetry as if she hadn't even noticed that anything was so terribly, critically, crucially wrong.

"What use has a boy for *Shall I compare thee to a summer's day*?"

"A poem, Charlotte, is many things for many people. For some men it is merely an illusion used to feign culture and refinement, and for others it can be a trick to appear in love or worse—besotted. More than a few women have been known to use a poem as a yardstick to measure the affections of their suitors, always finding them inadequate when compared to Mr. Shakespeare. A teacher employs a poem as a test of memory and devotion to study. An intellect, praised be the lonely soul, can be amused, fascinated, and entertained by a poem.

"For Master Flannigan it will be a tool with which to train the tongue."

He snapped shut the green cloth volume that had lain open on his lap. In gold lettering across the cover, the title proclaimed the volume to contain the *Practical Treatment of Stammering and Stuttering.* Illustrated, no less.

"You will remain in this room until you have repeated the alphabet no fewer than five times, noting, on a tablet, in one column, which of the letters cause you difficulty and, in a second column, those sounds that do not."

The boy's eyes widened, his split lip trembled.

Cabot closed his eyes and shook his head in utter disbelief. "You don't write, do you?"

"No, s-s-sir."

The disappointment on Cabot's face was replaced by a

grin so sly that Charlotte squinted in search of yellow feathers sticking out of the man's mouth while he handed Davis a book.

"Copy the letters in this book. Fill three pages with the smallest letters you can make. We'll make sense of them tomorrow."

"I could teach him his letters," Charlotte offered. "After he's . . ."

"He's what, Charlotte?" Cabot asked. "What is it you're thinking?"

"Davis," she said, bending slightly so that she was on eye level with the boy, "I'd like to file a suit against your father."

The boy shook his head, as vehemently as she supposed he could do without causing himself great pain.

"He's hurt you again," she said softly. "I can't let him do that. You deserve better than this and I can—"

"No!"

Well, she'd found a way to cure his stammering. Just threaten to take him away from his father.

"I can't let your father do this to you," she said.

Again he shook his head.

"You will stay here," Cabot said. "And I'll work you twice as hard as your father ever did and you won't enjoy a moment of it. But you won't have any scars to show for it, I promise you that. You'll have diplomas and degrees."

The boy looked doubtful.

"Don't let Mr. Whittier frighten you," she said. "He only wants what's best for you. As do I."

"You'll file the papers on Monday, Charlotte, when you get the extension in Ashford's case," Cabot said, beginning to wheel toward the door. "And you can do an extra page for the trouble you've caused," he shouted over his shoulders at the boy. "As small as you can do it."

"Cabot, there's no reason to punish the boy," she said as she closed the conservatory door behind them.

"Really? Then why do you suppose he stays with his father?" he answered. "And if he's so eager to be punished for something, at least I can oblige him in a way that won't do him any harm."

She wondered whether Cabot might be right as she followed along behind his chair, studying the top of his head. When she'd met him, his hair had been dark and sprinkled with the occasional silver strand. Now it was more silver than black. Ash's hair was a soft brown. Soft on the eye, anyway.

She had never touched a man's hair, never thought about it, or wanted to before now. She bet that Ash's hair was as soft as it looked. Lost in thought, she took several steps after Cabot's chair had stopped moving. Her knee hit the back of his chair with enough force to jolt him and send a sharp pain running up her shin. It also brought her hand down against his head.

Wiry. Coarse. But his hand was smooth and soft as he took hers and removed it from him.

"Are you quite all right?" he asked, holding her as far away as his arm could place her.

"Your hand is really soft," she said before he jerked it away and glowered at her. "I mean your grip is very strong, but your skin is soft."

"I'm sorry," he said, fighting with the knob on the door. It was a difficult maneuver for him, getting close enough to hold the knob and then backing up to make room to open the door without crashing it into his chair.

"For squeezing my hand, or for letting it go?" she asked. "Or for never having held it before?"

He fought harder with the door, backing up against her boot until it was clear that she had him trapped. She reached out and put her hand within inches of his tightly closed fist.

"Am I soft too?" she asked.

"Of course you are," he said, still maneuvering his chair.

"How do you know?" she asked him, offering her hand.

"I don't know," he said, looking at it without taking it.

She swallowed. Pride had left a big lump in her throat, but she spoke around it. "Shouldn't you want to know?"

He grasped the door handle and pulled back again, the door slamming with a resounding crack into knees that felt nothing. "Get my brother," he said while he pushed his chair back against her, the wheel running over the toe of her boot before she could retract it. "We've got work to do."

Her fine kid boot came to a point long beyond her foot, so his brusque movements did it no harm. Her heart, however, was another matter.

"Cabot, wait," she said as he braced his hands against the door frame and propelled himself out of the room.

He stopped and turned to look at her. The corners of his mouth, nearly hidden by his mustache, were turned down. "Do you want to see my brother go to prison?"

The knot that had been in her stomach for days tightened.

"It's in your hands, you know. That's the price of being a lawyer."

"Maybe it wasn't even arson," Ash said. He didn't know what had passed between his brother and Charlotte, only that yet another barrier had fallen between them. Charlotte's chair was so close to the wall that the back legs rested on the edge of the molding, and she tottered slightly every time she shifted her weight—which was often enough for Cabot to demand she sit still as if she were some ill-behaved child who was being kept in at recess.

"Of course it was arson," Cabot said, throwing some papers in his direction. " 'Two separate and distinct locations,' the report says. 'Accelerant,' the report says. For Christ's sake, they found the cap to the kerosene. *Not even arson!*" He exhaled hard enough to ruffle the papers on his desk.

"Sam Greenbough sold those coffee beans to someone," Charlotte said. "My guess is for a lot more than he put on those books. There's no question from the way he was living that he's been robbing the company blind."

"And the company *was* blind, wasn't it?" Cabot asked, staring at Ash as if trusting his partner was now a crime. "But if your theory is right, Charlotte, why bother burning down the place if the books had already been altered? Can you tell me that?"

"Don't take it out on her," Ash said. "How's she supposed to know how someone like Greenbough thinks? He's the scum of the earth, and she's—she's . . ." He held his tongue. Cabot ought to know what his wife was, damn it! He shouldn't need to be told.

"You don't have to roll in the mud to know how the pig got dirty," Cabot said. "What would Greenbough have to gain if he burned down his own warehouse?" he asked Charlotte.

"For one, he'd be able to get rid of any evidence that might incriminate him were Ash to find it," Charlotte suggested. Her chair inched away from the wall as she continued. "For another, if he were able to frame your brother, he could wind up with the whole business instead of just his half interest."

"Weak," Cabot said, his hands folded on his desk. "Can't you do any better?"

"I don't know," Charlotte said, throwing her pad down onto the desk top and coming to her feet. "If, as usual, you know the answer, why not just tell us and stop playing with me like I'm still a student?"

"You are a student of the law until the day you die, Charlotte. Now, sit back down and learn." Cabot held out her tablet, waiting for her to take it from him.

"I am not *your* student anymore, Mr. Whittier," she said, folding her hands over her chest. "The sign says I'm your partner. If you have a reason to think it wasn't Greenbough, tell us. If not, I think he's our prime suspect."

"It's common sense," his brother said. His tone was conciliatory; his eyes studied Charlotte's face as if he'd never seen it before. Or perhaps as if there was something new to see there. "The books that burned up would have been the perfect means by which to prove his innocence. Doctored, they would have provided chapter and verse of the fictitious sale. In fact, we're probably fortunate they went up in the blaze."

Charlotte reluctantly took back her notebook and regained her seat.

"You know, Charlotte may still be right," Ash said, hoping to bolster her sagging morale. Should the woman ever give up the law—and he thought the world would be the worse for it if she did—he surely hoped she didn't take up poker playing. He'd have promised her the moon to curve the corners of her mouth up again. He'd have promised her his soul for a smile. "Greenbough isn't any smarter than he is honest. He could have panicked that I was back, feared I would discover his deceit, and set fire to the place to cover his tracks."

"In law, as in life," his brother began to pontificate, leaning back far enough in his chair to cross his hands over a belly that had added a few annual rings since Ash had been home last, "there are only four basic motives. Naturally, the most common is greed—the crime for profit. We'll skip the second for the moment and come to the 'cover-up' crime—the one committed to prevent the discovery of some other deed, to protect another, or to destroy the evidence that would prove guilt. That's your theory, Charlotte. The last, not nearly as common as we defense attorneys would have people believe, is compulsion—insanity, temporary insanity, the need for the thrill."

Ash shook his head. His brother always broke things down to the point where all other ideas were reduced to the ridiculous. There was a time, when Ash was young, that he'd thought of Cabot as some sort of magician. With a wave of his hand or his wand he could turn black into white or wrong into right. And nothing had changed.

"But the most common motive, the one you've naturally overlooked, is the one that speaks to man's greatest weakness. Anger. Anger that stems from jealousy, lust, or better still, revenge. Revenge is a powerful motive, Charlotte," Cabot said, pulling his eyes from Ash to study quite the sort of woman who could drive a man to the edge of disaster just to keep a smile on her face. "If one man felt wronged by another, his trust violated, his honor impugned, there are no lengths to which he might not be pushed by his need for revenge."

Charlotte shook her head. "Yes, but in this case—" she began.

Ash knew what Cabot was after, knew even why he had chosen to have the conversation in front of Charlotte. The man was no fool. Anyone with eyes in his head could see that Charlotte had begun, like so many other women, to find Ash in need of her special attention and care.

"I've given him no reason to seek revenge," he said

simply. He sat back in his chair and crossed his legs. *Don't pursue this,* he thought. "Ever."

Cabot tapped against the arm of his chair, his fingernails making a clicking sound. "Really?"

Ash nodded. Sam's wife wasn't happy about the fact, but he'd never so much as run a finger through that curly red mane, never brushed against those ample breasts, even by accident. He believed, whether Helena Greenbough did or not, in the sanctity of a true marriage. "Really."

Cabot looked at his wife and pulled at his lower lip. "A man, by nature, doesn't like to share. Look at the infant with his rattle, the toddler with his ball. What's his is his, and he wants to keep it. Of course, if everyone felt that way, there would be no need for courts, would there? It's when the bully comes to the park and says, 'What's mine is mine and what's yours is mine, too,' that the penal codes come to be necessary."

"A rather simplistic explanation of mankind and the law. All you've omitted from that park is the serpent and the apple," Ash said.

He did not wish to have a discussion of the purity of his soul in front of Charlotte, any more than he'd like to meet his maker and, right at that moment, explain to him his transgressions.

"I'm not worried about the serpent or the apple," Cabot said. "I'm worried, hypothetically, about what belongs to me."

"If the child leaves his hypothetical ball in the park he shouldn't expect it to be there when he returns. If the ball matters to him, he should cling to it tightly."

"Or leave it at home?" Cabot asked. "Would that keep it safe?"

Ask knew what his answer had to be, for all their sakes. And yet he couldn't bring himself to utter the words.

Maria's knock came to his rescue. "That man is here again," she said to Cabot. "The investigator. You want me to tell him you are busy?"

Ash opened the curtain and studied the back of the man who waited on the front porch. His coat was dirty and rumpled and his shoes worn down at the heels. Beneath the brim of his hat his hair fought for freedom in several different directions.

"Tell him to go around to the back and I'll see him in the conservatory. It's best that you don't meet him," Cabot said to Ash, and began the process of coming out from behind his desk.

"A third wheel—" Ash began, sure that a smaller wheel at the back of Cabot's chair, able to pivot in any direction, would increase his mobility enormously.

"I don't want a third wheel," Cabot snapped at him. "Do you understand me?"

Charlotte and he stared at each other for a moment after he was gone. "Wheels and balls. How clever men think they are," she said with a sigh.

"And do you know so much about men?" he asked as she stood tapping her foot in annoyance.

"Not enough," she said, opening the door she had closed behind Cabot. "And not yet."

She meant it to be the end of their discussion, going out in a dramatic flourish, but he followed hard upon her heels like some lovesick puppy and asked, "What's that supposed to mean?"

"It means that a ball can be as abandoned in the cellar as it can in the park. And a doll left on a shelf gets mighty dusty. And how dare he not care whether I'm soft? I'm so soft, I'm rotting! Feel this!" She put her palm against his face and ran her hand slowly down his cheek, turned it over, and ran the back side down against his neck.

And with the gesture all the fight seemed to go out of

her, there in her office, with a hundred little ceramic animal statues watching them and papers piled high on her desk and hairpins in a dish on the windowsill.

He didn't answer her question with words. Instead, he ran his own hand against her cheek, imitated her move by caressing her neck, feeling the blood rush beneath his fingertips. *Was she soft?* Van Gogh's fur was a sisal mat beside her. Rose petals were sandpaper. She was like talc itself, silky and smooth and so soft, you weren't certain it was there at all—that you'd touched anything or just imagined the sensation.

His lips had to make sure of what his hands had judged. *Just her cheek*, he warned himself. Then just her neck. The smell of her! Clean. Sweet. A hint of something exotic he guessed he'd probably bought her himself on one of his trips. Soft? Oh, no—there had to be another word for her skin, the tip of her ear, the lid of her left eye.

A tiny gasp escaped her lips as she offered them up to him. Those huge hazel eyes begged him to teach her more. Two wayward locks of hair fell across her face—no doubt he'd loosened something with his explorations—and she brushed the locks away with her left hand. The simple gold band on her finger glinted in the sunlight. How much brighter her office was than Cabot's.

Bright enough for the light of day to shine in, and too bright to hide what was growing between them. He backed up, letting his hands drop away from her with more difficulty than he'd have had raising the mainsail on the *Bloody Mary* single-handedly.

"Oh, please don't stop," she said softly. "I've so much to learn."

"I cut your husband off at the knees once," he answered, wishing he could look away, not watch her lip tremble, not see her bite on it to make it stop. "I can't do it again."

"No, of course not," she said. "I'm married to your brother no matter what you told Kathryn about him breaking his vows. You know, I don't believe he'd ever intended to keep them."

"I'm sorry," he said, shoving his hand in his pocket to keep from touching her again.

"You Whittier men are always sorry," she said sadly. "And I'm sorry too."

She went behind the desk and sat down, reached back for a hairpin, and caught up the wayward locks.

"If you'll excuse me, I've work to do," she said, giving him a sad little smile and bowing her head as if she cared at all about the papers on her desk.

"I'll go see what's keeping your husband," he said, trying to remind them both that they had obligations they shouldn't forget.

"What?" she looked up at him, distracted.

"Where were you, just now?" he asked. *What do you daydream about? What time of day is your favorite? What color makes you smile? What song makes you weep?*

"I was remembering a line from Whittier," she said, trying to dismiss him with a wave of her hand.

"Ashford?" he joked. Lord, he thought, she was almost as pretty sad as she was happy. And then he corrected himself—happy she took his breath away. When she was sad, he simply didn't want to breathe anymore.

"John Greenleaf. *For of all sad words of tongue or pen, the saddest are these . . .*"

"*. . . It might have been.*"

She nodded and shooed him off again. "I've work to do."

There was no use arguing with her. She and her poet friend had summed up his life in a couple of lines.

* * *

"How much?" Cabot said to the man who stood in the shadows.

"Twenty. Thirty if you need physical evidence."

"Just get it lined up, in case. That's all."

"I know my business," the man said. "And it always turns out to be necessary."

"I know you've found a puddle of piss when you promised an ocean of information," Cabot said.

"This your investigator?" Ash asked. The man turned his back so that Ash couldn't see his face and Cabot reached quickly into his breast pocket, pulled out his wallet, and handed the man several bills. "You come to the back door next time," he told the man.

"Yeah, yeah," the man said, counting the money. "And you try to remember I'm not the one on trial and I'm not the one who's done anything wrong, yet."

*Yet.* The word hung in the air as the man strode purposely to the outer door and slammed it behind him, rattling the glass panes throughout the conservatory.

"Just what does that guy do?" Ash asked him. "Besides ooze pus?"

"Every now and then he saves a neck," Cabot said. "And the less you know, the less Brent can accuse you of. Just leave him to me."

"And leave my investigation and my neck to him? I think not, Cabot."

"I will take care of it." Cabot pounded on the arm of his chair. "You take more reassurance than a five-year-old!"

"Perhaps because you've given me all the authority and discretion of one," Ash snapped back. He'd be damned if he left his fate to some weaselly little man who used people's back doors.

Cabot shrugged as if that was all Ash merited. "Where's Charlotte?" he asked.

"I left her slaving away in her office," Ash said. "As usual. Do you have any idea how lucky you are to have such a beautiful and dedicated wife?"

"Dedicated?"

"It's Sunday, and the moment she got back from taking your mother to church she was hard at work."

"And that makes me a lucky man?" Cabot played with the spokes on his wheels as if Ash needed reminding. "And she's *your* mother, as well."

"I've never met a woman like her," Ash said. He kept to himself how soft she was, how good she smelled, how just the thought of her got juices flowing that he had to fight against with all his might.

"And you never will. I made her—shaped her like a sculptor. And while I'll agree I started with the finest marble, without my hand she would be some diplomat's wife dolled up in a fancy dress with a smile pasted on her pretty face and not a thought in that head of hers."

"You sound like Mary Shelley's Frankenstein. But I think you've forgotten the end of the tale."

"You might do well to wipe your drool before you call my wife a monster. It would have a more resounding ring of authenticity that way." Cabot's eyes looked straight ahead, riveted on Ash's row of trouser buttons.

"It was a cautionary tale," Ash said, refusing to let his brother intimidate him. "The lesson being that everyone needs love. So when the monster demanded it from his creator, and was denied . . . well, you know how the story ends."

"Oh! Am I in mortal danger from Charlotte?" Cabot hunched his shoulders and shivered dramatically, pulling on his suit lapels as if he were freezing.

"If arrogance were fatal, undoubtedly. But I'd say your person is safe. It's your marriage that's teetering on the brink."

"Thanks to a few kicks at the underpinnings, no doubt. Wasn't pushing me off the roof enough for you?"

His memories of the event were hazy. After all, he was six at the time, and the whole incident had happened so fast. And afterward there had been all that commotion, the yelling, the crying, his mother begging to be allowed to see her son, his father's thunderous voice forbidding it, his brother's friends scattering to the winds. But of one thing he was completely sure. He did not, would not have, pushed his brother from the roof.

He remembered backing away, yes. Remembered his brother making silly faces at him and dancing across the roof line in pursuit. His brother's face, filled with surprise as his last step took him over the edge of the roof, was etched forever in Ash's memory. But Cabot was far away from him, out of his reach as his short little child arms stretched out to catch him before he fell.

"I did not push you from the roof," he said, turning on his heel and passing Davis, who was just coming into the room with Liberty on his shoulder. Even in his anger Ash noticed how big the bird was for the slight boy. Ash wondered how many burdens Davis bore that were too large for those small shoulders.

"Did you come when I called you?" Cabot called out after him as Ash left the conservatory doors open behind him and took off for the stairs.

Once Davis had gotten the double doors closed—there was a trick to it that the mister had shown him—he returned with the parrot to the stand near the wheelchair.

"Your father will be here within the hour, I believe," Mr. Whittier said to him. He had a deep voice and spoke slowly, not like the men down at McGinty's, who spat words at him quickly and with anger. "Did you practice again today?"

"Yes, s-s-sir." Always the same. *Sir* wouldn't come out. But here in the garden room there was nothing to kick that wouldn't fall over or crack, so he just dug his nails into his palm and tried again. "Yes." So clear. The word was his, belonged to him. "S-s-s-sir." He opened his mouth to try again, but the mister waved away the attempt.

"I've given Mrs. Whittier permission to initiate a case for your removal from your present domicile. Do you understand what that means?"

He thought it meant that the missus was going to try to get a judge to make his father give him up and that he would come live here, but they were some pretty big words that the mister was using. Words he was going to own someday, just like *yes.*

"Yes, s-s-sir."

"And you have no objections? Now, I'm not asking about reservations, mind you, but objections. Do you understand the difference?"

Of course he didn't. "Yes, s-s-sir."

"No, you don't, but you are quite right that it isn't important. What is important is that I am about to make you a promise, something I do not take lightly, in exchange for a promise on your part. I have made such a promise before and I have kept my word, and now I give that word to you.

"For your part, you agree to do as I say, everything I say, and when I say it, without argument."

The sun would have to shine for a week straight in San Francisco for Davis to agree to something like that.

"And if you fulfill your part, I promise to make you the best lawyer in Oakland."

Davis wasn't born yesterday. He knew he'd be lucky to

wind up with a job cleaning up spilled beer on the floor at McGinty's or working at the canneries or the docks. Still, there was something about the way the mister was looking at him, right on, not sort of sideways the way people did when they lied.

"All right, perhaps not the best. There is me, after all, and Mrs. Whittier. But you will read, write, and argue the law, and I won't quit until you do. Unless, of course, you don't live up to your end of our deal."

It was the most ridiculous thing anyone had ever said to him. Sillier than where babies came from or that his ma could hear his prayers at night. And still he stood there, considering, listening, wishing.

"You think about it," the mister said. "And while you're thinking, you tell that parrot, *See you soon, sweetheart.*"

It wasn't right to promise the bird he'd be back. He struggled to get the words out that he might not. The mister waited patiently while he tried.

"Oh, you'll be back. Mrs. Whittier will see to it. And you will practice and work your tail off for me and make me very proud."

He opened his mouth to tell the mister he didn't think it was going to work, and that he wasn't so stupid as to believe he could ever become something so important as a streetcar conductor, never mind a lawyer, but the mister was already rolling toward the door.

"*See you soon, sweetheart.* Over and over until one of those *s*'s just slips off that recalcitrant tongue of yours. You know what *recalcitrant* means?"

He didn't know what half of the mister's words meant.

"Bet you wish you did," the mister said. "Bet you wish you could look it up in some book. I'd be willing to bet right now you're wishing you could tell me how much you hate me, or leave me a note saying as much. Without my help, though, you can't do a thing. With it you can rule the world.

"Up to you, of course," he said rolling his chair up the slanted board that connected the conservatory to the rest of the house.

Davis pulled the book with the pictures of mouths and tongues off the table and threw it to the ground. He stamped on it twice and then jumped with both feet up and down on the cover.

He didn't deserve the chance. Could never take the mister up on it.

But it would sure have made his mother happy.

"S–s–see ya s-s-soon, sa–sa . . ." he told the parrot, who listened happily and then told him to shut up.

# Chapter 12

It had been the longest week of her life. Of all the years to throw in an extra day, this one had to be leap year? The last three days of February had been spent trying to see Judge Mallory, without any success. On the first of March, Cabot had intervened and a hearing had been set for the following Wednesday. Then Davis had shown up on Friday night, his old bruises so faded that one would suppose he'd never been touched. Charlotte should have been relieved, of course, and the fact that she wasn't weighed heavily on her conscience.

But without the physical evidence of his father's abuse, coupled with the poor boy's inability to articulate the situation even if he were willing (which she rather strongly doubted), her chances of getting the boy removed from his father's custody were slimmer than a woman getting into a voting booth. In fact, they were about as good as getting a woman elected to office.

And while she had certainly made his case her highest priority, the truth was that Davis Flannigan was not the only thing on her mind—not during the week and not over this weekend, either, despite a houseful of people, all of whom seemed to have suddenly decided she needed watching.

Kathryn, always independent before, had uncharacteristically demanded Charlotte's time and attention for everything from accompanying her to church to the color of her new dress. The woman had then abruptly and unilaterally decided that it was time Charlotte took her rightful place as the lady of the house and promptly left Sunday dinner in her hands. Unfortunately, this sudden relinquishing of authority didn't stop Kathryn from inviting Dr. Mollenoff and Selma to join them once again for dinner on Sunday afternoon.

But it wasn't just Kathryn. Davis, bless the sweet boy's heart, had spent the entire weekend delivering at least a hundred messages from Cabot, every one of them seeming to start with the letter *s. Starch in his shirts,* the poor lamb had tried to tell her. That had taken the better part of half an hour and in the end had meant rather little. More? Less? *S–s–some st-st-st-starch in his sh-sh-shirts.* There is? He wants? And on it went, a million interruptions she suspected were designed to keep Cabot abreast of where she was and what she was doing.

Though why he would have any interest was beyond her. Except, of course, that she was feeling guilty. But even if that had been Cabot's intention (which presupposed that he was jealous—an utterly ridiculous presumption), how could the boy manage to tell him what it was she was up to?

Which naturally was nothing but work, anyway, so the guilt was out of order.

*Oh no,* her conscience shouted—*overruled.* That guilt

was well founded and earned anew every time she looked at Ash Whittier. Each time she called up the memory of his breath on her cheek, every time she imagined his hand stroking her throat, and all the while she ached for the scent that clung to his hair. It was a wonder to her that after all these weeks at shore, he continued to smell to her of the sea and faraway places. Eau de Freedom.

And if all those thoughts weren't distraction enough from his case, she was expected to make the dining arrangements for Sunday dinner with the Mollenoffs and Davis and Cabot and any other strays that Kathryn could manage to drag off the street and place around the table to keep her farther from Ash than she wanted to be.

And since when didn't Cook know what to make and where the serving pieces were kept? And who had ever decided to place at the top of the breakfront that silver platter with the animals around the edge that might amuse Davis?

"Let me help you with that."

And what had ever possessed her to try to get it down herself? Oh, really, Charlotte, *what indeed,* she chastised herself as she allowed Ash to reach up along with her and hand the silver tray into her waiting arms, brushing now against his. *What indeed,* as his hands encircled her waist and lifted her from the step stool to set her on the floor only inches from him.

"I thought Davis might like it," she explained, setting it down on the table and tripping over her feet as she backed away from the man whose nearness made her ears burn and her fingers freeze.

"He's talking to Liberty," Ash said, steadying her with his hand and leaving it under her elbow years longer than it needed to be, then taking it away eons before she was ready. "I'm not sure which of them is more tortured, but the boy won't take a break."

"Do you think Cabot could be right?" Charlotte asked.

Ash was standing much too close to her, studying her shirtwaist with more than idle curiosity. *All the women were doing it,* the seamstress had told her. Just two rows of ruffles on the underlayer and even the least endowed woman became instantly shapelier. When she'd resisted, the seamstress had tempted her with promises that her suit jackets would fit all the better for the bit of fullness the hidden ruffles produced.

"New blouse?" he asked, dousing any hope she had that he hadn't noticed that overnight there were two oranges where her pair of grapes had formerly been.

"Yes," she said as brightly as she could. "It's the latest style. All the rage."

"It's very nice," he said. He tilted his head and looked at her from first one angle and then the other. "Flattering."

"Thank you." She studied the silver platter, unable to look him in the eye.

"Be even more lovely with the lace on the outside," he said with just the slightest smirk, as if he couldn't resist teasing her.

"Cabot doesn't care for lace," she said, putting the platter down and crossing her arms over her chest as if that would end the discussion.

"So you had to put it somewhere." His smile was wide now, broad enough to include her in its shelter. "Well, you picked a good place to hide it."

She had allowed Hedda to talk her into the blouse for Ash's sake, to show him that she really was a woman, but the plan had plainly backfired. "Is it that obvious?"

"Only to someone whose eyes are roaming where they don't belong." He pulled them from her chest and met her gaze. "But everywhere I look at you does funny things to my insides. Your earlobe, for instance, drives me—"

* * *

He stopped midsentence and stepped back a foot. Just over Charlotte's right shoulder he could see Davis, standing in the doorway, waiting and watching. And very obviously disapproving. The boy was Cabot's if he was anyone's, and Ash took an extra step back and another to the side as if to show that his hands were off Cabot's wife. Well off.

"Hi, there, Davis. Miss Charlotte was just getting down a special platter she thought you'd like."

"I'm going home, now," the boy said with several interruptions before the sentence was fully uttered. He added something about not wanting Charlotte to go to court.

"Mr. Whittier tell you not to go ahead with this?" he asked.

The boy shook his head.

"So then you just like being a human punching bag? You know there's not much future in it—those bags don't last all that long."

"I'll be okay," the boy answered in only two tries.

"You ever get a good look at old Moss Johnson's face?" Ash asked.

Davis's eyes widened, but he didn't flinch.

"Your father wear gloves when he works out his liquor on you? Those bare knuckles are the ones that leave the worst scars. Why, I once saw a man with only one eye. Lost the other when a man's finger—"

Beside him Charlotte swayed and reached for the wall to steady herself but found it too far away. He caught her just as she lost her balance. Without being told Davis pulled out a chair and pushed it up against the back of her knees until Ash let her go softly and she all but fell into the seat.

"Don't get no worse than I deserve," Davis said after getting stuck on almost every word.

"For what?" Charlotte asked, her heart breaking her words in two. "What could you do that would justify anyone raising his fists to you?" She reached out and traced a thin scar by the boy's eyebrow before he backed away.

" 'Nough." The word rang clear as a bell. "Sh-sh-shoulda b-b-been hung."

Ash nodded gravely and pulled out a chair for himself and one for Davis, gesturing for him to sit. "You know, you've got to do something very serious to be hung." He thought about the charges that he faced and how very lucky he was that at least he wasn't contemplating the noose. "And you've got to have meant to do it."

Davis looked at Charlotte for verification. She was as white as her starched shirt with the augmented bodice. It was utterly ridiculous how happy it made him that she wanted to look more womanly. Stupid even, because he enjoyed the thought that maybe it was for him that she'd bought the blouse. As if her dimensions mattered to him. If the circumstances were different, he believed his brother would actually be proud that he'd risen above such shallow standards for assessing a woman's value.

He doubted it would be politic to point it out to Cabot now.

"I didn't mean it," the boy said, his eyes getting overly bright. "I I–I–I–" He gave up and gulped back a sob.

"Things happen," Ash assured the boy, "that we never meant to happen. We leave a lamp burning and start a fire. We leave a toy on the stairs and someone tumbles down." He searched for other things that Davis might hold himself responsible for. Just what could a boy so young, so small, have done that would make him think he needed to pay with his own well-being?

"Sh-Sh-Sh—"

Ash's skin crawled with the wait as he let the boy push the words from his mouth. Of all God's afflictions on man, all the scars and pains and disabilities, he thought Davis's must be up among the worst, and he wasn't going to make it any harder with his impatience. Not guessing what the boy wanted to say was almost as hard as not taking Charlotte's hand as together they waited for the child to spit out the awful truth he carried beneath his scars.

When he'd gotten it out, Charlotte had grabbed the boy and was hugging him to her chest while Ash patted his back. All the while the boy cried, Ash tried to organize his thoughts, find a way to help the boy forgive himself.

"You were how old?" he asked when the tears subsided and Davis wiped at his face with Ash's hankie, pulling away from Charlotte now in embarrassment.

"S–S–S—"

Oh, Lord! *S*'s were the hardest for Davis. Ash wished the boy had been five at the time.

"Six."

"And this little six-year-old boy's terrible crime was that he stood up in a boat."

"My ma," Davis began.

"Your ma fell out of the boat and drowned, and that was a terrible, terrible thing," Ash agreed, reaching out to take Davis's hand, only to be denied. "But all you did was stand up. Could your ma swim?"

Davis shook his head.

"You?"

Again he shook his head.

"Your papa?"

Davis nodded, but with a face that said his father wasn't ready to cross the bay without a boat.

"So your papa, a grown-up, took you and your mama out in a boat on the ocean even though you couldn't swim, and you stood up."

"But—"

"Do I have it right so far?" *Ash saw himself out on the roof, his bare feet hugging the tile shingles.* "And you wanted to sit near your ma." *He moved farther out onto the roof where he'd hidden Cabot's birthday present.* "And you stood up."

Davis covered his ears with his hands. "Sit down! Sit down!" he shouted, the words ringing true and clear.

*"Come here, you little twerp! Come on, Ashtord, you little ferp!"*

"You were just a baby," Charlotte said softly. "A small child. You didn't do what you were told right away, and something went wrong. You were guilty of not listening, like every other child at one time or another, that's all."

"Sit down! Sit down!"

*Cabot was laughing, placing one foot in front of the other down the ridge of the roof. "Com'ere! Com'ere!"*

Ash pulled Davis's hands down from his ears. Guilt was something he understood better than love, better than life. "It was not your fault," he told the boy. "Your memories are punishment enough, aren't they?"

Davis shut his eyes tight rather than meet Ash's gaze.

"Aren't they?" He shook the boy gently. "Do you need your father's beatings to help you remember?"

Davis shook his head.

"Believe me, son. There aren't enough beatings in the world to make you forget."

# Chapter 13

The rain was wet and cold, but Charlotte was numb to it, numb to everything around her but the pain. She'd watched Ewing Flannigan charm Judge O'Malley with his lilting brogue, and then leave the courtroom with the collar to Davis's coat balled in his fist and his son nearly dangling from the strong hold.

O'Malley had called her a frustrated woman, warped by guilt at turning her back on her true destiny, and hoping to steal away someone else's child for her own. He claimed that the mother in her would never be denied, but the course she had thus far chosen to pursue went so against nature that he feared she was actually unable to see the great injustice she was petitioning the court to effect. That just because a man had seen to his duty by raising a child up right in a world where anything had become permissible . . .

She couldn't remember the rest. All she could recall

was the hollow look in Davis's eyes as she and the court and the world all betrayed his trust and left him to the mercy of his father.

She had filed the notice of appeal that Cabot had made her prepare just in case. Now all they'd needed was some grounds to base it on. And then she'd left by the side door as Cabot had told her to. He'd had his concerns about the case from the beginning, but she'd insisted on forging ahead. He'd advised her to wait until he could take care of the whole matter behind some chamber doors, but she had been adamant.

She clutched her coat around her more tightly. Cold rain slipped down the back of her neck and the rawness of the day crept into her bones.

If Ewing Flannigan didn't stop at a bar on his way home, she'd be the next mayor of San Francisco.

It might just as well be her own fist that pounded that poor boy's sweet face, her own hands that boxed his ears. Whatever that man did to his son tonight, she had brought on him herself. What had all her high talk and overconfidence gotten that boy tonight? A bloody nose? A split lip? A broken bone?

She fought with the cast iron gate that separated Whittier Court from the street, Argus squawking at her as if she were some intruder bent on destroying anything beyond herself.

She had failed.

And she had to face Cabot and Kathryn and Ash and tell them all that Davis wouldn't be brightening their lives anymore and that they had lost their opportunity to brighten his.

The gate conceded and reluctantly allowed her entry. But Argus was less accommodating, pecking at her unmercifully, chasing her up the steps and into the house. When she turned to glare at him after Maria let her in, she found him happily picking apart her newly cropped navy hat. "You are the meanest thing that ever lived, Argus Whittier," she shouted at him, "and someday you'll get yours!"

Gingerly and without a word Maria helped her out of her coat, as if the poor woman was just a little frightened of Charlotte's mood.

"Where is everyone?" The house was quiet enough to hear the rain slipping down the windowpanes, and Charlotte's sniff echoed in the silent foyer.

"The mister is in his office," Maria answered. "The Mrs. Whittier, she's not feeling so good. Her eyes they are smarting and she is in her room, where the other mister is reading to her."

"Is she all right?" Charlotte asked, pulling a soggy scarf from around her neck and handing it to the maid. "Has Mr. Whittier been told she's not well?"

Maria held the scarf away from her body, not pleased by the smell of the wet wool. "I think she is liking Mr. Ash's company. She don't want the mister and so he told her 'fine' and went to his office and yelled at Mr. Arthur to get out of his way."

She gestured toward the inner hall, where Arthur sat in the chair usually reserved for Kathryn and stared at the closed office door.

Charlotte rubbed her hands together, but it was no use. She would never be warm again. Not until she had managed to make Davis safe. She thanked Maria, nodded at Arthur, and went through her office into Cabot's. He started at the interruption and then nodded his head toward the seat across his desk, signaling her to sit.

"Oh, it was dreadful," she began, her lip trembling uncontrollably.

He put up one finger. "In a moment, Charlotte. Just let

me finish this thought." He wrote furiously on the pad in front of him. And she waited.

"It was O'Malley," she said while he continued to write. "Luck of the draw, huh? First Mallory and then O'Malley. And he wasn't interested in—"

"I said just a moment, Charlotte." He didn't bother looking up.

"He's going to beat that boy, Cabot. And it will be my fault." When the words were out they seemed even more awful than the thought had been.

"We'll take care of it, Charlotte, but not now. I need another few minutes. Why not have a cup of tea and see if you can't compose yourself while I finish this up." Again he didn't bother raising his eyes to her.

With a ragged sigh she pushed forward slightly on her legs, only to find that they were too rubbery to hold her up. She sat back in the old leather wing chair with the cracks that pulled at her clothes, and caught her face in her hands.

What had she done to that innocent child?

"Oh, my God," she said, seeing with closed eyes the boy's face the way it looked when Eli Mollenoff had first brought him to her. "What have I done, Cabot? What in heaven's name have I done?"

"Beside interrupt me for the fourth or fifth time?" he asked, finally looking up at her. "Raining, is it?"

"It's raining in my heart, Cabot. It's pouring in my soul." She fought to swallow and choked, coughing until she was nearly dizzy. When she was done she leaned back against the seat where a thousand clients' heads had rested before hers.

"You did file for an appeal?" He flipped the days on his calendar, waiting for her response.

"What about tonight, Cabot? What good will the appeal do Davis tonight?"

"Calm down. Will the tears do him any good? Did you remember to change the date of Ash's jury selection?"

"I've done a terrible disservice to that little boy, thinking I could win a motion on my own. And he's going to have to pay for my hubris. My pride will be his downfall!"

"I'll take the appeal," Cabot said. "I should have gone down there in the first place. You get a date?"

She nodded. It wasn't for three weeks. By then Davis could be in a hospital. Dear Lord, he could be dead!

"When?"

She couldn't recall the exact date. When the clerk had told her she'd been so distressed, she'd had to write it down rather than commit it to memory.

"You have to go to court, Cabot," she said, jumping up and pushing things on his desk out of the way. "You can convince them to change their minds. Make him a ward of the court. Get an ex parte order or a temporary restraining order or—" He wasn't moving. "Cabot, come on! I'll tell Arthur to get your coat. It's terrible out there."

"Sit down, Charlotte." He waited while she raced around the office like some sort of lunatic just let out from the asylum. Or maybe just committed, as the walls moved in and the room got smaller around her. "Sit down!"

"I will not sit down," she cried. "There is a boy out there who needs us!"

"It's four-thirty, Charlotte," he said, pointing to the clock on the mantel whose ticking had often driven her to distraction. "By the time I got down to court, the building would be closed."

"We could go to Judge Pollack. You've done him enough favors, Cabot. Call one in."

"I will not even discuss this with you when you are in this state. I will take care of the boy, Charlotte. Sit down. You are acting like a blubbering female!"

She took a step toward the chair and then stopped. "I

*am* a blubbering female," she said. Couldn't he see that? No one else in the world had failed to notice she was a female. Only this man seemed to be oblivious to the fact.

"Well, Charlotte, that's nothing to be proud of."

"It's nothing to be ashamed of either," she said. She wondered if she meant it, truly, and decided that she did indeed. "I do have feelings like a woman. And right now I'm cold, the kind of cold that a woman gets that makes a man pull off his coat and offer it to her. And I'm sad. I'm sad enough to cry and need comfort. I lost that case, Cabot, and it breaks my heart that Davis will have to pay for my failure."

"Charlotte, believe me, I'm sorry that you lost this round. Sorry for you and sorry for the boy, and I'd cry along with you if it would do a damn bit of good. But a lawyer can't come apart with every setback. Lawyers don't cry—they file appeals, they—"

She put her hand out across the desk. "Please, Cabot. I don't know what to do."

He focused on her hand, but didn't take it. Instead he backed the chair away from the desk and she thought for a moment he might come around and take her in his arms.

"Go wash your face," he said. "It'll be all right." And then she watched as he wheeled his chair from the room.

Ash thought that Kathryn would never fall asleep. It had taken the whole volume of *Sonnets from the Portugese* (of all things for her to choose!) and two of Robert Browning's poems as well, but finally she was snoring lightly and Ash could tiptoe from the room without having to discuss with her his need to make sure that Charlotte was all right.

From the moment Maria had brought them their tea and told them that Charlotte had lost her case, it had taken every ounce of willpower to stay nailed to his seat. And then there was his mother to help convince him, tightening her grip on his arm and assuring him that when it came to the law, at least, Cabot would be her refuge.

Now he was going to make sure that Cabot hadn't let the woman down.

They weren't in their offices, or in the parlor or the dining room. Maria said she was preparing a tray to bring upstairs, as everyone was taking their meals in their rooms. Would he like that as well?

"I'm not hungry," he grumbled at her, trying not to imagine Cabot and Charlotte taking tea together in the bedroom. "I had enough tea with my mother to float a boat to China." He sounded sulky, even to himself, and he took the stairs two at a time, racing past the second floor without even looking at their doors.

Whose room were they in? he wondered, baffled by how his brother could pass up the chance to share a room and a bed with Charlotte. Didn't he want her to be the last thing he saw before he shut his eyes? Didn't he want to watch her sleep in the first strains of daylight, her hair every which way, those long eyelashes of hers resting on those soft pink cheeks? Just because he couldn't fill her womb with children, didn't he still want to unlace her boots? Unfasten the buttons that ran in a row down her spine?

His mother was right—someone was adding more steps to the third-floor stairwell every day. Today the flight went on forever and he could barely drag his feet to his door.

Liberty, that fickle flirt who batted his eyes at both men and women, began his greeting before Ash had even opened his door. "The swell's here! The swell's here!" he shouted, following it with so much banging about the room that Ash had to wonder if he was stashing some lady bird in the closet.

Jeez, it had been a long time since either of them had been free birds with room to fly.

The room was dark, despite all the windows. The sky had turned grayer and grayer with the day as if in sympathy for the people beneath it. He lit the lamp beside his bed and stretched out, his hands behind his back, his eyes closed, and prayed that he would wake up from the nightmare of his life.

It was cold, cold and wet, and reluctantly he opened one eye to find that the window had been left ajar. With his foot he swung the edge of the bedcover up and over his legs and watched the curtains blow in the wind until the chill forced him up.

Two hands on the sash, he'd nearly closed the window before he saw her, huddled in a ball in the rain like so much wet laundry. "Charlotte?" he whispered into the wind.

She nodded. At least he thought she did, as he squinted into the darkness trying to make out her shivering form. He didn't bother waiting to be sure. He was out the window almost before he'd gotten it fully open again, and had her collected up in his arms. "Charlotte, Charlotte, Charlotte," he kept repeating, gathering her soggy woolen skirt up with her and carrying her back through the window.

Her blouse was soaked through. Her wet skirt probably weighed twenty pounds. He put her down onto the bed and she just sat there, shaking from the cold, not saying a word, those goddamn hazel eyes growing bigger as she stared up at him silently.

He opened the top button on her blouse, the two under it, and one more still, so that his hands were working between her breasts. "I could get Maria or Rosa," he offered when she neither resisted nor offered help of her own.

She shook her head, water droplets flying, and he

pressed her against him, trying to dry her hair with his shirttails. Without letting go of her, he leaned toward the foot of his bed, grabbed the towel off the footboard, and wrapped her hair in it. Limply she sat in front of him, shivering wildly but making no move to warm herself.

"Christ!" he said, taking one of her hands and placing it on top of her head to secure the towel. "Hold this. I'm going to get you out of these wet things."

"He told me to stop crying," she said shakily, shuddering breaths interrupting her as she spoke.

He unfastened the remaining buttons of her blouse and peeled it from her body, her wet skin fighting to keep it plastered to her. The hook of her skirt fought him as well, and he had to dry his fingers twice before he could convince it to let go. When it did, he pushed her gently onto her back and wiggled the skirt from beneath her hips.

"No. He called it blubbering," she told him, sniffing and rubbing her nose with the back of her hand. "He called me a blubbering female, as if I had no relation to him. Like I was some stranger in the jury box who'd been swept away by some misplaced sentimentality."

"Put your head on the pillow," he ordered, swinging her feet up and trying not to notice that her underthings were soaked through and that he could see what little nature had endowed her with, and how perfectly it suited her.

She took a big shuddering sob and squirmed around on the bed. After she was settled, he folded the edges of his coverlet over her.

"Get the rest of your wet stuff off," he said. He meant to turn away then, not to watch her movements under the blankets as she gyrated her hips before bending and straightening her legs several times. Finally her twisted little cotton drawers appeared against his footboard in a soggy heap. "All of it," he directed as he flicked the drawers out straight and then laid them over the back of his chair to dry.

"I can't stay here," she said, the covers pulled up to her armpits as she held out another wet piece of cotton with a trembling naked arm.

"No one knows where you are," he said, half a statement, half a prayer.

"No. It's not that. I have to go find Davis before it's too late." She began wrapping the covers more tightly around her and inching toward the edge of his bed.

"Too late for what?" he asked, pushing her back with very little effort. She was frozen, her bare skin still damp as he reached for his dressing gown at the foot of the bed and wrapped it around her shoulders.

"His father. Oh! What have I done to that boy!" Dissolving in tears, she fell back against the pillows and turned her head away from him.

"His father isn't going to lay a finger on him tonight," he said, uncovering just her feet and rubbing them hard. "You're an icicle! We need something warm here." He sat on the edge of the bed and unlaced his shoes, pulled off his socks, and slipped the warm soft wool stockings onto her tiny feet.

"That feels wonderful!" She was still shivering, each of her words shaky when she spoke. "Ewing Flannigan was mad, Ashford. I really better—" She tried to sit up again, nearly losing the blanket in the process.

He could feel his jaw drop, he just couldn't seem to do anything about it but stand there like some besotted fool. He tried swallowing, but with his mouth open couldn't manage so difficult a trick. If just the small swell of her breast left him breathless, he could only imagine what seeing what else hid under his blanket would do to him.

He told himself this was ridiculous. Why, in the islands he'd seen more naked women than clothed ones. Once, two of them—he stopped the thought before it fully took shape. That was another lifetime.

"Ashford?" She was slipping into his dressing gown, one naked shoulder at a time. Had her teeth not been chattering, her lips not been blue, her whole body not been shuddering wildly, he might not have been able to control himself. "Do you think you could sneak down to my room and get me some clothing? I have to get to the Flannigans."

"I told you he's safe for tonight," Ash repeated. Safer, he thought, than they were. "Moss is waiting at home for them. He'll be camped outside the door all night."

Her eyes glistened, then spilled over, tears streaking her face. "I should have known," she said, and picked up the pillow behind her to hug against her chest. The trembling continued, her breathing quavering with each breath.

"Should I send for some tea?" he asked. "I could go down and send Rosa up to you."

She shook her head nervously.

"Then let me warm you." There was a huskiness to his voice that unnerved him. He could only imagine its effect on her.

Slowly, deliberately, she set the pillow aside and moved from the center of the bed so that there would be room for him. "I'm freezing," she told him when he sat down on the bed. He carefully propped himself up against the headboard, keeping the quilts between them, and rolled her against his side. "I've been freezing forever."

She was awkward against him and he had to guide her to where her body would fit neatly against his.

"He's never held you, has he?" he asked. He felt her shake her head against his chest and pushed her away so that he could see her face. "Why have you stood for it,

Charlotte? Why haven't you demanded more of your marriage?"

She averted her eyes, unwilling to meet his own. "He can't," she said softly, trying to burrow back into his armpit like one of her furry creatures.

"Can't do this?" he asked, rubbing her arm briskly to warm her up. "Can't do this?" he asked again, planting a kiss on the top of her head.

"Won't, then," she admitted, pushing herself closer against him until one of Liberty's feathers couldn't have gotten between them.

"What about this, Charlotte? Can he do this?" He tipped her head back and kissed her hard on the mouth, no teasing of lips, no brushing cheeks or rubbing noses. Just a hard, demanding kiss that deepened until his lips were asking her for promises of now and forever, deepening still further until his tongue demanded that she be his alone for always.

She was stronger than he would have guessed as she eased down onto the mattress and pulled him along with her. Her arms wrapped around his back, pressing him closer against her, every piece of her so hungry for affection that he felt as if he were somehow taking advantage of her need while slaking his own.

With little effort he rolled her onto her back and hung above her, looking down at her as he would if he were about to take her. "Can he do this?" he demanded, searching for her breast with his kiss, running his lips against the silk dressing gown until he felt the pebble beneath it, toying with it until the pebble became a stone and the woman's hunger began to match his own.

She pressed up against him, arching her back, the full length of her against the full length of him.

He snaked his hand between them, tracing her ribs, one after the other, always lower and lower still until he reached the soft expanse of her belly. The spread of his hand spanned her whole being there, and he tipped and twisted it until down was up and up was down and his fingers came to rest at the soft curls of her femininity.

"Are you still cold?" he asked, his fingers poised to make her warmer yet. Her answer came with hard breaths, her mound thrust up toward him.

"Don't stop," she said, willing beneath his touch. "Oh, please don't stop."

"Don't stop!" Liberty shouted from the windowsill, where he had courteously turned his back until now. "Oh! Oh! Oh! Don't stop! Shut up, you stupid bird!"

Charlotte was up before he could stop her, pulling the robe against her bare skin, her eyes frantic as she searched in the darkness for her things.

"Ow! Ow!" she yelped as quietly as she could, hopping around holding her toe and affording him a view in the lamplight that was worth going to hell for—no doubt the price he would pay for seducing his brother's wife.

"Are you all right?" he asked, averting his eyes and holding out her still-dripping undergarments.

"No, I'm not all right," she said, clutching the wet things to her breast and starting to shiver all over again. "I'm married to your brother, for heaven's sake! What did I think I was doing? My God! I've given myself to my husband's brother!"

"Okay," he said, one hand up to calm her down. "Whoa, there. You haven't given yourself to anyone. We did not actually do anything . . . really. I mean, not anything like you're feeling guilty about. . . ." She knew what they hadn't done. Did he have to spell it out? It wasn't as if he'd docked his boat in her slip.

*Shocked* didn't quite describe the look on her face. *Incredulous,* maybe. *Flabbergasted.*

"We didn't kiss? You didn't—" She pointed in the general vicinity of his lips and then her breast. "And you did touch my—my—" She clutched his robe more tightly around her middle.

"No. I didn't touch your—your—" They were beginning to sound like Davis. "I nearly touched your—your—but I stopped before—" He made a rolling gesture with his hands to indicate that there was plenty more he hadn't done.

Her eyebrows came down over troubled eyes. "Before what?"

Jeez, Louise! Didn't the woman know anything? "Before I *really* touched you."

"You mean fornication."

He opened his mouth to speak, but no words came out. He waved his arms, but still the words were stuck in his throat.

"Right?" She looked at him with obvious confusion.

"No," he said slowly. "I meant that I didn't touch the parts you are worried that I touched. And *fornication* is a very ugly word, young lady."

"Oh, please! And what we were doing was all right?" She dropped her righteous indignation for a moment. "And I know you touched what I think you touched."

"There's a lot more to it!" He ran his fingers through his hair. Was he really having this conversation with his brother's wife? "You've got better parts!"

"Oh, good glory! There are only so many parts and you covered them. Not that I couldn't have stopped you—*should* have stopped you—I'm a married woman. What do you think this band means?" she asked, holding out her left hand.

"I only got as far as the gangplank," he said, sitting down on the bed with his hands in his lap. He had a bad feeling he was never going to regain his original proportions if they didn't drop this subject. "I never got on board the ship."

She pointed to her chest. "Am I the ship?" She seemed highly insulted.

"They call ships 'she' for a reason," he said, hoping she wouldn't ask what it was.

She did.

"How the hell should I know?" he said, throwing up his hands. "Maybe because they can give you a good ride and then kill you. And the way I see it," he added, "you are certainly no married woman."

"Oh, really? Maybe you ought to tell your brother that." She was juggling her wet underthings, trying to keep his robe closed, and still maintain her dignity. She simply couldn't have all three. Ash was hoping the closed robe would be the one to go.

"I did. But it doesn't seem to me that either of you knows what marriage means."

She turned away, staring out the window into the darkness. "We took vows, Ash. Signed a wedding license and a marriage certificate."

"And he broke that contract. Has he loved, cherished? Has he honored and obeyed? Charlotte, there is no marriage here. You got to be a lawyer, and he got a partner he doesn't have to pay."

"I knew what Cabot couldn't do before I married him, Ash. Don't think that he tricked me or anything. Your mother explained the way things were with Cabot, and I accepted that."

"Did you know he wouldn't touch you?"

She shook her head.

"Did you know there would be no kisses, no hugs, no touching your—your special places?" She blushed, but he had to admire her honesty when she shook her head.

"No," she admitted, "but I didn't want any of those things from Cabot."

"And now you want them?"

Her hair was drying in ringlets around her face, curls that hung down and brushed her shoulders, and they danced as she spoke.

"Not from him," she admitted shyly.

"Affection is a good thing, Charlotte. Now that you finally know how good, you should demand it."

"I don't think so." She stared down at her feet, the ends of his socks empty and bent beneath her. "Not from Cabot."

"Well, don't look at me, honey," he said, stroking her cheek and lifting her chin so that she had to look into his eyes. "For one thing, I'm probably going to prison for the rest of my life, and then where would you be?"

"Don't say that! Don't even think it! Cabot will get you off. Your brother would never let you go to prison for something you didn't do."

*Ah, but how about for what Ash wanted to do? Something he wished to the heavens he could do? And which involved Cabot's own wife?*

"And for another, he's my brother, Charlotte. I cut the ground out from under him once before. I can't do it again."

"So what was this about?" she asked, waving her hand over his bed. "Why did you kiss me and touch me and—"

"I just wanted to show you," he lied. "Didn't I tell you all the while I was doing it that Cabot could do it as well? Someone had to show you. Now you've just got to make him love you, Charlotte, and then we can all be happy."

She ran from his room in tears, as he'd suspected she would. Slowly he lowered himself to the bed and sat there in the dark, only his memories to keep him company.

*Come'ere twerp! Come on, Ashtord, you little fwerp!*

He'd hated Cabot that afternoon all those years ago. The thought surprised him, but he didn't dwell on it. He'd only hated him half as much then as he hated him now.

# Chapter 14

"You might try the *California Penal Code* instead of Garner's *Estates and Trusts,"* Cabot said to her as she came down the ladder in his office with Garner's in her hand, nearly falling as her heel got caught in the hem of her skirts.

"And you might try steadying me," she grumbled back at him, massaging the elbow that had crashed against the shelf to stop her fall.

Cabot's teacup seemed frozen in midair. "Are you all right?" he asked.

"Of course I'm all right," she all but barked at him. "As if it matters to you," she added under her breath as he set down his cup and returned to work. She still missed her mother's cup. Now she just passed on tea when it was offered. The pleasure was gone.

"The *Penal Code,"* he said, reaching his hand out for it without even lifting his head to look at her. "Where's Ashford, anyway? I've got some questions about Greenbough, and if you can't find the damn code, I'm sure he can just—"

Oh, yes—Cabot and Ash and her all in the same room. That was what she needed. The man had touched her breasts. And every time she thought about those moments she felt a tightness, tingling, almost as if he were touching them again.

"Charlotte! The book?" Cabot had thrown off his reading glasses and sat with his hands crossed over his chest. "It would help me immeasurably if you would keep your mind on your work today."

She had lain in bed with his brother, the silk of his dressing gown the only thing covering her nakedness, and Cabot wanted her to restrict her thoughts to the law. "Is that all you ever think about?" she asked him, handing him the book and standing close enough to smell the bitters he'd mixed into his tea. "The law and your flowers?"

"What are you getting at, Charlotte?" He always began or ended a sentence with her name, it seemed, as if he wouldn't know who she was otherwise.

"Are you sorry you married me?" Her voice squeaked like a little girl's, embarrassing her.

"What would make you ask? Have I done something that makes you feel that way? Have I asked too much of you? Kept you up working too late? Canceled your charges at Capwell's or Pennoyer's? What have I denied you that you've requested?" He rubbed at his brow as if the entire subject was tiresome but that he would deign to discuss it because he was a more patient man than she deserved.

"I didn't ask if you were good to me, or generous or kind. I asked if you're sorry you married me, and I want an answer, not an evasion."

"Why?"

"That's an evasion." And worse, something she refused to answer, couldn't answer. Why did she want to know? Was *she* sorry? Or was she seeking his permission to look for love elsewhere if he wasn't willing to offer it to her himself?

"No, it's a request for clarification."

"The question is simple. Do you regret making me your wife?" She took a step closer to him, so that now her thigh pressed against his upper arm. If he merely turned his head, his face would be lost in the folds of her skirt.

His fingers worked the spokes of his wheels furiously. "Is your name not on the sign with mine in front of this very house? And did I not give you that name? What greater proof could you be seeking?"

She squatted beside his chair, ignoring for once the degree to which he despised the action as condescending. Her face inches from his now, close enough to notice that the tea still glistened on his mustache, the skin around his nose was chafed, and the whites of his eyes were bloodshot and yellowed. "I'd like a kiss," she said softly, praying that Cabot could erase the memory of Ash's lips burning her own. "You could prove it with a kiss."

"How sad," he said touching her cheek gently and cupping her chin as if she were a small child come to learn at his knee. "You've confused love with desire. Did you get these thoughts from that Ebell Society of Women? Or your Halton case? *Fornication without procreation*—isn't that their motto? A bit base, don't you think?"

She said nothing, rising with the slight swish of petticoats and serge.

"It's not something you can't work on, can't rise above."

A short bitter laugh escaped her. "It's so very easy for the man who isn't hungry to say no to the dessert tray."

The thought seemed to give him pause, but she

watched him rally, just as though he were in front of a jury. His voice strong, yet quiet enough for only her to hear, he said, "And I would imagine it equally easy for the woman who has never tasted cocoa to refuse the unattractive brown offering."

Through the pebbled glass of the office door Charlotte could see the silhouettes of Ash and Maria heading their way, Maria carrying a tray. Wishing she could be swallowed by the curtains, absorbed by the walls, she backed up as they entered the room.

"Tea and coffee," Maria said, setting the tray on the sideboard. "And Mrs. Mason, she baked some little cakes. The yellow ones, they are lemon, and these, they are choco-lat."

Charlotte rushed past him, pushing him aside as she went. Everything in him wanted to go after her, but somehow his shoes stayed nailed to the patent tapestry carpet that covered the area in front of Cabot's desk. He waited impatiently for Maria to leave him alone with his brother.

"What was that all about?" Ash asked. He didn't dare give away any more than Charlotte had. His brother could put a bullet through Ash's own double-crossing heart anytime he wanted, but Ash had no desire to put Charlotte at her husband's mercy.

"She isn't feeling very well," Cabot said. He fingered the small plate of cakes that Maria had removed from the tray and set on his desk. "For such a brilliant woman, she still can't rise above her sex in so many small but significant ways."

"Well, women are plagued by cycles we can hardly fathom," he said. "They can hardly be asked to rise above the physical. . . ." Jeez, women were entitled to feel awful every few weeks. If what happened to them happened to men . . . Ash didn't even want to think about it.

But apparently that wasn't what Cabot meant. "Always at the mercy of her emotions. You should have seen Charlie when I met her—a silly little schoolgirl trying to be a grown-up matron. She had on the ugliest shoes I have ever seen."

Cabot was looking beyond him at some speck on the wall, and seeing a past only he remembered.

"She wouldn't take a break, you know. Not for tea or dinner or even to stretch her legs. Insatiable. *Teach me more, more. Are you proud of me? Did I get it right?* When the lessons were over and I'd send her home, I'd watch her out the window, her feet dragging, her nose in whatever book I'd loaned her to study.

"There were days, weeks, when I gave more thought to her lessons than to my own cases. Her challenge became mine, her goals were my goals. Imagine! A woman lawyer practicing in the courts. Could I pull it off?

"Oh, rabbits out of hats for my guilty clients were everyday occurrences for me by then, but this was putting the beautiful lady in the locked box and, with all the flourish of the great magicians, pulling off the cloth to reveal"—he paused, waved his hand in the air and continued—"a roll of the drums, please . . . a fanfare . . . I give you—ta da—the lady lawyer!"

His brother was breathing heavily, a contented smile on his face as close to satisfaction as Ash imagined Cabot got.

"Well, you should be very proud of yourself. Charlotte appears the consummate lady lawyer."

"I showed them all," Cabot said, and Ash knew the words were not for him, but for Cabot himself and all the people who had ever seen him in that wheelchair and taken pity on him. "She'd been educated to be nothing more than a competent wife, schooled in the graces that enhanced a woman's value as an ornament, the best mare in a gentleman's stable, as it were. And I taught her to think, to analyze, to consider. . . ."

He stopped there, grimacing as he looked at Ash, as if deciding whether or not to continue.

"The intellectual stimulation excited her, the mind puzzles were challenges—you don't know how I loved to watch her struggle with a problem, wrestle it out in her mind or on paper, and come to me to see if she had won."

"Did I hear you use the word *love*?"

"There seems to be a lot of doubt about that suddenly. Do you doubt that I love Charlotte? And do you think putting all these doubts in her head will make her any happier?" He sighed. "I've worked so hard with her, Ashford, to make her better than the rest. Above them all. And don't think I don't know who's been filling her head, and what's weighing on her mind."

The accusation hung there in the stuffy air of Cabot's office. Finally Ash answered it as best he could. "I don't doubt you love what you have created. What I doubt is that you love who Charlotte is."

"Charlotte is what I have created," Cabot said. "And that, dear brother, is what makes her so worthy of my admiration."

"It's a good thing this house was built with double doors, or you'd never fit that head of yours through the doorway. Were you always so pompous an ass, or has it grown on you with age like the mold on cheese?"

"It's so very like you to attack what you can't comprehend. Haven't you ever yearned to do what those around you cannot? Don't you ever long to sail faster, climb higher—ah, I forget myself. Here's one for you—don't you want to cover more women in one night than the next man? Don't you want to reach that peak again and again and again until she begs you to stop and then once more to prove you can?"

"You don't think very much of me," Ash said. "But then that comes as no surprise. No, dear brother, I have no grand desire to fuck my own brains out, nor those of some poor woman along with me."

"Crude, but to the point. All right. Don't you wish to win for yourself the most beautiful woman in the world?"

Ash imagined Charlotte as he pulled her in from the storm, and pictured her in the lamplight as she stood before him. "The most wonderful, yes," he agreed.

"Well, let me tell you this. If you were to win her, being the man you are, you would find that with that challenge faced and conquered, you would grow tired of the success and seek out a new woman, more beautiful than the first woman. And the attempt to seduce her would begin again."

"Ah, but the first woman was the most beautiful. How could there be one even lovelier? I would be more than satisfied, I assure you."

"Not you, Ashford. No more than me. Men need a hill to conquer, and once they've climbed it, they must go seek a mountain."

"If I could stake my claim on that first hill, there is nothing that would make me look beyond it."

Cabot looked at him dubiously. "Before you go planting your flagstaff, little brother, I suggest you check that there isn't a prior claim on the land. Trespassing carries a pretty stiff penalty."

Ash shrugged his shoulders as if none of this mattered to him at all, as if it was all just hypothetical and they weren't talking about the woman who gave him reason to breathe. Deciding that there would be no work done that morning, Ash rose and opened the door that connected Cabot's office to Charlotte's. "Aren't there any statutes regarding abandoned property?" he asked over his shoulder as he started to leave the room.

"Just a minute," Cabot said, and gestured for him to sit. "The flowers in Charlotte's office. I don't recognize them as ours. Do you know where they came from?"

"They're from a little shop near the wharf," Ash said. "Why? Were you hoping to send her some yourself, after all?"

"By the wharf," Cabot said, ignoring Ash's challenge. "Naturally you had Moss pick them up for you."

Ash was silent. That investigator of Cabot's wasn't making any progress at all, according to Charlotte. Was he supposed to remain confined to his room, twiddling his thumbs, while the man who had set fire to his business walked free?

"Tell me that Moss picked up those damn lilies." Cabot's face was red, his nostrils flared, as he spoke.

"I only meant to show her my appreciation, Cab. They're called stargazers, and I've seen her, once or twice, staring out the window and dreaming. Haven't you?"

"You went out," Cabot said, the flared nostrils now the softest of his angry features. "Didn't you?"

"For God's sake, there's a man out there somewhere who set my business on fire, wiped out my stock, convinced my partner I was a goddamn firebug, and killed people in the process. On top of all that he's left me holding the bag. You're damn right I went out, Cabot, and I'll be going out again. You know, for example, what Jack Perry is selling Cuervo for? Twice what I was getting. What do you think of that?"

"I think if you go out again, you're on your own. I don't like cases I can't win, Ashford, and I'm beginning to dislike yours a whole lot."

* * *

"All right, Kathryn, I've had quite enough of this game you're playing," Charlotte said the following day when she'd finally cornered the older woman with her nose pressed up against her embroidery board near the fireplace in her bedroom. "Mrs. Mason has chased me up and down this house half the day asking me whether I wish to serve oysters on the half shell with soup *à la reine* or *croûtes aux champignons* with mock turtle soup. Maria suddenly doesn't know one set of sheets from another, and Rosa isn't sure the floor is polished to my satisfaction. I'm only waiting for Arthur to find me and ask me what time Cabot wishes his bath."

Behind her there was a knock, and she turned to find Arthur in the open doorway, a basket in his hand and a clean towel over his arm. "Pardon me, ma'am, but—"

"I don't know," she said angrily without waiting to hear the question. "I have no idea. Ask Mr. Whittier. Ask Miss Kathryn. Ask Rosa or Maria or whoever might know, but don't ask me!"

"You really do have to learn to run a household, dear," Kathryn said with a sigh. "I won't live forever, and you are the woman of the house. What is it, Arthur?"

"Might I speak to you, ma'am?" he said, addressing Charlotte nervously.

"Arthur, if this is about Mr. Whittier—"

He cut her off. "It's about the rabbit, ma'am," he said, holding the basket out to her. "I was cleaning up Mr. Whittier's old chair as Mr. Ash had asked me to, and I didn't see him there by the wheel and—"

"Oh, good glory!" she said, rushing to take the basket from him and set it on Kathryn's bed.

"He isn't dead, is he?" Kathryn asked.

"No, ma'am," Arthur answered. "But I've cut up his foot a bit."

"I thought rabbit's feet were supposed to be lucky," Kathryn said, peering over Charlotte's shoulder.

"Not for the rabbits that have to part with them," Charlotte answered. She wasn't superstitious to begin with, but if a person believed that there was some force out there that would keep a person safe at the expense of a rabbit, she said poo on any such force and stepped on every crack she could in that person's presence.

Van Gogh whimpered as she examined his paw. Apologizing to him over and over, she gently tried to trace the tiny bones within his fur and concluded that she knew next to nothing about a rabbit's anatomy.

"I'll need some gauze for the bleeding, and a splint might be a good idea," she told Arthur. "Do you think that you could find something I could use in the conservatory?" Cabot had all sorts of sticks for training his plants to grow the way he expected them to.

"I'm afraid that Mr. Whittier is in there with the investigator again," Arthur said, screwing up his nose at the mention of him. "But perhaps Mrs. Mason has something you could use."

"That man!" Charlotte said through gritted teeth. "I don't know why Cabot needs him when just one look at Ash's face ought to be enough to convince a jury of his innocence. Why, just the idea that he could do something as awful as set a fire anywhere but in a woman's heart . . ."

Kathryn gasped.

Arthur coughed.

And Charlotte turned three shades of red.

"That'll be all, Arthur," Kathryn said, and waited for the servant to leave before continuing. She raised one eyebrow at Charlotte and pursed her lips. "So you think if people just got a good look at Ashford that would do it?"

"I think that the truth ought to be obvious and that

Cabot's sneaking around trying to buy something that merely resembles the truth is sordid and implies that he doesn't believe fully in Ash's alibi or his innocence."

"So Ash has done nothing wrong, but in your eyes, Cabot has?" Kathryn's eyebrow had not come down yet. Perhaps she was remembering a time when Charlotte wouldn't have thought Cabot could so much as throw a cigar band on the sidewalk, when the man walked on water for her. He'd taken a few dips since then. Like during the Murphy case when he'd threatened to reveal the parentage of a certain small child unless the child's mother cooperated with his investigation. He had been looking for the truth, of course, but it didn't make his tactics more palatable.

And there was the time that a witness for the prosecution mysteriously failed to show up in court and everyone was baffled but Cabot. And what had he offered her in his own defense? *The ends, Charlotte. The ends . . .*

He ought to just have Machiavelli's words printed below his name on the letterhead.

"Charlotte, be a good girl and take the rabbit and go. I'm very tired." Kathryn sat down in the overstuffed chair by her fireplace, closed her eyes, and leaned her head back. Her hair had lost some of its silvery glow in the last few weeks and looked more white and less abundant than it had always seemed. Her skin, too, seemed whiter, thinner, like parchment over her bones. "I think I'd like to just rest awhile."

"I'm sorry if I've upset you," she said as she touched the old woman's hair and then laid a kiss atop her head.

"I just can't see how this will work out all right for all of you, Charlotte. I just don't." A dainty sigh parted her lips, and then her breathing evened.

"Sweet dreams," Charlotte whispered, unfolding the

patchwork lap blanket that Cabot's grandmother had made and covering her mother-in-law with it.

"Aren't you freezing out here?" The screen door slammed behind Ash as he joined Charlotte out on the back porch. "It can't be more than forty-five degrees and you haven't even got a shawl around you."

"I didn't want Cabot finding me," she said. She'd assembled everything she needed to wrap poor Van Gogh's foot, and supposed she ought to be grateful for the help Ash would be able to offer her with the rabbit, but just having him near her hurt—hurt her heart and her head and her pride. She told herself it was only the cold that left her feeling numb as he came up behind her, the breeze that made her shiver as his hand brushed her arm when he reached out and petted the rabbit's soft fur.

"Why didn't you go up to the high room?" he asked, pulling the winter throw from the wicker rocker and wrapping it around her shoulders.

She left the question unanswered. He'd made it clear he didn't want her, that his obligations to Cabot ran deeper than his passing interest in a woman who didn't even know how intimately she'd been touched. Well, they didn't say that blood was thicker than water for nothing, but she'd never known how true that old saying was.

Or how much it could hurt to know that even though he wanted her—it wasn't only her breath that was quickening as they stood there together looking down at the pathetic rabbit whose eyes were locked with theirs—he would never betray his brother.

Even if his brother didn't want her any more than she wanted him.

She shrugged the ratty cloth off her shoulders. "I can't work like that," she told him, concentrating on wrapping

Van Gogh's paw tightly enough to protect it while it healed. The rabbit fought her and backed up within the basket. "Do you think you could . . ." she asked Ash, gesturing at the bunny.

"Oh, of course," he said, reaching into the basket and grasping the rabbit's middle. "Where should I hold him?"

"Well, just because I have to hurt him doesn't mean I want to get hurt myself." She moved Ash's right hand—a big mistake—and tried to place it where it would do the most good.

"You're doing it for his own good," Ash reassured her. Oh, but his hand was warm, despite the cold, and pliant under hers, as if he'd do with it whatever she wished. But he wouldn't do what she wanted most, and even if he did, without loving her, what would it matter?

"He doesn't know that," she answered. "Be sure to hold his head in place so that he can't bite me."

"He does know," Ash said.

"Well, when I hurt him, he isn't going to care about how much better he'll feel in the long run. He's just going to want to take a chunk out of me, and I don't think I can stand any more pain than I've already got."

"I won't let him hurt you," he said, as if a little rabbit bite could compare to the damage Ash himself had already inflicted. She finished with her doctoring in silence, but continued to fuss over the rabbit rather than look at the man who was making her breath come out in ragged little gasps she preferred to blame on the cold.

He put the chair cover over her shoulders again. "Why is it you always seem to need warming, Charlie Russe?"

Oh, how he made her lose herself with just his low soft voice, his pet name.

The poor rabbit was losing patience with her, but still she adjusted the bandage rather than look at him.

"I was surprised to learn that Cabot has an interest in

your warehouse," she said, unwilling to let the conversation get out of hand, to let herself be toyed with and turned away yet again.

Ash let the rabbit's head go and pulled her away from the poor creature. All it took was his hands on her upper arms to bring back all the feelings she'd felt in his bed. She fought hard to keep her wits about her.

It wasn't easy with him running his hands up and down her arms and pretending that all he was doing was trying to keep her warm.

Was the woman never warm? he wondered, and remembered a time when he felt her melt in his arms. He closed the gap between them until his legs made waves in her skirts.

"Cabot's interest?" she repeated, waiting patiently for him to answer her.

He let his arms drop. *Cabot's interest. Cabot's wife.* "Yeah, well, I was pressed for money when the opportunity to go into business with Sam came up. Kathryn offered me a loan, but Cabot intervened. He convinced me that I couldn't risk what money my father had left my mother and offered to loan me the money himself."

"Have you ever paid him back?" she asked.

However did Cabot resist those eyes? When she was happy they glowed until they warmed his soul, and when they were sad, like they were now, he felt as if he'd sell his soul just to put the sparkle back in them.

"No," he said. "I tried several times, but he never let me." Of course, it was no surprise when he thought about it. After all, Cabot's need to control those around him was bigger than the state of California. And as long as he had given Ash his start, and never let him repay the loan, Ash could never really take credit or pride in the business he would build.

"So in a way the fire served to sever a cord he refused to cut himself."

She nodded at him, shivering and reminding him once again of the other night in his room. Hell, everything reminded him of that night. Not a moment went by when he wasn't feeling the softness of her skin, the silkiness of her curls, not a second passed that he didn't remember the look on her face when he told her she'd have to get her loving from her husband. He imagined it hurt her nearly as much as it had hurt him.

He touched the tip of her nose to take her temperature. "You should go in," he told her. "You're always freezing."

"I just want to find Argus and give him one of Mrs. Mason's brioches from breakfast. I'm trying to bribe him into better behavior." She called to the peacock and strode out onto the back lawn in search of the wretched bird. Ash followed along behind her, carrying Van Gogh in his arms and whispering to the rabbit about how he supposed he'd follow the woman right into Lake Merritt if that was where she wanted to go.

The peacock sauntered out from behind the eucalyptus tree dragging his tail behind him, and looked at Charlotte suspiciously.

"You're a nice peacock," she told the nasty animal. "So pretty! You just need a little more attention, don't you?" she said, reaching out to pet the bird behind its regal crown.

Quicker than Ash could react, the peacock had snapped at Charlotte's finger and then pecked again at the side of her hand. Grabbing at her wounds, she dropped the biscuit and yelled at the bird.

"I was just trying to be nice to you." Her eyes glistened with unshed tears. "Stupid bird!"

He pulled her hand to where he could see it and wished he could wring the bird's neck himself. Instead he waved at the bird like some madman, sending it running and squawking across the lawn toward the lake. Then Ash guided Charlotte back to the porch, where he blotted at her hand with the leftover gauze.

"I was just trying to be nice to him," she told him, more angry than hurt.

"Well, maybe there are some creatures that just can't accept love, no matter how hard a person tries to give it to them."

Oh, the look she gave him!

"Yes, well," she said, pulling her hand away and rising quickly, "there seems to be a lot of that going around, doesn't there?"

"More than your share, I'd say," he said, and watched as the tears that had wet her lashes began to fall.

# Chapter 15

"Where's Charlotte?" Kathryn asked, her steely eyes pinning first Cabot and then Ash himself to the wall. "It is seven, is it not?" She checked the watch that had been pinned to her blouse for longer than he could remember.

"I haven't seen her since early this morning. We've got Ash's case closing in on us and Davis's appeal, and I don't know what she's up to," Cabot said. "Nasty cut on her hand," he added out of the blue, and joined Kathryn in staring at Ash accusingly.

"Is she hurt?" Kathyrn reached for her cane, ready to go see to the woman who had obviously become a daughter to her.

"She tried to befriend that deranged lawn ornament you've got out there," he said, pointing toward the window.

"And it bit the hand that fed it?" Kathryn leaned her cane back against the table edge once again.

Cabot laughed abruptly and said something about turnabout being fair play. Then he yelled for Charlotte as if she were a tardy child who'd forgotten her time.

There was no answer.

"I don't think I've seen her since breakfast myself," Kathryn admitted. "You don't suppose she's sick, do you?" Again she reached for her cane.

Sick at heart, maybe, he thought to himself, recalling how she looked down by the water, where he'd caught a glimpse of her in the late-afternoon sun. As always, she was without a shawl, and she stood with her arms wrapped around herself, braving the wind to watch two swans drift across the lake. Her hair was blowing behind her, fighting to be free of the bun she had confined it to, and her skirt was flattened to the back of her body and billowed wildly in front of her.

He could almost imagine her with child, standing there, her skirt pretending it was full of life. He had leaned against the window frame and watched her for several minutes before she sensed him up there, turned, and, shielding her eyes from the sun, sought him out.

She didn't wave, didn't acknowledge his presence, but turned instead and watched the swans and geese swim off in pairs. He'd considered joining her but thought better of it. It was a sorry state of affairs when two grown people were envying the waterfowl.

"I'm sure she'll be all right," he reassured Kathryn without conviction. "I mean, she'll be down soon, I'd suspect."

"Charlotte!" Cabot yelled again, rattling the goblets and Ash's nerves. "Supper!"

"Supper!" Liberty yelled from what had become his dinner perch, just inside the kitchen doors where he often stole food just as Rosa was about to serve it. "Come and get it!" he shouted, following the words with a very authentic belch.

"You're next," Cabot said calmly as he unfolded his napkin and placed it on his lap. "Charlotte! We are not waiting any longer!"

"I'll just go check on her," his mother said, struggling to push her chair back and escape the confines of the table.

"I'll go," Ash said, sensing immediately that it was a mistake. The room went silent, but no one tried to stop him and so he had no choice but to leave his napkin on his chair and go after his sweet Charlotte Russe.

"Charlotte?" he called loudly enough for his mother and brother to hear. "Are you in here?" He poked his nose into the darkened offices and then headed for the stairs. He hoped she'd had the good sense to come in out of the cold. He took the steps two at a time. She couldn't have stayed out at the lake this late. It was dark, for heaven's sake. He raced around the newel post at the landing and hurried to her room. The swans had all found shelter by now. The geese would be gone.

"Charlotte?" He tapped softly on the closed door. No light came from beneath it. "Are you in there?" Perhaps she'd lain down for a nap and fallen into a deeper sleep than she'd planned. The cold air could do that to a person. Especially one as small and delicate as his Charlotte.

Not *yours,* he told himself silently. Not *your* Charlotte.

He pushed the door open. Silence and darkness greeted him.

"Damn it, Charlotte, where are you?" Blood pulsed in his temples and his heart thudded in his chest. Every time she was out of his sight he worried about her. And that was only half as much as he worried when she was around.

Above him he heard a creaking and he raced to the

stairs. A faint light meandered down the stairwell and he hurried up to his room.

The door was ajar, a cold breeze flickering the lamp on his side table and chilling the sweat that had gathered at his temples.

"Charlotte?" he called softly, entering his room like a trespasser afraid of discovery. "Charlie Russe?"

A lump of fur sat on his dresser in front of the mirror, and for a moment he mistook it for Van Gogh. There was something awful about it, treacherous, and he came upon it slowly, his hand poised and ready, but unwilling to examine it. There was no movement, no rhythmic breathing, and he knew the dark thing was dead before he reached his hand out to it. Silkier than fur, finer, smoother, he stroked it once and felt no resistance. The mass had no form, no body.

He felt sick to his stomach and fought to swallow the bile that rose. Clutching the mass he lifted it from the dresser and held it up, watching the chestnut strands unfurl from his fingertips.

He could see her out there, just beyond his window, the moon shining for her alone, and he held the cluster out to her. "Why?" was all he could force past his lips. Then, "What have you done?"

"No one wanted the woman," she said, her chin thrust out proudly as if there were no tears streaking her extraordinary face. "So I got rid of her. You and Cabot should both be very happy."

She looked almost like a pixie—some sprite, standing there in the moonlight, the wind ruffling her short dark cap, and he thought that if only he could catch her, she could grant his fondest wish.

"Not that it matters to you any."

She had been lovely before, but he hadn't realized how truly exquisite she was until now. If she'd hoped to make herself unattractive, she'd failed miserably, horribly, tragically.

"Well"—she sighed—"as always, I'm freezing." She ducked her head and slipped in through the window like some thief come to steal his heart. "I just wanted to throw some covers over my plants. It's a bit cold for begonias."

"And as long as you were here you thought you'd just . . ." He held out the hank of hair that was still in his hand. He imagined it tied with a blue ribbon and tucked away in some chest that would follow him to prison.

"I saw the scissors," she said, shrugging, as if the act were inconsequential.

"It's surprisingly lovely," he said, reaching out with his empty hand and hesitatingly touching what little hair remained. He had been intimate with many women—hell, many, *many* women if he were held to the fire—but nothing was as purely carnal, as erotic, as running his fingers through the cap of short dark hair that surrounded her upturned face.

"I can't imagine what Cabot will think," she said nervously, touching the wisps that teased her cheek. "Do you suppose I can somehow pin it back on for court?"

Her hand reached for the curls she'd so cavalierly severed, expecting him to relinquish his hold. He had but one small part of her, these locks of hair, and a memory sullied by his rejection. He did not let go.

"You smell like rain," he said, taking a step closer so that just inhaling let his body touch hers. "It's wonderful."

"It's just beginning to mist outside." With him so close to her she had to tip her head back to talk with him. It was an offering he couldn't resist, and he dipped his head and touched his lips to hers.

She answered back with a passion that nearly staggered him, and he had no choice, it seemed, but to pull her against him and plant his feet firmly against the rocky seas.

"If only," he began, wishing away their past—Cabot's accident, all the women he'd lusted after and left, her marriage to his brother; wishing away their futures—his in a jail cell, hers here with a cold man who never so much as took her in his arms.

"Ssh," she said as his lips traveled across her cheek, traced her chin, and began a trek down her neck to unclaimed territory. "Don't let me go again, Ash. Don't ever let me go."

He leaned down into her, his lips brushing her temples, his fingers winding their way through her short locks. "Charlie . . ." he said, trying to pull himself away.

She couldn't have him forever. She understood that. A few weeks and his trial would be over, and with any luck at all he'd be back to sea. But for this moment, these few minutes in her special room where all her girlish wishes still had room to roam free, she could touch his cheek and know what he felt like at this one hour of the day.

And if maybe, by chance, she could see him in the morning, accidentally touch his arm, and then casually brush the hair from his eyes, she could know, too, how he felt in the morning. And then, perhaps at lunch . . .

She tipped her lips up toward his and admitted to herself what she suspected he already knew all too well. She was in love with him, head-over-heels-like-some-ridiculous-schoolgirl in love. She loved everything about him—the good things, like how he left her flowers and pretended he didn't know what she was talking about when she tried to thank him; the bad things . . .

Oh, Lord! She was so in love, she couldn't think of any bad things. Especially not when he was placing tiny little kisses on the ends of every strand of hair she'd cut.

"I shouldn't . . ." he murmured, taking a step back from her and shaking his head as if to clear it.

"No! Oh, God, don't stop," she said, pushing against him, rubbing her head against his chest, and standing on her toes to reach for his lips.

"Ashford?" Kathryn's voice was shaky as her cane hit the bottom step. "Are you up there? I don't want to climb up there for nothing."

Charlotte pulled away first, her hands flying to her lips and then her freshly shorn head.

"I'm up here," Ash called out to his mother. "Don't bother climbing."

"Have you found Charlotte?" Worry rang in her voice like church bells on Sunday.

"Yes." He made no mention of how far away they'd been, how very lost.

"I was seeing to my begonias," Charlotte chirped, her voice cracking. "And I lost track of the time."

"Come to dinner," Kathryn said. They heard her pull open the elevator door. "Cabot says he has a surprise for you."

"Well," Ash said, ruffling her hair and trying to restore the distance that belonged between them, "I'd say you have quite a surprise for him."

It took her more than a moment to realize he meant her hair.

At first they didn't say a word. Oh, poor Kathryn's jaw dropped a couple of inches at the sight of her, but Charlotte was impressed with the older woman's restraint. She didn't scream or tear her hair out, or point a finger and laugh.

Cabot, of course, didn't need to resort to words. He sighed heavily, rolled his eyes theatrically toward the ceiling, and shook his head. Charlotte had the feeling that there would be a wigmaker at the door come morning.

"Moss convinced Ewing Flannigan to allow Davis over next weekend," Ash said, breaking the silence at the table. "I think he intimidates the man. Anyhow, with St. Patrick's Day and all, I suppose Flannigan will be laid out cold."

"How could you have—" Kathryn began, pointing in Charlotte's general vicinity.

"What ever possessed you—" Cabot said now that the floodgates were open.

"Oh, Miss Charlotte!" Maria chimed in.

"Saints preserve us!" the parrot called from the other room.

"Charlotte, really!" Kathryn said, summing up all their opinions in just two words.

"Clara Foltz wears her hair bobbed and is taken quite seriously," Charlotte said in her own defense. "I would have thought this would please the lot of you!"

"Basis?" Cabot asked as if she were arguing a case instead of defending her right to wear her hair any way she damn—yes *damn!*—pleased.

"It's self-evident," she snapped back. Who in this house wanted her to be a woman? Surely not Cabot, who had stripped her of lace and finery and given her serge and cigars in their place. Surely not Kathryn, who had convinced the tailor to duplicate men's suits for her daughter-in-law, and who had until just recently encouraged her daughter-in-law to leave the running of the house to her so that Charlotte could concentrate on her work. Surely not Ashford—oh, no, not Ashford, who, while he obviously enjoyed kissing her, had foisted her back on Cabot as a problem of which he didn't want any part.

"Self-evident? Pray go on. Don't stop now," Cabot said, gesturing with his hand for her to explain.

"Oh! Oh! Oh! Don't stop!" Ash's parrot shouted from the kitchen. "Oh, God! Don't stop!"

Charlotte felt her cheeks pinken, then deepen to red. The heat of them burned until she had to press her hands against them to stop the fire. She could feel Cabot's stare and refused to meet his gaze as she glued her eyes to her plate and fought to regain control of her racing heart.

Ash, she could see without raising her head, had shakily put down his water goblet and was reaching for something stronger.

"Oh, God! Don't stop! Shut up, you stupid bird!"

Charlotte dropped her head into her hands.

"Well, well, well," Cabot said softly while Ash opened and closed his mouth several times.

"I'm just so embarrassed about this hair," she said, fussing with it and rising to look in the mirror. Actually it didn't look nearly as bad as she'd expected it would in the light. Behind her she could clearly see the looks pass between the Whittier brothers and felt at once the guilt that Ash had been bearing alone.

"I don't know what you could have been thinking," Kathryn said quickly. "You couldn't have expected Cabot to like—that is, it just isn't seemly. What I mean is that—" she tried again.

Charlotte fought to summon some righteous indignation. Cabot had rejected her, after all. But he had always stood by Ash, even after his brother had caused his accident. And now he had been betrayed.

"We'll skip the damn soup, Maria," Cabot said when she came through the door with the silver tureen. "I'm sure by now it's cold, and I won't have the main course spoiled. Sit down, Charlotte. I don't want you to miss this."

She took her chair reluctantly, wishing she were on the moon, or at the North Pole, rather than at her own table seated between her husband and his mother and directly across from his younger brother.

*"Rosa, abre la puerta,"* Maria said from within the kitchen. *"Ayúdame."*

"What have you got up your sleeve, Cabot?" Kathryn asked. "You seem quite pleased with yourself."

"Well, Mrs. Mason couldn't find Charlotte this morning and so I took the liberty of planning our supper myself." Maria came through the door with a big covered platter. "Ah! What shall we do with it? Take off the cover and show it around first, and then you may put it on the side-board to carve."

"Ah! What shall we do with the drunken sailor?" Liberty shrieked from the kitchen just as Rosa took the lid off the platter that Maria held.

Charlotte stared, shaking her head in disbelief. The hot cider and crackers she'd had at three raced each other up her throat. She covered her mouth with her hand and ordered her body to rise and run. Rubber legs couldn't so much as push her back from the table.

Across from her, held low enough for everyone at the table to see, on a bed of his own feathers and propped up as if he were proud to be there, sat Argus, the peacock, roasted to a deep golden brown and drizzled with Madeira wine gravy.

# Chapter 16

It had taken a week for her to get up the nerve to ask him for money. Well, it had taken her five days to talk to him at all after the Argus fiasco. And then two more to find a moment they weren't immersed in Ash's case, which was scheduled to begin in less than a week's time. She'd waited until they had some semblance of a defense, what with Perry turning up trumps all over town with all of Ash's old accounts, Greenbough's beans about to pan out, and more than a few tongues willing to wag down by the wharfs now that Cabot had upped the ante considerably.

And now she'd asked, plain and simple, lawyer to lawyer, partner to partner, man to man.

And he was just staring at her as if she'd grown another head. "I'm not following your argument, Charlotte," he said, as if she'd pulled a new concept out of thin air. Well, for Cabot she supposed it was. "What exactly do you mean by compensation?"

"A salary," she said trying not to let the look on his face intimidate her. "Or a share in the profits, since I am your partner."

"A roof over your head isn't enough? Food on the table and clothes on your back aren't enough? Tickets to the San Francisco Opera House, my mother's pearl earring bobs, all those things are not enough?" He flung some papers toward the out bin that sat on the desk between them.

"If I were simply your wife," she said, looking at the papers and not taking them, "all of that would be more than adequate. I don't mean to imply for a moment that you are not a generous husband." At least when it came to monetary matters. "But I do believe fervently, ardently, and justifiably, that I am entitled to funds of my own for use at my discretion."

He returned the pen to the well and set the papers he was working on aside. "Why?"

"Because I put in a day's work and that entitles me to a day's pay. In fact, I put in a good deal more than a day's work most days. Because the only time off I've taken in the last five years has been for illness, and even at that I recall copying your briefs from my bed."

"That's unfair, Charlotte, and you know it. I offered to send you abroad with Mother, didn't I? For a grand tour? And not just once. And did I not sit by your side when you had that fever? It was only to keep you abed when you thought you were ready to get up that I let you copy the briefs."

"You've been very good to me, Cabot, but that doesn't change the fact that I should have been paid for my work."

"And were you ever charged for your education? You

and I both know that the cost of Hastings far exceeded the measly inheritance your grandmother left you. Without me you would never have become a lawyer at all, never mind a better-than-average lawyer with beyond simply adequate skills. Have I asked recompense for that?"

Too stunned to answer, she just looked at the man she had married for all the right reasons. He was noble, honest, good hearted, and kind. She had admired his passion for the law, and even his love of his precious flowers.

She had thought him anything but petty. Until now.

"Are we even, then?" he asked, pulling the papers back in front of him. "And can we actually get some work done this morning? We do have a major case I suspect will affect us both."

"This smacks of indenture," she replied. And, she supposed from his side it smacked equally well of ingratitude. Still, being without funds left her without options. And it would be worth conceding on the past if she could still get her hands on some small sum that would allow her to start a practice of her own in the future. "But let's say that I was willing to set aside all demands for a salary when I was learning the law. What about once I was admitted to practice, once I began to handle cases, and write briefs, and argue before the court—haven't I been responsible for the generation of revenues? And aren't I entitled to a share of . . . said revenues?"

"Why?" he asked again when she paused to take a breath. Leaning forward, pulling himself upright in the extreme, he appeared to hold his breath while he waited for her answer.

"I think I've explained my position adequately," she began.

"Yes, I believe you have. And argued well for it too. But my question remains why. Why do you need the money, Charlotte? To what end? Are you thinking of leaving? Is that it? Because before you answer me, I think you should know my response to such a move on your part."

Where anyone else would have seen a man simply resettling himself in his chair, Charlotte watched Cabot's mind racing, just as she'd watched his movements in the courtroom and had learned to read them. Ordinarily, this would be the moment she would choose to bring him a file, or a glass of water, or provide a distraction that would give him the time he needed to collect his thoughts and present an argument that would appear seamless as a result of her intervention.

But she wasn't about to help him now, not against herself. Instead she let the moments hang like hours, waiting for him to continue.

"Should you be entertaining the notion of ending our partnership, understand that I would never ask you to leave here empty handed. On the contrary I would insist you take with you your fair share, which would be all of your cases." He put up his finger to hold her words at bay while he continued, his anger getting the better of him.

"That means that Davis Flannigan, poor child, will remain on your caseload. But then, you've learned all you need to from me, so I'm sure that you'll be able to convince O'Malley to take the boy from his surviving parent and give him to . . . well, the boy could be a ward of the court, anyway, since the situation here would be altered considerably.

"And then there's that ridiculous Halton case. Frankly I'd be happy to see that one go, though you know your involvement does worry me more than a little. Still, the same precautions could be exercised.

"It's Ashford's trial that really concerns me. Do you think you can win that one on your own? It's a pretty thin defense we've got so far—a few aspersions cast on Greenbough and little else."

"Ashford's case would be mine?" she questioned. "Why?"

"Really, Charlotte," he said with one eyebrow raised, "do we need to spell it out? Dot *i*'s and cross *t*'s and account for hours that are simply unaccounted for? Wouldn't you prefer to simply remain unaccountable? Consider me a generous man, Charlotte. The cases are yours."

He was bluffing. She knew he was, even if he wasn't picking lint from his suit or stretching out his knuckles, which were his usual signs. But he'd made his point nonetheless.

O'Malley would never even hear her reargument in Davis's case. She'd only been granted the reargument because Cabot's name had been on the Notice of Appeal. Alone there wouldn't be anything at all she could do for the boy.

And Ash! She could never get Ash off by herself, had no illusions that she could. Working together with the strain between them all would make things difficult enough, but Cabot would be able to pull it out. Cabot could make magic happen. Hadn't he made a lawyer out of her?

"I'm not going anywhere. But I still do feel that it devalues my work not to receive pay for it," she said, trying to give him some reason other than the fact that at the moment she hated him over a stupid bird she'd had no kindly feelings for in the first place.

The room was silent, save for that droning clock that ticked on and on, winding her nerves as tightly as its spring.

"I see," he said at last. "I'm glad. And sorry, too, Charlotte, if I've ever made you feel less than essential in any way. Ironic isn't it, that I can be so eloquent in court and yet here I find it so hard to say the things I feel. And so instead I say ridiculous things about the price of your education. I suppose in truth I should have paid you just to come into this room every morning for the good it did my heart."

"It isn't the money," she lied, rubbing her sweaty palms against the green velvet skirt she wondered what had ever possessed her to wear. "It's the . . ." she searched for a word other than *independence,* but none stumbled into her path.

"—tangible sign of appreciation and worth," he finished for her. "I've been a boor, haven't I? What do you say to a little vacation? When Ash's case is over? We could take a ship somewhere, perhaps. Or a train. Would you like that?"

"I think we'd better win his case before we plan the celebration," she said, wishing she could get on a boat or a train and never come back, never see another law book, or courtroom, or lawyer—her husband included.

"However it ends up, I think it wise we get away. Can't you smell that ocean breeze?" he egged her on. "Salt spray in your hair, and all that. Maybe Ashford could recommend a place. Though I suppose we wouldn't be looking for the same sorts of things."

"We should get back to work." She stood and took the papers from the out basket and turned toward her office.

"I'm sorry, Charlotte," he said, and she stood perfectly still with her back to him. "I'll try harder. I'll notice the things I ought to and comment on them."

The harsh light of day had revealed the butchering she'd done to her hair, and no green velvet skirt or striped shirtwaist was going to make it look any better. Still, she wouldn't have minded someone at least acknowledging the change in her appearance this morning. Kathryn had simply stared, Ash had held his tongue, and Cabot had dashed extra bitters in his tea upon her entrance into the dining room.

"Yesterday's memo was well done," he said, tapping his desk with a pencil. "Well done indeed."

*Especially when you consider what you paid for it,* Charlotte thought bitterly. But then, the memo had been for Ash, who had caressed her with his eyes even while he was holding his tongue.

They were all in the dining room waiting when Ash came down to dinner. As always, he was seated next to Selma and across from Charlotte. The intention was for him to entertain Selma while Charlotte made polite conversation with Eli on her left and Kathryn on her right. Cabot, pontificating at everyone, sat at the head of the table with Davis on his right, since the child needed the most edification from the master.

The chip on Ash's shoulder was so heavy, he was surprised he could walk upright into the dining room, make his apologies for being late, and take his seat, all without breaking under the weight of it.

"You're late," Cabot said. "Which is amazing, considering the fact that you can't leave this house."

Ash tried simply ignoring him.

"Equally amazing is the fact that someone whose description is remarkably close to yours was seen down on the docks last night."

Ash watched Charlotte's eyebrows rise, but busied himself with his napkin. The closest he'd come was a woman named Jamaica, who'd told him about a blonde who'd moved farther south to ply her trade in the better weather.

"A man of low moral fiber, this one was, consorting with those of the same ilk."

"That is an exceptionally pretty dress," Ash said to Selma, without so much as a look in Cabot's direction. "It seems to make you glow."

"That's not the dress," Eli said with a slight grimace. "That's her *goyisher* beau, you should pardon the expression but I feel I am among friends."

"Eli, he's not a beau," Selma said, blushing to her widow's peak. "He's a nice man I see every now and then."

"For vhat?" Eli demanded.

"For tea, or a little supper. You're always at the office and I get lonely. Why shouldn't I eat with whomever I please?"

*"Goyim?"*

"We aren't out eating pig's feet, Eli. At least I'm not. What does it matter if the man is not Jewish? I'm eating dinner with him, not standing under the *chuppa.*" Ash was surprised Selma could turn any redder, but she managed it at the reference to the bridal altar.

"You're breaking bread with us, Dr. Mollenoff," Kathryn reminded him. "And we're not of your faith."

"It's different," Eli said. "And you know it. We're friends here, a group of people not looking for more than that. Now if I vas to vork up the nerve to ask if you should maybe one day vant to go for a sip of tea vit me down in the city, and you should maybe take leave of your senses and say yes to an old fool like me, then maybe ve vould have something to compare.

"But even then it vould be different. Selma is, you should take no offense, much younger than you or me, and children are not so distant a possibility for her."

Next to him Selma threw up her hands, but what caught Ash's attention was that his mother's cheeks had taken on the same pink tinge as the woman next to him. "Now he's got me calling in the midwife! Eli, we had tea, that's all. The man delivered my mail at the warehouse and then when we moved to the new building, there he was again. He smiled, I smiled, and from this you've got little crosses hanging around my children's necks."

"God forbid!" Eli said, his hand shaking as it covered his heart. "Better you should be dead."

"Dr. Mollenoff!" Charlotte shook that pretty little head of hers, smaller now without that ridiculous bundle of hair piled atop it. He couldn't look at her without thinking of rolling her about in the grass, tumbling down a hill with her like two carefree children. Thoughts he clearly had no right to.

"Religion," Cabot said with a huff, the way he said most things of late. "Just another weapon to divide people from one another. Race, sex, religion. All excuses for discrimination and hate."

"All sources for unity and progress. People banded together with the same cause can achieve great things," Charlotte said. It was simply amazing to him that such brilliance could come out of the same darling little mouth that had nearly accused him of stealing her honor. "Look how close the women are to the vote."

"Oh, yes," Selma said sarcastically. "In the meantime the man who stables my horse has more say about our President than I do."

"I think we tend to write off people too quickly," Ash said. What was it his father had told him when he'd handed him a nickel to give the man who begged by the church? *There but for the grace of God go I.* "How many people thought Charlotte, here, could never make a fine lawyer because she's a woman? How many would have said that my brother could never become a lawyer because he's stuck in that chair? Look at all of us—"

"But that's just man fulfilling his potential," Charlotte said. "Selma's asking why those who don't achieve their full potential still have rights that others of us have proven we deserve."

"Because if we had to use reaching their potential as the criterion for the right to vote, my dear Charlotte, only you would be allowed to vote!" He raised his glass to salute her.

"Here, here," the doctor seconded, and everyone drank to a clearly embarrassed Charlotte.

"I think what we're really at here is suitability," Cabot said. "Eli probably has nothing against Selma's friend personally, but I can certainly understand his concerns regarding whether the friend is an appropriate one for his sister and whether condoning a relationship between them is not inviting trouble in the door."

"Come, now, Mr. Whittier. You wouldn't try to decide what was right and appropriate for your brother, would you?" Selma asked.

Ash noticed Charlotte's pale face, the way she busied herself lining up her spoons against the edge of the table, the way her gaze refused to rise and meet his own. "I think," he said, "that you and I suffer the same fate, Miss Mollenoff, and that what was once a blessing has become a curse."

"Because we raised you," Dr. Mollenoff said, nodding his head. "A parent and yet not a parent. Fine lines, we draw, and then we cannot seem to cross them, eh, Mr. Vhittier?"

"Am I your curse?" Cabot asked, erasing everyone from the room but the two of them.

"Of course not," Ash was forced to say. Cabot had been there too many times for him, smoothing over rough spots Ash himself had created.

Cabot snorted quietly, apparently deep in thought. "Just your albatross, then, is that it?"

"Don't be absurd," Ash responded, recognizing for the

first time the millstone his brother had become, the weight of the guilt that he had dragged around the world with him, and denied to Cabot's face because it upset his brother so.

"You know," Cabot said abruptly, addressing Selma as if the private exchange between him and Ash had never taken place, "Davis's father is a mail carrier. Perhaps he knows your new beau."

"The man is not a beau," Selma said, crossing her arms and grimacing. "He's merely a friend I would just as soon not discuss."

Davis had no doubt his da would know Miss Mollenoff's beau or friend or whatever she wanted to call him. His father knew everyone, knew everything. To hear him tell it, there wasn't a shamrock in all of Oakland he didn't hear growing before it broke the ground. Like he knew that big fellow Moss would be waiting at McGinty's Bar for him to come in after court, and that the man would follow them home like a shadow on a summer afternoon. Like he knew that Mr. Ash had someone searching all over the bay for some dish like it would prove he hadn't set fire to his warehouse.

Da had been different all week. So different that when Mr. Johnson had said he was taking Davis over to the mister's place, his da hadn't even blinked. *Yeah, go,* he'd told him, and he hadn't opened the bottle until Moss had knocked on the door.

"How'd you like to sleep up in the high room?" the mister asked him as Maria was circling the table with a platter of something that smelled extra good. Fish in papillote, old Mrs. Whittier had told him, and warned him to take the paper off like he'd never gotten fish or chips wrapped up in a newspaper before.

The missus's fork fell against her plate with a clang and a clatter, and she chased it to stop the noise in a hurry. "The high room?" she asked. "But that's your brother's room. Where would Ashford sleep?"

"The carriage house," the mister said, like it had all been decided already. Except Davis guessed it wasn't, since the mister added, "Unless, of course, you object, Ash. It's clear you're feeling a bit confined by now. Perhaps a little space, a little distance, might make you more comfortable. And keep you on the grounds."

"If you're implying that I've been out pleasure seeking—" the brother—Davis thought he was real nice, and surely liked the man's parrot—started to say.

The mister took in a big breath and acted like he hadn't said what Davis was pretty sure he had. "Never!" he said, shaking his head slowly back and forth. "But you don't mind the carriage house, then, do you?"

The brother said he didn't, and then told Maria he didn't want any more food.

"Good, good," the mister said, and winked at his brother real big so everyone else at the table could see. "Maybe we can slay two birds with the same stone. Give you a bit of the privacy you must be craving after all those years at sea and all."

"Well, Liberty ought to appreciate the chance to spread his wings," Ash said, smiling right at Davis when he said the bird's name.

"Not to mention you as well," the mister added, then looked at the missus and smiled real private, like it was just the two of them in the room. "And then, Charlotte, you'll be able to get up there every now and then like you used to. Tend your animals and such."

"My animals?" The missus tilted her head and leaned around the doc and Davis to get a better look at her husband. "What animals?" she demanded, just like he was the one hiding them.

"Oh, the little one-eared fellow, and the blind one, and the rodents you can't bear to catch in traps. Need I go on?" Davis had figured that the man had to know at least about that stupid rabbit who was always getting loose. The mister seemed real pleased with himself for having kept the secret so long, but the missus didn't seem to appreciate it at all.

"The blind one is dead," she said through gritted teeth. "He died about a year ago in the cellar. How long have you known about them?"

The mister shrugged and winked at Davis. "I'm no idiot, Charlotte. Not blind, not deaf. The first one I can remember is that squirrel you called Bristles. Not counting the cat I agreed could stay in the cellar after our urn-filler got to him."

He waved at the peacock feathers filling the jug on the sideboard. It was too bad that bird had died. The missus was all broke up about it, which surprised Davis because he didn't think anyone liked the mean old buzzard all that much.

"Not counting the cat you *relegated* to the cellar," the missus said with her eyes all squinty. "Where the poor thing died. If you've known all along, why didn't you say anything? Do you have any idea how hard it's been for me to take care of them surreptitiously? Getting up in the middle of the night to feed them just to accommodate your edict of no pets in this house—do you have any idea how many stairs I've climbed, trips to warm things up and back again, all after you've gone to bed. Do you—"

The mister threw back his head and laughed. "You make it sound like it was my fault that you were a sneak and a liar. As if you could sneak anything past me, Charlotte! As if I don't know everything that goes on under my roof. And here I was all this time letting you get away with your little deception."

"Why?" she asked, her fists so tight up, they were turning white. "What was the point of making my life so hard?"

"Nobody made you take in those animals, Charlotte, so don't go blaming me for the work of them," the mister said.

"Vas she supposed to just let them die?" the doc asked. "Come on, now, Mr. Vhittier. You know your vife better than that. She didn't have no choice but the one you left her—to hide them."

It seemed to Davis that the doc had a point. Even in the little time he'd known the missus, he'd seen that she couldn't even turn on a spider. She sure looked silly chasing the hairy little thing under the sofa and warning it to stay there cause Maria was on her way and would be sure to step on it.

"It's my fault?" the mister asked, his eyes real big like it was the silliest thing he'd ever heard. "She sneaks these things into the house against my express wishes and I'm the one guilty of something?"

"She asked you why, Cabot," the other mister said. If Davis didn't know better he'd swear that man was sweet on the missus, the way he kept looking at her like she'd just baked him a birthday cake with three layers and a whole lot of candles. "And I'd like to hear the answer. We know why she tricked you—her nature wouldn't let her do anything else. Why did you trick her?"

It seemed like everyone was ganging up on the mister, but Davis figured the man could take care of himself, so he rested his head in his hand and just watched the man wheel that chair of his back away from the table a little.

"I should have expected you would leap to her cause," the mister said to his brother. "For all the good it'll do you. You can look at me and ask why I don't want animals around here, Ashford? It's just one of the many little annoyances this chair has caused in our life. Seems you were right about how much I'm forced to disappoint her. Not that it's your fault in any way, Ash, but I'd expect you to at least be aware of the limitations imposed on me by—"

"You want to get into this in front of our guests?" Ashford asked. Davis was beginning to think of him by his first name, since that was all most people called him. "Because I doubt she does."

"No, he does not," the old lady said, stomping that cane of hers against the floor.

"Then I'll just be moving my stuff on out to the carriage house, if anyone needs me," Ashford said, getting up from the table and throwing down his napkin. "And we can finish this later."

"Just wait until our guests leave," the missus said, signaling him to sit back down. "And I'll give you a hand. I've a few things up there that—"

"I think not, Charlotte," the mister said, rolling his chair back up against the table and waving for Maria to take away their plates. "We have a great deal of work to do if we hope to win Ash's case. If you really want to be of help to him, I think it would be best if you and I did some work together tonight. And left Ash to himself and your various other animals."

It made sense to Davis, but there must have been something he was missing, because Mr. Ash stormed across the room while the mister yelled at Maria for more wine. And Davis saw the old lady pat the missus's hand gently, giving the mister the evil eye like he'd done something she was real ashamed of.

"I was just wondering, Cabot," Ash said before he left the room, "what made you tell her now?"

# Chapter 17

She'd helped settle Davis into the high room, which consisted of little more than introducing him to a few more animals Ash had been willing to put up with, and pointing out some books he might enjoy leafing through. And then she'd gone down to her office, only to find the lights turned out and no sign of Cabot at all.

Twice today she'd felt that he was threatening her. Of course, looking at it rationally, she was being ridiculous. All he'd said was that she could take her cases with her if she left. How could that possibly be construed as a threat? Especially since she wasn't going anywhere. Or putting Davis in the high room and suggesting they needed to do some work on his brother's case. What kind of threat was that?

Still, something was afoot. They had become adversaries suddenly, on opposite sides of a nameless case.

Her head was just poking through the neck of her

nightgown when she heard three short taps. Davis? She lowered her gown, and clutching it around her neck, she opened her door to an empty hall. Again she heard the rapping and like an idiot she ran to the window to look out at the dark night.

"Charlotte?"

She heard the low voice, but saw nothing.

"Charlotte, can you hear me?" It was Cabot's voice. She poked her head out the window and looked in the direction of his room.

"Cabot?" she said out into the night.

"Charlotte?" He tapped again and she realized he was knocking on the wall that separated their rooms. "Are you in there?"

She put her head against the wall. "Cabot? Are you all right? Do you need something?" She was reaching for her robe and trying to remember where it was that Arthur slept, when Cabot answered her.

"Come next door. Please."

A chill went through her and she pulled the wrapper tighter around her. "Is something wrong? Should I get Arthur?"

"God, no! Just come in. I can't talk to you through the damn wall."

"I'm not dressed," she mumbled, looking down at herself and realizing she was as covered from her neck to her toes as ever he'd seen her.

Sneaking out her door, looking both ways like an errant child, she hurried to his door and knocked so quietly, she suspected he wouldn't even hear her.

"Come in," he whispered like some coconspirator.

He lay in his bed. To the best of her recollection she had never seen him ready for sleep before. He was propped up with several pillows behind his head and lay on the left side of the bed, leaving the right empty. He had on a blue dressing gown and white nightclothes, which peeked out from beneath it.

"Close the door. If you don't mind, that is." And then he cleared his throat and smoothed out the empty side of the bed.

With one hand on the knob and the other near the edge, as if that would make it any quieter, she closed the door and then stood inches from it, fighting to swallow. "Is something wrong?" she asked when he just lay in the bed staring at her.

He opened his mouth to speak and then shut it.

She bit at her lip and waited.

He opened his mouth again and, once more managed to clear his throat.

She pulled at the ties of her robe until she nearly severed her top half from her bottom and made it almost impossible to breathe, which she wasn't doing anyway. She took a step back and hit the door with her heel.

"What are you doing way over there?" he asked. "This is hard enough."

"What is?" She felt her legs getting rubbery.

"Maybe it would be easier if you came and sat here," he said, pointing to the chair at his bedside. "Or on the bed."

"Are you going to fire me?" she asked. "Because I'd just as soon hear that from over here."

His eyes widened and his jaw dropped and then he threw his head back against the pillows and laughed. "Is that what you thought? You poor child! No, no, I'm not going to fire you. Now come and sit."

She did as she was told, taking in her surroundings as she did. It was a Spartan room. She supposed he needed a great deal of space to maneuver around up here, what with the difficulties involved in getting him dressed and undressed and all. It wasn't easy to move his heavy legs, shift his uncooperative torso, lug him from his chair into his bed.

There was a notebook and pen on his nightstand and she reached for it.

Again he laughed, this time nervously. "You won't need to take notes."

"Cabot, what is this all about?" It was late and she was tired, and being in Cabot's room gave her the willies.

"I think there's something going on between you and my brother."

Just like that he said it. No preamble, no leading up to it or letting her see it coming.

"And I want you to know that I don't blame you. You don't know Ashford all that well, but he's been a ladies' man since he was in knickers. No doubt he told you that he loves you, and no doubt you think that you are in love with him."

She studied the small checks on her dressing gown and fiddled with her belt but said nothing. Cabot had been the one to teach her never to show her hand until she knew just what the opposition held.

"You know, of course, that you weren't his first, and that you won't be his last. You're no fool, but neither are you an expert when it comes to love. Neither am I, of course. But I do understand human nature and I do have compassion for your needs."

"Cabot, I'm not sure I understand what you're getting at. Are you forgiving me my trespasses? Because I don't think there was anything to forgive." She corrected herself. "Not what you think, apparently, anyway."

He sighed deeply. "I'm glad to hear it. My brother is not a bad man, Charlotte, but he has bad habits. Using women is one of them. If he ever hurt you, I think our vows would override my blood ties to him. Do you understand what I'm saying?"

Of all the scenarios she could have imagined, this was the worst. She could have faced his anger, his outrage, even his indifference. Not his caring, his kindness, his protectiveness.

"Are we finished, then?" she asked, beginning to rise. "It's very late and I—"

"Would you stoke the fire for me?" he asked, handing her the poker and explaining that he had rapped on the wall for her with its end.

She took the poker and awkwardly moved the screen from the fireplace.

"Put on another log, if you're able," he directed, turning on his side to watch her. "Careful of your robe."

She held her clothes away with one hand and tried to juggle the log with the other.

"Take off your wrapper," he said. "It'll be easier with just the gown."

"I can do it," she insisted, losing her balance and dropping the log, which missed her toes by inches.

"For heaven's sake, Charlotte. You can take off your wrapper. I am your husband, after all. You're certainly safe with me. And when you're done, I think perhaps you should come lie on the bed beside me."

She couldn't look at him, and so she stared into the fire, her face flushed by the heat and her body beginning to sweat despite how cold and clammy she felt. When she could breathe again she hurled the log into the fire from a few feet away and then poked it toward the back. Sparks flew wildly, and a wall of heat came toward her.

"It's all right, Charlotte. I couldn't hurt you if I wanted to. Come now. Close the curtains and stretch out beside me." He patted the spot beside him and waited patiently while she stood in front of the window. "Are the lights on in the carriage house?"

She could make out Ash's shape in the window, as she

supposed he could make out hers. Was he counting from the corner, wondering whose room it was she stood in? She hurried to shut the curtains and dragged her feet over to sit on the far edge of the bed.

"It's best he know that you aren't his to toy with. We'll all be more comfortable if we all understand . . . Charlotte, are you all right?"

She was shaking uncontrollably, her hands twisted in her nightdress and clutching each other. Unless she was wrong, and she was sure she wasn't, he was going to touch her any minute now. Her *husband* was going to touch her, and all she could think, the only words that swam in her head, were *too late. Too late.*

"Lie back. I'll put the cover around you. It must be eighty degrees in here. I don't see how you could be so cold." He eased her back against him and pulled the covers up and over her. Then he touched her forehead lightly with the back of his hand.

He was checking for a fever, she knew, just as her father had done so many times when she was a sickly little girl.

"Let me feel. When Ash was little . . ." he began to say, then stopped abruptly as he leaned over her and placed his lips just above her eyebrow. "No fever," he reported, but he kept his face so close to hers that she could feel his shallow breathing on her cheek.

"I'm fine," she agreed, and lay perfectly still in his arms as he fiddled with the ruffle of her nightdress idly.

"You look like a little girl with all these ruffles and that short mop of hair," he said, tucking the covers down some until they were under her armpits. Abruptly he slipped his hand within the covers and rested it on her breast. After a minute or two he began to move his fingers, much as if he'd lost something and was trying to find it. Maybe, she thought, it was the past he was searching for but couldn't seem to find. She had no trouble recalling how it felt when Ash had touched her, but one seemed to have nothing to do with the other.

When Ash had touched her she was fire.

Cabot's touch had left her like stone.

"Perhaps it will get easier with time. Now it's late," he said, then briefly touched dry lips to hers. "I'll get the light."

She fought against the covers, trying to sit up. "Did you mean for me to stay here?" she asked, unable to keep the shock from her voice. "I mean we've never . . . that is . . ."

"Would you prefer to return to your room?" Maybe it was the dressing gown, but he seemed so much more vulnerable than in his navy suit within his wood-and-wicker wheelchair.

"If you would prefer me to stay," she said deferentially. "Or go," she offered as well, perhaps with a bit more hopefulness than the first option.

"Actually, it's time you got to bed and I'd like a cigar and to read a bit. I know how the smell bothers you, so perhaps if you'd like to return to your own room . . ."

In thirty seconds she was out of his room, in her own, and leaning with her back against her closed door, trying to catch her breath. Dear God! It was like lying in bed with her own uncle! Her father! The water in the pitcher on her dresser was ice cold, but she stripped to her skin and washed in it anyway, washed places he'd touched and those he hadn't. And then, God help her, she went and stood by the window and wished for Ash to want her again.

He'd tried to be glad she'd been in his brother's room. It was where she belonged, after all. He'd told her as much and he was glad she'd listened. He'd virtually ordered Cabot to see his duty through with her, and now it appeared that Cabot had taken his words to heart.

Of course, it would be that for twenty-eight years not a soul on the planet had done what he'd requested of them, with a few notable exceptions who'd been paid for the pleasure. And they'd chosen *now,* of all times, to listen to him?

*Good, good,* he tried to convince himself. With Charlotte being so hungry for love and Cabot finally willing to feed her, he could feel proud that he'd been able to do something right for his brother to help make up in some small measure for the wrong he'd done him.

Then he made the mistake of looking up again.

Nothing billowed around the slight form that was silhouetted in Charlotte's window. No full sleeves, no shapeless chemise. And his heart ached and his loins burned, and he would have given anything he would ever own to scale the walls of her fortress and abscond with the princess who had captured his heart and soul.

Not that it could make any difference, but as always in his life, his timing left a little to be desired. Just this morning Cabot had finally been honest enough to tell him that, as things stood, it would take a miracle to get him off scot free. His brother might be able to get him off on the manslaughter count by preying on the jury's sympathy—it was simply bad luck that anyone had been trespassing at the time. But the fire itself had all the earmarks of an insurance arson, and he'd be lucky to get away with five years.

*Five years,* he thought, as he tried without success to pull himself away from the window.

As long as Charlotte had been married to Cabot.

A lifetime.

# Chapter 18

When he heard the banging at the door and opened his eyes, it took Ash a moment to realize where he was. He hadn't slept all night, images of Charlotte and Cabot twisting his gut, the vision of her naked at the window torturing him lower still. Shortly after sunup he'd headed down to the temporary space Moss had leased for the goods that had followed the *Bloody Mary* back to Oakland and arrived after the fire. The second floor of a bar down by the wharf had been willing to trade them some space for a few cases of liquor until something better could be found. Or until Ash went to prison and the business was dissolved.

He'd slipped out without notice, hoping that there was something he might see in the light of day that had evaded him in the darkness. Maybe, too, he wanted a quick taste of freedom again before it was too late. On his return he'd fallen into bed. And now with the light streaming in from the window blinding him after perhaps an hour's worth of sleep, he barked at whoever was knocking to come in, adding that it had better be important.

In the doorway Davis stood stoically, but no one could miss the pain in the child's eyes, even from a good ten feet away.

"What is it?" Ash asked him, halfway into his pants and shoving his feet in his shoes before the boy could even begin his stuttering. "Charlotte?" he demanded. "Cabot?"

Each question was met with a shake of the boy's head.

Ash stopped his frantic circling of the room in search of this or that and took the boy by the shoulders. "My mother?" he asked, facing the fact that with that ivory-handled cane of hers, the woman was poking harder at old age every day.

"Fire," the boy managed to get out without stuttering.

"Good God!" Ash said, rushing past the child and out onto the grassy lawn that separated the carriage house from the main one.

There was no sign of fire—no acrid smell in the air, no cloud of darkness hanging over the house. The window to Charlotte's bedroom was open just a crack and he could see the fresh air ruffling the curtains within.

"Where?" he demanded, shaking the boy. "Where's the fire?"

The boy swallowed, obviously preparing to talk. He exhaled, and at the end of the breath spit out, "The new warehouse," without his usual struggle.

Ash thought of the pathetic little floor above the seedy bar at the wharf where he'd been just a few hours before.

Again the boy took a deep breath and let most of it out. "Miss Mollenoff's hurt." He'd seen Selma there. She'd been surprised to find him there and he'd asked her to keep it to herself.

"Damn it to hell and back," he said, kicking at the

fence posts that lined the drive. "If they want me so bad, why the hell don't they just come after me? Or burn out the damn *Bloody Mary*?"

He followed Davis up to the house, assuring him more than once that he'd had nothing to do with Sam Greenbough's wife, that he wasn't undercutting his competitors, that he'd done nothing wrong, as if the boy cared.

"How bad?" he asked when he found Cabot and Charlotte preparing to go out. Cabot's hat was already in place and Charlotte was working in front of the mirror in the hall, attempting to secure hers to her head without sufficient hair through which she could run her hatpin.

"Eli's with her at the hospital," Cabot said. "Arthur's having the carriage brought around. Couldn't have come at a worse time with your case just days away and the boy's appeal in the middle of all of it."

"Oh!" Charlotte said, running up the stairs with her skirt hiked up in a very unladylike, albeit efficient—and provocative—manner. "I'll be right back."

Ash and his brother waited for her in silence, Ash rocking back and forth on his heels, Cabot running his hands along the spokes of his wheel.

"Sleep well?" Cabot finally asked, just, Ash supposed, to break the silence, and not because he was interested. Unless of course he was hoping that Ash would ask him the same question in return—which he wasn't likely to do before San Francisco was swallowed by the bay.

"Good fresh air out there," Ash said. "Wonderful view." He thought of Charlotte at her window, moonlight reflecting off two tiny breasts, and repeated himself.

"Whatever are you doing with my prize striated rose velvet gloxinia, Charlotte?" Cabot asked when she came down the stairs with the most magnificent plant Ash had ever seen. "You weren't considering bringing so precious a plant to the hospital, were you?" he asked while Ash took the plant from her so that she could put on her coat.

"It's not your prize anything," Charlotte said, taking the plant back now that her coat was on. "It was just some runty little seedling you told Mr. Newcomb to throw out."

Ash fixed her collar for her and managed to touch her neck just by accident—twice. "So you don't just rescue wounded animals," he said. "You can't let plants die either?"

As she shrugged shyly at him, Cabot examined the plant in her hand, turning a few leaves over and examining the rose and deep-maroon-striped flowers. "I never threw away this plant," he argued. "This is a rare specimen. I would never throw away something so valuable and precious."

"Well, you did," Charlotte said over her shoulder as she walked toward the door.

"And you would," Ash added, racing to get the door for the little lady who always managed to put everyone in their place.

"Can't you bring her one of the red ones?" Cabot asked, rolling through the door that Ash held open.

Charlotte hugged the plant to her navy double-breasted coat protectively. "No, I cannot. And if Selma is well enough, I'll go down to court on Monday to demand a hearing date be set for the Halton case. The sooner the better. That might give Selma an incentive to get well."

"Charlotte, that case is dangerous," Cabot said. "And that plant cost more than my coat. Arthur could run in and get a lovely—"

Charlotte let Arthur hand her up into the carriage, and Ash climbed in next to her. While Arthur secured the ramp and pushed Cabot's chair up into the specially designed coach, Ash made sure to comment loudly on how lovely the flowers really were and added that he was sure Selma would appreciate Charlotte's generosity.

Cabot seethed, and that was just fine with Ash, whose thigh was pressed up tight against Charlotte's. Despite the layers of coats and skirts and trousers, he was sure he felt the warmth of her leg through them all, and he removed his hat and unbuttoned his coat.

"And this time, Charlotte, while you're at the courthouse, you be sure to change the date Ash's trial is set to begin. Tell the clerk I've a conflict. Jack likes to accommodate me whenever he can."

"He likes the Chivas Regal he gets for accommodating you," Charlotte said, looking for a place to put the potted plant.

"Would you like me to take that for you?" Ash offered, reaching out and letting his fingers touch hers. He took the plant and placed it on his lap, finding it ridiculously stimulating to think that it had just rested on her own.

Good God! If holding the same plant she had could make his stomach fly and flop like flapjacks, what would touching her again do to him?

Resolutely, he planned to never find out.

The hospital was bustling, too busy for its size and too noisy for its patients. At first the nurses thought that Cabot was injured, being wheeled into the front hall in an invalid's chair, which he found profoundly humiliating. Being horribly petty, Charlotte considered it nothing more than he deserved after trying to stop her from bringing her very best friend in the world a plant that she had nurtured herself on the roof outside the high room.

Well, at least there had been no mention of what had occurred the previous night in Cabot's room. Tonight she would be sure to tell him she had a headache and needed to get to bed early. Tonight and tomorrow night and every night for the rest of her life if need be. And she'd hug herself until she broke before she'd answer another knock on her wall.

Ash spoke to the nurse at the front desk. She smiled up at him as if they were old friends, and rose to point the way down a corridor, her hand on his sleeve. It was a simple gesture, overly friendly, perhaps, but men and women did it all the time. *"I heard your husband's aunt was ill. I'm so sorry,"* someone might say, adding a pat of the hand. Or *"Let me help you with that,"* and arms would brush arms.

It was something she and Ash needed to avoid, that contact that set her on fire and made her think reckless thoughts. She envied the nurse who stood so close to him, leaning her head toward his as she pointed straight and left and right.

"They try to keep the burn patients together," he said when the nurse had finally let him go. He looked at Charlotte and stood just out of her reach. "I think you'd better just wait here."

"Don't be ridiculous," she said as if she spent half her days and all her nights at the hospital.

"Cab, I think you ought to make her wait here," Ash said, leaning over and whispering something to Cabot that she couldn't hear.

"You're so used to your damsels in distress, you've lost sight of just who this woman is," Cabot said proudly. "Despite that ridiculous haircut, this is one of the best lawyers in all of northern California."

She took off her hat and shook her hair, what there was of it, out. "Thank you very much," she said a little too sweetly, and forged forward down the hall.

From behind her she could hear Ash disagreeing with his brother. "Well, then, I hope she's got one of the strongest stomachs," he said finally, and seconds later he'd caught up to her.

"Left?" she asked him, trying hard to keep from seeing into any of the rooms, trying even harder to block out the sounds of moaning and the calls for help that echoed down the hall.

"Just follow the screams," he said, then shook his head tightly. "I think this is a mistake."

"She's hard," Cabot said, urging Arthur to push him faster to keep up. "She's tough as ice in winter."

"And she appears to be melting," Ash said, just as she began to feel the corridor tilt around her. *This is hell,* she thought, voices all around her calling out in pain, crying for help, praying to die. *I'm in Dante's damn inferno.*

She leaned against the wall and swallowed hard, the edges of her vision darkening, seeing two of everything, and all of it turning an unnatural yellow.

"I'll take you back to the waiting room," Ash said. He sounded miles away, though she could feel that he was close to her, touching her, holding her up so that she wouldn't slip to the floor in a puddle of serge. She inhaled deeply, trying to fill her lungs with the scent of him instead of carbolic acid and decay.

"Don't be ridiculous," Cabot said, ordering Arthur to her side. "Treat her like a woman and you see what happens?" he said to Ash. "Which room is it? This one?"

"Let me take you back," he said. His hand gripped her upper arm and one leg had her pinned against the tile wall where the cold was seeping through her coat and into her bones.

"No." It was all she could manage. She was afraid to try to say more. If she opened her mouth again, it might be a scream that emerged. Or her breakfast biscuit.

"For him?" Ash asked, backing away just a little as if

testing whether she could stand under her own power. "Or for you?"

"I want to see Selma," she said. She pulled herself upright and stood squarely on her own two feet. "And Eli will need me. I'm all right."

"You're better than just all right," he said softly, moving his hand so that he now only guided her by the elbow. "I'll be right here."

Cabot coughed and held out the potted flowers to Ash. "Hold this. I don't want it to fall."

It seemed to Charlotte it was perfectly all right with him, however, if she went tumbling to the ground.

She grabbed the plant from his outstretched arms and tiptoed into the room, where Eli sat by the bed, his familiar back bent, his head hanging low. In the bed was a mass of gauze and padding that all but hid Selma's small body. A portion of her face was bandaged as well, and the piece of cheek still exposed was white and tight looking like a rubber water bottle about to burst. She appeared to be asleep, but her breathing was labored and heavy.

"Eli?" Charlotte whispered. "We came as soon as we heard. How is she?"

Eli's face when he raised it to hers was old. Deep lines ran like dried riverbeds down his cheeks, and the remnants of tears still glistened within the crags and ruts. His eyes were rimmed in red and he clutched a damp hankie in one hand. He shook his head slowly from side to side. "She's gonna be fine," he lied, loud enough for her to hear it in her dreams.

The back of Charlotte's throat itched, her nose did as well. Her eyes smarted as she fought off tears, and she bit on the inside of her cheek to concentrate on simply not going to pieces in front of her friend.

"She was awake a little while ago," Eli said. "They gave her enough laudanum to put a horse down, and still she was in pain. I had to sing her to sleep like when she was a little girl. We had an Irishwoman who watched her while I was at work and her favorite lullaby was 'Too-Ra-Loo-Ra-Loo-Ral.' Imagine! An old Jewish fool like me singing 'Too-Ra-Loo-Ra-Loo-Ral.' But she finally fell asleep."

He wiped at his nose with the wet hankie and then accepted a clean one from Ash, who put a hand under his elbow and tried to get the old man to get up. "We'll sit with her, Eli. Go get some fresh air and something to eat."

He shook his head at Ash's suggestion. "Never me," he said softly. "I pray to God let it be me, and he doesn't hear."

"That's because he's listening to me," Selma said, her eyes still closed, her voice a raspy whisper.

"I thought you were asleep," Eli said. "Charlotte's here. And the misters."

Selma's one visible eyelid fluttered and she raised her eyebrow as if it could pull her eye open. Her thick dark eyelashes were gone, the hair that was visible lay in short clumps. Her right eye opened and suddenly the woman in the bed was Selma again as she focused on Charlotte.

"I brought you some flowers," Charlotte said, holding them where Selma could see them. "Cabot tells me they're very special."

"All the donations," Selma said, her words interrupted by a coughing fit that racked her body. "I tried to get them, but—" Her words petered out, and she closed her eyes once again.

"It's swollen in her chest," Eli explained. "In her lungs there's fluid. We have to turn her soon." He pulled his watch from his pocket and winced as if he could see the time running out.

"The money," Selma said again between wheezy breaths.

"You rest," Charlotte ordered her. "And stop worrying

about the money. On Monday I'm going to demand a hearing. You're going to have to hurry and get well so that you can cheer me on."

Selma didn't bother to open her eyes, and in her voice Charlotte could hear defeat settling in. "You win it for me, Charlotte," she said so softly Charlotte had to strain to hear her.

Tiptoeing in with shoes that hardly made a sound, a nurse appeared with a small bouquet. "Handsome gentleman sent you these," she said to Selma, and Charlotte looked up at the doorway. He was there for a brief moment only, and when she blinked he was gone. Had she not recognized him, even with all that pain etched on his face, a blink would have erased his face from her memory.

But his was one countenance she would never forget, since his actions were ones she could never forgive.

"Shall I read you the card?" the nurse asked, pulling it from among the flowers.

"I'll read it to her later," Charlotte offered, plucking the card from the nurse's hand and shoving it into her pocket. Good glory! If Eli only knew!

"Better," Selma agreed, and let the nurse help her drink a bit of water through a bent glass straw. As she sat up slightly, Charlotte could see the skin on her neck, blackened and puffy as if it had been toasted.

"They've scheduled a second escharotomy," the nurse told Eli. "There's more flesh they'll need to cut down."

"You should go," Eli said, cupping Charlotte's chin in his hand. The next instant he was barking instructions at the nurse and ministering to his sister.

"We'll go now," Ashford said, putting a hand on Eli's shoulder. "You take care."

It was unclear whether he was talking to Eli or Selma,

but it was Selma who responded. "I don't know what happened," she said, as the nurse held up her shoulders and helped Eli to turn her. "It wasn't half an hour after I saw you that the whole place was in flames."

# Chapter 19

"Of all the stupid, senselessly asinine stunts you've pulled in the past, this one tops them all," Cabot said to him as they entered the foyer, Charlotte running ahead and hurrying up the steps so quickly that she nearly tripped on her hem.

It hadn't been easy just watching her all the way home from the hospital, sitting there with those small hands of hers folded stoically in her lap because his brother was too foolish to reach out and take them in his own.

Twice he'd asked her if she was all right, and twice she'd assured him that of course she was. But she hadn't fooled him for a moment.

"Are you going after her or shall I?" he asked when her skirts had vanished from the top of the stairs. It was clear that the reality of what had happened to Selma had crawled under Charlie's skin and she was fighting it with all the strength she had to keep it from soaking right into her bones.

Cabot looked at him blankly. "Oh. Charlotte," he said finally. "Let her be. A decent cry and she'll be good as new."

"Talk about stupid and asinine," Ash said, shoving his hat at Arthur and heading for the steps. He stopped on the lowest one and turned to his brother. "I'm going up there if you're not, because I don't think she can make it alone."

Cabot rolled his eyes as if he were talking to an idiot. "Do you have any idea what happened in that hospital room? Do you realize that woman put you at the scene of a second crime? In front of the nurse yet! You think I'm some kind of goddamn miracle worker? It's one thing getting you out of your little peccadillos. This could cost you years, Ashford."

Even with his brother's yelling he could hear it. Deafening. "Don't you hear how upset she is?" he demanded.

Cabot was quiet for a moment, then shrugged. "I don't hear a thing. In fact, she seems to be handling it well, I think." He headed for his office, apparently oblivious to the tears Charlotte had yet to shed.

"I'm going up." If Cabot was right—and when wasn't he?—soon enough he'd be unable to help her. While he could, he wasn't about to exile himself when she needed him.

Cabot stopped his chair again, waved Arthur off, and sat straining to hear in the silence. "I don't hear a blessed thing. Is she crying? I thought we'd conquered that. No doubt if we ignore it, it'll go away after a time and she'll come down right as rain with only a red nose to show for her time."

Ash wondered for a fleeting moment if there was some law against hitting a man in a wheelchair, wondered further if he cared. After all, they could hardly hang a man twice. "No, she's not crying," he said. "She's not doing a damn thing."

Cabot looked at him as if he'd lost his mind. While that was certainly a possibility, it seemed to him that if Charlie was in such a hurry to get upstairs, she ought to be doing something now that she'd gotten there. And all the silence said she wasn't.

And how did he explain that to his brother?

"Go after her," he begged, wishing he were free to do it himself. "She needs you."

"Arthur, would you ask Mrs. Whittier to see to Charlotte?" He looked up at Ash as if that settled it, and gestured for him to follow him into his office. Clearly, *Mrs. Whittier* never referred to Charlotte. "We've work to do I hadn't counted on," he said.

Ash had felt it from the first, but had kept the thought buried deep within him. It hadn't been any of his business in any event, but having been the one to put Cabot into his chair, he had a special obligation to look the other way.

Now obligations pulled at him from another direction and keeping silent meant abandoning Charlie Russe to a life of loneliness.

"You can't send your mother in your place. She's your wife, dammit, Cabot, not your ward."

Cabot never looked happy. His eyebrows had always curved down seriously and his mustache drooped. But Ash wasn't sure that despite the wry smile, Cabot had ever looked quite that miserable. "And you thought I never made mistakes," he said, with more of a snort than a laugh. "Come on. We've work to do. This is going to be hard to pin on Greenbough. If you hadn't been there, been seen, we could have made it work in our favor—after all, the new building wasn't yours. But, no, you had to go for a morning constitutional. . . . Ash, let's go. I don't know how much time Charlotte will be able to buy us."

Charlotte bit at her lip harder still. She would not cry. Crying had never helped anyone in the past and wasn't likely to help Selma now. It hadn't brought her mother back and hadn't kept her grandmother from slipping away day after day and leaving her all alone in the world with only Cabot Whittier, her mentor, to tell her what to do.

Kathryn, wringing her hands and getting smaller and smaller as the chair she sat in seemed to swallow her up, wanted to hear every detail of Selma's injuries and yet cringed with each one. When the knock at the door interrupted them, it was Kathryn who rose to answer it.

Charlotte could see Ash's face clearly over the top of his mother's head. Such a good, kind face, so full of concern for her, when what he should be worried about was himself.

"She's fine," Kathryn was telling him while he strained his neck to see for himself.

"I'll be down soon," Charlotte added. "I know we've got work to do."

"Just take care of yourself," he said, giving his mother's shoulder a soft squeeze. "See that she gets a little rest, will you? She's had a hard day."

"Me?" Charlotte said, her voice coming out a squawk. "What about you? Do you realize—"

He cut her off with a knowing nod. "So Cabot's been telling me. Don't you waste time worrying about me. Get some rest, will you?"

Not worry about him? She spent her days and nights worrying about him in one way or another. How she would live with him around, how she would live without him.

"I'm fine. I'm coming now. Did you know that L and P Imports has been involved with the law before? And that Bekins had a fire that was ruled arson last year? We've only got a couple of days left and now there's more work to do than ever," she said, rising from the bed on whose edge she had been perched.

Kathryn shifted slightly so that she was blocking the doorway and, with it, Charlotte's view of Ash. "She'll be down later," her mother-in-law said.

Charlotte leaned to the left just as Ash leaned to his right, and once again their eyes met. If she could just look at him until she was a hundred, then maybe, she thought, that might be enough. Or nearly, anyway.

"I'll tell Cabot you're all right, then," he said, breaking the spell. "He was worried."

"Naturally," his mother finished for him. "And that's why you came up." Charlotte wondered if any of them believed it.

"I'll see you later?" he asked. He seemed to hang on her answer.

She nodded. "If you like," she said, looking down to see how badly rumpled she must look to him.

"I like," he said softly, almost as if his mother weren't there at all. Then, as if realizing it, he added, "You, too, Mother."

Kathryn shook her head sadly and closed the door behind her, leaned against it for a moment, and then walked slowly over to the wing chair that was set in front of the fire.

Her movements were slow and deliberate and resigned as she sighed heavily, sat, and pensively watched the fire. "Remember last year when I had that awful influenza? How death came knocking at the door and you barred the way?"

"I remember the only thing we could get you to eat was

your mother's apple leek soup," Charlotte said, coming to sit at the old woman's feet and letting the heat of the fire warm her face. "And you insisted that if I cooked it, you'd eat it."

"I knew you'd put love in there, dear one, and that would save me if anything would."

"I still think it was rather extreme of you to get me to try my hand at domesticity, Kathryn, but I'd hardly claim the credit for defeating death. That victory most assuredly was all your own."

"Maybe I shouldn't have fought quite so hard," Kathryn said thoughtfully, as she ran her fingers through the short strands of Charlotte's hair. "Maybe I defeated death only to have life defeat me."

"Are you afraid for Ashford?" Charlotte asked. "Cabot won't let him be convicted. You know that."

Kathryn looked into the fire as if she would find the answers there. If they'd ever been there, though, they had gone up in smoke. "I'm worried that Cabot has very little incentive to save his brother's neck," Kathryn said, addressing the glowing embers. "When saving his brother might mean losing his wife."

Charlotte swallowed hard. "I don't know what you mean. How could Cabot lose me?"

"The way any husband loses any wife. And you've more reason than most, my dear one."

"But I would never—" Charlotte began, stopped by Kathryn's raised finger.

"In some ways, Charlotte, you already have, despite your best efforts to the contrary. I only have to look at you, dearest, to know. And Cabot's crippled, child, not blind. No one this side of the bay can miss the way your breath catches when you're within ten feet of my younger son. The question is, what are we going to do about it?"

"There isn't anything to be done about it but try to hide it better until it goes away."

"Goes away?" Kathryn looked at her closely as if trying to decide whether or not she could be serious.

"No one feels like this forever," Charlotte said. If they did they'd never eat or dress or work. They'd spend their lives staring into each others' eyes and wishing on stars. They'd daydream about forever while holding on to now with all their might. "It'll pass. And then, too, Ashford will be off to sea again before you know it and life will return to normal."

Kathryn cupped Charlotte's chin and waited until she met her gaze. "Is that what you want? To remain here with Cabot forever?"

Why was forever so much longer when it involved Cabot than it had been just a moment ago when she'd been thinking of Ash? "Of course," she answered matter-of-factly.

"I wish I was so sure of what it was I hoped for the future," Kathryn said. "And mine so much shorter, at that."

Charlotte put her head down on Kathryn's lap and let the older woman stroke her hair. For a time they were silent, and then Kathryn spoke quietly.

"I love both my children, Charlotte, and I've come to love you, too, almost as if you were my own. Did you know I had two daughters once?" she asked, and continued without waiting for Charlotte to acknowledge the picture she had seen in Ash's room all those weeks ago. "The diphtheria. I still can't talk about it. But somewhere along the line you slipped right into their place and I began to tell you what to wear in much the same way I would have told them, and told you what to eat as I would have fed them. Your dreams became my dreams.

"And now I look at you and feel my heart ripped and

torn and bleeding for all my children. Over and over I remind myself that I am not your mother and that my allegiance must be to my sons. But even that doesn't help me, does it?"

Charlotte nestled against the woman's lap, noticing how bony Kathryn's thighs felt against her head.

"Cabot does love you," Kathryn continued. "As best he can. And I've always felt that my loyalty to him had to be unquestionable, unshakable. After all, he is my crippled son. Crippled in body, crippled in spirit. He had to become the man of the family so quickly after the girls and Charles all died. And he did it at the cost of any softness he had in him.

"But, Charlotte, I've always known he wasn't the only one hurt in that accident. He had the visible scars, but Ashford carried the ones on his soul. And those are so much easier to hide, to deny, especially from a mother who doesn't really want to see what's always been right in front of her nose. I knew, though, knew when he took off to places where I wouldn't see his hurt. And I watched as he went around the world and back without finding relief until he looked at you.

"Someone's got to lose, Charlotte dear. And I'm *damn* glad the choice isn't mine."

Charlotte started at Kathryn's words. "I don't see that there is a choice," she answered, getting to her feet and staring out the window at the carriage house. "I'm married to Cabot and I owe him everything."

"That debt was paid the first time you made him smile. And a million times over when you made him laugh. You owe him no more than you owe yourself."

"He made all my dreams come true," Charlotte said, her fingers spread against the glass as if she could reach out and touch the man who was striding across the lawn to his quarters.

"But Ashford gave you new ones, didn't he?" Kathryn asked, coming up behind her. Charlotte turned quickly, ashamed at having been caught in the act of wishing. "Cabot may have made your childhood dreams come true, but you're not a child anymore, Charlotte, and the dreams Ash can make come true are those of a woman."

"I don't want to hurt Cabot," Charlotte said, forbidding herself from even imagining what her world would be like if Ash could be in it.

"No, and neither does Ashford. And so you'll hurt each other by your denials. And Cabot will be hurt anyway. You've a long life ahead of you, God willing. Don't be so quick to throw that particular type of love away."

"That particular type?"

"Oh, come now, Charlotte! I am not so old that I don't remember how a man's touch could make the temperature rise fifty degrees in a buggy in January. That memory can keep a woman warm long into her final years. . . . What's going to keep you warm?"

Ash was lying on his back in the darkness when he sensed her coming toward him. He'd had the dream before—heck, he'd found the line that separated dreaming from wishing growing finer every day. He kept his eyes shut tight and imagined the noise the squirrels made was the sound of the carriage-house door opening and shutting. He inhaled deeply and convinced himself it was her scent he smelled. He turned over on the cot and let himself believe that the slight pressure against his thigh where it hung off the bed was caused by her own leg.

He refused to have the dream again, and forced himself to sit up, throwing the covers off his chest and gulping for a breath of fresh air.

"You're awake," she said softly, and whatever followed

it was drowned out by his groan. If this was a dream he wanted to stay asleep forever. If he opened his eyes and she was gone, he would never allow himself to drift off to sleep again. To see her here was worth the risk. He opened his eyes.

She was there.

"Ash?" Her voice quavered. "Should I leave?"

"That all depends on why you're here," he said, shocked at how gruff his voice came out, how raw his need could sound. "Did you come to discuss my case?"

"No."

He took her hand and pulled at her until she sat on the edge of his bed within the curve of his body.

"The weather?"

Gently he pulled her with him as he moved back on the small cot. He looped his arm about her legs and pulled them up until she lay against his side.

"Did you want to talk about Kathryn or Cabot or your woman suffrage?"

She shook her head against his chest and laid a tiny hand on the side of his neck, where she no doubt felt his blood racing, just as her head must have heard his heart beating a double-time tattoo.

"Why are you here?" he whispered against her hair while his hands began searching for the answers beneath her nightdress.

"For this," she admitted, slipping the buttons through their holes until she'd reached nearly to her waist.

His hands found their own way, his lips traced new paths where no other man had been. She let him do what he would, her only move a bold one in which she lifted his shirt so that his skin would touch her own.

He rolled onto his back and took her with him so that she rested on the length of his body. Then, after he had raised her slightly so that her lips were within reach of his own, he asked her again, "Why are you here?"

"So that I'll be warm when I'm old," she said, leaning down and touching her lips to his. She kissed him tentatively at first, and then instinct overcame her and she kissed him with all the passion she had stored within her, all the fire he had stoked with every look he'd ever given her, all the love he had promised her with each of a million silent smiles.

"What about now? Are you warm now?" he asked, easing her nightdress down over her arms, slipping it over her hands until she was free of it, until it was a puddle of white around her waist. He sat her up on him to glisten in the moonlight like some sprite rising from the sea with her nightclothes all foam around her.

Her breasts were just the right size and shape for his hands. Nothing could have felt more perfectly made for him. Her legs straddled him and her knees hugged at his hips. Only the blanket between them was saving her from ruin, only her innocence was keeping her fear at bay.

"Now are you warm?" he asked her again, pulling her down against him and taking the tip of one breast in his mouth, teasing it with his tongue and then tracing a path to the neglected one.

Her hands roamed his chest and she pulled herself away from him to shimmy down until her face was once again resting on his chest. With her fingers she searched out his own nipple and then caught it between her lips. She sucked ever so gently and rocked against him slowly, while he fought the rising tide, until nothing, not even all he owed his brother, could stop him from insinuating his hand between them and searching out her femininity.

He would do nothing his brother couldn't do, he decided. Life had been unfair enough to Cabot. And he would take no further advantage. Maybe, he admitted in a haze of want and need, it was a foolish line to draw when his hungry fingers were poised to storm the gates to what long ago should have become the stronghold of his brother's passion.

It was a game he had always played with his own mind to allow himself some small pleasure in life that Cabot's condition otherwise denied him. He could enjoy the ocean breeze against his cheeks because Cabot could do the same. He could drink until he puked, he could stay up until dawn, all because, while Cabot might not, still he was able.

And now Ash could bring this woman to heaven and pretend that she belonged to him for just this moment in time.

She was silky and soft and, oh, so willing as he touched her gently, trying not to frighten her with his boldness.

God, how he loved this woman! Not merely her lovely little body, which he wanted, nor her kind, sweet heart, which he needed, but her soul itself, which made his own soul sing with the joy of an innocent six-year-old who had never disobeyed his brother's commands.

He rolled over with her once again, this time laying her on the cot and crouching above her to keep his weight off her small frame. He kissed her everywhere, letting her moans fill him with a relief he'd never known. He kissed her on into the night, and when he felt her satisfaction as his own, he held her against him and let her joy wash over him like a balm that could soothe his guilt.

Cabot could have done it all, had he chosen to. Before he'd gotten in so deep, Ash had actually wished his brother would.

Now it would take the California prison system to keep Ash's hands off his brother's wife.

And the way things looked, they'd be happy to do the job.

# Chapter 20

"You what?" Ash heard his brother yell from inside his office. He jammed his hands in his pockets to keep from opening the door. What kind of idiot promises the woman he loves that he'll just *stay out of it*? What kind of man agrees that what had happened between the two of them the night before had to be buried and forgotten for Cabot's sake? "Tell me you're joking, Charlotte."

"I wish I was," she said more evenly than Ash ever could have. She hadn't even allowed him to say he loved her before she'd made him promise not to breathe a word to Cabot. At the time she could have asked him for the moon and he'd have promised that too. Could a man be held responsible for the promises he made when the woman he loved was crying and vowing the moment they'd shared would never happen again?

"And what's your excuse?" Cabot demanded. How the hell was she supposed to answer that? *Your brother started kissing me and . . .* He shook his head. He reminded himself that he hadn't exactly seduced her, after all. She'd been the one to come to *his* bed, nuzzle against *his* side, beg for *his* warmth.

But it didn't assuage his guilt any. It was still his fault. All his fault. A woman so starved for affection . . . a man who knew what a kiss could lead to . . .

"There is no excuse," he heard her say. "I mean, I could tell you I was worried about your brother, heartbroken over Davis, horrified with what's happened to Selma. I could tell you that being spat upon and vilified for doing what I believe in, and working day and night, have tied me up in knots that can never be undone. I could tell you that being served Argus for dinner was the last straw. I could tell you a million other things, but you wouldn't understand any of them, would you?"

"I understand the part about there being no excuse, Charlotte. That I understand quite well. This is that for which the word *inexcusable* was created."

Ash had heard enough. If it wasn't something they could put behind them, keep secret and sacred unto themselves, then so be it. But he wouldn't have it made tawdry and cheap. And he wouldn't let her stand there alone and face Cabot's outrage.

"I don't suppose saying I was sorry would do me any good here," she said. "So I won't bother. I've never condoned this sort of behavior and I've made no secret of it. But you've bullied me and bossed me and I've had to bear it silently time after time."

He opened the door and stood in the doorway, confused. *Time after time?* What in hell was she talking about?

"Decide to finally get out of bed this morning?" Cabot asked, more than a touch of sarcasm tingeing his voice. "Get what you were looking for last night, did you?"

He bit his tongue rather than say in front of Charlotte the only word that came to mind. *Ass.* His brother was an *ass.*

"I forgot to do something for Cabot down at court," Charlotte said quickly, pleading with her eyes for him to hold his tongue. "And he's rather angry. Not that I blame him with all the work there is to do and only three days left to do it in."

"And why are there only three days left?" Cabot shouted, pounding his fist on the arm of his chair so hard, it shook his body and made it look as if his legs had moved. "Because instead of doing what she should have been doing, *what I told her to do,* she was off fighting battles that have no relevance to her own life, and endangering herself in the process. It's not enough I have to worry for her safety, but I've your rattle-pated exploits to make things even worse. I suppose you were off again last night to scour the docks? No one listens to a word I say and then they expect me to make it all work out in the end." He rolled his chair to the bookcase, turned, and rolled back toward the desk. "One thing I asked of you, Charlotte. And you couldn't do even that."

"Stop yelling, Cabot. Now." Ash took two steps toward the desk, enough to stand between his brother and the man's wife. "One thing you ask of her?" Ash asked and followed it with a sorry laugh. "You ask more of her than any man could expect of ten women, and she—"

"—gets damn little in return? Is that what you were going to say?" Cabot asked.

"No. But there's something—" he began, until Charlotte cut him off.

"We've less than seventy-two hours to get ready for jury selection and prepare a case that will keep an innocent man out of jail. Is this how you two intend to spend it? Like two bull seals at the pier?"

"What I intend is for you to go down to the courthouse in the morning and get one more day, Charlotte Reynolds! And I expect that you won't come back here without it."

"So you can spend the day drinking? So you can get so full of Scotch that you pass out in here and leave me to clean up what you can't hold down?"

Cabot's eyes widened and he shook his head. "You don't know what you're talking about. Arthur—"

"Arthur! Arthur thinks the sun rises with you and the moon sets when you say so," Charlotte said testily. "Would your mother let him see you compromised?"

Ash felt, not for the first time, like a stranger in his own house. As if there were rules and rituals that had been kept secret from him and in which he was forbidden to take part. He stood there silent, stupid, watching his brother's marriage unravel.

"And could I let your mother see to you? Could she get you out of your clothes and into your bed? It's time this ridiculousness stopped. You want your annual oblivion, Cabot, you go to the courthouse and have the trial date changed. And then you can lie in your own vomit if you like. I've got more important things to do."

"No one asked you to see to me." Cabot rubbed the spokes of his wheels so fast that Ash could hear them sing in the quiet of the room. "I will get drunk this March twenty-second, just as I have gotten drunk every March twenty-second, and not you, not him," he said pointing at Ash, "not my father, not the entire California court system, is going to stop me."

If they said anything else, Ash didn't hear it.

Just like tumblers in a safe, each gear fell into place in Ash's head and unlocked that part of his heart that hurt like hell. Closing his eyes, he watched it all happening again. But this time he wasn't six years old. This time he understood what it was about his big brother that had frightened him so much that day on the roof.

And in the silence the rage that was bottled in his chest boiled over. He took the few steps that separated him from his brother, and with a yank on Cabot's lapels, Ash lifted him from the very chair he'd always held himself responsible for putting Cabot into.

"You bloody bastard," he said, eye-to-eye with his brother for the first time in their lives. "You were celebrating your birthday, weren't you?" Cabot stared at him, silent, and Ash shook him and shouted into his face. "Weren't you?"

"Ashford, my God! Put him down," he could hear Charlotte saying, but she was far away. Years away. Twenty-two years away.

"All this time," he said, feeling the weight of his brother pulling at his wrists, sagging his shoulders, as the man just hung there, his useless feet at twisted angles, "you let me think it was me, what I did—"

"I always said it wasn't your fault," Cabot answered back, his hands clutching at Ash's arms to keep from falling. "I always told you not to blame yourself."

"And Mother? She let me think—"

"She doesn't know," Cabot said, looking guilty for the first time. "Father didn't think she'd want to know and so he kept it from her. It was an accident no matter how you look at it—to assess blame now . . ."

"You're quite a piece of work, Cabot Whittier. Letting me owe you and owe you, all because you couldn't face the truth yourself. So all along you were the one who couldn't take the responsibility you always accused me of running away from." Ash lowered the older man back into his chair without regard for whether his legs were where they ought to be, and stepped back toward the door. "Well, big brother, I've paid my dues and then some. I don't owe you one damn thing anymore. Not even the time of day."

He could hear Charlotte calling after him but he couldn't stop, not even for her. There was too much anger in him, too much malice. When he claimed her as his own, and he had no doubt he would, he didn't want vengeance crawling into bed with them.

He heard his mother call out to him, too, from the dining room as he went past the door. But he just kept walking. Out the back door and past the carriage house and right on down to the lake.

And even then, he walked on, his shoes soft and wet, his feet icy cold. He walked still, turning to see whether he could see the roofline yet, rising up over the carriage-house weather vane. He was up to his chest in the frigid water before he could see the roof in its entirety.

No ghosts stood on its ridge. No child clung to its ornamental rail.

There were only flowers there, turning their faces to the sun.

Ash hadn't come to luncheon or dinner, and Kathryn finally demanded to know what had caused this latest rift. Charlotte watched as Cabot tried to brush off the whole thing as typical of Ash's overreaction to something that was completely insignificant. Like twenty-two years of guilt.

If Cabot fooled Kathryn, it was only because she was begging him to whip the devil around the stump and he was more than willing to oblige. Kathryn, even as she appeared to accept Cabot's words, still insisted on sending Maria to make sure that Ash was all right. And she appeared less than content with Maria's report that her younger son was huddled with Moss Johnson in the carriage house poring through stacks of paper.

Kathryn told Maria to take off her wet coat and apologized for having sent her out on a wild goose chase in the rain. When the girl was gone, she turned to Cabot. "What do you suppose they could be working on?"

Cabot was quick to answer that between them they hadn't as much sense as a box of rocks, and added that whatever they came up with couldn't be worth more than a hill of beans.

Maria, her hair still damp, rushed to offer Charlotte more peas, managing, as she did so, to drop a note in her lap. *Ask Cabot about the progress on the coffee beans,* it said.

"Speaking of beans," Charlotte said as innocently as she could, "did your man ever find out anything further on Sam Greenbough's sale of those coffee beans?" Of course the note made no mention of love. Wasn't that what they'd agreed? And wasn't Ash just honoring her request? she thought as she balled up the note, covering the noise by rubbing her fork against her plate.

"My *man,* as you call him," Cabot said carefully, "found that the beans were sold in Sacramento for ten times what Greenbough told Ash. He didn't cover his tracks as well as he thought, apparently."

"Well, some people are better than others at hiding things," Charlotte said with equal care. "For years."

*"People in glass houses . . . ,* Charlotte," he started for her, but she wasn't playing.

"I think it would be a sin if someone did something and let someone else take the blame," she said instead.

"You mean Sam Greenbough?" Kathryn asked. She was aligning her silverware with meticulous care.

"I mean that a man who doesn't own up to something

for which he is responsible isn't much of a man," Charlotte said, baiting her husband.

"*What's good for the goose . . .*" he started.

"Are you accusing me of something?" Charlotte asked. Let him spit it out, dammit! Nothing happened in Whittier Court that he didn't know, after all.

"No." He said it firmly, simply, with finality.

Kathryn broke the ensuing silence finally. "Things look very bad for Ash, don't they?"

Cabot nodded. "They do indeed. This may be one fire I can't pull his chestnuts out from."

She'd worked with Cabot until ten, the strain between them palpable as they went over Ash's case from every angle they could think of. They had Greenbough where they wanted him, right in the hot seat. Apparently Sam was convinced that his wife and Ash were involved and that he was "owed" as a result. He'd just been helping himself to his due. Even if it was true, which Ash had assured them it wasn't, and which she, as opposed to Cabot, believed, it gave Sam a motive for setting up Ash.

And then there were the suppliers who were benefiting from the shortages the fire created. She'd outlined them all for Cabot and he'd nodded, so she assumed that they, too, could help, even if Cabot wouldn't say as much.

Provided the police didn't try to pin the second fire on him, Ash had a chance, small, but real, of clearing his name, though she knew he wanted more. Didn't they all want to know who really did it now that Selma had been hurt? Of course, the rest of them weren't facing the blame.

The big hole in their case was that even though Cabot's man had checked out every brothel within a carriage ride of the bay, he'd turned up no one who remembered seeing Ash Whittier that night. Many of them, though, swore they knew him on sight, Cabot was quick enough to tell her, as if to say he'd told her just what kind of man his brother was.

He was the kind of man who'd let a one-eared rabbit share his sleeping quarters, while Cabot would banish it to unseen realms. The kind of man who would bring her gifts and pay her compliments and hope she was happy and do what he could to make her so. She had already learned what kind of man Ashford Whittier was, and it made her all that much more desperate to find a way to prove him innocent.

When she'd tried once again to broach the subject of herself and Ash, Cabot had thrown up his hands and admitted that they weren't getting anywhere. He'd told her she was tired and sent her off to bed like an errant child who had tricked him into letting her stay up late by inventing a problem where there had been none before. In the way he always did with her, with silence, with deaf ears, with unseeing eyes, he also made it abundantly clear that he did not wish to discuss or hear about her relationship with his brother.

And so she'd brought her notes with her to her bedroom to try yet another way to see what it was that they had missed that would prove to the world what she already knew about the gentle man who left a flower on her chair each morning, who put one of Mrs. Mason's cookies by her bed each night. But sitting by the window and watching the candles flicker in the carriage house hadn't brought any of the answers she needed.

She waited for Cabot and Arthur's voices to fade, heard the servant bid his master good-night, and listened for the door next to hers shut tight. If he called out to her tonight, asked her into his room, she would simply ignore him. Pretend she was asleep. Wish she were dead.

The rap was faint at first, dismissible. Coward that she was, she climbed into her bed and hid from it. A stronger tap sent her head beneath the pillow.

Faint though it was, she could still hear his voice calling her name.

"Yes?" she said finally, sitting up on her bed and hugging her pillow against her chest. "Did you need me, Cabot?"

"I just wanted to tell you not to worry," he shouted through the wall. "Get a good night's rest and we'll tackle the problem in the morning."

Warily her body came back to itself—her shoulders let go of her ears, her toes uncurled, her heart returned to beating. And with all of that came a calm she couldn't remember feeling in all of her adult life.

Cabot wouldn't ask to touch her again. She was sure of it.

"Charlotte? This *is* what you want, isn't it?" he asked in the silence she had left to him.

"Yes," she called back to him. "Thank you, Cabot."

Relief flowed through the wall, and she wondered which of them felt it more.

"Good night, then," he said more softly.

"Good night," she agreed, pushing her bare feet into the slippers by her bed and reaching for her robe before she quietly pried open her door and ventured out into the dark hall.

"What about some target other than us?" Ash asked Moss, grasping at straws that turned to dust in his hand. "Maybe someone whose business would be hurt when they didn't get their stock. If we presume for a minute that the target wasn't me, or G and W—"

The carriage house door opened a crack, and he signaled for Moss to be silent. While Cabot's chair could never make it to the outbuilding through the mud, one couldn't be too careful. He was not about to put his fate into his brother's hands again.

A tiny head peeked around the door. "Davis?" he asked. Would Cabot have sent Davis to spy on them? Davis was surely bright and would do anything for Cabot, still . . .

"Ash?" Even with a quiver in it her voice was unmistakable.

"Charlotte? What are you doing out here in the middle of the night?" he asked, as if he hadn't had on his mind the thought that maybe, just maybe, she'd come to him again, despite everything. "Moss is here," he warned.

"Are you working on your case?" she asked softly, stepping out into the light to glow there like some angel. "Can I help?"

"Come and sit down," he said, pulling himself from the stupor her presence always seemed to put him in. "Moss, give her a blanket. It's damn . . . I mean it's a little cold out here."

"Mmm," she agreed with that Cheshire-cat smile he found so irresistible. "*Damn* cold."

He could have sent Moss home, but he wasn't looking for one night with Charlotte. He was looking for a lifetime together, and if he had to sacrifice tonight, well, so be it.

"I'm thinking that we could be looking at this all wrong," he told her over his shoulder, figuring it would be better not to look temptation in the face—not when it had lips like that and when the top two buttons of her nightgown seemed to be—he caught his mind on a hook and reeled it back in. "What if they were actually trying to ruin someone else's business with the fires—or even just the first fire—and were using the second fire as a cover-up?"

It was a thin rope to hang on to, more like a slender

thread, but it was a direction to work in, and Lord knew he needed some hope, no matter how slim.

"Have you gone over the inventory that was lost?" she asked, pulling her chair up behind his and Moss's so that she could look over their shoulders at the lists they were making. Beside each name was a symbol Moss would recognize, and then a drawing of what it was they'd imported for that particular company. There were bottles, kegs, piles of rice, trees . . . or maybe those were pineapples. "I was thinking—did you lease any of the space to anyone else? Or maybe were you holding any merchandise for anyone? I think it's not very likely that those poor people who died were the target, do you? What about—"

"Whoa," he said. "If you're going to ask such good questions, you better be willing to wait for some answers."

"It's about time you took some interest in your defense," she said, getting up onto her knees and leaning against him to reach a pad and pencil.

He turned, and her face was inches from his own, lit by the lamp to an enthusiastic glow that could warm all of Oakland even on a night like this. "Oh, Charlie my love. We're gonna win this case. We've got to. I've too much riding on it now. And so do you."

Each prospect he and Moss offered seemed more far-fetched than the last, but she didn't rule any of them out and offered one or two of her own. *Could someone have been after Greenbough? How about those crazy temperance zealots? Could they have been after the Cuervo?*

Moss was snoring lightly by around midnight, and noisily by one. At two Ash roused him and sent him on home, lists of possibilities for him to investigate stuffed in every one of his pockets. And then he turned around to watch Charlotte, hunched by the lamp, still scribbling, stopping for a moment to arch her back and stretch out her shoulders and arms.

If there was a more beautiful woman on the entire planet, Ash had never seen her, and he'd looked awfully hard, back in his old days, before this morning in Cabot's office when the world had righted itself and his demons had been washed away.

He didn't even hate his brother anymore, though he'd only trust the man as far as he could walk. If history meant anything, Cabot had a strong sense of self-preservation, and Ash didn't doubt that it probably extended to Charlotte as well. Charlie Russe could drive a man to steal, to cheat. It was what she had Ash doing, after all, lying to his brother, stealing the man's wife. It was what she had Cabot doing, lying to himself, cheating his wife out of love itself.

And his Charlie—caught in the middle by none of her own doing.

"Tired?" he asked, coming up behind her and rubbing her neck. "Should I walk you back to the house?"

She shook her head and put her pen down. Her first finger and her thumb were nearly black with ink, and she rubbed at them with her other hand.

"Then what is it you want, Charlie Russe?" he asked her, planting a kiss atop her head. While he had loved that chestnut mane, had wanted her from the moment he'd run his fingers through it, he hoped she'd never let it grow out again—so incredibly intimate was it to touch, and kiss, and nuzzle the short little locks. "Why are you still here?"

She twisted around on her chair awkwardly, her body obviously cramped from sitting on her knees all these hours, and turned her little face up to him. "I want to spend as much time as I can with you now," she admitted, her lip trembling as she fought off tears. "I'm so scared that you could get convicted. Ash, I won't be able to live with it. If you have to go to prison . . ."

"No one's putting me away," he said, pressing her head

against his chest and rubbing at her back. Another minute of this and he'd break down and kiss her again, touch her. Another night of this and he'd take her, love her. "Let me take you back to the house now."

"No," she begged him, her words dancing against his skin beneath his shirt. "Let me stay with you longer. Don't make me go back."

"If I don't—" he began. He knew the catch in his throat and the ragged breath that ruffled her hair told her what would happen.

"Let me stay," she begged him again, and again, one tiny little stream of pleas against the boulder of his resistance. It was how the great canyons were made, and he was surely no stronger. Hadn't he told his brother he owed him nothing? Hadn't he meant it?

He allowed himself to taste her lips, lick the salty wetness of her tears away. He permitted himself the luxury of running his fingers across her soft cheeks, tracing her jaw, and trailing down her neck.

"Charlie," he said softly, the words getting lost in her neck, the edge of her gown, the perfume of her skin, "you should go now. You'll be sorry tomorrow."

"Tomorrow the world could end," she said, unbuttoning her gown until he could see the slight curve of her breasts through the opening. "And I don't want to die without knowing you love me."

"You already know that." He put his hands on her shoulders, massaging them and keeping her nightgown where he knew it belonged. "And what if the world doesn't end? What then?"

"Are you afraid I'll be sorry tomorrow if we do something here tonight?" she asked, the shoulder of her gown slipping and neither of them stopping it as it rolled down her arm. "Because I'm afraid I'll be sorry for the rest of my life if we don't."

"Honey," he said as she reached up and wound her arms around his neck, drawing him down toward her, drawing him in, holding him down beneath the surface with her until they were both drowning, "it's not something you'll be able to take back. Not something you can just tell yourself didn't happen."

"You don't want to make love to me?" she asked, pulling back while those huge hazel eyes searched his face. "Is that it?"

"I don't want to hurt you," he said, unable to stop himself from running his hands down her arms and dragging her gown along with them. As much as she wanted him, he wanted her that much more. But not at the price she'd have to pay if she thought she was doing wrong. "Ever."

"Is it going to hurt?" she asked, the slightest wince crossing her face.

He let go of her gown and backed away from her, letting a moan escape through his lips. He hadn't meant hurt her physically. Somehow he'd managed to forget about it being her very first time, had forgotten the fact that she was a virgin bride.

Her face fell. "That much?" she asked, and her throat bobbed as she swallowed.

Had he ever been with a woman for her first time? He didn't recall and couldn't believe it was something he'd forget. He shrugged his shoulders. "I've heard that it does," he answered honestly.

"But you've . . ." she said, those wide eyes melting places he didn't realize had ever hardened.

"Yes, I've made love," he admitted. "Too many times to too many women."

"Did it hurt them?" she asked, not seeming to be troubled by the fact that he'd actually done everything Cabot had ever accused him of—and then some.

"It only hurts once," he said. "Just the first time."

She ran her tongue over her bottom lip, thinking. "So then this must be your first time too," she said, uncoiling her body and stepping down from the chair. "The first time that it was for the first time."

Somehow it cleansed him just to be with her, as if her very breath could blow away his sins.

"Are you sure this is what you want?" he asked. "It can only be your first time once, and if I do get convicted, if I get sent away . . ."

"I want my first time to be with you. I want every time to be with you." She shook her shoulders slightly and the white gown billowed about her and fell to the ground around her feet. "And if you do get convicted, then I want my only time to have been with you."

Her words were eloquent, moving. But the sight of her there, some sprite rising from the dirt floor—that was beyond all words.

He put out his hand to her and she grasped it tightly with warm fingertips. Willingly, she followed him to the bed, let him lift her and place her down gently on the cot, let him stare down at her nakedness while he pulled his shirttails from his pants and hurried out of his shirt.

It was a wonder to him that the world didn't stop revolving at the sight of her—that judges and lawyers continued their business when she was present in the courtroom, that merchants could still show their wares when she entered their shops, that butchers could speak with her about meat or tailors about clothes.

His world stood still.

While he turned his back and shimmied out of his trousers, she shifted onto her side and moved toward the far edge of the cot, making room for him. Looking over his shoulder he saw her fuss with the pillow, run her hand over the sheet, and bite at her bottom lip.

"Don't be afraid," he said, lowering himself to the cot and pulling her against him.

"I'm afraid *for* you," she admitted, shifting to fit snugly against him. "But not *of* you. I could never be afraid of you."

It was tight on the bed, but she was a tiny thing, and he rolled her onto her back and lay on his side, running his hands over her breasts, her belly, her thighs. In turn she touched his chest, and for a while he thought she was counting his ribs. He bent his head and kissed her lips, letting his tongue hint at what his manhood would do when she was ready.

All the while she continued to trace his ribs, but he had the feeling she was losing count often and starting over.

He drifted from her lips to her neck, from her neck to her collarbone. From there he traced with his tongue down the center of her chest and made a sharp left turn to grasp a small nipple between his lips.

She moaned softly.

Clearly she had lost count.

The skin on her thigh was satin smooth as he inched his way toward her femininity, the circles he made getting ever closer to her curls, until his fingers were tangled in them and the heel of his hand pressed softly against her belly.

He felt the change in her and attributed it at first to fear. "I won't hurt you," he promised, his fingers creeping lower, seeking out her treasures for them both to share.

Her breathing was tight, her muscles tensed.

"Charlie? Do you want me to stop?" He held his breath waiting for the answer, knowing before she said it what was to come.

"I'm so sorry," she said, sitting up and pulling away from him. "I love you, Ash. I do. With all my heart and soul. But I'm his wife. I married him for better and for worse. Forsaking all others."

Tears were streaming down her cheeks as she blindly felt around beside the bed. Reluctantly he handed her the gown she sought and turned his back while she donned it. "He's not a husband to you, Charlotte," he said, his voice coming out more harshly than he intended.

"You're right," she said, laying one of those tiny hands on his shoulder. "But it doesn't make me less a wife."

"Even Kathryn thinks you've a right to some happiness," he said as he covered her hand, now cold, with his own.

"Do you know the truth? I think even Cabot would agree with that," she said with a sad little laugh. "I think he'd be relieved."

"We'd all be relieved," he said, shifting his weight slightly. "It's a marriage in name only, Charlotte. You never even saw a priest, did you?"

"I'm married in the eyes of the law."

"And I may just be found guilty in the eyes of the law. That doesn't make it so, Charlotte. That doesn't make it real."

"It's real enough," she said, looking around. "So real, it hurts."

"No matter what we do, I seem to promise you pain, don't I?"

She looked around again, embarrassed about something.

"What is it?" he asked, standing and looking down at her. "You can tell me."

She chewed at her lip for a moment and then shrugged up at him. "I still want to spend the night here, with you . . . without . . ."

*That's it, Charlie Russe—don't just plunge the knife in to the hilt. Twist it.*

"Wrap yourself in the blanket," he instructed her, helping tuck it in around her. He didn't want to come in contact with an inch of that silky skin, even by accident. "And scoot over. More."

She was nearly off the edge of the cot when he finally eased himself down onto the bed.

He waited through the tears, through the ragged breaths and the sighs, until her breathing evened out and he was absolutely certain she was asleep. And when he was sure, he took her into his arms and held her and let his own tears soak the pillow beneath their heads.

# Chapter 21

One minute she was in heaven, and the next she was in hell. At least that was how it seemed to Charlotte as she'd made her way back to the house just before dawn. Waking up in Ash's arms, seeing his face before even the ceiling came into view—well, everyone knew if wishes were stars, the night would be as bright as the day. What life could be!

And then she'd sneaked up to her silent lonely room and crawled into her cold bed, Cabot just on the other side of the wall. This was her life, for now and for always, it seemed.

She wished that she could just discuss it all with Cabot, thrash it out like it was one of their cases, ask him what he thought and seek out his advice. But how could she ask her husband what she should do?

She wished she could tell him how she felt when she was with Ash. How there were bows and ribbons on her every thought. How the air was crisper, the sun warmer, the world kinder, just because he was there. And when he smiled!

Not exactly the sort of thing one's husband wanted to hear about his brother.

There was a piece of her that honestly believed that Cabot would be happy for her—that he'd tell her to leave the old coot and go after some happiness.

And it was just that piece, that man, that would keep her in her bed swearing she'd never go out to the carriage house and betray him again.

All the while she dressed in the clothes that Cabot had chosen for her, she thought about what she'd given up. It had seemed so little at the time. Children. Physical love. A hand to hold and a shoulder to cry on.

She brushed her hair, thinking about what she'd gained. The respect of an entire community. The ability to make a difference. A precious friend in Kathryn. A partner for life.

She hugged the poster of her bed and rapped her head gently against it several times in the hope of juggling her brains back into working order and knocking some sense into her head.

The noise continued even after she stopped.

"Señora Charlotte?" Rosa's soft voice called through the door. "You are in?"

"I am in," she answered. "Deep."

Rosa opened the door a foot or so and poked her head into the room. With the door open Charlotte could hear Cabot's voice drifting up from the front hall. She caught a word here and a word there, but the tone told her enough.

"Thank you, Rosa," she said, hurrying past the maid and rushing down the stairwell.

In the foyer with Cabot were two uniformed policemen

and the district attorney, who held several papers in his hand.

"What took you so damn long?" Cabot was asking Brent. "I expected you here before the ashes were cool to revoke his bail."

Brent didn't look as pleased as Charlotte would have expected. "Just waiting for the charge," he said, looking up at Charlotte and then gesturing toward Cabot's office. "It might be best if we—"

"Whatever it is," she said, coming to stand next to Cabot, "I want to know. If Mr. Whittier is in more trouble—"

Brent nodded. "He surely is. But it's not just that, ma'am. I'm afraid I've some bad news for you. You might want to sit down."

She stood her ground, all Cabot's training holding her upright when all she wanted to do was collapse in a heap on the floor. "What is it?"

Brent exhaled hard enough to raise the dust Rosa had missed on the hall tree. One of Liberty's feathers flew up off the glove box and came spiraling down slowly while they all looked on in silence.

Charlotte held out her hand for the summons, but Brent handed it to Cabot. "I'll just have him out again this afternoon," Cabot said, but there was no muscle behind his words.

And if she had any doubts about just how bad it was, the fact that Brent nodded rather than argued latched the lock for her. Reaching over, she tried to take the summons from Cabot, but his fingers refused to release it. She pulled harder, until he finally shrugged and let go so abruptly that she nearly lost her balance.

She was familiar enough with summonses to cut right to the heart of the matter with one glance. *The People of the State of California* were arresting Ashford Warren Whittier for the murder of Selma Mollenoff.

Selma was dead.

"I was going to see her this morning," Charlotte said to no one in particular, "after we got some work done on Ash's case. I was going to stop at court on the way over to the hospital and get a date for Virginia's case so I'd be able to tell her. I was going to bring her a bouquet of Liberty's feathers in that lovely bottle Ash brought me from South America. And I was going to tell her about the letter from Clara Foltz."

No one said anything.

"You can't think that Ash would ever have hurt Selma," she told Brent. "He was going to start reading *Little Lord Fauntleroy* to her this morning. He was the one to give her a job when no one else would. Remember, Cabot, how everyone said she was a troublemaker and they didn't want their women roused?"

"They're going to take him in," Cabot said softly. His mother was just coming down the stairs and he motioned for the officers to move back toward the door. "He's out in the carriage house," he told them.

"You aren't going to let them," Charlotte said, coming down hard on her knees by Cabot's side. "Cabot, he's free on bail. Tell them. Tell them he's been remanded to your custody."

"It's a capital offense, Charlotte," Cabot said, his hand touching her wayward locks. "Bail is revoked and further bail will surely be denied."

On the stairwell Kathryn's cane rapped softly. "But you will see him found innocent, won't you?" she asked, holding the banister so tightly that her knuckles were white.

"I'll do my best to see him found not guilty," Cabot corrected. "But I'm a lawyer, Mother, not a miracle worker."

"Selma dead. Poor Eli!" Kathryn said, sinking down to the third step as if it were her chair. "Charlotte, tell Arthur I'll need the carriage brought around and someone to drive me to Dr. Mollenoff's. Where's Maria? I'll need something baked right away to bring with me. And Rosa can come and serve. What is it they call a Jewish wake? A cold?"

"Shivah," Charlotte said. "Appropriate, isn't it?"

"Well, I wonder what Eli will think of his God now," Cabot said.

Kathryn, who had gotten up with Charlotte's help and then turned around on the steps, heading back up, paused. "I don't want to see my son taken from here," she said, more to herself than to Charlotte and Cabot. She shook her head, slowly took a few more steps, and then called over her shoulder. "Cabot, see that he's released in time for supper."

Cabot chewed at the corner of his mustache. "Of what year?" he mumbled, shaking his head at his mother's back.

"Ash and Moss were working on some new possibilities," Charlotte said, positioning herself so that she could see through the dining room windows even though she remained in the vestibule.

"Really?" Cabot's eyebrows lifted slightly. "When was this?"

"Last night," she said. "After you went to sleep."

"Yes, I thought I heard you three talking down here after I went up. What did those two legal beagles sniff out?"

"It was very late, Cabot," she said softly. "In the carriage house."

"And then they came back here and told you what they'd come up with," he insisted. "What was it?"

Cabot Whittier was a complicated man, but he was

nobody's fool. He believed nothing that he didn't choose to believe, of that Charlotte was certain.

"Charlotte?"

"Hmm?" If he wished so clearly to remain in the dark, was it fair for her to turn up the lights?

"Lawyers do not daydream, Charlotte. Daydreaming doesn't win cases." She supposed he didn't understand that dreams were all that were left to her.

"Can we win this, Cabot?" she asked, watching for Ash to emerge from the carriage house with the men who had gone in after him.

"Win it, Charlotte?" he answered. "We'll be lucky to survive it."

"Would it be all right if we just stopped off at the main house for a moment?" Ash asked the district attorney, who'd reluctantly agreed to let him get into his clothing as one of the men opened the box Moss had left on his dresser.

"Your lawyers can visit you in jail," Brent said, signaling the officers to get going.

"Can you give my brother a message for me, then?" he asked as they put his hands behind his back and fastened his wrists together. Brent was right. Kathryn wouldn't want to see him like this. And Charlotte . . . All he wanted was to keep Charlotte out of the sordid details of his past, to keep her safe, separate. "Can you tell him I don't want some woman defending me? Tell him to keep his wife at home and do the job himself, or I'll get myself some other lawyer."

She'd hate him for shutting her out. But he was going down and he wasn't going to take her with him to the bottom, or allow her to be there to watch him go under.

*I want you to be my first. My only.*

He was grateful they'd stopped when they had. No good ever came from opening up someone else's gift.

He was glad. Hell, maybe someday he would be anyway. When he was too old to remember what had really been between them.

# Chapter 22

"Look," he said as they stood in the lobby of the courthouse, two guards watching his every move. "She's said herself a million times that no judge takes her seriously—"

Cabot, like the rest of them, was caught between a rock and a hard place. Not that Ash gave a damn where Cabot was caught, just so long as Charlotte was kept out of it.

"And you?" Charlotte asked, just the hint of a quiver in her voice. She might have been looking at him. He supposed she was, from the way his skin warmed and his bones went soft. But he kept his eyes riveted to his brother at all costs. "Don't you take me seriously?"

"Well, you might be able to do some good outside the courtroom," he said as casually as he could without risking a look her way. "There are the notes Moss and I left in the carriage house, if you want to go through them."

"Maybe I ought to take a look at them," Cabot said, his

eyes shifting to Charlotte with no thought for what Ash would give to study her face just one more time.

"At least it's something I can do to help you," she said. "But don't think I don't know why you're doing this."

Even laced with pain she had the loveliest voice he'd ever heard—somehow it was strong, yet soft. Or maybe it was soft, yet strong. He concentrated on what the difference was, if any, while he studied the floor beneath them.

God, but it hurt to stand there as if she meant nothing to him. He watched her shadow on the floor and studied the curve of her cheek, the tilt of her nose, the way her new short hair capped her head beneath her hat.

"You find anything that might help me, Cabot?" he asked, still studying the floor. There were sixteen pieces of black marble in a square around her shadow. Within the sixteen black tiles were eight white. Her shadow fell across six of them. In the center was another black tile about where her heart would be. He moved slightly so that his foot could touch the shadow of her hem while his brother cleared his throat.

"A host of things," Cabot said unconvincingly. "Myriad lines of defense. And a suspect to throw at the jury, to boot." One wheel of his chair was lined up perfectly against the edge of the black marble. The other missed by several inches. The imperfection of it must have irritated him to no end.

But not as much as seeing just the tip of Charlotte's brown kid boots was bothering Ash.

"I heard this brother of mine is thinking of taking you on a vacation when this whole mess is over," he said as cheerily as he could, allowing himself to look in her direction for just the quickest moment.

She'd been crying. Her eyes were red rimmed and her nose matched them well.

"Where might you go?" he asked. He liked the thought

of her on a ship sailing to the South Seas, where she would drink milk from coconuts and turn brown from the sun.

She looked at the watch on her breast. His eyes followed. Through the brown wool jacket, through the starched white shirtwaist, through the underthings beneath that, he could still see the contour of her breast, feel the slight weight of it in his hand, taste its sweetness on his lips.

He groaned and pulled his eyes from her.

"I thought perhaps Chicago," Cabot said. "Or St. Louis." He pronounced the *s* at the end.

"Chicago?" he said, nearly choking on the word. "Why the hel—" He caught himself. None of his business anyway. He surely couldn't offer her anything better, now, could he? Chicago beat visiting him in prison, if only by a little.

"There's a seat on the Federal bench opening up there," Cabot said. "And another in St. Louis."

"Well," Ash said, swallowing hard. She'd be hundreds of miles away. Thousands. The air he breathed would never have touched her first to carry a kind thought to him. He risked another look at her. "At least there'd be one judge on the bench who took you seriously. Even if it is in Chicago."

"Better than Wyoming, don't you think?" Cabot asked. "Though from what Charlotte tells me, they'd welcome anyone to the bench there—even her!"

"You'd get your vote there, anyway," Ash said, looking only at the top of her head.

"Time!" one of the clerks told Cabot. "Judge is coming in now."

Cabot nodded. "Ready?" he asked Ash.

"You might as well go pay our respects to Eli, Charlotte," Ash said.

"Oh, but I—" she began in the voice that he heard with his heart.

"Tell him how sorry I am. Not that—you know what I mean. Tell him I'd like to find the man who did this to Selma and watch him swing from the end of a noose."

"I know." That voice again.

He wished she wouldn't say another word. And he wished she'd never stop speaking.

"Please let me come in."

"We can't stop you from sitting in the back," Cabot said, already beginning to wheel himself toward the courtroom doors. "But if the client doesn't want you at the table, there's nothing I can do."

Ash made room for her to pass and as she did, she touched him. All right, perhaps it wasn't even a touch—perhaps her skirts merely brushed against his leg—still he felt her softness one last time.

"Don't be part of this," he begged, his voice so low that only she could hear.

"I won't get in Cabot's way of defending you," she said. "But don't think I won't be doing everything I can."

"It's not your fight," he said, bending down to tie laces that didn't need retying so that Cabot would get farther and farther ahead of them. "Stay out of it."

She looked down at him with her tiny breasts heaving, so that he could only see part of her face. "Cabot's right," she said, stepping on his lace as he rose so that this time it was truly undone. "You are an idiot."

She crossed in front of him, nearly knocking him off balance, just as the guards who had kept their eyes on him from the distance came to escort him to the defense table.

He stood, straightening his jacket and vest, his tie. He checked the cuffs of his shirt to see that they looked presentable, and then stole one last glance at the woman he couldn't bear to see witness his debacle.

She was sitting with her arms crossed over her chest in the very last row. Seething.

Davis stood against the wall in Dr. Mollenoff's parlor and watched as the old women threw black cotton cloths over the mirrors. He watched as they pulled out small stools and fussed with platters of food that made his mouth water.

He was ashamed to think of food when Miss Mollenoff was dead, but he'd left his breakfast on the table when the news came spreading down the street hours ago, and he hadn't eaten since.

Old Mrs. Whittier had shown up around eleven or so. She'd been surprised that the doc wasn't there, but she'd rolled up her fancy sleeves and joined right in with the other ladies, ordering him around, telling him to go here and go there and do this and do that. He didn't mind much, though, since it gave him something to do.

He wasn't really sure why he was even there, except that the doc had been good to him. And then again, he sure didn't want to be home when his da got back. Not the way he'd been carrying on since Miss Mollenoff had been taken to the hospital. Davis was pretty sure from the looks of them that his father had broken a couple of fingers when he'd slammed his fist against the wall.

"Put this just outside the door," Old Lady Whittier told him, pointing to a small table covered in more of that thin black cloth.

He pointed toward the door and cocked his head. Whyever did she want the table outside?

"I've no idea," she whispered with a shrug, and gestured with her head toward the old women. "They said it had to go outside. And they want a basin with some water there too."

He wiped his hands on his pants. The doc's side table was a real nice one, with turned legs and carved roses around its edges. Miss Mollenoff was always rearranging the gewgaws on it and the doc was always telling her to leave his books where they were. Davis backed away from the table and right smack into the old woman, nearly knocking her over.

"Take it outside," Mrs. Whittier told him. "And put a towel out there too."

*A towel? Was someone gonna bathe out there?*

"And don't argue."

Was he arguing? He hadn't said a word. He didn't suppose anyone was going to tell him where the doc's towels were kept.

Like it had a dozen eggs upon it, he lifted the table carefully, moved it a few inches, and put it down. It wasn't all that heavy, there was no question he could move it, he just didn't want to bang it into any walls or anything.

"I'll help you," a young woman said, and took up the other side of the table. She was dressed like the older women but she didn't seem to Davis to be more than fifteen or sixteen. Except maybe around her eyes, where she looked a lot older.

He took a deep breath in the hopes of spilling out all his words at once, but by the time he was ready to answer, she had the table halfway out the door. As fast as he could he wiped his hands dry and grabbed on to the opposite side, more trouble than help, he supposed. Carefully they set the little table down together, and she went after a bowl while he searched around the kitchen for a towel.

"He deserves better," the girl said, sniffing back her tears while Davis put the cloth beside the bowl just as the doc's carriage pulled up at the front stoop. Dr. Mollenoff came out of the carriage slowly, his steps even heavier than they usually were—and that seemed like he had lead in his boots.

Two men, all in black like the women, with hats and overcoats and solemn faces, hurried down from the coach and stood by the doctor's side while more men—there were two carriages full of them—escorted him up the stairs and waited while he washed his hands in the water the girl had put there for him and then dried them on the towel Davis had found.

"So you're learning the rules of shivah?" the doc said to Davis, cupping his chin and twisting his head gently this way and that, as if Davis's bruises were the only thing on his mind. "Ach. Does it hurt much? No?" The doc shrugged and moved slowly toward the door. "Later we'll have to see to that cut."

Behind the doctor each man stopped to wash his hands before they, too, went into the house.

Davis followed them, dipping his hands quickly in the water and wiping them on the damp towel. Before he did it, washing seemed like a pretty dumb thing to do, but when he walked into the house clean, it made him feel good. He could almost remember his mama's voice telling him that cleanliness was next to godliness.

He took up a position against the back wall, as far from the happenings as possible, and closed his eyes. Around him, men and women cried and he felt the tears well up in his own eyes too. Because his mother had been swallowed by the sea, there'd been no body for the wake. Miss Mollenoff was already buried, so here again, there was no way for him to say good-bye. And a ride up to Mountain View on the horsecar would cost him a dime, which was ten cents more than he had.

Across the room he saw Charlotte and fought the urge to run to her. He was too old to bury his face in some woman's skirts. Even if the woman was an aggie. He didn't know when Charlotte had slipped into that pile, only that she was there, like his ma. One of the ones you just wouldn't think of trading. Sometimes though, like with his ma and Miss Mollenoff, the "keepers" got stolen away.

"Ah, that's the *Yortzeit,*" some man in black said softly to him, pointing to a candle that the doc was lighting. "That will burn for seven days. All through shivah. You remember that."

*Shivah. Yortzeit.* It was a stupid religion that had words that sounded like sneezes, but he kept the thought to himself.

He was keeping more than ever to himself these days.

Charlotte waited for the candle-lighting ceremony to be over before seeking out Kathryn. She was certainly in no hurry to tell the woman how court had gone that morning. Bail revoked. Bail denied. Just as Cabot had said. And jury selection to start the next morning.

Without her.

Not only didn't he want her at the defense table, he didn't want her in the courtroom. *Bring her again,* he'd told Cabot as the guards were taking him back to his cell, *and I'll change my plea to guilty.*

Cabot had just nodded.

And she had had to stand there as if her heart weren't bleeding on the floor, as if Ash's were just another case, as if she didn't know that he was trying to protect her.

Not ten minutes later a clerk informed her that Virginia Halton's case had finally been scheduled. Oral arguments would be heard at ten the next morning.

Of course, Cabot could have made that happen all along. He'd chosen now to get her out of the way. And if that was the way he and Ash wanted it, that was the way it would be.

Kathryn was busy with Eli, her hand on his arm as she spoke. Eli was nodding at whatever it was she was telling him, and he stopped to lift a stray hair away from Kathryn's eye.

It was nothing. An innocent gesture. And yet it was so intimate that the breath burned in Charlotte's throat.

"Want some?" Davis asked, appearing suddenly at her side and holding out a glass of wine to her. When she took it, he wrinkled up his nose a bit and rolled his eyes. "Kosher," he warned.

She took a small sip. The wine was thick and sweet, and felt heavy on her lips. It coated her tongue and she felt it inch down her throat and disappear.

"The mister?" Davis asked after a big intake of air. Cabot was making great progress with the boy. For a second she wondered if Davis would like to have Liberty.

Wonderful. She already had Ash tried, convicted, hanged, and was giving away his things. The reality smacked her hard enough to snap her head back. Frantically she gulped for air. Davis, clearly alarmed, nearly pushed her into a chair while people looked on sympathetically, most of them in tears themselves.

Selma was dead. Sweet, tough Selma, who wasn't afraid of anything. Even in the hospital she was more worried about the contributions for "the cause," as she called it, than she was about herself.

"Are you all right, dear?" Kathryn asked, Eli having left to go off with nine other men to pray. "Was court an awful scene?"

"Kathryn," she said, taking the woman's hand in her own, "things look very bad."

"Cabot will take care of it," Kathryn said, refusing to look at Charlotte. "He always has and he always will."

"I'm sure he'll do his best," Charlotte agreed.

At that Kathryn raised an eyebrow. "Of course he will. Why wouldn't he?"

"Excuse me," a young girl said, bending over with a tray of food for Charlotte and Kathryn. "Aren't you Mrs. Whittier, the lawyer?"

Charlotte nodded, for all the good being a lawyer did her. He'd banned her from the courtroom! Her courtroom, to which she'd fought so hard to be admitted.

"Oh, Miss Mollenoff just thought the world of you! And now your husband's brother has gone and . . . I mean . . . not that you can be blamed for that . . . It's just . . . Well, it's really nice of you to come, considering . . ."

"I thought the world of Miss Mollenoff too," Charlotte said. "As did my brother-in-law. And Ashford Whittier wouldn't hurry a squirrel out of his way, much less hurt a woman. I hope you'll remember that, despite anything you hear."

Charlotte wondered how many times over the course of the next few weeks she'd have to say those same words. And whether there would ever come a time when everyone would know that Ash had had nothing to do with either fire. Even Cabot had wondered after the first fire—not that she felt he was justified. But the second fire had to have convinced Cabot, and everyone else, that a man like Ash wouldn't have risked hurting Selma for any amount of money.

"Are you a friend of hers?" Charlotte asked the girl.

"I know the doctor," she answered, her cheeks reddening while she busied herself examining the little fish balls on the platter she held. "He—"

Charlotte stopped her. She didn't want to know what Eli had or hadn't done, or which one of the women this young girl was. Was she the one whose father had brought her to him bleeding and near death from another doctor's attempt to rid her of a problem? Was she the one who had punctured herself with a coat hanger? Was she the one who had swallowed a bottle of Nature's Own in the hopes of helping nature take the course she wanted it to?

"He's a good man," the girl said. "A good doctor."

Charlotte agreed wordlessly.

"Still, he's lucky to have a minyan today to say Kaddish," she said, pointing to the group of men who stood rocking on their heels and mumbling. "In our faith it takes ten men to pray for deliverance."

In Ash's case it would take twelve men—a jury—to give him the same.

Hell. That was where he was. And if he'd ever thought he was there before, he was a fool.

Oh, the look on her face when he said he didn't want her at the defense table! At least, as far back as she was, he couldn't see her face when they'd started hurling charges at him. Couldn't see her expression when the district attorney brought up his associations with women all over the waterfront who might help him run if he wasn't locked up like some animal. They certainly hadn't been leaping to his defense yet.

He paced off his cell again, making sure it hadn't gotten any smaller in the last few minutes. Twelve steps in one direction. Eight in the other.

What must she have thought of him when Brent pulled out his record and listed the brawls, the public drunkenness, the *lewd and lascivious conduct* charges?

And Cabot! Had his brother used his objections any more sparingly, Ash would have suspected he was sleeping with his eyes open. For all the help he was, his brother might just as well have spent the whole day at home drinking himself into oblivion as he'd planned.

At least Ash had made it clear that Charlotte wasn't to be in the courtroom again. Cut the ties. Let her loose.

Eight feet in one direction, twelve in the other. He took the knife from his dinner tray and scratched one short vertical line into the wall over his cot. And then he lay down on the bed, shut his eyes, and watched the tears course down Charlie Russe's face until he finally fell asleep.

Cabot was waiting in the foyer when Charlotte and Kathryn came through the door. "How were things at Eli's?" he asked.

"Charlotte tells me it didn't go well in court," Kathryn said, ignoring Cabot's question.

"I suppose Eli was beside himself with grief," Cabot responded.

"She says that your defense is tenuous at best." Kathryn allowed Rosa to help her off with her shawl but waved the girl away when she tried to lead her to a chair.

"Was the boy there?" he asked Charlotte. "He was just beginning to like Selma, you know. Said something about her maybe not being an aggie, but still he didn't think he'd trade her."

"An aggie?" Charlotte asked. Cabot and Davis had actually had a real conversation? About Selma Mollenoff? Her Cabot? And Davis? She was too stunned to hear Cabot's answer. "What?" she asked, realizing he'd asked her a question.

"Marbles," he said. "You ever play marbles as a little girl, Charlotte?"

"If you can just get him out on bail again," Kathryn

said, "he could escape to the islands. A person could lose himself there forever, don't you think?"

"I cannot get him out on bail while he is on trial, Mother," Cabot said. "Nor do I relish the thought of my brother as a fugitive from justice."

"Do you suppose he should have run? I mean now, with hindsight?" Charlotte asked him. She wished with all her heart and soul that he had, and more than a small piece of her wished that she had run with him, no matter the cost.

"As I was saying," Cabot said, "aggies are marbles. They're the special ones that no self-respecting marbles shooter ever trades away. They're the ones you don't bet because you feel their loss for a long, long time."

"Then he won't be home tomorrow either?" Kathryn asked, finally sliding down into the chair as if the strength in her legs had deserted her.

"No, Mother. He will not be home tomorrow. Or the next day, or the day after that. He's on trial for murder, and these things take time. You know that. You've seen me through a hundred like cases."

Kathryn took the cup that Rosa held out to her, leaving the girl to hold the saucer. She took a sip of the tea, her eyes keeping contact with Cabot's over the rim. Slowly she replaced the cup without looking down. "None of those involved my son," she said sharply.

A heavy sigh, a brief moment with both eyes closed, and then softly, with a small sad smile curving his lips, Cabot shook his head. "Yes, Mother," he said in answer. "Every one of them did."

After a cold supper that they all just picked at, Charlotte had helped Kathryn up to bed. Reality was hitting Kathryn hard, and Charlotte wasn't sure she had any strength left to lend her mother-in-law. But then she'd helped her to undress and saw the paper-white skin hanging in tiny, empty pleats around the woman's bony frame. Kathryn, with her fine features and lovely silver hair, hadn't been able to cheat time as well as she pretended, and as Charlotte tucked the older woman beneath the covers and kissed her forehead, Kathryn had reached out and clutched Charlotte's hand.

"Promise me you'll do whatever you can," she begged.

Charlotte swore she would, surprised that Kathryn thought she needed to ask.

"Whatever it takes to make Cabot win," she said, gripping Charlotte's hand more tightly. "Whatever that is."

Charlotte agreed to that as well.

"I'll check on you later," she promised Kathryn, then returned to Cabot's office to help him prepare for the next day's voir dire for the jury selection.

He looked up, startled when she came into the room, almost as if he didn't expect her to be there at all. Motioning for her to sit across from him, he put down his pen and rubbed at his forehead.

"Was the boy very upset?" he asked.

"Davis? He seemed to be all right. For a child his age he's had too much practice, don't you think?" she asked.

"His appeal comes up next week," Cabot said, flipping pages on his desk calendar. "I'm going to ask Hammerman for a short recess so that I can argue it."

"Have you any use at all for me?" Charlotte asked. "Perhaps I can carry your briefcase between courtrooms for you."

Cabot gave her yet another sad smile. Each one seemed to cost him, but still he offered them. "We haven't that good a shot at either, Charlie. And you take losing so to heart. Sometimes I'm sorry I ever agreed to any of this.

You were such a happy little thing when you first came here—so full of passion and excitement."

"You may be sorry I'm a lawyer," she said, shocked by his honest assessment of where they had been and where they'd come to, "but I'm not."

"What if you were to lose the boy's case?" Cabot asked. "The last loss cost us your lovely hair. What will be next, Charlie, your little fingers?"

"I'm going to win his case," she said evenly, understanding what she'd done wrong the first time. "You see, it's not the judge I need to convince. It's Ewing Flannigan. He, not the court, is going to give us that boy."

"And if you lose, Charlotte? Can you live with yourself?"

She nodded. "And you, Cabot? If you should lose Ash's case? Can you live with yourself then?"

There it was again, that sad smile. But instead of nodding he shrugged. "The real question, Charlotte, is, if I lose, could *you* still live with me?"

With her heart lodged firmly in her throat she nodded.

"Ah," he said. "That's a comfort."

She rose, ready to say good-night, but turned when Cabot cleared his throat.

"And what if I win?"

She'd already made the promise in her heart. If Cabot wanted her to, she would stay with him forever, forsaking all others just as she had vowed. Anything, to see Ash walk out of the courtroom a free man.

She nodded once again, but this time the sad little smile was hers.

# Chapter 23

The sun was just rising when Charlotte gave up trying to sleep. She threw the covers off and rose to stand by the window from which she had seen Ash watching her. The carriage house looked empty, abandoned, which, of course, it was. There was no smiling Ash, no serious Moss, not even irreverent Liberty, whom Moss was seeing to on the *Bloody Mary*.

She put on her robe and slippers and headed downstairs and out across the lawn for the papers she had promised to look at. Promises. She was good at making them, even better at keeping them, and undoubtedly best at allowing them to strangle her to death.

As she pushed open the door to the carriage house, she took a deep breath. Knowing he wouldn't be there filled her with warring emotions. More than anything she wanted to see him, be held by him, touched by him.

But not at the cost of facing him. The fact that she'd

been banned from the courtroom had become a comfort in its own way. At least she wouldn't have to tell Ash that she had promised to stay with Cabot in exchange for his freedom. Would he understand that Cabot was their last, best hope? That she'd had no choice?

Van Gogh greeted her at the door, happy to see his mistress. She'd resented it when he'd switched allegiances and left her for Ash, only showing up at the kitchen now and then for a free handout. But now—now she resented nothing Ash had ever done. She only regretted what he hadn't done.

The papers were where they'd been left when Moss had gone home and left them alone. Hugging herself, she smiled at the memory. Maybe she shouldn't have stopped him. Maybe they should have made love to each other the whole night long and maybe he should have left his seed inside her to grow.

And then she realized he had planted something inside her after all—in her heart, where her love for him grew every day. And which she knew would stay there until she took it to her grave with her, and even after that.

Beside the papers was a box with a ribbon tied hastily around it. Perhaps it wasn't even meant for her, she warned herself, lifting the box and shaking it gently. "What do you think, Van Gogh?" she asked the rabbit, who was nuzzling her ankles. "Should I open it?"

The last few days had held only sadness for her, and she fondled the box as if its contents were somehow magical and would turn her world around. Her hopes built so quickly and so out of proportion to what could possibly be in the box that she was tempted to put it down and leave it, unable to face another disappointment in her life.

"Go ahead and open it," a deep voice said, and she spun around to find Moss standing in the doorway, Liberty on his shoulder. "It weren't a easy thing to find. But he was determined. The man's a determined man, all right."

"Then it is for me?" she asked, pulling the sash at her waist a bit tighter and making sure she was covered up properly.

"Everything be for you, Miz Whittier," Moss said. "The sun, the moon—the way he tell it, they all for you. But that"—he pointed to the box on the table—"that be especially for you alone."

"He's in big trouble, Moss," she said, fingering the ribbon and watching the bow fall away. "And I don't know how to help him."

"It'll come, ma'am," he said softly. "Some things, it seem there ain't no hope for 'em, and then a miracle happens."

"I don't think we can wait for a miracle," Charlotte said, tears beginning to clog her throat.

"You don't just wait on a miracle, ma'am," he said softly, coming closer and pulling the cover from the box. "Sometimes you gotta help it along."

Charlotte stared down into the box, confused at first. Blinded by tears she thought she saw her mother's teacup nestled in some paper. Her finger traced the rim, smooth as the finest silk against her skin. As carefully as she'd ever lifted her baby birds, her newborn rabbits, her china figurines, she pulled the cup from its surroundings and held it in shaking hands.

Her mother's cup.

Moss was right. Sometimes when there was no hope, a miracle happened.

"You go ahead and have a cry," Moss whispered. "Then we gots lots of work to do before you get on to the court."

* * *

Well, they always said bad news traveled fast, but Ash had never expected to be living proof of it. There didn't seem to be a man in Oakland who hadn't heard about the fires or wasn't familiar with the defendant's *reputation,* as Cabot called it. Ash wished he'd had half the fun that was attributed to him.

His thoughts drifted to Charlotte, as they always did. His worst sins were in his mind, desires that, if a jury knew, would no doubt send him from the gallows to the bottom of the bay.

"And are you familiar with the defendant?" his brother asked yet another man in the jury box.

"Not as familiar as Tess the Whiting," he said, causing chuckles and guffaws around him that egged the man on. "Or Slant-eyed Annie. Or—"

"Thank you," Cabot said, cutting him off. "You seem rather well acquainted with these women yourself. Might make it hard for you to serve as an unbiased juror, don't you agree? I ask that juror twenty-four be excused for cause."

Brent stood, raising a hand to slow down the proceedings. "You ever see these women you mentioned yourself?" he asked the man in the box, who got a bit red faced and blinked in response. "Socially, that is?"

"I ain't on trial," the man said, crossing his arms over his chest.

"Ah, but if you were, you surely wouldn't want someone holding it against you that every now and then—not too often, of course—you might have taken a stroll down the wrong street and been tempted to exchange pleasantries with a pretty young woman intent on keeping the cold away, now, would you?"

"Your Honor!" Cabot groaned. "What Mr. Brent portrays as an act of charity now will no doubt be a heinous sin when it becomes my client who might have once, on some isolated occasion, helped fight the chill of a January evening. I again request the juror be excluded."

"Would you hold it against him?" Brent asked the prospective juror, ignoring Cabot completely. "Or might you even have a little sympathy for a lonely bachelor with no obligations to hold him elsewhere?"

"Your Honor," Cabot again called out, "the district attorney is tainting the entire jury pool. He begs for a mistrial before we've even—"

Judge Hammerman looked at Cabot hopelessly over his half-rims, shrugged as if it were suddenly beyond his powers, and addressed the juror. "You can answer the district attorney's question. Would you hold the fact that the defendant is of questionable moral character against him?"

Cabot threw up both hands as if to ask God Himself what was happening in his courtroom. "Your Honor!" he said, disgust dripping from his words. "Might I approach the bench?"

"You may," Hammerman said, popping the remnants of the lunch he'd been eating since noon into his mouth and talking around it, "but it won't do you a bit of good. I've seen Brent's case, Mr. Whittier. Let's just move on and get it over with. My wife's hoping I'll take her to her sister's in Sacramento for Easter."

Apparently things hadn't been going badly enough. Now Cabot had managed to lose favor with the judge.

"We can at least take heart that Mrs. Whittier won't be here for the details. I don't know how many times I've told that woman she doesn't belong in this courtroom. That a normal woman's sensibilities prohibit—well, we took care of that, anyway. Juror accepted." He raised his gavel and then hesitated. "Unless you want a preemptory—but if it were my brother's head on the block, this isn't the one I'd toss back in the ocean. He's apparently been on the hook once or twice himself."

Ash rested his forehead in his hand. For the better part of his life he'd had all the time in the world and nothing worth doing. Now he had everything to live for, and the real possibility that there'd be no time to do it.

Well, between her case and Cabot's they had filled the courthouse to capacity. Even the courthouse steps were crammed with reporters from the various papers and wire services. They were calling it a double-ender, like those boats that were the same at bow and stern, claiming there was a Whittier at either end of the courthouse.

She couldn't imagine what the street cleaners were charging the city of Oakland to keep the place from looking like a shanty town. Papers littered the lawns around the courthouse. Vendors circled the block selling fresh-baked cookies and washed fruit. A man on the corner shouted verses from the Bible and warned that the wrath of God would be visited upon the earth and to watch for signs of pestilence. With the fruit attracting the flies and the orator threatening plagues, Charlotte thought the end of the world seemed just a courtroom away.

She pushed her way out the courtroom door, grateful that the arguments were over for the day and she'd have time to regroup. Cabot had asked for no help on Ash's case and offered her no pointers on Virginia's. Kathryn said she felt like a messenger sent behind enemy lines wherever she went and whenever she spoke to either of them.

Outside the courtroom, the buzz of the crowd pressed against her until she couldn't make out what anyone was saying. There were some words of praise, she thought, from someone standing too close to her. Others called from farther back for her to be banned from the courthouse along with her client.

"This way," a man said, and grabbed at her just as an egg went sailing past her ear. He yanked on her arm with authority. "I said come this way!"

"I don't care what you said," Charlotte answered, trying to shake him off. "Let go! I'm not—" A tomato hit the wall inches from her.

"Your carriage is waiting out back," he said, turning so that she could get a look at his face. Cabot's private investigator, and apparently he had no patience for the likes of her. "Come on!"

"But I wanted to—" she said, pointing to the courtroom in which her husband was picking twelve men to decide whether Ash would ever hold her again. She doubted that would be exactly the way Cabot might have described the point of the jury selection. Doubted, but didn't rule it out entirely.

"He's already been returned to his cell, Mrs. Whittier," the man said, sending a chill down her spine. Was she so obvious that a stranger knew where her heart was headed? Or did he just mean that court was over for the day? "And your husband's waiting in the coach."

"Let go of my arm," she said, yanking her elbow from his grasp. Something hard thudded against her shoulder, catching the bone and sending an unpleasant tingling down her arm. Yellow slime ran down her brown jacket in a slow rush toward her skirts. If an egg was hard enough to hurt, and it was, why then did it break so easily?

"Oh, he's going to love that," the man said, rubbing against her chest with his sleeve in an attempt to get rid of the evidence. He pushed her against the wall and shielded her as several apples splattered and splintered around them, then shoved her out the back door in front of him, nearly dragging her to the carriage. Arthur helped her up and around Cabot, who pressed her to his far side, all but hiding her with his bulk.

Cabot gave the man a quick nod while Arthur climbed in and shut the door behind him, "Let's go!" he yelled up to the driver, and Charlotte was thrown back against the seat as the horse took off like his tail was on fire.

When they'd cleared the courthouse area and the businesses around them changed to grander and grander estates, Charlotte began to breathe again. Allowing her gaze to meet Cabot's, she found him staring at her with tired, sad eyes. Still, when he sensed her studying him as well, he smiled softly.

"And how was your day?" he asked, reaching into his breast pocket and taking a quick dose of his least favorite bitters. "Things went well for you, too, I trust?"

# Chapter 24

Jury selection took two long days. Days in which Ash, like a dying man, saw his life flashing before him. References were made to his penchant for wine, women, and song, or more accurately Scotch, whores, and bird calls. His business pursuits were bandied about; the fact that he had no real home was noted. While Cabot fought to keep his prior run-ins with the law from the jury, Brent managed to ask potential jurors enough questions about brawls and knives to more than pique their interests and suspicions.

Another full day was spent on what Cabot called opening arguments. Ash dubbed them eulogies, and much preferred Cabot's to Brent's, though the man the district attorney described was far more interesting (and an awful lot closer to Ash) than the paragon of virtue (who read stories to his mother and mended wounded animals) Cabot's client was portrayed to be.

The meat of the trial started on Friday, with the prosecution's case. By lunch even Ash was convinced he'd set two fires and killed four people, one of whom he regularly had dinner with.

"I know it looks bad," Cabot told him as they shared a lunch from home in a small locked room in the courthouse. "But you are not to worry. The advantage is ours."

Ash played with the food on his plate, pushing it around without eating it. "How do you figure?" he asked.

"Law is a game, not unlike baseball or soccer. Just as in sport the right combination has been worked out to give one team the advantage. In baseball the home team has last licks. Just so, the defense has last licks in the law."

"It seems to me I haven't even gotten to bat yet, and I'm already out of the game," Ash said.

"Not necessarily," Cabot said. "It just seems that way because the prosecution gets to go first and lay out its entire case. The jurors believe most of what they are told and are ready to hang you." He paused, waved his fork in the air as if to erase the words, and then continued. "Metaphorically speaking, of course. Then we get to present our side of the case. We refute all their claims and show the jurors how you couldn't possibly have committed the crimes, how someone else could have, and they then believe us. Well, the prosecution's shot its wad, so to speak, and can only bring up issues they've already discussed. We get to rebut those, and then they close first, leaving us to convince the jury in the end and win the case." He dusted off his hands and tossed his napkin over his plate.

"And all we need to hit is a six-run homer," Ash said. "Great. Too bad that's impossible."

"There are very few things I've found impossible," Cabot said. Both of them stared at his inert legs.

"Can you prove I didn't commit these crimes, that I

didn't kill Selma, for God's sake, and get me out of here so I can find who did?"

Cabot sucked at the corners of his mustache. "Working on it," he said.

"Can we offer them someone else? Greenbough? Some customer? You know Moss and I—"

Cabot nodded. "Charlotte's working on it. She's got Sam nailed to the wall, and enough other innuendoes to confuse the jury even if we can't quite convince them. She should wind up the last of the arguments on that damn Halton case today, and she'll devote the weekend to it."

"Don't put it all on her shoulders, Cab," he said. "If—hell—*when* I go down, I don't want her feeling she helped dig the hole."

"Worried about her feeling guilty?" Cabot asked. He was digging through papers in his briefcase and didn't look at Ash.

"She has nothing to feel guilty about," Ash said. He could still see the moon shining on her skin as she lay waiting for him, her wide frightened eyes intent on trusting him even while she'd bitten nervously at the corner of her lip.

"She'd like to come to your trial when her case is over," Cabot said. He fished out a small envelope and held it in his hand.

"No."

"I can't bar her from the courthouse," Cabot said. He seemed genuinely sorry that he could not. "I've even agreed to her taking the boy's appeal. . . ."

"You think she won't win it?"

"It's a risk I don't really want to take. If I didn't believe I could buy the father off if we lose, I wouldn't even consider it."

Ash felt his jaw fall. "You think you can buy Davis?"

"You'd be amazed what you can buy if you have to," Cabot said. "And last resorts are always a risky business."

"So you think you can buy a kid," Ash said. His brother's moral code struck him as very bizarre. After all the years of looking up to him, all the years of comparing himself and falling short, Ash was finally beginning to see the true Cabot Whittier. And the more he saw, the less he admired. And the less he admired, the more he seemed to find sympathy for. Perhaps after all the years of thinking otherwise, he was learning that his brother was simply a man.

"Would you prefer Charlotte in your courtroom or down the hall?" he asked. "I can't lock her in her room, Ashford."

"What if she loses?"

"I'll take care of it," Cabot said. "I've been taking care of her since her grandmother died, and before that as well. And I'll keep taking care of her."

"Promise me this," Ash said softly, "—that won't change if we lose this thing."

"Win or lose," Cabot agreed with a nod, "nothing will change."

It was in the judge's hands now, and while Charlotte wasn't sure she'd won, she was sure she'd put forth the best argument that could have been made for the case. By anyone. And that felt good.

Good, too, was the fact that Moss Johnson was waiting for her at the back of the courtroom, ready to escort her next door. If she couldn't help defend him, she could at least show herself in Ash's corner. And there was a good chance that their case would have broken for lunch and she would be able to at least see Ash and thank him for the teacup. Tell him how much it meant to her in person rather than settling for the little note she'd had to write so carefully, lest anyone get hold of it.

"I think you done real good," Moss said when she'd gathered up her belongings and found him at the back of the room. "Real good."

There was something about the way he said it, some underlying something that made it sound like compensation. "What's wrong?" she asked.

"And you is smart too," he said. "No question about it."

"What is it, Moss?" she demanded. She didn't need compliments, she needed facts to deal with, and overcome somehow.

"Mr. Greenbough," Moss said, grimacing. "He done broke his leg."

Charlotte shrugged. It was too bad he hadn't broken his head. And she knew Moss felt the same way. So then . . . "When?" she asked, realizing the significance.

Moss nodded with his whole body. "Week and a half ago. Hasn't been outta bed since."

"So I can prove he was cheating Ash blind, and it won't do us a bit of good. There's no way he could have set the second fire. Is that what you're saying?"

Moss continued that same nodding of his body that she'd seen the men do at Selma's shivah. It was as if he were already mourning for Ash. She put a hand on his arm and steadied him.

"Then we have to find someone else," she said firmly. "I know we're missing something here, Moss. And it's so obvious that we just don't see it."

"Yes, ma'am," Moss agreed, but without any conviction at all.

"We just have to widen your list," she said, pulling a hankie from her skirt pocket and dropping out the card she'd prevented Eli from seeing at the hospital. The one she suspected was from Ewing Flannigan.

* * *

He saw Moss Johnson slip into the courtroom out of the corner of his eye, trying to hide Charlotte with his bulk. *Damn!* He'd begged her not to come. Told Moss he was to take her directly home. He hated that he couldn't just get up and go back there to where she sat and demand she leave. He hated that he had to sit impassively at the big oak table and simply take notes on what Cabot might miss.

She was back there and it all but stopped his ability to breathe. The pencil in his hand, which he had forgotten, broke in two and he stared down at it, surprised to find how hard he had been clenching it.

"So then you're saying that from the angle that the canister was thrown, it would be your guess that the man who set the second fire was left-handed?" Brent asked, hurrying with the question so that the jury would no doubt see the broken pencil in Ash's left hand.

"Your wife is here," he whispered to Cabot, putting down the pencil as inconspicuously as he could.

"I don't care if Lillie Langtry is here," Cabot responded. "You had to be a lefty, didn't you?"

"Get her out of here," he said, imagining her last memories of him tainted by accounts of his illicit affairs.

"Don't worry about it," Cabot said. "It's not likely she'll hear anything that isn't true."

Ash studied the man next to him as he busily took notes. Naturally it wouldn't bother Cabot if Charlotte were to hear the worst. He reminded himself that this was the man who had let him believe that he was responsible—at six, yet!—for crippling his brother. This was a man who would offer a father money in exchange for his son.

Slowly he stood up and waited for the judge to take notice of him. In the meantime he glanced back and looked quickly at Charlotte, enough for her to realize what he was doing and yet leave everyone else in the dark as to why.

She shook her head, that sweet little mouth opening in horror.

"Mr. Whittier?" Judge Hammerman said. "Is there something . . . ?"

"Yes, Your Honor," he said, clearing his throat to give her a moment. "I'd like to change—"

He could hear the rustling of her skirts, the tapping of her feet, the slap of her hands against the courtroom doors, and she hurried out.

"—my seat, if that's all right. I'm having trouble seeing the witness from here. . . ."

"I don't think you ought to come again," Cabot said to her after she'd played with her dinner and refused dessert.

"I'm sure you're right," she said. She'd never noticed that the tablecloth had a floral pattern within the white-on-white damask. She traced one of the flowers with her finger.

"How did your argument go?" he asked after Rosa had cleared the dishes and brought them each a cup of tea, hers in the cup that matched her mother's pattern.

"Fine." The word came out slowly, longer than it needed to be.

"Your worthy opponent—his argument anything special?"

"Nothing he hadn't said before."

"Mmm," he said, as if what she'd told him required deep thought.

She traced another flower. Someday, she supposed, this tablecloth would be hers and she could pass it on to—no, she could never pass it on. She sniffed. What a stupid thing to make her cry. An old tablecloth that already had two wine stains marring its beauty.

"Charlotte? Are you all right?" He waved away Rosa and they sat in silence. "Charlotte? Answer me, please."

She nodded. If he didn't like nods he could sue her.

"Did you see Mother after you got home from court?" he asked.

She nodded again.

"Is she ill?"

She shook her head. Talking was too difficult. Breathing was too hard.

"Where is she? Eli's?"

"Bed."

"Mother's in bed?" he said as if he needed to guess from her response. "But she isn't ill?"

Charlotte shrugged. "Sad."

"This is like talking to some prepubescent—" He stopped midsentence as if something had suddenly occurred to him. "You're certain you are all right?"

"Tired," she said softly. "Very tired."

"Charlotte, if there's something you need to tell me, something I ought to know—I realize that I can seem rigid sometimes, difficult, even. But this is your home and I am your family. And furthermore—"

*Furthermore.* She could just imagine Cabot making love. There would be parties of the first part and parties of the second part and whereas clauses and . . . Not that he would ever make love to her. Not in any way.

"You're crying," he said without any annoyance in his voice. He sounded surprised, confused. "What is it?"

"I like this tablecloth," she said, feeling the tears roll down her cheeks and make patterns of their own on the white damask.

"The tablecloth?" he said, wheeling over to where she sat and taking her hand in his. "It'll be all right. You'll see.

When you're older, things will look different to you—better. You know what they say about time. . . ."

He waited for her to finish the line, but she was too busy gulping back tears to answer, and so he did it himself.

"How it heals all wounds? We'll be fine, you and me. I was thinking about that little vacation I promised you. Does Europe sound better than Chicago?"

She was racked with sobs now, and he let go of her hand so that she could tend to herself, blow her nose, wipe her tears.

"Wouldn't you like to see England? France? If you're up to it, of course."

He put the back of his hand to her forehead, then to each of her cheeks.

"And if you like it, we can plan on going back sometime. Maybe bring Davis. Can you imagine him at the Tower of London?"

She looked at the tablecloth again and laid her hand over one of the flowers, petting it gently.

"Where's your rabbit, anyway?" he asked. "Do you suppose that a dog would bother him any? I've a client who raises Afghan hounds and I was thinking about getting a pair for you. Would you like that?"

She dissolved into a heap on the table, her head in her arms as she wailed and gasped for breath.

"Charlotte, this is wholly unlike you," he said, patting her gingerly on her back.

"Maybe this is the real me, Cabot. Maybe I'm just a blubbering female. What if you were stuck with that?"

"Do you remember that I promised you I'd take care of you? Have I ever not kept my word? Maybe we weren't meant to be happy, Charlotte. But we'll be all right."

# Chapter 25

Had Cabot really sat beside her bed while she'd cried herself to sleep? Or was it a dream that he had tucked her tightly in and whispered that she not let the bedbugs bite? Wouldn't it have been her mother in a dream? But then why look for logic when what had sent her over the edge was an old tablecloth?

So now it wasn't just lost cases that reduced her to tears. Fat lot of good falling in love had done her. She'd been better off before.

She dragged herself out of bed and down the hall to the washroom, passing Cabot's open door on her way. His exasperated voice carried down the hall from Kathryn's room.

"It's one thing, Mother, to find a witness who saw Ashford somewhere else that first night. It's quite another to find someone who saw the torch being thrown by someone else the second time. I can't prove he wasn't where he was, can I?"

She couldn't hear Kathryn's response.

"No, I don't," he said with a heavy sigh. "Not when he knew that Selma was in there. There's only one person he's ever been willing to hurt, and that's himself. I'm sure he was gone when the fire broke out or he'd have risked his own neck to save hers. I've no doubt of it. The fact is, the way the timing worked, he probably passed the murderer himself."

Kathryn must have muttered something in response, or maybe she didn't. Charlotte didn't care. Cabot was right. Ash probably saw the killer!

No one had ever dressed as fast. She threw on a fresh shirtwaist and the skirt she'd worn the day before and ran a brush through her uncontrollable mop. It was never going to be long enough to pull back again, but suddenly that didn't seem to matter. Ash loved it short and wild and if he wanted her to, she'd hack it off whenever he asked.

She'd promised him that she would not show her face again in the courtroom. But she hadn't said she wouldn't visit him in jail, and grabbing up the notes she'd been poring over, she hurried down the steps and out the door.

"What are you doing here?" he asked, buttoning his shirt and tucking it into his pants. "They said my lawyer was here to see me," he explained, running his fingers through his hair to straighten it.

"Would you leave us alone?" she asked the guard the way she'd seen Cabot do a hundred times. "I need to speak with my client in private."

"Charlotte, don't," he warned, but he didn't stop the guard from leaving and closing the door behind him.

"You're losing weight," she said, touching his cheek where the hollow had grown deeper.

He stood perfectly still and let her run her fingers over his face. His Adam's apple bobbed furiously, but his hands stayed at his sides. "Cabot know you're here?" he asked.

"It was Cabot's idea," she started, then felt a pang of guilt. "That's not exactly true. I've come because of an idea that Cabot had. He's home with your mother."

"She must be pretty bad if Cabot's with her," he said.

Charlotte nodded, unable to lie to him. Then, with her fingers crossed for luck, she told him about Cabot's theory. "Can you remember seeing anyone after you left the warehouse?"

"You mean someone I know?" He pulled out a chair for her and one for himself, coming to life for the first time since his arrest. "Wouldn't they have been hiding?"

"Only if they got there before you. But then they would have heard you talking to Selma and have known she was inside. And who would want to hurt Selma?"

She meant it rhetorically, but the question hung in the air.

"No," he said finally, with the hint of a laugh. "If you knew Selma well enough to hate her, you'd have had to love her."

"So then you and he probably crossed paths as you were walking down the street. He broke a window, so you had to be far enough away not to have heard it. Of course, he kept walking and so did you after you passed, which means you didn't have to be blocks away at the time to be—"

"No one," he said, and hit his fist into his palm. "No one I remember. No one who stood out. Just your usual assortment of riffraff that the morning brings out. Plus the iceman. The milkman. The mailman. The—"

*The mailman.* Charlotte reached into her pocket and

pulled out the small envelope that she had taken from Selma's flowers. She slipped her finger under the seal and pulled out the card.

"What is that?" Ash asked, leaning closer to her to get a look.

Oh, but he smelled of cheap lye soap and frustration, and Charlotte thought if they could bottle it and sell it they'd be richer than Midas. She inhaled deeply while he read the note aloud.

*"I'm so sorry this happened to you—Ewing.* Where did you get this, Charlie?"

"What?" she asked, trying to pull herself away from the warmth his body gave off, the hard arm against which her breast was pressed. She looked at the note in her hand. "Think! Did you see Ewing Flannigan that morning, Ash? Was he the mailman you passed?"

"Flannigan sent this to Selma?"

She nodded. "Mr. Flannigan was the beau that Eli was talking about that night at dinner. Of course, he didn't know it was Davis's father she was seeing. But the truth is he was the one sweet on her. What if she'd spurned him?"

"That wasn't the way Eli was telling it," Ash said.

"What if Eli had convinced her?" Charlotte asked. "And in his anger Flannigan decided if he couldn't have her, no one could?"

Ash shook his head. "Flannigan fights with his fists. He might have hit her if he was mad enough, but setting the place on fire? It just isn't his style."

"We know he's violent. Maybe he does all kinds of terrible things when he's drunk."

"And why would he have set the first fire?" Ash asked. "Selma hadn't even started seeing him then."

"Maybe she'd turned him down," she insisted, unwilling to give up this first shred of hope. "And maybe he's a pyromaniac."

"A pyromaniac who sends flowers?" Ash asked skeptically. "And I'd remember seeing him, don't you think? He isn't likely to be someone I wouldn't have noticed."

"He says he's sorry, doesn't he? Isn't that an admission of guilt?" She studied the evidence in her hand.

"What did you write on your card?" Ash asked her. "With your plant?"

"I don't remember."

"Liar," he said, touching the tip of her nose. "I bet it was pretty close to what Flannigan said."

"So what if it was?" she said, lacing her fingers through his and brushing her cheek with his knuckles. "It's reasonable doubt, I think."

"Because a man sent a woman flowers?" He brought their joined hands to his lips and kissed the back of hers. "I would send you flowers if things were different."

"And I would learn to bake so that I could make you cakes and pies," she said, her thigh pressed against his.

"Would you sneak a file in one of them?" he asked, his mouth against her ear.

"A file? That, and my heart and soul," she said, turning her face so that his lips were a hairbreadth from her own.

He pulled back, and she could see in his face what it cost him to do it. "Don't go giving those away to the likes of me," he said. "Not if I'm convicted. You go on with your life if that happens, Charlie Russe. Promise me you will."

"I brought the list of customers with me," she said, fighting tears as she dug into her satchel. "Maybe if you see a name, you'll remember passing him that morning."

"Cabot will take care of you, just like always," he said softly, looking at her as if it was the last time he'd ever see her. As if he had already given up. "He's promised me that."

"And is that good enough for you?" she asked as the

guard worked the key in the lock of the door. "Should it be good enough for me?"

"It may have to be," he said as he rose and shoved his hands into his pockets.

"Kathryn," Charlotte said, standing by the woman's bed holding a dress in either hand, "which one are you going to wear today?"

Kathryn rolled over, turning her back to Charlotte, and burrowed deeper under the covers.

"So you're folding," Charlotte said letting her disappointment show. "All those times you told me to try a little harder, stand a little straighter, all those lectures about the good I could do women with my example—was that all just to keep me out of your hair and out of your house?"

Kathryn's head whipped around and wide eyes stared at Charlotte. "You're trying to make me angry. You've never doubted that I wanted what was best for you. You got stronger and stronger—look at you! You have it within you to help Ashford." She sighed helplessly and picked at the covers. "I can't do a thing to help my own son."

"Oh, yes, you can," Charlotte said, throwing back the covers and kneeling beside the bed. "You can do something I can't. You can go into that courtroom and sit right behind your sons. Brent will think twice before he disgraces your own child in front of you. He's a decent man, and your presence will make him very uncomfortable about bringing up Ash's indiscretions.

"And if he does, the jury won't like him for it. They'll have sympathy for you and it will spill over to Ash. They'll see you think he's innocent and they'll give him the benefit of the doubt. It's all they need, Kathryn—reasonable doubt."

The old woman grabbed her hand and pulled herself up with it, easing her legs over the side of the bed and feeling about with her feet for her slippers.

"The lavender one," she said, pointing at the dress that rested at the foot of her bed. "It's grown a tad large and I look more pathetic in it."

"I'm proud of you, Kathryn," Charlotte said, giving the woman her arm to help her rise.

"I don't want to hear them say awful things about my son," she said when they were eye-to-eye.

"I don't want to hear them either," Charlotte said, "but I'd give my right arm to be able to sit in the courtroom and let him know that I don't care what anyone says about him."

Kathryn patted her hand and stood up straight. She arched her shoulders and threw back her head. "I'm proud of you too," she said softly. "Cabot and I did a good job."

Charlotte, who had begun to pull out the underthings that her mother-in-law would need, turned and put her hands on her hips. "You did have a lot to work with," she said with a smile.

Davis's da was passed out cold on the sofa in the front room. Since Miss Mollenoff's accident on St. Patty's Day, he wasn't saving his drinking for Friday nights. Mostly, he was too drunk to hit Davis, but it didn't stop him from trying.

"And where were ya thinkin' of going?" he roared as Davis tiptoed by the couch.

Davis swallowed twice, breathed in, and said, "Miz Whittier's got work for me."

His father opened one eye. "Ah, but can ya be sayin' it three times fast?"

The smell of urine and vomit rose from the couch along with his father.

"You're doin' better," he admitted, going to unbutton his pants and finding them already undone. "Get me a bottle and a piss pot."

Davis brought the chamber pot from beneath his bed and handed it to his father. A creeping stain on his da's trousers showed he was a little late, and his father grabbed the pot and finished his business before reaching out to take a swipe at him.

"She still dead?" he asked, coughing up some phlegm and spitting it into the pot by his feet.

"Course sh-sh-sh . . ." he began.

"Ah, and has the lease run out on your tongue?" his father asked. "Where's my whiskey?"

"You're out," Davis told him, ready to dodge the blow that would follow.

Instead his father put his head in his hands. "It's just as well, I suppose. The doc—he's all right, Davey?"

Davis went to nod, stopped himself, and said, "Yes sir," with only the slightest hesitation.

"You tell that man he best be taking extra care. There are people out there that are wishin' him harm, there are, for sure."

"Who?"

"A stand-up gent don't name no names," his father said, tucking his privates back into his damp pants. "Suffice it to say I got ears and eyes and he'd do well to be watchin' his back."

"I gotta go," he said, inching back toward the door. His father was always pretending to know stuff he didn't, and Davis didn't want to hang around for the mailmen-know-things speech.

"Where's my bottle?" his father asked again. "I'll be

damned if I'll be stoppin' in that bar to shoot my mouth off after this."

"After what?" He picked up his father's chamber pot and placed it behind the door to the water closet.

"My fault." His father came to his feet, teetered, and fell back down onto the couch.

Davis took a deep breath. "Which bar?"

"And on a saint's day! They'll all be rotting in hell for what they did to her." He slid to the side and his head fell onto the arm of the sofa.

"Who, Da?" he asked, taking several steps toward his father.

The man was sleeping once again, snoring lightly while he no doubt lost his job. Davis considered waking him up, but remembered what Mr. Whittier had told him about letting sleeping dogs lay.

Behind Ash something was happening in the courtroom. Before he could turn around, Cabot grabbed his arm. "Don't look behind you," he warned. "Keep your eyes on the jury and sit up straight."

"Don't worry, I'm not about to change my plea this time," he said, shifting in his seat to look for Charlotte and instead being treated to one of his mother's gracious smiles. "What is she doing here?" he hissed at Cabot through gritted teeth.

Cabot shook his head, apparently baffled. "Smile at her," he whispered. "The jury's watching you."

"Is the defense prepared to call its first witness?" Judge Hammerman asked.

"A moment, Your Honor," Cabot said, and began hurriedly sifting through his notes.

"What's wrong?" Ash whispered.

"My first witness was the hooker you spent the night

with on February eighth. I can't call her with Mother here."

"You found her?" Ash asked, more than surprised. "Where is she?"

Cabot nodded his head in the direction of a stunning woman whose deep eyes slanted slightly and whose black hair shone. Ash didn't recall ever having seen the woman before. "You're sure?" he asked.

"*She's* sure," Cabot answered. "But the jury won't like Mother hearing her testimony."

"Counselor?" Judge Hammerman asked.

"Yes, Your Honor," Cabot said. "My wheel here seems to be jammed."

Ash watched as he slipped the brake in place.

"Can't get it to move. Might I ask the court's indulgence for a short recess?"

People behind them began to shift in their seats as if the judge had already granted the request. Ash realized that if the judge refused, the jury would be sympathetic to Cabot, and consequently to him. And if he agreed, Cabot had bought them some time. He was definitely getting the hang of this trial thing. Just in time to be hanged himself.

"Arthur," Ash said, calling Cabot's man over when their request had been granted, "go back to the house and get the new wheelchair as fast as you can."

"What new chair?" Cabot asked.

"Who are you going to put on?" Ash asked in response.

Cabot studied the jury box, hesitating only a moment.

"Mother," he said, with just the hint of a smile.

# Chapter 26

"I love both my sons," Kathryn said pointedly in response to Cabot's question. "Though neither of them is perfect." There was a titter from the crowd, and Cabot turned his new three-wheeled chair around easily to smile at Ash.

"She never did care for your table manners," he said.

Ash's brain raced for a comeback. Was there anything about Cabot his mother hadn't liked? "She hates the way you suck on that mustache," he said, figuring no one could like it.

Cabot looked shocked, and the courtroom erupted in laughter, which only quieted with the banging of the judge's gavel and an order to proceed with the case at hand.

"Do you think that Ashford Whittier could have set either of the fires of which he stands accused?" Cabot asked their mother.

"I do not," she said, looking down her aristocratic nose at the jury.

"What makes you so certain?" Cabot asked.

"I know every mother is sure that her child could do nothing wrong. And they can't all be right, because bad things do happen. Obviously, someone's son did those awful things. How do I know it wasn't my child? Because in all Ash's crazy wild days, in all his wanderings about trying to find the meaning in his life, he has never hurt anyone but himself. His crimes, if you want to call a man's weaknesses that, were without victims."

She turned to face the jury. "When my son was a very young boy, he was playful and full of life. He had a streak of mischievousness that always made us laugh. Told to do something, he didn't always obey. Called, he didn't always come. Without going into it, let me just say that on one particular occasion it resulted in a terrible tragedy. He was six. He never forgot and he never forgave himself and he'd never talk about it."

She looked straight at him then, and smiled slyly. "Now I suppose he has to at least listen to me. I watched him as he carried his sadness around with him for years, across oceans. And nowhere he went and nothing he did seemed to free him.

"Until recently. Within the last month or two I've seen a serenity replace his pain, a satisfaction replace his hunger. He's finally stopped running from a guilt he should never have felt. I know my son could never have set fire to his warehouse, because it simply isn't within his nature, and because there is nothing that would have made him risk that newfound peace."

Ash didn't know when he had closed his eyes, but when he reopened them, his mother was only a blur of regal bearing. He'd disappointed her over and over again, and yet there she sat in the witness box with her head held high as if Ash were someone of whom she could truly be proud.

"No further questions, Your Honor," Cabot said in the hushed courtroom, and then wheeled himself back to the defense table with ease. "You know, this works remarkably well," he said to his brother, loud enough for the jury to hear. "Thanks."

Ash just nodded. What a time to find out what he meant to his family. Just before he would break all their hearts by getting convicted and hanged.

"So your son has had a sudden conversion, shall we say," Brent said as he came to his feet and addressed Kathryn. "Why?"

Next to Ash, Cabot's fingers went back and forth on the spokes of his wheel.

"I believe he's fallen in love," Kathryn said, her eyes meeting Brent's.

"Really?" Brent threw a gaze their way, lingering a moment on Cabot. "With whom?"

Cabot sucked at his mustache. Ash studied his fingernails. The courtroom was silent as a tomb.

"He hasn't confided in me," Kathryn said carefully.

Ash held his breath, waiting for Brent to ask her to guess. Who'd have thought that his mother would be a match for the district attorney?

"No further questions," Brent mumbled, and all eyes watched his mother come down from the stand and stop at his table to place a kiss on the top of his head and squeeze Cabot's shoulder lightly as she passed.

"Defense calls Nora Mui to the stand." Cabot wheeled out from behind the desk, leaned over to get a better look at the third wheel, and did a sharp little turn on his way to the witness box.

Nora was sworn in and Cabot went through the pleasantries and preliminaries with her.

"Do you know the defendant?" he asked.

"We passed an evening together," she said.

"You saw him socially, then?" Cabot tried to clarify delicately.

"You could say that," she agreed.

"Actually I'd prefer it if you did."

"I saw him socially," she said amiably. Ash thought if Cabot told her to say they swam the bay, she'd say that too. And he figured the jury felt the same way.

"Where?"

"We went to his ship." She looked down at her hand. "The *Bloody Mary,* it's called."

"You're sure that was the man?" Cabot asked, pointing at Ash, who by now was sure he'd never seen the woman before in his life.

"I remember the bird," she said.

"The bird?" Cabot asked, wheeling near the jury as if he, along with them, were hearing this for the first time.

"A big red-and-yellow one. He called it a macaw, but I think it was really a parrot, if you ask me."

"He had a parrot there?" Cabot asked.

"Mm-hmm," she agreed. "And we tried to teach it to say something new."

"This parrot talks?"

"Does it ever! Ashford said it belonged to a sea captain and had a very salty mouth."

"Did you succeed in teaching it to say anything?" Cabot asked.

The girl nodded. " 'See you soon,' " she said.

"And this was when?" Cabot asked.

"The night of February eighth. I remember because it took nearly the whole night, and a woman in my position doesn't forget something like that."

There were a few guffaws, but they ended abruptly when Ash turned and looked apologetically at his mother.

She shook her head as if it didn't matter in the slightest to her. Perhaps it didn't, perhaps she knew the truth of it, but it mattered to him, and he hung his head as Cabot continued.

"Your Honor, I'd like to introduce Defense Exhibit A at this time, if it please the court."

Hammerman nodded and Cabot signaled to the back of the room, where Moss Johnson was coming through the doors with Liberty perched on his shoulder.

"Oh! Oh! Oh!" Liberty shouted. Ash slid down in his chair with the full intention of slipping right on through the floor and pulling every piece of the marquetry wood over him.

"That's enough of that, Liberty," Cabot said.

"Shut up, you stupid bird! Awk! Shut up!" Liberty shouted. The crowd behind him roared their approval of the bird. On Moss's shoulder, Liberty nodded his head vehemently as if he were taking bows.

"Now, what was it you taught him to say?" Cabot asked the woman on the stand when the crowd had quieted enough for him to continue.

"See you soon," she said, her shoulders up and her back pressed into the chair.

"S-s-see you s-s-s-soon! Oh! Oh! Oh! He's so big!" the parrot shrieked.

Cabot put his hand up to his forehead. "Get him out of here, Moss," he directed.

"S-s-see you s-soon!" Liberty shouted. "Shut up, you stupid bird!"

It took several minutes of gavel banging to restore order to Judge Hammerman's courtroom. Finally the judge looked at the time and simply adjourned court for the day, but not before the crowd had subtly shifted into Ash's corner.

* * *

"Oh, Charlotte, I wish you'd been there," Kathryn said over dinner. "I'm quite sure I did him some good, didn't I, Cabot?"

Charlotte was barely paying attention. She'd spent the day at home with Davis, going over papers and looking for something to hang her hope on. Maybe she was seeing things that weren't there, mirages in the distance on a landscape barren of hope, but she was convinced that Davis knew something about Selma's case. She wasn't sure what, or how much, he might ever be willing to tell her.

Naturally she didn't want the boy to implicate his own father, but if he could just point her in the right direction . . .

"And then when Liberty started in," Kathryn was saying. "You know, at first I didn't believe that girl. I mean, I'm fully aware that Ash hasn't led a monk's existence, but that woman uses kohl on her eyelids, I've no doubt! Then when the bird—"

"Liberty was in court?" Charlotte asked. She had tried not to pay attention to Kathryn's rattling on about Ash's exploits, but this bit of news was impossible to ignore.

"Oh, yes," Katherine said. "Cabot had him there to prove that Ash had visited a friend on the night of the first fire and that the bird had been with them."

"Really?" Charlotte asked despite herself. Was that where the bird had learned to shout, *Don't stop*?

"Charlotte, are you ready for the boy's appeal?" Cabot asked her, steering her artlessly away from the subject of Ash's liaisons. "I've arranged for a longer-than-usual luncheon break tomorrow, so that I could actually do the argument if you want me to."

"What was the point of all my training, then, if you are going to take my cases? Why did we do all our hard work? You've given me wings, Cabot. It's time you let me fly," she said.

He ran his finger around the rim of his wineglass. "Do you see yourself caged?"

Her heart spent its nights in a barred cell with the man she loved. She was locked out of the courtroom. "I'd like to do the argument," she said softly.

"And so you shall. I'll be in the back of the room if you need me."

"You have your own case to worry about. I know you and Ash think that I'm seeing things that aren't there, but Davis told me today that since the accident his father has changed. Did you know that Ewing Flannigan was that mysterious beau of Selma's? And Davis says that there are men at the bar who are asking about him but he won't go there anymore. Don't you think there's something to it?"

Cabot tipped his wine goblet slightly, watching the deep red liquid coat the glass.

"And Davis says that his father asks after Eli. Don't you think that's strange?"

"Well, he liked Selma. Selma loved Eli. What's strange about that?"

"Eli hated him. And with good reason."

"That doesn't make him a murderer," Cabot said.

"Will you at least look into it?" Charlotte asked. "I went to the bar myself today, but they wouldn't let me in."

"Women aren't allowed in those bars," he said, shaking his head at her. "And for good reason. A lot of drunken men can only mean trouble. Don't you have any fears?"

Charlotte thought about Ash spending the rest of his life in prison, or worse. She thought of herself, spending night after night alone in her narrow bed. Lining up her knife and spoon carefully with the edge of the table, she took a moment to pull herself together before looking up to meet his eyes. *Had she no fears?* Fear was her constant companion, her closest ally and her most hated enemy. It was what she conquered every morning when she opened her eyes, it was what fueled her energy when she wanted to give up working on Ash's case and what left her hoping long into the night.

But was she afraid of the men in McGinty's?

"Do you want to go there, Cabot, or shall I try again?"

# Chapter 27

Charlotte wiped her sweaty palms on her skirt and stood up. This one was for all the marbles, as Ash always put it. She smiled down at Davis and pointed out to him that Cabot was in the back of the courtroom. Across from her table sat Ewing Flannigan. Even spiffing up for the occasion, he looked a great deal worse than he had the last time they had met in court.

"Mrs. Whittier?" Judge Mallory asked. "It was my understanding that your husband would be presenting the argument this time."

"Your Honor," Cabot called from the back of the room, "as you undoubtedly know, I'm trying a case next door and may be called away at any time. I beg the court's indulgence and stand ready to answer any questions that may arise."

Mallory was clearly not pleased, but he nodded at Charlotte. "You may proceed."

"First, I'd like to apologize to the court and to Mr. Flannigan. I made a terrible mistake at our last hearing and I want to acknowledge it."

She came out from behind the desk and stood in front of Ewing Flannigan.

"I made a great many assumptions I had no right to make. Having gotten to know Davis better over the past few weeks, I want to apologize to you for assuming that you didn't love or value your son. He couldn't be as wonderful a boy as he is, as trustworthy, as honest and good natured, if you and his mother hadn't put in the time that being a good parent takes."

Ewing Flannigan acknowledged with a nod that they had done their best. She could see the hurt on his face at just the mention of his wife, and she knew she was on the right track.

"Times are tough, Mr. Flannigan, and life can be unfair. Losing someone you love, love desperately and beyond all reason, as you must have loved your wife, must leave an emptiness that nothing can fill. I don't blame you for trying to dull the pain with alcohol. I'm not some zealot who thinks that liquor is the instrument of the devil or that your indulgence shows a weakness of character. I imagine that I, too, could be driven to the bottle after a loss such as you have suffered.

"But when you are drunk, sir, you hurt the boy you love. And it is the duty of the court system to protect that child. Indeed, if someone else raised a hand to your son, you would turn to the courts to see justice done, I'm sure. And the truth is that you cannot control your anger and your pain when you are drinking. And further, it is true that you cannot control your drinking.

"And because you love your son, I'm asking that you voluntarily give him into the court's care with the stipulation that he come and live with Mr. Whittier. That sweet child of yours has had to survive the loss of his mother. Don't make him bear up to the betrayal of his father. If you truly love that boy, Mr. Flannigan, and I believe you do, it has to be slowly killing you inside to see him hurt. And to be the one inflicting that pain.

"Being the one who loves him the most doesn't mean holding on the tightest. It means wanting what's best for him, not what might be best for you. It means wanting to see that child be all that he has the potential to become, and as happy as he has the capacity to be. Can you give him that, Mr. Flannigan? Or can you offer him work in the canneries ten hours a day when he's lucky, and a beating every night when he's not?

"If you love him, Mr. Flannigan, you'll let him go."

She took her seat without looking at Cabot, and felt Davis's fingers slip into hers. She squeezed gently and he squeezed back.

"Come up here, Davis," Judge Mallory ordered, and with a quick look at her first for permission, Davis slid from behind the table and approached the bench. Charlotte was struck by how small he seemed in front of the massive judge's podium. Of course, she wasn't more than an inch taller than him herself. "How did you get that bruise on your face?"

Davis turned to look at his father before answering the judge. "Banged into a door," he said softly.

"A door, huh?" the judge said. "Come around the side here and raise your shirt, boy."

Davis dragged his feet as he made his way around the witness chair and up the two steps of the judge's dais.

"And would I ever be seein' the boy again?" Ewing Flannigan asked in the quiet of the courtroom before Davis had a chance to show the judge the bandages that held his ribs.

"Dinner is at three on Sundays," Cabot said from the back of the room. "If you're sober, you're welcome."

"I'm going to sign the order, Mr. Flannigan," Judge Mallory said. "Do you understand that Mr. Whittier will then have custody of Davis Flannigan and will be responsible for his upbringing and support until he reaches his eighteenth birthday?"

"He won't be workin' in the canneries, now, will he?" Flannigan asked Cabot. "Had a brother that lost his hand there when he was a lad."

"No, Mr. Flannigan," Cabot agreed, "he will never work in the canneries."

"And he's not one for vegetables," Flannigan added.

"He'll learn," Cabot said softly, allowing Arthur to push him to the front of the courtroom. "We'll all learn."

"Sign it," Ewing told the judge, staring at his son while the sound of Mallory's pen scratching his name onto the order filled the courtroom.

"Just another minute, Mr. Flannigan," Cabot said as the beaten man turned to leave the courtroom. "I believe this gentleman has something for you."

Charlotte held her breath as the court clerk handed Ewing Flannigan a summons.

"I believe we're all wanted in courtroom number one," Cabot said, reaching out for Charlotte's hand. "That was very eloquent, my dear.

"But never settle for flying, Charlotte, when you may soar."

"Defense calls Ewing Flannigan to the stand," Cabot said. It had taken Cabot a while, but he'd convinced Ash that she ought to be in the courtroom to see what all her work had come to. He'd even given in and allowed her to sit at the table next to him. And so there she was, at the defense table, her leg inches from Ash's, trying to keep her eyes glued to her husband when what she wanted more than anything was to drink in the sight of Ash.

As he swore on the Bible and took his seat in the witness box, Flannigan glared at Cabot. Behind them Kathryn sat with Davis at her side and she could hear them whispering.

Cabot wheeled to a spot near the jury so that they would get a good look at Flannigan's face as the man answered his questions. "Please understand, Mr. Flannigan, that you are not on trial here. Would you state your occupation for the record?"

"I'm a mail carrier," Flannigan said. He sat tall in the stand as he said it, daring Cabot to make something of it.

Cabot did. "Just a mail carrier?" he baited Flannigan.

"And there be no *just* about it," he said addressing the jury in his heavy brogue. "It's a common man that thinks bein' a mail carrier is next to bein' a pissant. Beggin' your pardon, but that's how it 'tis. Have ya any idea what a mailman's privy to? What a man who pays attention can learn just from the mail he's pickin' up and deliverin'? Love letters, past due notices, I've seen 'em all."

"And what did you see coming and going from both the G and W warehouse and then again from offices above the Charter House Bar?" Cabot asked him.

"I don't recall," he said, crossing his arms over his chest.

Davis stood up and leaned forward, whispering to her. Dutifully she wrote down his request and passed it to the clerk to hand to Cabot.

"Did you know Selma Mollenoff?" Cabot asked after he'd glanced at the note and put it in his pocket.

"I didn't kill her, Davey," Flannigan said to his son. "It weren't me and don't you be thinkin' it was."

Beside her, Ash turned in his seat. "For God's sake, take him out of here," he told Kathryn.

His mother rose and she and Davis argued quietly until Ewing began to talk.

"It was that damn ladies' stuff. Those Halton pamphlets with the doctor's instructions. And those pictures of . . . well everyone knows what kind of information it is she's sending to ladies."

Charlotte heard herself gasp. Selma had been one of what Charlotte always referred to as her "silent supporters"—women whose hearts were in the right place but who wouldn't stand up and be counted. But all the while Selma had appeared to be standing on the sidelines, she'd really been sending out Virginia's mailings, using Ash's office to receive the donations and disseminate the information. She'd been pulling the wool over Charlotte's eyes, and Ash's, and everyone else's too. And somehow it had cost her her life. "I saw some initials on the envelopes at both places and I couldn't help asking the lady what it was she was sending. I remember the smile she give me, and the wink, and saying she couldn't be tellin' the likes of a good Catholic like me."

"Then how did you know what was in the envelopes?" Cabot asked.

When Brent objected, he let it pass, but Flannigan blurted out the answer anyway.

"I weren't openin' the mail, if that's what you're thinkin'. But glue ain't the way it used to be and every now and then a letter finds its way out of an envelope, and that's what happened once or twice with Miss Mollenoff's mail." He folded his arms across his chest, then let them drop to his sides as if it didn't matter to him anymore what people thought.

"And what did you do about it?" Cabot asked.

"Take the boy out of here," Ash ordered his mother.

Cabot raised his hand. "Let him be," he said to Ash, and then addressed the witness again. "You didn't do anything about it, did you, Mr. Flannigan? Neither my client nor you would have hurt Selma Mollenoff for the world."

"That, sir, Mr. Whittier, is the God's honest truth. I'd as soon have cut off me own arm as hurt a hair on that woman's head, no matter how misguided her efforts mighta been."

"Unless of course, you were drunk and showing off, which you were, weren't you?"

"I've been know to tip a few, as you well know. But I had nothing to do with the fires."

"I'm not accusing you of setting the fires, Mr. Flannigan. But you were drunk and shooting off your mouth a bit, weren't you?"

"And how was I to know that it would lead to this? Fires and killin' and him bein' blamed?" He pointed at Ash. Charlotte came to attention and leaned forward in her seat, everything clear to her now as she silently cheered Cabot on.

"And how do you know that this man is innocent?" Cabot asked, looking over at the table and no doubt seeing Ash's hand reach out for Charlotte's beneath the table. It didn't cost him a beat as he went on. "Please, Mr. Flannigan, for Selma's sake, don't let yet another tragedy come out of this. Someone killed that dear young lady and it wasn't my brother, was it? Tell the court how you know this man never set those fires."

Ewing Flannigan shrugged uncomfortably. "They were braggin' in the bar, they were. How they'd stopped the sinnin' and the fornicatin'. How the 'act' was meant for makin' babies and not for women enjoyin' themselves."

"Are you saying that these men admitted to setting fire to both warehouses in order to stop the dissemination of materials vital to the concerns of women?"

She and Ash smiled at Cabot as they recognized her words flung out into the courtroom. Tears stung her eyes as Cabot smiled back and she gently slipped her hand from Ash's and returned it to the table.

"Your Honor," Brent interrupted, "is this witness willing and prepared to name names?"

Flannigan leaned back in the witness box. "I can be givin' you their names and their address at work and at home. I know how much they earn and where it is their relatives are writin' from. You know people think a mail carrier is as low as a pissant, beggin' your pardon, but—"

Cabot put his hand up to stop Flannigan's tirade. "Your Honor, I request that all charges against my client be dropped. I could continue this case to its logical conclusion at great waste to the taxpayers of the State of California and—"

"The state agrees to drop all charges," Brent said, "providing Mr. Flannigan here is willing to cooperate with the state in the apprehension and arrest of the party or parties responsible for the murder of Selma Mollenoff."

"You thought I did it, didn't you, boy?" Flannigan called to Davis over the pandemonium that had broken out in the courtroom.

Cabot reached into his pocket and handed Ewing the note. On it Charlotte had written Davis's request to leave his father alone. Cabot had done better. He'd exonerated him before his son's very eyes.

They'd been lucky to get out of the courthouse alive, which was becoming the normal course of events for Charlotte these days. But this time she'd had Ash to protect her, while Moss had seen to Kathryn. At the carriage the private investigator had been waiting with a smile on his face.

He'd shaken Cabot's hand and then Ash's. "It was a pleasure uncovering the truth for a change," he'd said to Cabot. Over his shoulder as he walked away, he'd added, "but now we're even, Whittier."

And now they were back in the house where she and Cabot would grow old together as she'd promised. Ash had looked surprised and hurt when she'd taken the seat next to Cabot's chair in the carriage and had rested her hand on his arm all the way home. He couldn't know what it had cost her to do it, how much she longed to simply touch him, feel the texture of his skin against her palm, to look deep into his eyes and see the love she felt reflected there.

"Charlotte, may I see you in my office?" Cabot said when they were all in the foyer and had given up coats and hats to Rosa and Arthur. "There are a few papers before we're quite finished with this whole affair."

"Couldn't they wait?" Kathryn asked. "It's quite the day for celebration."

"Indeed it is," Cabot said, but his face didn't match his words. "We won't be long."

"Davis, why don't you see if you can find Van Gogh?" Charlotte suggested. "I've made him a bed in the carriage house." At the mention of the carriage house her insides tightened. If she lived here until she was a hundred, nothing on earth would send her into that building again.

"Bring him back into the main house," Cabot told the boy. "With this extra wheel I think we can manage to stay out of each other's way."

Charlotte felt her jaw drop, and drop again, farther, when Davis answered, "Yes, sir, Mr. Whittier."

Cabot nodded at the boy. "I owe you one of those little circles in my chair, son," he said, indicating one with his pointer finger. "Remind me tomorrow."

"Charlotte?" Ash whispered from just behind her.

"Haven't you told him about how you feel? Doesn't he know about us?"

"Oh, he knows," she said softly, allowing herself the luxury of looking at his incredible face before pulling away. "And you're free. But I'm not."

He looked more angry than hurt as she pulled away to answer Cabot's call.

"Charlotte? Are you coming?"

"Yes," she called to him, hurrying to his office without looking back.

He was waiting for her there, in the semidarkness, and watched her every move as she came into the room.

"Sit," he said, and gestured toward the chair across from his desk as if that weren't where she always sat when she worked with him.

She did as she was told.

"You were perfection in the courtroom today," he said, referring to the job she'd done on Davis's case. He was studying her hair, her eyes, staring at her shirtwaist, considering her hands.

She complimented him back. "As were you." She shifted in her seat. Was he imagining how it would be between them now? Now that Ash would be off to sea again and they would be alone at Whittier Court?

"Ah, well, it was your work that set me on the right track. I couldn't have done it alone." He pulled his eyes from her and began to go through the papers that cluttered his desk, reaching for books behind him and making notes.

"What is it that we still need to do?" she asked him, anxious to toast the victories and then crawl up to bed. Alone.

"As I said, you were perfect," Cabot repeated. "I don't think before that moment in the courtroom I—"

Things would never change for her. She would spend

her days listening to Cabot analyze their cases and her nights dreaming of what might have been if things were different. "Cabot, I appreciate your praise, but they are all waiting for us. What is it we still have to do?"

He put his hands together, almost as if he were praying, and touched his fingertips to his lips.

"Face facts," he said, pushing a hastily scrawled document at her. "Read it."

Across the top of the paper Cabot had written *Petition for Annulment of Marriage.*

"I've loved you, Charlotte, from the day I met you. You were such a silly child then, so serious about wanting to be the best attorney in all of Oakland. I loved you when you were learning the law and I was so proud of you when you were admitted to the bar."

"Are you saying you don't love me anymore?" she asked him, her eyes seeking out the grounds for the annulment and finding only the truth—that the marriage had never been consummated.

"I love you more today than perhaps I ever did. Enough to open the cage, Charlotte, and let you soar."

"I promised that I would stay," she said, reaching across the desk and feeling the warmth of his hand as he took hers.

"It was never quite right between us, Charlotte. But it was never as wrong as when we tried to play at man and wife. That isn't the way I love you, and it will never be. I listened to you in that courtroom describe how a father should feel about his child, and for the first time since I'd married you I understood what was between us."

He pulled a hankie from his jacket and handed it to her. Until then she hadn't realized she was crying.

"It doesn't have to be my brother," he said softly. "You're free to go anywhere, you understand."

"It has to be your brother." Ash's strong voice had a crack to it as he stood in the doorway.

"I thought perhaps it did."

"I'd promised him, Ash," she explained as he came to her side and knelt by her chair.

"Make your promises to that Whittier," Cabot said softly, easing out from behind his desk. "Sign the paper and I'll push it through. I'd like to give you away before I take Davis to London."

He did a small circle on his way to the office door.

"Love this third wheel," he said, tears clearly glistening in his eyes. "I'll miss you, Charlotte, every day of my life. . . . Of course, while I'm in London I may be too busy. . . . And then there's Paris . . ."

He wheeled out the door to a good deal of commotion in the foyer.

". . . and Naples . . . and Rome . . ."

"Sounds like you're missing out on quite a lot," Ash said, rising and pulling her with him.

"Oh, no," she disagreed, her face pressed into his chest while he stroked her back. "I've got everything I want right here."

"I'll never be able to give you the things he did," Ash admitted with a heavy heart. "Trips to Europe, this fine house. My business is in shambles and I've nothing to offer you."

She looked at him incredulously, then reached across her desk and picked up the teacup he had finally found to replace the one that had broken. Pressing it to her chest, she spoke softly, but her words still rang out clear. "You have the keys to my heart. You have the map to my soul."

"It's just a teacup," he said, easing out from her grasp

and putting it down so that he could take her into his arms. "I want to give you so much more."

"I have everything I want right here," she told him, her arms around his neck. "I don't need a grand tour or a grand house if I have you."

"Still, I could try to make it up to you," he said, tipping her head back so that he could press his lips to hers.

"You could," she agreed.

"I could bring you flowers," he said, his hands running through the cap of curls and pressing her lips harder against his own until he couldn't talk at all.

"Mmm," she said again, and he pulled back just far enough to promise her chocolates.

"Oh, chocolates too?" she said, undoing his collar button and the one beneath it so that she could reach the hairs at his throat and feel him struggle to swallow at her touch.

"I wish I could promise you jewels and pearls," he said, pressing up against her and cupping her bottom close.

"Is that what you think I want?" she asked, then clarified her question. "Pearls, I mean?"

His head dipped to her shoulders, her neck. Unceremoniously he lifted her to the desk and buried his face against her bodice. "Is this what you want?" he asked.

"Come on!" Davis yelled from somewhere a million miles away but close enough to bring them to their senses. "Cake!"

"Come on," she said, pulling him by the hand until they were through the door, and then letting go.

"Come on!" Liberty yelled. "Come on!"

"I suppose this is going to be rather awkward," Ash said as he followed her, not too closely, into the foyer. He pulled her back for a second, and while he buttoned his collar he asked, "When am I supposed to show you just how much I love you?"

In the dining room everyone who loved them both waited to help celebrate.

"Don't worry," she said, running a finger along his neck and feeling the heat rise up to envelop her. "We'll have the rest of our lives."

# Epilogue

*SILVER PASS, WYOMING TERRITORY*
*MARCH 1890*

"So?" Ash asked, putting his arm around Charlotte. "Was it as wonderful as you'd been anticipating?"

"Oh, it exceeded even my highest expectations," she said with the grin that always melted his heart.

"It was that good?"

"Better!"

"So then it was worth waiting for?"

"Well, I'd have liked it a long time ago, and I still don't see why I had to wait," she admitted.

"Was it worth coming to Wyoming for?"

She nodded happily. "How did you like it?" she asked, batting those long eyelashes at him.

"Well, it was hardly my first time, Charlie Russe," he said. "But, of course, having you there made it special."

"You did vote for me, didn't you?" she asked as they left Town Hall, waving to several neighbors as they made their way down the sidewalk together.

"Oh, being a justice of the peace hasn't been exciting enough for you? Being woken up in the middle of the night to set bail for Olaf Williamson? Being woken up in the middle of the night to see Raymond Rochman do his duty by Leila Singer? Being woken up in the middle of the night to—"

"I only like it when you wake me up in the middle of the night to—" she started, her cheeks turning a bright shade of pink as they walked along Main Street toward Whittier Dry Goods. "Oh, Ash! I voted! I stepped behind that curtain and cast a ballot!"

"And if you win that judgeship by only one vote . . ."

She slapped him gently on his arm. "It's going to be a veritable landslide. Don't you read the newspaper you sell?"

"Speaking of reading . . ." he said, fishing around in his pocket for Cabot's latest letter and waving it beneath her nose. "This one's from Paris, France."

She grabbed for it, but he held it out of her reach and opened the door to the store.

"Let's go on upstairs and get settled before I read it to you. How's that?"

"Fair, I suppose," she said, with her bottom lip pouting. "I did get to read you Kathryn's letter last week."

Ash couldn't help smiling. His mother's words had sounded so joyful as they poured from his wife's lips. Maybe it was the way Charlotte sang Eli's name each time his mother mentioned it. Or maybe it was how excited she got when she read that Kathryn was thinking about coming out to Wyoming for a visit in September before Cabot and Davis returned from the grand tour. "You can close your eyes and rest while I read."

She seemed to think that was a good idea, and she lazily let her cape fall from her shoulders as she headed for the stairs. He caught the wrap as it hit the floor and reminded her that he was not Maria.

"No, but you'll do," she said. Her voice was light, but it didn't escape him that she was nearly pulling herself up the stairs by the railing. Wyoming wasn't an easy life. The winters were harsh. For that matter, so were the summers. For his part he enjoyed the challenge, but of late it seemed to be taking its toll on his wife.

At the top of the stairs they could hear Liberty talking to himself in the back room. "Come on, Liberty," the bird was saying. "Stupid bird! Say it! Say it! Come on, say it!" It was all he'd said for a week now. They'd tired of hearing it, but the bird didn't care. "Come on, Liberty! Please! You stupid bird!"

"Shut up!" Ash yelled to the bird while he bent to tend the fire, and Charlotte put up the kettle.

"Say it!" Liberty shouted again as Charlotte, her feet dragging, set two places at the little table between the wing chairs that faced the hearth. "Ash? You're not sorry we're here in the middle of nowhere?"

"No," he said honestly, a little worried that Charlotte might miss the mild weather and the faster pace of Oakland. "Are you?"

She shook her head. "You don't miss your family?"

"Cabot and Mother were always more your family than mine," he said, coming to sit beside her and placing one finger beneath her chin. "Silver Pass has just what I searched all over the world to find."

She dipped her head shyly. He could compliment her all day, every day, for the rest of their lives, just to watch the color rush to her cheeks, and never tire of it.

"And being a shopkeeper after all the excitement you used to have? You don't mind that?" she asked, stretching and settling back into the soft chair sleepily as he placed a cup of tea beside her. She fingered the rim of the treasured cup contentedly.

"Mrs. Fagan came in today," he said, trying to explain what Silver Pass meant to him. "Her little one had the croup last week. She paid me with a dozen eggs. Glen Shumacher came in about noon. They're looking to start a collection for the Grange Hall and he thought I'd want to know." The town amazed him with their warmth and their inclusiveness. "For the first time in my life, Charlie, I feel like I'm part of a community. Like I'm part of a family."

"A family," she said, and her smile grew to be a yawn as she closed her eyes and motioned for him to read her the letter from Cabot.

Ash cleared his throat. *"Dear Ash and Charlotte,"* he began, after he'd settled back himself and gotten comfortable in the chair beside her. *"I hope this letter finds you both well. Davis and I are soggy, at best. Paris in the spring is not as beautiful as the guidebooks promise. It has rained nearly every day since we arrived."*

She *tsk*ed at his brother's penchant for always pointing out the worst first.

*"But,* he continues," Ash said, rallying, *"it has provided ample excuse to drag poor Davis through the Louvre twice and even get him to services on Sunday at Notre Dame. To tell the truth, in Latin and French it was more palatable than I remembered, and I do believe we'll continue the habit at home—for the boy's sake."*

Charlotte's mouth drooped open enough for him to realize that Cabot's letter had put her to sleep. He put it down on the table between them and gently slipped his arms beneath her body to lift her and carry her to their bed.

* * *

She felt his familiar hands wriggling between her tired body and the chair and offered no resistance. What a day she'd had—casting her first vote, and her name among those on the ballot! She put her arm around Ash's neck as he picked her up and carried her to their bedroom, setting her gently on the lacy spread that topped their bed.

"In the top drawer," she said with her eyes still closed, as she listened to the sounds of him rummaging for her buttonhook.

"We'll have you out of these in a jiffy," he said, working at her boots with a good deal of huffing and puffing. "Why do women insist on buying their shoes a size too small? Don't they hurt?"

She opened one eye to look down at her swollen ankles and wished Kathryn wouldn't wait until autumn to come for a visit.

"You seem awfully tired," he said as he worked at her shirtwaist buttons. "You feel all right?"

"Better than all right," she said, reaching out for him and pulling him to her. "How do *you* think I feel?"

After her buttons were undone, he worked the blouse out from her waistband and spread it to expose her chemise. Trailing the ends of the ribbon against her collarbone, he toyed with the bow, then ran his hands over the exposed skin above her corset cover. "Soft," he said almost reverently. "Softer than soft."

They'd been married nearly two years, and still every time he touched her, warmth rushed to her belly and spread through her like a prairie wildfire. And if she was the meadow aflame, he was the fire itself—white hot, raging, and out of control.

Like now, as he bent down to rain kisses over her neck, her collarbone, her chest, to trail his lips across her breasts and down her ribs. And all the while he kissed her, his hands were pulling at what was left of her clothes, and tucking the covers around her and pulling her against him once again.

*"Judge,"* she corrected him, struggling to turn on her side and press her bottom against him, ". . . with any luck," she added before starting to drift off to sleep.

"Hey!" he complained, shaking her gently. "Aren't you hungry? What about supper? How do you think they'd feel about their new judge letting her husband starve?"

She yawned, rousing herself just enough to turn over within the circle of his arms and open one eye.

"How do you think they'd feel about their new judge having a baby?" she asked.

Oh, what a smile that man had! What pure delight was written all over his face, mirroring her own. "I think," he said after giving it a moment's thought, "they'll be almost as happy as we are."

"Awk! Happy!" Liberty squawked, strolling in from the other room and climbing up the footboard of the bed to look down on them. "I love you, Charlotte! Come on, you stupid bird! Say it! I love you, Charlotte! Oh! Oh! Don't stop now."

Charlotte's giggle turned into a yawn. "You're a little late," she told the bird. "We already did that part."

Liberty paced back and forth on the footboard, rocking his head to and fro. "Shut up, you stupid bird! S-S-see you s-s-soon!" He worked his way, beak over claw, down the bed and waddled toward the kitchen. "I want some of that!" he shouted as he passed the new cat with the sore ear who was lapping up milk from a saucer by the sink.

"I do love you, Charlie Russe," Ash said as he brushed the short chestnut locks off her cheek. "And I'm a very happy man right now."

"Do you think Silver Pass will really be as happy as we are?" she asked nervously as a big yawn escaped her lips.

then at his own—as if they didn't have all the tin
world to lie naked in each other's arms.

She loved his hurry and his need for her. Lovec
there naked with him as he stoked her fires and brc
her back from the edge of sleep with the warmth ot
touch. Brought her back to hold him close.

He traced the mark the seam of her chemise had le
down her side, ran the tips of his fingers in the myriac
lines that crossed her waist from skirts and petticoats and drawers. "But how do you think the good people of Silver Pass would feel if they knew their justice of the peace was going about without her corset again today?" he asked as he began to kiss the marks her clothing had left upon her body.

He was driving her crazy, mumbling against her skin about what seeing her, touching her, did to him. The heat of his breath, the roughness of the stubble on his chin—his need was fueling her own and she pressed herself up against him until he simply gave up on her underthings and just raised the last of her petticoats to circle her waist.

"How do you think they'd feel about their justice of the peace in such a rush she can't even get properly undressed?" What did she care? Who mattered but him, as his kisses fell everywhere—her eyelids, her neck, lower and lower still? There wasn't a place he neglected, a spot that didn't burn at his touch.

And she did for him what he was doing for her, until there was no distinction to where each one's pleasure began and ended.

And when the fire was over and only the glowing of the embers remained, she cried in his arms, shaking against his chest while he held her.

"Not to mention how they'd feel about their justice of the peace crying every time it was good for her," he said,

"Nah," he said softly, easing her down by his side and letting his hand drift to her belly, where, deep inside her, their future was growing. "They'll be happy, but not half so happy as we."